DIGITAL VELOCITY
McAllister Justice Series
Book One

by
Reily Garrett

Acknowledgments

This book is dedicated to Darius, Leyna, and Raptor, the incredible trio, loyal, kind, and energetic. Three incredible beings who don't understand the words "give up." To Faith, whose love and compassion changed my life.

Special thanks to beta readers Lori Sickles and Siobhan Caughey. I appreciate your time and insights.

To my readers, each one of you who selects and reads one of my books, thank you for the opportunity to share my work.

For information on updates, new releases, deals, bonus content, and other great books, sign up for Reily's newsletter at reilygarrett.com.

Chapter One

"If God wanted you to tie the knot, he'd give you a near-death experience to better appreciate life, along with a craving for procreation. Then he'd smother your soul with the essence of venison, squirrel, frog legs, and taters to attract a likely counterpart from the sticks. No, wait. The latter has already happened, hasn't it? Sorry." Ethan narrowly kept his balance on the green-slicked, handmade bricks leading up the two-story, mauve-colored Victorian. If his 210-pound mass ended up sprawled on the steps, no doubt the picture would be splashed all over the precinct by noon with various unsavory captions.

"Maybe you should try it. The stick up your butt has to cause at least minor discomfort." Larrick's early-morning snark was a common greeting.

"Hey, I'm a *normal* guy." Ethan glared over his shoulder.

Larrick snorted.

"Still wet from our early-morning storm. Watch your step, it's slippery." Scanning the myriad amorphous shadows lurking in the wood line, realization struck that he and Larrick were sitting ducks if a sniper perched among the loblolly pine and oak trees lining the front and side yards.

His partner's reply came in equal measure of soft tones. "Either that or a large flock of birds dropped in recently to help her redecorate. Great detective work."

"Bird droppings are—"

"Sought after for facials. Especially the Japanese Nightingale dung." Larrick grinned.

"Only you would know that." Ethan adjusted his tie, an acknowledgment of the apprehension filling his mind.

"Are we whispering because your paranoid gut can't

assimilate food well enough to distinguish indigestion from an outside threat? This woman lives alone, gonna think we're a couple of perverts and liable to shoot us."

"Word has it she's a pacifist."

"Fine. You're one to talk about signs—dragging my butt to a stranger's house at this ungodly morning hour. I love knocking on someone's door and asking, 'Lady, are you all right? We're police detectives who received an anonymous tip that you might have a hangnail. Perhaps we could lend you a pair of nail clippers...' then ask if she needs the gutters cleaned." Derision and humor warred for dominance in Larrick's tone, yet his sharp gaze continually scanned the perimeter in consideration of his partner's unarticulated hunch.

Yin and yang, they fit together, a clean-cut detective and his partner whose hair length had passed regulation specs weeks ago.

"You know this isn't the first tip we've gotten, not to mention the fact that the other leads were solid and led to arrests. And while we're at it, why don't you step to the side? Standard police procedure when approaching an unknown situation." Ethan turned sideways, standing by the door with his hand poised to knock on the solid oak.

Ethan's hand paused in midair. Moisture coated his palms, a rare occurrence. Scrutinizing the interior through the narrow sidelights yielded nothing more than expected.

Upscale furniture, gleaming hardwood floors, and delicate bric-a-brac adorning the thick mantle and each side table completed the picture of elegance.

"Don't see any problem. Maybe she's fallen and can't get to a phone," Ethan murmured.

"You expected an old lady brandishing her curling iron?

As for leads, I get *mine* from three-dimensional people while you get yours from a bunch of ones and zeroes. Why can't our IT department trace your anonymous texts further than the loony bin? Though that's probably appropriate since your secret admirer's last present consisted of a flower basket bigger than my TV along with fur-lined cuffs.

"I've never laughed so hard I pissed myself. I thought that was hogwash, a myth made up by old ladies." Larrick leaned over the iron railing to peer through the window. "Can't see squat, bottom sill's too high."

"As my partner, you're supposed to have my back, not stab me *in* the back. You didn't have to broadcast it through the whole department by hanging the cuffs from the sprinkler system with a bunch of roses twined in them."

"But it was funny."

"Now my brothers won't let up, and I've been subscribed to every kinky magazine known to the publishing world. You think *I* should know why some whacko chose me for their personal marionette?" Ethan suppressed a shudder before his partner gained more verbal ammunition. If his suspicions were correct, his informant was in fact a beautiful enigma with waist-length chestnut hair and an emerald gaze capable of melting steel.

"Maybe because you were the youngest to make detective? Rising star, golden boy, and all that crap."

"No. Probably afraid your redneck ways would rub off on them, or maybe because I'm the biggest sap." Ethan's gut rumbled, more of a warning sign from a well-heeled intuition than hunger.

"Larrick, this doesn't feel right." Behind him, the slide of metal on leather let him know his partner had palmed his Glock. Three years of working together circumvented the formality of dissecting gut reactions.

"Side windows are lower. I'll take a look." A creak of leather sole betrayed his partner's backtracking to scrutinize the surroundings.

"Hood of her BMW is cold. Didn't go anywhere recently." Larrick's harsh whisper halted a nearby squirrel scampering up a tree, its head cocked to one side while studying the strange human interlopers.

Sunshine warmed the first spring buds on the low shrubbery bordering the walkway to complete the idyllic setting. Nothing but peace and serenity, yet Ethan's heart hammered against his ribcage like an aggressive punk drummer.

With his partner disappearing around the corner, he again scanned the perimeter while the morning's corrupted equanimity formed a sour wad in his chest.

A lazy March breeze combed its cool fingers through his short hair while the deep foreboding received with the initial text message blossomed into multiple horrific scenarios, leaving one of them a corpse, their life's essence forming macabre shapes on gleaming hardwood floors.

"I see bare feet beyond the kitchen island. Toes up. Probably female." Larrick's disembodied whisper just provided probable cause. "Backup?"

Ethan backtracked then trailed his partner to the rear of the house. "Let's check for signs of forced entry first. The informant's message stated this woman has been threatened."

Two large windows remained intact and locked while a slider and windowed personnel door revealed no signs of tampering. Yet they couldn't ignore the anonymous text when a previous anonymous tip led to the psychopathic killer terrorizing the Pacific Northwest. There hadn't been anything unusual in approaching those homes, either.

"I'll go first, your turn to follow." Larrick smirked, their mutual understanding of tempting fate playing out. "She might've had a stroke or something. Let's find out before we call central."

A city like Callouston saw little violent crime within the upper crust style of living. Those depravities were usually drug related and found in less influential neighborhoods.

A spirit's survival depended on the seasoned blend of adventure, risk, contentment, and fear. So far, Ethan's experiences waded in the tepid middle ground of each, as if fate deemed him not ripe for the headier aspects of life. He'd never minded taking point.

The back door's glass inset revealed a small swath of open floorplan with the kitchen to the right and a curving stairway adorned with an ornate banister separating it from the hallway on the left. No broken lamps, overturned chairs, or rug stains indicated a struggle, yet the grim portent of violence hung like a dark nebula, a warning of caution.

Pasty-white lower legs protruded from beyond kitchen cabinets, their delicate structure indicating a thin frame. The rest of the body was left to the imagination.

"Let's go through the front," Ethan suggested.

"All right, the likelihood of it making a difference to her is slim." Larrick's tone declared it a foregone conclusion.

Ethan's wearing a suit to work lent a dual advantage, an air of professionalism if the need arose, and a counterbalance to his partner's camo jacket and cowboy boots. The fact Larrick's longish hair pushed the captain's buttons provided a perpetual source of amusement for the entire department.

A removable layer came in handy to protect vulnerable flesh, like in the present scenario or when faced with a lunatic wielding a knife. Leather gloves from his pocket would prevent adding fingerprints inside the home and aid in protection from protruding shards.

Shattering glass announced forcible entry before the sidelight's glass fragments tinkled across the hardwood medallion inlay of the grand foyer.

I hope my tipster hasn't turned to the dark side and set me up.

At the very least, he could receive several days of suspension.

Seconds later, he shook out then shrugged back into his jacket before opening the front door. Though his partner's advance was equally silent, he felt Larrick's presence stepping up beside him.

Knowing something was off and defining it left a wide range of possibilities. The kind that could leave one or both detectives dead. Irrational apprehension had never been one of Ethan's shortcomings.

The carpeted staircase to his right wound its way to the second story, its bordering wall bearing vintage pictures of men and women in coattails and jeweled gowns, smiling as if confining secrets and arcane knowledge within their canvas prisons.

Larrick's frown indicated his own perception of *wrongness.*

Ethan motioned his partner to circumvent the large, ornate dining table capable of seating a dozen. On the opposite side, the redneck smirked. The multi-tiered crystal chandelier was a far cry from Larrick's six-antler whitetail counterpart.

Sparsely placed furniture granted a partial view of the kitchen where the woman's lower legs extended beyond the island. Blood spray clotted the tile and grout lines while spattered crimson patterns forming grotesque inkblot tests on white cabinets suggested a barely controlled rage.

A victim, but not of a stroke.

The limited view changed both their perspective and method of approach, being careful to not disrupt trace evidence.

A grandfather clock measured seconds in muddled chaos. Ethan remained vigilant while Larrick rounded the island and checked the body.

"Dear God in heaven. Who would do *this*?" A slight headshake conveyed the obvious before he knelt.

Too late for help, and details would come later. They'd clear each room one at a time before ferreting out the why of the murder.

Off to the right, several large rooms with wide, arched doors surely contained more heavy furniture fit for royalty. Such a waste their queen had no further need of their presence.

Several narrow boards protested his partner's weight on the floor's tile-to-hardwood transition. Larrick rolled his eyes and shook his head before moving closer to the wall where lingering shadows incorporated secrets of previous activities.

A quiet snap of Ethan's fingers brought the older man's attention back, wariness in his features. Despite no heavy breath or stealthy movements suggesting another presence, Ethan's gut foretold a different scenario. He frowned and shook his head, conveying his concern.

Larrick nodded and closed the distance while still

maintaining room to maneuver.

Stepping wide of the stairway, Ethan noted the first doorway slightly ajar. No light spilled from within as they stood aside and each took a deep breath. He nudged the door a few inches.

A slight squeak of the hinges announced their intent just before the portal slammed shut with enough force to shatter the morning quiet.

In the next heartbeat, a shotgun blast rang in Ethan's ears as splinters flew from the newly made Cyclops door.

"Police, dirtball. Put down your gun."

"Language, partner, what would your brothers think?" Larrick's hardened gaze belied the lightness of his words.

"That I shouldn't have drawn a partner who uses a toilet seat as a horseshoe."

In answer, another roar splintered the quiet, the second shot completing an obscene pair of eyes in the oak planking. The third blast blew a hole below it and would've finished anyone who'd fallen in the short hall.

Shells shucked from a shotgun fractured the quiet, giving Ethan a second to reposition himself and kick the door's remnants inward.

A solid thud from wood connecting with dirtball boosted his adrenaline-infused strength. Grabbing the frame, Ethan shoved harder, satisfaction filling him when the door gave way with his opponent's stumble backward.

"Not today, prick." Filtered morning light spilled through the floor-to-ceiling windows and emblazoned the intruder toppling to the hardwood.

The black ski mask covering the thug's face contrasted white sclera surrounding pupils and irises darker than sin. As he raised the shotgun to aim, Ethan fired two rounds into his chest and eliminated the thug's ability to shoot.

Kicking the gun aside and securing the assailant's bloody hands while Larrick stood watch allowed for a small expenditure of excess energy. If his partner saw his hand shaking or fumbling with the cuffs, he didn't betray it in a cheeky quip.

"I was supposed to go first, cheater," Larrick whispered. Two wingback chairs and a large leather sofa hid no other intruders.

Neither detective spoke while Ethan searched the downed man, unsure if another assailant lurked in the bowels of the home in hopes of finishing what the first had begun.

Rubbing his palms on his slacks and several deep breaths prepared Ethan for the next phase of clearing the residence. Larrick's hands remained steady while a half smirk declared Ethan the equivalent of a babe in the woods.

Redneck.

The faintest of telltale thumps in the distance warned of another presence. The nightmare wasn't over. A quick hand signal alerted his partner to the new plan.

Larrick frowned but nodded.

In the hall once more, Ethan glanced to the second floor. No moving shadows or press of small air currents alerted him to danger. His second step caught him halfway between two covers, the stairway in front and the office just vacated.

Sunlight streaming through the kitchen's slider illuminated a second intruder stepping out and taking aim at the same instant Ethan swung his Glock's barrel in defense. Pain blasted through his right leg just as his pistol barked in kind.

"Ahhh!" Piercing tentacles of pain stabbed his upper

thigh into his groin and down his calf.

Larrick provided cover fire from the office while Ethan's staggering steps ended with the stairway's protection, its bulk between himself and his shooter.

Booted strides rumbling on bare floorboards signaled the intruder's retreat toward the back door. A second later, its slam was a welcome sound in a world where gray encroached from the periphery of Ethan's vision.

"You all right?" Larrick asked. "Christ, I do *not* want to have to explain this to your older brothers. Crap. Matt's gonna have my nuts in a sling."

"Son of a bitch!" It appeared Ethan's shot had winged his assailant, but sudden pain had skewed his aim for center mass.

"You missed him?"

Fire shooting down his thigh forced a hobble-step back to the office while heat draining from his face left him lightheaded.

Nothing could take away the compulsion to groan. With his hand covering his mouth, soft expletives slipped past tingling lips. He'd dealt with minor injuries before, but not this mind-rending perdition.

Several deep breaths helped clear his head and regain control. He shouldered his weapon and looked at the intruder on the floor, wondering where the killer's pain level registered.

"I was more concerned about you...Here, sit on the floor in case you pass out. Lean against the sofa and hold pressure on your boo-boo." Larrick's narrowed gaze took in the tableau before shrugging out of his jacket.

"Ya know, if you're as quick off the mark at sex as you are jumping turns, it'd explain why you don't have a long-term woman."

"And if you're as bad an aim with your joystick as you are your gun, you don't need condoms."

"Hey, the world can only handle one Robertson."

"Damn hick with a third-degree black lip. Why'd I get partnered with a redneck?" The makeshift pressure bandage successfully stopped the bleeding, but not his partner's list of complaints about the paperwork they'd just incurred.

Caring came in many forms.

"*Arrgh*, that hurts. Go see which direction the creep ran." Remnants of the morning's bagel lurched to the back of Ethan's throat. Swallowing hard only encouraged its reappearance.

"I'll clear the upstairs first. Don't pass out, or I'll tell Matt and Billy you cried like a baby." Fast, light footfalls belied Larrick's six-foot-two frame.

"*Aw*, you used your best camo jacket on my leg. I'm honored." When his vision cleared, Ethan took stock of his surroundings, thankful he wasn't in the first shooter's shoes.

All of this stemmed from another anonymous tip from the as yet unknown source. Former prompts had led to the arrest of a psychotic predator with incriminating documents hand-delivered to his doorstep.

On another occasion, evidence had led to catching the murdering co-conspirators bent on claiming an early inheritance. It seemed unlikely the tipster had set him up to be murdered. In counterpoint, they couldn't track the mysterious source.

So how did his snitch know the homeowner who lived in elegance and style and also held a respected position at the hospital? If today's informant had also fed him the earlier tips, maybe he could find the common denominator. Surely he couldn't have two anonymous digital sleuths wanting to humiliate him in front of his peers.

In his gut, he knew his source enjoyed a complex sense of humor and was the minx sending wacky, embarrassing gifts. A prankster and tipster rolled into one confusing brainteaser he intended to decipher. His addled mind assembled images and sensations of delving his fingers through thick mahogany hair and thoroughly enjoying all the delights his mysterious enigma could offer.

Maybe this was an entirely different ballgame, one where his invisible assistant called the shots and held a more complex agenda. He wouldn't know until he'd traced the early morning text message. Pain and the hole in his leg declared that might take a while.

Blood seeped between the downed intruder's fingers, the loss of life's essence soaking his shirt and staining the hardwood. Harsh breaths and a face twisted in agony seemed the least of what he deserved considering his past night's activities.

Soiling the beautiful lap blanket probably entailed a wasted effort, but Ethan reached back and yanked it off, toppling the decorative pillow wedging it between the sofa cushions.

It's not like the owner cares. Helping the perp live might provide answers and closure for the victim's family.

Pressure on his chest snapped the man's eyes open.

"W-why—are you—helping me?" Each breath rasped as if accompanied by extreme pain and produced a foamy dribble from his mouth. It seemed unlikely he'd win the battle for his soul.

"There are no words for how much I want to just lean against this sofa and watch you bleed out."

"Y-you won't. You want information."

"Let's not be hasty on the first assumption. Why'd you kill her?"

"An-answer the riddle, and you'll find the clue to the next victim."

"Riddle? What riddle? Listen, prick, you're probably gonna die right here on this cold, hard floor."

Most likely very soon.

"Why not meet—whoever you're destined to greet—with an unburdened mind?"

"Because even in death, he'll get to me. Rather face the devil himself." Though his eyes closed, the shooter's breath continued in uneven rasps and foamy wheezes.

Larrick's low whistle preceded his appearance in the doorway. Disappointment etched his brow. As expected, he was alone. A silent moment passed while the older man removed his belt and secured Ethan's makeshift bandage. "Sorry. I figured you'd have sense enough to do this."

Another explosion of agonizing pain accompanied the buckle's fastening. "You're enjoying this."

"Oh, shaw, man. Look at this. You might even get a couple of stitches. Gonna ruin your swimsuit bod."

"Didn't hit an artery. Thanks for asking."

"Hey, we're partners, equals." Larrick's brand of dealing with stress equaled snark.

"Then why am I the one with all the pain?"

"You think this isn't painful for me, too? The entire department knew you'd be the first one of us to get shot. Those dark Hollywood looks were a sure bet for a psychotic stalker."

"Redneck. Next time, we go in the back door." Though every nerve ending in his thigh screamed, Ethan recognized the banter as a distraction to keep him conscious. He shuffled aside as his partner moved and pulled back the blanket to inspect the thug's wounds.

"One, Charlotte's not the type to share. And two, you wouldn't like a woman's back door." Larrick scrutinized Ethan's face before continuing. "Ya know, you're getting old, moving too slow."

"You're one to talk. Where's my shooter?"

"Vanished in the woods. I've no idea which direction, too darn much underbrush. I didn't even get a look at him."

"Beer belly, tall, masked."

"We'll need dogs to track him with all the trees and briars. Looks like it wasn't indigestion after all. I called it in. Do you think your secret admirer set us up?" Larrick's measured words reflected his doubt.

"No...I think we just had bad timing. This dumb creep's going on about answering a riddle that'll give us some type of clue to the next victim."

"More? Oh great."

Sirens in the distance forewarned of the advancing wall of blue. Ethan's sigh of relief had nothing to do with easing pain. "I'll watch over Mr. Cryptic here. Go see if you can find this riddle before the cavalry tramps over everything."

"Your brothers will probably be first to arrive."

"So I'll tell them you shot me. By accident, of course."

"Son of a deer slayer. You've always been trouble." Larrick's half grin belied his words before he shoved to his feet. At least they'd both survived to face the whirlwind of commotion after an officer-involved shooting.

The vibration of Ethan's phone signaled an incoming text. Since word of the incident had gone out on the air, he'd expected one of his older brothers to text with some snarky comment underneath their collective concern. Puzzlement over the message furrowed his brow.

OMG. I had no idea what was going on. Are you and Frannie okay? She's important.

Staring at the text, Ethan discerned neither the significance of the words nor any clue of how to pin down the anonymous informant. "Important how? To whom?"

Adrenaline washout followed the primal protection response and settled the matter of position as soon as paramedics followed responding police officers through the doorway. He relinquished pressure on his leg wound and settled back against the sofa with a groan.

The fact his hands shook while lightheadedness tunneled his vision in diminishing shades of gray would be fodder for the department if known.

Stay conscious.

Vaguely, he remembered Matt, his oldest brother, and the paramedics scooting him around and pushing him supine amid bodies rushing and other orders being carried out. Someone unbuckled his pressure dressing to study the wound.

Matt, go away and stop inspecting me like a side of beef.

"Okay, sir. You're going to be fine. Can you tell me your name?" Confidence in the medic's tone matched the self-assurance in his quick and efficient movements.

Ethan closed his eyes, inhaling cool air as the paramedics took over his care.

"Answer the damn question, Ethan." Matt's no-nonsense demeanor earned a chuckle from one of the officers.

"Mud. My name is mud."

"Damn right, it is." Matt snorted and stood, barking orders about not contaminating evidence.

Disembodied voices continued above the sound of blood roaring in his ears. Considering the circumstances, he'd never live it down.

"Sir? Your name?"

Cool metal rested briefly against Ethan's ankle before the sound of ripping fabric echoed in the room. Brisk, efficient movements saw his leg bared to the thigh and cool air caressing his skin. He couldn't contain the violent shaking in his limbs.

An odd coldness seeped to the depth of his marrow, but he had no strength to cover himself. "Ethan. My name is Ethan."

Damn, he hated needles, but the IV the paramedic started would deliver much-needed sugar to his system, depleted in the backwash of his reaction.

"A painkiller would be real nice about now."

"Twit." Matt's murmured word spoke volumes.

Emotional extremes flowed through his consciousness. He couldn't make out the words before blackness narrowed his world to a void.

Chapter Two

Sudden jolting leg pain woke Ethan, the groan escaping his throat despite clamping his mouth shut.

"Ahhh. Crap that leg hurts. I'm not in the mood for calisthenics." The pressure around his leg tightened while something cool lay across his forehead.

"Ethan, welcome back. My name is Kevin. We're on our way to the hospital. You've been shot in the leg, but we're going to help you through this."

"H-how's the perp I nailed? Still alive?" Frequent thumps jarred the stretcher beneath him as the speeding ambulance failed to navigate multiple potholes.

"Don't know. He's in the wagon behind us."

Once again, Ethan's world narrowed in pain and confusion as blackness pulled him into its welcoming grasp.

Waking up had never entailed such a miserable experience. Grogginess gave way to confusion, which paved the way for incredible thirst. His tongue felt swollen and dry, but his leg no longer rejected the idea of living. In fact, Ethan couldn't feel it at all.

Panic took root as he fumbled with the blanket covering him. Curling to a semi-sitting position, he looked first at his thigh, covered in white gauze with a small rubber tube protruding from between the layers, then at his surroundings. A foggy haze of dizziness brought nausea and more confusion.

Several stretchers bearing unconscious men and women of varying ages surrounded him. Each wore a blue gauzy surgical cap. Bodies in scrub uniforms moving between the oblivious clarified his venue among the living as nurses checked blood pressures, administered medications, and monitored the status of others in various states of waking up post-surgery.

Strong hands pushed him back to the mattress. "Lie still, Ethan. Your operation went well, and you're going to be fine. Take a couple of deep breaths for me, please."

Following the line of cartoon figures up the scrubs, Ethan found the kind voice behind the directive. "Hmm, a sight for sore eyes, someone not pointing a gun at me. I like Chinese food." In the back of his mind, something registered as *off*, but he couldn't discern the reasoning for the delicate cough hiding a smile.

"Actually, my husband and I enjoy Chinese takeout on a regular basis considering the hours we both keep." Humor danced in her gaze and the quirk of her mouth.

"Come on, Ethan. Deep breaths."

With no reason to argue, he took a few deep breaths before asking. "Everything still in good working order?"

Several chuckles at the long nurses' station brought his attention to the other recovery room attendants.

"Yep. I suspect you'll be chasing down bad guys within a month's time."

Those last words settled something in his head, allowing the fuzzy edges of sleep to drag him back to oblivion.

Voices droning in the background denied Ethan the privilege of undisturbed rest as intermittent ribald laughter punctuated lewd jokes. The summation of those things equaled family, just as it always had.

"Come on, youngin', we're tired of waiting for you to open your eyes. Two more minutes and we'll douse you with ice water." His oldest brother, Matt, existed as a short fuse even while demanding the impossible.

Ten to one, his other three brothers waited to verbally abuse an injured sibling. Only his sister, if present, would prevent their jesting from becoming a reality.

"I'm awake, already. Go away." Ethan opened his eyes to see his family, some surrounding the bed and reading the labels on his IVs while others sat in the chairs dotting the room. Billy examined the chart attached to the footboard.

"Huh, somebody sprung for a private room. I'm touched."

"You certainly are—but not in a good way. That's why we insisted on private digs, might be the only way you get lucky again, some poor nurse feeling sorry for you." Lucas jarred the bed as he sat, his hand hovering over the thick gauze bandage. "What's with this drain sticking out? Do you think he still needs this thing?"

As fate would have it, a nurse walked in bearing a small cup in one hand. "Hey! What do you think you're doing?" Her stride toward Lucas likened more to a drill sergeant bent on educating an errant recruit than an angel of mercy.

Lucas held both hands up. "No harm done, darlin'. I was just worried if you let all the gooey goodness out of Ethan here, he'll turn as sour as Matt."

"Off the bed, unless you'd like a reason to need one?" With brows drawn down and together, lips pursed and a gaze that could bore to Earth's middle core, she hadn't meant that in a sensual way.

"Well, now that you mention it—" Lucas fell silent as he stood and stepped back under the nurse's advance.

"Mr. McAllister, I have a pain pill here for you." She hesitated after narrowing her gaze at Lucas. "Two of your brothers said you have a high tolerance, but in light of seeing this interaction and Matt's suggestion, perhaps you'd like something a little stronger than what I have here?"

Clear gray eyes scrutinized him, declaring her ready to do battle with them all, and win, on his declaration.

"Thanks, Mrs.—" Ethan groaned as he tried to sit up, his body not responding well to the command. The last thing he needed was for his brothers to witness him puking in front of a beautiful woman.

The taunts would never end.

"Wait, Mr. McAllister. Let the bed do the work. I'm sure you're perfectly fit, but you've been injured and are under the influence of anesthesia."

A slight metal grinding accompanied the head of his bed raising after she pushed a side-rail button. "My name is Carrie Jackson. You can call me Carrie." Before rearranging the pillows behind him, she set the white paper cup down and poured a glass of water from the pitcher on his overbed table.

"Carrie, you might want to get him something a lot stronger, like morphine—or a sledgehammer." Comments from Lucas generally paved a pathway to hell. "And as far as influences, you'd be surprised at the extent of Ethan's vulnerability."

The nurse's glare could've frozen Hades in one pass. "You, sir, can call me Ms. Jackson." Turning her attention back to Ethan, she smiled sweetly. "Do you feel up to eating some gelatin? Everybody responds differently to anesthesia. Some experience nausea when they first wake up."

"And others might enjoy spontaneous orgasms or suffer anal seepage?" Caden suggested.

Ethan didn't miss Lucas and Caden's suggestive gestures made behind the nurse's back. "Maybe after my family's gone. I don't think I can stomach food on top of them."

"Boys, knock it off. Ethan's having a rough day." As matriarch, Janice McAllister's admonishment halted sibling shenanigans.

"Very well." Turning to the room at large, the nurse announced, "You have ten minutes before I kick you all out."

Grumbles and protests rose, instantly silenced by her raised brow.

"Hmm, can't say I've ever liked being in a hospital, but I certainly like you, young lady." His mother's quiet words carried the weight of final judgment. From the corner chair in the room, she rose with an air of quiet dignity.

Quiet footfalls stood her face to face with the nurse, each gaze assessing the other before smiles graced both expressions.

"Thank you for taking care of my son. I'm afraid none of my boys have much sense, especially one that would allow himself to be shot." Having said her piece, Janice McAllister approached her son and kissed his forehead.

"Next time, be more careful. I am an old woman now and cannot take such nonsense. You need to find a woman to care for you and give me grandchildren."

A smile took the sting out of her words before her calculating gaze slid to the nurse. "With good people like you to bring them back to health, the world is a better place. Thank you." Turning to the older male present, she added, "Come along, John, let the boys talk."

"Mother…" Ethan's drawn-out warning elicited a round of chuckles from his four brothers. He didn't need anyone's help in the romance department. "Where's Abagail?" His only sister, the sibling closest in age and temperament, wasn't present.

How odd.

His father stepped forward, keen eyes assessing even as he leaned over for a manly hug. "She'll be back in a bit, had to make a quick stop. Take care, son. We'll return later when you're fully awake. I'll call first to see what we can bring."

"Thanks, I'll see you later." After taking the offered pill, Ethan watched Carrie leave, the slight sway of trim hips distracting enough to draw his siblings' attention.

"Maybe he won't need his blow up doll right away." Caden's appreciative stare followed Carrie through the doorway.

"Nuh-uh, hound dog. Hands off. Ethan needs all the help he can get, and this is a golden opportunity. Do we need to have *the talk* about the birds and the bees, Ethan?" Lucas' ill-timed humor failed to spark a rise in temper.

"Enough, we have work to do." Matt's no-nonsense command ended the levity. "So, what did the shooter look like?"

"I already told Larrick. The mask—" Ethan began, his head still fuzzy from anesthesia.

"We talked to him. The only reason he's not in the room next door is because you both followed procedure, somewhat. Now tell us what happened." Billy, two years Matt's junior, acted more like the eldest sibling every day.

Relaying the scene as it unfolded in his mind allowed Ethan to sift through the morning's events, one frame at a time. Both men had followed standard practice, but that was part of the problem—dirtballs never followed a predictable routine, which necessitated a fluid and flexible approach.

Next time they entered a hostile environment, instinct would guide his movements. His gaze drifted outside, the scenery animating his memory of the morning's incident.

Dark clouds swept across the sky by the stiff breeze bending small saplings in preparation for another storm parroted the commotion now felt within. Nature and nurture worked in tandem. The arena outside mimicked the upheaval in his room.

His family would always surround him, scrutinizing and influencing his decisions yet curving around his path and offering support however they saw fit.

Three of his brothers, police officers in the same department, along with Caden, a PI, dissected each move he and his partner had made, nodding and commenting along the way. By the end, each appeared puzzled and at a loss for words.

"Huh, first time I've seen you all speechless. No derogatory comments? I know each one of you is all over this. Tell me what's been going on."

"Well, since you've been sleeping on the job, we did find a few things a bit...odd," Billy began.

"Well? Do I have to beg?"

"Naw, you can save that for Carrie, and make sure you're down on one knee. Always did want to do a nurse..." Lucas sat on the bed despite his oldest brother's frown.

"Let's go over this again. We're missing something. Tell us more about this anonymous tip. Our IT guys still can't trace it." Matt rubbed his forehead as if trying to fend off a headache. "Carl's even working on his own time, trying to get a line on the snitch that's been helping you."

"Look, I've no idea who's sending me the texts and...stuff."

"No new women in your life? Or men?" Caden snickered under Matt and Billy's glare.

"Hey, when a woman sends you fur-lined cuffs, she's

looking for some serious playtime. If you need any advice, I'd be glad to step in and assist." Lucas' wistful tone declared his desire to help.

"No. If I did, I wouldn't go to the infamous Caden or Lucas McAllister, the family's hound dogs. What'd you find out about the victim? I've met her before, and she presented as a straight arrow."

"We were hoping you could tell us more. So far, we have a middle-aged hospital administrator attacked between late last night and early this morning. Some inventive psychos tortured her. You guys apparently interrupted them before they could get clear." Matt took a deep breath, shoving his hands through his close-cropped hair.

"What do you mean?" Unlike Larrick, Ethan hadn't been able to walk the crime scene, which necessitated playing catch up. "She was dead. Larrick didn't mention details."

"Probably because you were laying down on the job," Caden quipped.

"He was shot. That earns him some leeway," Matt retorted.

Billy turned toward the window, disgust in his stiff-set shoulders as he explained the gruesome scene. "Got a call from Larrick. The guy you shot had a note in his pocket, destined for the kitchen counter or table, I imagine. Had a typed riddle on where to find a clue to the next victim's identity." Billy glanced at Matt before reciting it aloud.

"*I move frequently—but gain no distance. I am warm, moist, and dark, but give no comfort. I can stretch and shrink, giving or taking at will, bringing both pain and pleasure with each.*"

"What does that mean?" Ethan's confusion echoed around the room in varying gestures of grimaces, curled lips, and fisted hands.

"By the time we got it, the intended clue had been pretty much decimated." Matt shook his head.

"What? Our crime scene techs are good. I've yet to see them spoil evidence." Disbelief that CSI could be careless brought a surge of heat to Ethan's face.

"The riddle's answer—her bowels. Which is where the coroner found another paper when he examined the wounds in her belly. Unfortunately, body acids destroyed some of the evidence, words written on fake money from a child's game." Matt scrubbed a hand over his jaw.

"Dear God. Those sick pricks." With the earlier levity gone, Ethan felt the weight of the morning's proceedings and recent anesthesia. "I remember hearing Larrick cussing from the kitchen area...But I'd only seen her lower legs."

"Yeah, she was still handcuffed." Even Billy, who had an ironclad stomach, looked a bit green.

"They'd taken their time, at first slicing her, not deep, just enough to create lots of pain and an unholy mess," Matt added.

"What about the scumbag I shot?" Ethan asked, his mind conjuring an image of the strange scene with updated information.

"They're getting ready to bring him up from recovery. Don't know if he'll make it or not." Matt turned to face the bed once again.

"I vote for—not," Caden advised.

"Hey. None of that crap. We're cops, and we'll see this done right, regardless." Matt glared at his younger sibling.

"Uh, forgetting something? I'm a private investigator, not a cop anymore." Caden shrugged off his big brother's warning.

"We'll cuff you to your bed if we have to, bro. We're not gonna screw up this investigation." Billy, considered the other hothead of the four, faced off with Caden until Matt stepped between, giving each a not-so-gentle backward shove.

"Fine, but my way works better and faster. Larrick said you winged the other gunman, but there wasn't any blood. Are you sure you hit him?" Caden's smirk deserved a punch.

"Yeah. What did the fingerprint scanner turn up?" Ethan wished he was having this conversation with a clear head.

"Michael Collins. He does have at least one alias, maybe more—Dooley Sonnenfeld is what we have so far. We're running background checks on him now. We'll know more when it pops up." As he spoke, Matt pulled Caden's hand away from the IV pump that buzzed with each button pushed.

"You forgot to tell him about the dog." Billy sat in the chair his mother had vacated earlier.

"Dog? We didn't see any dog." Ethan readjusted his bed lower for comfort. Between the after-effects of anesthesia and his brothers' vivid descriptions, he was glad he didn't have anything in his stomach.

"Yeah, out in the yard, a doberman. Drugged. He's still at the vet clinic," Matt added.

"Wow. So the attack was planned well ahead." Ethan briefly closed his eyes to the images running forefront in his mind.

The re-entrance of his nurse signaled the end of visitation with a mere hand-on-hip stance. Each brother filed out with get-well wishes and promises to return amid jokes about varying uses of gelatin dessert.

"Here's something to start you out, Ethan." The red,

jiggling semi-solid appeared about as appetizing as a lettuce salad.

He smiled dutifully as she raised the head of his bed.

"I know you're exhausted. Do you need a hand with this?" She hesitated before continuing. "I have the rest of my med rounds to finish, but I'll be back shortly just in case. Don't get out of bed the first time without help, the anesthesia in your system will make you woozy."

Pushing the overbed table closer, she set the cup and spoon down before grinning. Warmth and kindness radiated from a smile that built slowly. A slight flushing along her cheeks and brightness from her gaze indicated a certain amount of curiosity. He was used to the latter.

"I'm good, thanks."

"So you're the youngest of five? That's gotta be tough." A cryptic smile spoke of commiseration.

"Actually, I'm fourth of six. I have a younger brother and sister, though she hasn't been in to see me yet." Brotherly bonds were strong, but Abagail was the one who'd worry most about him. According to Matt, she'd paced the waiting room until the surgeon had emerged and predicted a full recovery.

"Don't worry. When she comes in, she can stay as long as you're not overtaxed. So, how long have you worked for Callouston PD?"

"Three years. I started out in Portland, thought it best to learn somewhere away from my older brothers. After Caden was injured on the job, I moved back to help him out. Apparently, cheating husbands don't like to be photographed."

"Imagine that. Yet it's great to have a large support system. You all seem very close." Even white teeth delineated her smile. "I'll be back in a bit." Carrie checked his IV before leaving.

Yeah, sometimes we're too close.

Normal sounds of patient care—a stretcher wheeling down the hall, drawers opening on the med cart visible through the doorway, and wrappers being torn open—dwindled with the closing door.

A determined disregard allowed Ethan to sniff the red, squishy substance that should taste something like cherry, strawberry, or one of a hundred other flavors but in fact issued no aroma.

In his mind, men just didn't do gelatin or any other food lacking real substance. As soon as Abagail arrived, he'd ask her to sneak up something solid, even if only a burger and fries.

At least he could lay his head back and rest a bit. Who knew undergoing surgery could be so exhausting? The mental to-do list lengthened as he closed his eyes to enjoy the peace and quiet that allowed him to concentrate.

The low peal of sneakers on linoleum snapped his gaze open to collide with deep green irises speckled and rimmed with gold.

"Greener than an avocado." He hadn't heard the door open.

Chapter Three

"Hmm, I've been compared to a lot of things before, but not a fruit." Laughter danced in a face he'd first seen months ago across a parking lot.

Blinking away the mental fog, he took in his visitor's attire. A white lab coat covered her body from neck to knee, allowing little definition of the shape underneath. Judging by the slim face and neck along with the delicate finger she held to her mouth in a quieting gesture, he assumed her height would allow her to carry much more weight before giving way to obesity.

A quirky smile and devilment in her gaze spoke of unique pranks and an endless sense of humor.

His world tilted. He just *knew*.

"Your eyes…You're not a nurse."

"Well, you just called me a fruit. So be thankful I don't work here. And you can tell that by my eyes? I came to check on you." Small furrows lined her forehead, her smile vanishing underneath a frown as her gaze sharpened to dissect his very breath.

Intuition guided his assumption that she intended no harm. Rolling his shoulders to relieve the swelling tension, he put a name to his visitor. His anonymous enigma, tipster, and giver of prank gifts.

As a rule, he didn't care for long hair but seeing hers in a ponytail, he silently wished she'd turn to allow him a glimpse of its length down her back.

"Sorry. Anesthesia has done a number on me. Your eyes are so *green*. I…know you."

"Yeah, gotta love a post-anesthesia *loopiness*. Tell me what happened this morning." Pulling her bottom lip between her teeth prevented words spilling not meant for his ears.

Obviously not accomplished in the art of deception, she displayed several other *tells* signaling anxiety while avoiding his unspoken question. Sometimes, direct approaches yielded the best results.

"So you're my secret admirer." *Yeah, that came out wrong.*

Humor flickered in her eyes as her gaze roved over his form. "Huh, you wish. I just like messing with your head." A sad amusement lined her face. "You know—you should eat the red stuff, so they'll give you something solid." Without hesitation, she picked up the cup and spoon then devoured his snack with not a speck of remorse.

"Thanks, I couldn't stomach that. What's your name?" Maybe the remnants of drugs in his system were clouding his judgment, or maybe it was due to his fascination. Either way, the intensity of her nonverbal cues pricked his investigative instincts.

Her beauty wasn't that of a runway model, but there radiated such an honest sincerity, something he rarely saw in his line of work. *A diamond in the rough.*

She hesitated as if weighing something heavily in her mind. "Lexi."

"What made you pick me to receive the tips? I don't think we've met." At this point, he didn't remember a heck of a lot.

"I did a little research and found that you and your hick associate have a great record. It was either you or your *smatterchew* partner." The tone declared it a foregone conclusion.

"Hmm, he is a bit of a redneck. Okay. So why greet me in person? Your anonymity is obviously a high priority."

Again she paused before answering. "First, I guess—guilt. I didn't mean to send you into an ambush. Saying that in a text doesn't carry the same sincerity. Second, you collared the pimp I'd been avoiding for years, removing my number one necessity for anonymity, which isn't an appropriate discussion now."

"The prostitutes you helped free from their pimp by sending me that evidence? He would've killed you if he'd had the chance." If not for Lexi's intervention, more girls would've ended up in the morgue. As it turned out, they'd stopped a killer and solved multiple murders throughout the state.

"He *did* get the chance, but I got away and left you the evidence." After setting the empty cup down, she picked up a baseball cap left by his older brother. Turning it idly in her hands offered a reference point on which to focus her attention.

"Yeah, another anonymous tip."

"Hey. It panned out. You got him behind bars."

"There's more to it than that." Ethan saw no signs of deception in her nonverbal, but instinct told him she held something back.

"How'd Frannie die?" Averting her gaze, she swiped at the tear spilling to her cheek, nothing fake about her unadulterated grief.

"I can't discuss an ongoing investigation. Are you a relative?" Though he hadn't seen the victim recently, he'd met her before and didn't detect any physical resemblance.

"Not by blood, but yes. She is, or was the only family I have." Again, she rotated the cap in her hands.

"I'm sorry for your loss. Do you know if she had any enemies or anyone that hated her enough to want her dead?" What he wanted to ask was how she'd known the victim was in trouble, but he was in no position to mentally catalog everything she said. *Priorities.*

"No, none. Everybody I know loved her. She'd never hurt a soul." The cap in her hands contorted under her anguish.

"Everyone makes an enemy along the way, someone who's jealous, or just plain crazy."

"Wait, she was in line for a step up in the hospital's management hierarchy, maybe someone wanted it more. She'd said she had *words,* as she described it, with an associate who wanted to climb the corporate ladder."

"Did she mention a name?" *How many people are vying for the position?*

"No, but she called me last night. Said someone broke in and left odd stuff on her kitchen countertop. She thought it was someone playing a sick joke, but her dog was inside and all right, which didn't make any sense. Her dog is *not* friendly. I told her to report it to the police. She said she'd call in the morning."

"Do you believe…?"

"I don't know anyone who would do this, but she was not the kind to make enemies, and no one she'd call friend would pull that type of crap."

The sudden announcement blaring over the PA system startled them both. "Code red, room 401. Code red, room 401." Three more times, the wooden voice announced its emergency with cold, monotone indifference.

The rush of heavy footfalls and rolling carts in the corridor told him the patient who'd just arrived next door was flatlining.

"Um, it wouldn't be good if I'm discovered here." Lexi looked around nervously.

"Yeah, especially if that's the slime-ball who shot me this morning. I think it's best if you leave." To encourage her departure went against every police policy he could imagine, but the instinct guiding his action was something he wouldn't ignore.

"I didn't do anything! I just came to make sure you're okay." Her harsh whisper held the panic evident in her gaze.

"Yeah, but if they finger you for the informant, you'll be questioned to the nth degree. Meet me at my home tomorrow. I assume you remember where I live?"

Hushed, urgent voices heard from the next room signaled the staff's attempts to resuscitate a patient while adding more weight to her shoulders.

"Ah, yeah, but I don't think—"

"Hey, if you want information, you have to give like in kind, Lexi. Tuck your hair under that hat and take off the white coat before you leave. Otherwise, it'll look odd for you to be going the other direction."

"All right, I'll be there. So long as your brothers aren't visiting when I arrive." The cap's high crown contained most of her chestnut hair with small wisps escaping to frame her oval face.

Hurried movements slipped each button through its hole before she shrugged the garment off and tossed it on the back of a chair. As suspected, blue jeans hugged her hips and a flannel shirt concealed the perfect swell of her breasts.

In the instant when emerald depths held him in thrall, he speculated at the scope of an internal conflict held within by pursed lips and fisted hands at her sides. What knowledge did she conceal, and to what lengths had she gone to obtain it? Would he see her again, or would she live in his memory as the mystery who would taunt both waking and sleeping hours?

Light spilling from the hallway highlighted half her face when she glanced over her shoulder, the words she obviously wanted to say not coming. She merely nodded before leaving as if defeated.

Whether from exhaustion or medication kicking in, Ethan was grateful to close his eyes without the figurative knife in his leg. Against his will, the morning's scenario replayed in his mind, his subconscious looking for fault in his choices. Surely that job fell to his brothers and Internal Affairs, who'd grill him until satisfied no stone remained unturned.

A subtle scent lingered, aggravating his well-controlled libido and forcing him to sit up and reach for the chair where her discarded lab coat rested.

A slight squeak accompanied the wooden legs sliding toward the bed in his bid to retrieve the garment. An unknown compulsion to memorize the scent, possibly hers or maybe the coat's owner, saw the garment in his hands then pressed to his face to inhale the fragrance and keep it close. The crisp, clean scent of early spring flowers came to mind. From her shampoo?

A diminishing strength of will released his groan with a light rap at his door. If his brothers intended to sneak back to harass him, perhaps he'd test Carrie's resolve.

"Hi, Mr. McAllister. Mind if I come in for a sec?" Entitlement emanated from the intruder as he pushed the door open and strode in, not a hair out of place nor a wrinkle or smudge on his suit.

Ethan gestured to the chair.

"I'm Daryl Johanson, a trustee on the hospital board." Well-manicured fingers flicked an imaginary piece of lint from his shoulder.

All he needs is a stiff accent to match his demeanor. "Maybe it's the medication, but I think I know you from somewhere." Ethan scrubbed a hand over his eyes, trying to match a location or perspective with the familiar face.

"We met during the last fundraiser for the Art Council. I believe your oldest brother shanghaied you into appearing." Without hesitation, Daryl held out his hand in greeting.

Despite the visitor's friendly smile and warm welcome, fine hairs on Ethan's neck prickled. If this guy was important to Matt, then the face should've stood out. In his mind's eye, he'd endure another of his brother's lectures on the many ways the council helped the community's young artisans.

"What can I do for you?"

"Word is flying around the hospital that our administrator, Frannie, was murdered last night, and that you nailed one of the killers." Concern threading the tone was incongruent with the cold edge about his eyes.

"Since I can't give specific details of an ongoing investigation, let's leave it at this. Yes, your administrator died last night. That much will be public knowledge." *What is it about people wanting gory details?* "Did you know her well?"

An inscrutable expression flicked across his face before Daryl turned away and ambled to the window, a show of controlled nonchalance effectively putting his back to his interrogator.

"Actually, yes. When you check her phone records, my name will come up frequently, so I figured I'd put that information on the table right away. We've been involved for a little over a year, nothing emotionally intimate. It was more akin to meeting physical needs. I attended a charity function last evening, so I didn't get to see her. If I'd been there, maybe she'd still be alive."

"Or maybe you'd be dead, too. I see you're wearing a wedding ring. She wasn't married."

"As I said, physical needs. But now isn't the time for this conversation. I'll see to it that one of our security staff remains outside your door."

Without more visual cues to refute the visitor's statement and considering his current circumstances, Ethan surmised the schmuck's sole purpose had been to cover his butt, possibly save his marriage with every move he made calculated for maximum effect.

"Since there's still a killer on the loose who may think you can identify him, it's your safety now, in this hospital that concerns me."

"The department will probably post someone outside my door until I'm cleared for discharge."

"All right, then. If there's anything you need, just have your nurse let me know." Daryl's smile held the false sincerity reserved for assistants at the motor vehicle administration.

By dinnertime, he could sit up with a clear head and steady stomach. He hadn't realized the extent of his hunger until the door opened, bringing in the fresh-baked aroma of warm bread and seafood.

"Hey, Ethan. I heard you've had a rough day and thought you could use something good to eat besides the wiggly stuff." Carl, still in his forensics lab coat, deposited a bag on the rolling table.

"Hey, thanks."

"I brought your cell phone back. I noticed it was damaged

in all the hassle. I replaced it for you, transferred your contacts, etc. If you're like me, you'll feel naked without it."

Carl set the two phones on the table. "You might want to keep the old one for a spare, throw it in a junk drawer. It's iffy, but we packrats have trouble throwing anything away, right?"

"Yeah, thanks. Nothing like having a tech genius for a friend. The food smells great. Much appreciated." Ethan removed several takeout containers from the bag and took an appreciative whiff. "Smells great. I didn't expect to see you here."

"Hey, you're a hero now. I just wanted to rub elbows and make sure you're all right. Oh, and I asked them to go light on the spices."

"I haven't had salmon with herbed, shrimp sauce since you and my brothers helped me move back to Callouston. I love this. Anything new on my anonymous tipster?"

Experience with four brothers had taught Ethan to not broadcast his tells. Now that he'd met and hopefully made progress with his informant, he didn't want anyone else tracking her down and scaring her off.

Information she'd provided thus far had proven solid and direct. More than that, he didn't want to see her put in harm's way by drawing her out in the open.

"No. Your secret admirer is one clever hacker. Just like before, I can't trace any of your messages."

Now there won't be a need, as long as she shows up after I'm discharged.

Her anonymity, worn like a chameleon's skin, was probably just as precious to her as family was to him. "Well, the tip *did* lead us to a crime."

"Yeah, one in progress where you could've been killed."

After recounting the morning's nightmare once more,

Ethan repeated his desire to connect with his informant.

Mentally, he wished the tech master good luck in his search, suspecting that Lexi was a genius at her craft. What remained unknown was her endgame. Rarely did he meet such a Good Samaritan.

Chapter Four

Regardless of what horrors took shape in her day, coming home to Hoover's enthusiastic pup kisses and frisky romping instilled a different mindset, free of psychos, stress, or petty differences.

The three-year-old canine's unrestrained joy could bring a smile to the most stoic—and did when they made hospital rounds as a therapy team. A standard kneel and greet included much cooing, chuffing, and finally an offered paw.

In co-signing for the building, Frannie had helped her acquire it, then remained instrumental in guiding its transformation. During the past three years, the home had become Lexi's refuge where she could relax, work, and simply *be*.

As a programmer, she would've earned enough to pay her mortgage off in another five years. What would happen with her mentor's passing would be determined by a faceless, cold, and uncaring system, just as when her parents had died.

Frannie had no living relatives, had always looked at the *what ifs* of the future, caring deeply about those she helped rescue from the street. The fact that someone would snuff such a loving spirit bled morality and graciousness from humanity's collective soul.

Midafternoon shadows crawled across the cement floor of her converted warehouse turned fortress. Nothing could change the past, but the future remained open, and she had a murderer to catch.

It wouldn't be the first time she'd tipped off the police to a killer's identification, but she hoped not to land in dire straits again. This time she had the advantage of not just computer skills but also the backing of a cop who knew of her track record and determination.

At least I hope I do. She'd seen the edge of uncertainty in Ethan's gaze when the patient next door had coded.

Six years ago, she'd been a teenager, alone and newly orphaned. Unlike others in her predicament, she'd found herself taking refuge from the worst of street life with a group of prostitutes, something that continued for the next three years. They'd imparted their knowledge of basic survival skills along with a certain wariness for anything police related.

In stirring her vigilante side, she'd plucked karma's strings in stealing their murdering pimp's money and trophies, mostly odd pieces of jewelry, and delivering the latter to one Detective Ethan McAllister.

Subsequently, the girls were free, each with a split of the pimp's cash and a new lease on life. In return, karma and Ethan had intervened to keep her safe.

When Frannie had befriended her and infused hope for a better life, the girls had convinced her to go. The following years saw her safe and flourishing, her innate skills landing her a programming gig that allowed her to work from her secluded fortress.

The jingle-clink of keys dropping in the counter's clutter bowl pricked Hoover's ears and cocked the dog's head sideways. The canine could hear a cheese wrapper unfold from the next county but when called from across the backyard, selective hearing softened her friend's steps before Lexi had begun training in earnest.

It was times like these she wished she'd set up a mini gym in her spacious digs. Perhaps a ground-eating jog would induce the mindset needed for work.

"We should've gone to Frannie's last night, girl. Maybe

we could've scared the bastards off." The thought of acquiring a gun crossed her mind. "Looks like I need to keep up with the times."

Mostly shepherd with a bit of husky and something indeterminate on the side, her blue-eyed companion whined and rubbed against her leg.

With the graceless thud of a newborn foal, Lexi dropped cross-legged to the floor and hugged her precious companion tight until Hoover pulled back to lick her face.

"This place isn't much to look at, and it's not located in a ritzy neighborhood, but we're safe, healthy, and happy." She eyed the precious blanket lovingly laid across the back of her microfiber sofa. Flashbacks of receiving Frannie's gift filled her gaze with tears.

"We'll find that killer, girl. We'll find him."

Hoover finagled her muzzle under Lexi's hair, sniffing with the relentlessness of a tax assessor. Her twitching nose, wet with the moisture that helped capture scents, searched from head to toe, silently asking mom where she'd been.

"Yeah, I know researchers proved dogs can smell a teaspoon of sugar in a million gallons of water, but let me assure you, I'm not as sweet, nor have I been around anyone who is. You can stop taste-testing."

In her lifetime, there'd been a handful of beings that accounted for the preservation of her current sanity. Hoover's incredible communion assured her place among the canine Hall of Saints.

On the human plane, Lexi hadn't met anyone as altruistic as the hospital administrator who'd caught a snot-nosed kid red-handed, hacking a hospital's computer in hopes of erasing her friend's file. No record equaled no trail. Instead of calling the cops, the hospital administrator had delved deeper, finding some unknown quality worth nurturing.

"If it weren't for Frannie, I wouldn't be here, girl. Heck, you wouldn't either. All she ever did was help people. Why would anyone hurt her?"

Thinking back on Frannie's persistence in directing a mouthy kid to a decent path brought fresh tears to her eyes. She finally let them fall.

She'd known the shooter's room number from delving through hospital digital records, child's play. She also realized Ethan suspected her of *something* devious by the look in his eyes. "Think he believes I messed with the killer for revenge?"

She'd given Ethan no reason to trust her. "And now he's in the hospital and Frannie's dead." Lexi's list of suspected sins accumulated the weight of mountains, crushed and sheared into new shapes beneath the power of an oncoming glacier. The icy mass had a name—Ethan McAllister.

Even when physically compromised, he held the power to bore through the darkest reaches of her mind, sifting through her thoughts to pick at one for closer inspection. She'd have to consider her options carefully before confronting him again.

I bet he uses those sexy looks to his advantage.

"We'd better hack the path report if that shooter dies, just so we know what's happening. It's possible his partner didn't want to chance him talking to the cops."

She didn't expect good things in life, hence was rarely disappointed, but seeing the skepticism in Ethan's gaze had hurt. It wasn't as if they shared a common denominator. Any police officer would've doubted someone with her background and skills.

"According to the nurse's last digital notes before he

coded, the shooter was awake and in stable condition." *So what went wrong?*

Snooping through files gave her a start, a name. From there, she unraveled the shooter's past and pieced together a virtual frame of his life. His work and trading accounts confirmed his history as a day trader in the stock market, which meant his computer was his office. The divorce on record was final several years ago. *Who'd want to marry the creep?*

Trudging to her feet, she wondered about the deviant toys Frannie had found last night. "Got to be some kind of deranged psycho, Hoover. Nobody else could be that sick." The teenaged pup whined once and then headed toward the door where her leash hung low enough to grasp in her jaws, her signal when needing exercise.

"In a minute girl."

Chiming from her laptop on the table signaled an incoming email. The two-password system decrypting her 2048-bit private RSA key and personal mailbox occurred within her own browser using JavaScript to ensure anonymity.

Electronic invisibility provided comfort as well as refuge from legal eyes. The systems she'd previously hacked weren't for personal gain or with malicious intent; she simply wanted, *needed*, no, to learn how things worked and interacted. Unfortunately, the law wouldn't see it that way. Tor's snail pace induced nail-biting frustration as uncovering secrets on the dark net took time, not to mention patience. Hacking Frannie's network and retrieving her text message had led her down The Onion Router, a place she'd begun navigating long ago but still shuddered with the myriad levels of sick deviants found.

The current sender, from a .onion address, would remain unidentified unless she could garner favor from the right people, which was difficult but not impossible.

Again, it would take time.

Never considered a *people* person, she preferred computers and the simple honesty of animals to the lies and deceit of two-legged creatures. Now she had to curry approval from the very people she despised in order to solve the crime.

The unknown sender asked if she wanted to participate in the game. She'd sent out feelers concerning murder for hire but hadn't expected anything back so soon.

"What the heck? What game?"

The deep web started as a military project and now played host to infinite types of activities, many illegal, including pornography and black market weapons. "To which game is he referring?"

If she asked too many questions, the contact would assume her some type of cop instead of a referred peer. She was out of her realm and would have to work more closely with Ethan. Dealing firsthand with a cop wasn't something she'd ever expected to do.

From hacking records, she'd learned of Ethan's diligence and intelligence, but he was still a cop. The fact he compared her to a fruit attested to his lack of mental clarity, something that would probably embarrass him considering his general precision in both appearance and written reports.

Now that he has a face to match to his mysterious texts, how will he react once he's clear-headed?

* * * *

"Care to explain why some flaky administrator put a cop in the room next to his shooter?" Larrick paced back and forth at the foot of Ethan's bed. "I'll find out who's responsible for assigning room numbers. It smells dirty to me."

"There was supposed to be a guard by the door, maybe the hospital's idea of two-for-one budget cuts." Ethan rarely witnessed his partner's impatience take physical form. They'd already discussed the details but sometimes rehashing lit the proverbial shotgun lights inside the yokel's head.

"Yeah, a rent-a-cop who dodged his post to take a message, which just happened to coincide with the perp coding. We sure can't get any answers now. Our techs said they couldn't even trace the guard's communication back to its source. They did rule out the wife sending it. Which means it was a setup."

"Hospital security was only covering for city PD for an hour. 'Sides, the shooter was handcuffed to his bed, obviously not expected to go anywhere."

"Yeah, he's still handcuffed. Just dead." Larrick stopped and leaned over the end of the mattress, resting his hands on the footboard. "The nurses said he was going to be okay. What happened?"

"IA might want to look at me. They don't trust anyone." Pain in his thigh made Ethan wince.

"No, your nurse and one of the aides vouched for you, said you haven't been up yet. Even if you knew how to clamp your IVs and silence the pump, your heart monitor would've gone crazy if disconnected. Must be that McAllister karma."

"Thank God for small favors." Ethan sighed.

"I take it all your family has visited." A narrowed gaze gave away Larrick's speculation. Hillbilly did not equal dumb by any means.

"Yeah, except for Abagail." Too late, Ethan realized his mistake.

"What? Your nurse said a young woman wearing a lab coat visited, though your sister is neither a nurse nor a tech." Larrick, realizing he'd just latched on to the tiger's tail, grinned, waiting to pounce.

"Listen, I need you to do me a favor. Call Abagail and tell her not to visit today." If his sister showed now, questions about his earlier visitor might land him in hot water. "Now, please?"

"I'll send her a text and tell her your proctologist is busy butt mining." His dark chuckle declared that wouldn't be the end of it. "Then you're gonna explain about your mystery guest. I'm not leaving until you do."

Ethan had never lied to his partner and knew traveling that slippery slope wouldn't end well. The problem was he didn't have much information to give, and he didn't want his partner taking the wrong stance. In Larrick's mind, a wrong first impression would take a coon's age to change.

Once Larrick tucked his phone in his flannel shirt pocket and tapped the footboard rhythmically, contemplation time was up.

"All right, I had a visitor." Drawing it out allowed more time to think.

"And what did our little birdie have to say?"

"Her name is Lexi, said she was family to the victim. I'd appreciate it if we kept her identity just between us for now."

"Well, where is she?" Larrick held his arms wide.

"She left when the guy next door coded."

"Hmm, sounds like convenient timing."

"She didn't kill him." *Though she could have. White lab coat, in and out. Sending a text message to get the guard off his post.*

"And you know that how? Where is she now?" Larrick's grip white-knuckled on the footboard.

"I couldn't exactly cuff her to the bed now could I?"

"Been that long, has it? I know you're rusty. Maybe that's why she sent you fur-lined cuffs with the flowers."

"Larrick, her friend was just murdered. She wants to know who did it and why."

"And you don't think she could've sent an anonymous text and snuck into your neighbor's room for a little one-on-one vengeance?"

"Anyone could've sent the guard a text. Besides, you don't know the dirtbag didn't die from surgical complications. Chest wounds can be tricky."

"Time and the path report will tell." Larrick stabbed a finger in the air in Ethan's direction. "Sounds like you're getting in over your head. I'll check security cameras but let me guess. You're still too fuzzy from surgery to give an accurate description, and I'll bet we don't pick up any visual, right? The only glimpse I've had of her was from a good distance away and several months ago when we arrested that pimp. She's got long hair, skinny as a rail, and a sharp wit. I'm assuming this is the same tipster that led us to the psychotic pimp."

"I *am* still fuzzy. Anesthesia, remember? And maybe you should check the video recordings of this corridor." Considering her elite hacker status, Lexi was smart enough to avoid digital exposure but offering that for consideration made him appear more neutral.

"Any ideas about what might have been written on the phony-money clue at the crime scene?" Larrick finally sat in the corner chair, his right ankle bouncing on his left knee as he sat back and cradled his head on intertwined fingers. His demeanor underscored a contemplation and persistence that made him an equal partner in their working relationship. "Without it, we have no clue as to his next victim."

Ethan grimaced when images of the victim's likely last moments disrupted his thoughts. "Um no. Nothing comes to mind. Sick dirtballs, thinking up that kind of crap. You've been around awhile, and your girlfriend works here. Did you know Frannie?" Asking questions was the best way to sidetrack a steely persistence.

"I've met her a couple of times. Charlotte works in the ICU. Seems the administrator was both respected and well-liked by the staff." Larrick shook his head in disgust. "We didn't find anything to contradict that opinion in the victim's home, in her letters, email, et cetera. IT has her computer and cell phone. Nothing from the computer so far. There was a text message... that damned riddle."

"Let me guess, left by an unidentified sender that you believe could be my secret admirer." Ethan rubbed the shadow stubble forming on his jaw. "Maybe it was the killer's idea of an advanced warning."

"Sure as heck wasn't good tidings, and it could've been left by your newest friend. Think about it with your other head."

"She was family, not a killer."

"Yeah, and family never goes after their own. 'Sides, what if she's lying? Records show Frannie has no family," Larrick countered.

"They weren't connected by blood." Ethan .
doubt his own intuition. "There's a big age gap."

"Not connected by marriage, either. We checked. Frannie has no relatives."

Then what united two women who apparently had nothing in common? "You know anything about another hospital administrator, Daryl Johanson?"

"No, why?"

"Stopped by to tell me he was banging Frannie occasionally just to meet his *physical needs* and assure me I'd be safe. He also might've been in competition with Frannie for a step up in pay grade."

"Don't know him, but I know people who do. I'll start looking into him. Awful nice of him to come in and volunteer the information." Larrick's sneer asserted his opinion.

"Exactly. Lying in bed and a bit foggy, I wasn't in much of a position to ask questions."

"Think he had anything to do with assigning room numbers? As an administrator, he certainly has to have some computer skills."

"Don't know, but he was hiding something." Ethan shifted to find a more comfortable position.

"Well, while you're taking your undeserved vacation, I'll head back to the station and start digging into Daryl Johanson, Dooley Sonnenfeld's associates, and any other competing hospital administrators."

ɔpping sound of the metal plate against its
ɔd Diego's entrance through his electronic
Cold fur held the dampness from an early-
ɹ in grass needing its first spring haircut.

the advantages of large families equaled help when you needed it, though Ethan didn't want to ask. He now understood how Caden felt after his injury.

After setting the bowl of kibble on the mat, Ethan's hobble-step with a crutch carried him to his easy chair. Two thousand square feet had seemed modest when he'd built the rancher. Now the large space mocked his faltering step. He'd cursed both his weakness and the crutch.

"Despite what you may think, Diego, you are not part of the flooring. If you trip me again, I'm hanging a cow bell around your neck."

Two days into his two-week recuperation and boredom had sunk its talons deep. Still, he didn't want to be inundated with family.

Elicited promises from his brothers to not visit had only lasted hours upon his return, each bearing food of one sort or another, which meant his mother had cooked all day to provide each brother with a dish to bring. Adding insult to injury, they'd spaced their visits out to keep him hobbling about throughout the first afternoon.

When his sister had declared his fridge fully stocked and capable of feeding an army, she'd sworn to help ensure privacy for a few days to give him a break.

Unfortunately, his concerned informant hadn't visited as expected, which prompted more questions. He had no doubt the tears that had brimmed Lexi's eyes were real but was her grief so strong to compel her to take action?

"Well, boy, it looks like we're right back where we started." The white lab coat left behind probably contained Lexi's DNA along with who knew how many others. Besides, instinct told him that trying to track her down would induce flight, and she might hold crucial information.

A cloud of confusion fogged his mind, veiling any small tidbits or clues that might have illuminated a twisted reason for the killer's MO. Enforced time off allowed time to reassess his life, surroundings, and circumstances.

The end table's gory horror novel beckoned another long morning on the couch while his subconscious sorted details he hadn't yet fathomed. Still, it was better than enduring his brothers' ribbing.

According to Larrick, they'd learned nothing new about the victim, her lover, the perp, or Lexi. At least there were no new murders, as he suspected would soon occur. *Minds that sick won't stay dormant for long.*

Diego's excited bark alerting to an outside presence provided a surge of excitement despite Ethan's insistence on privacy. The dog's deep rumbling usually resulted from two-legged visitors.

Lack of skidding stones or tires grinding in dirt suggested no family members prepared to interrupt his quiet, contemplative morning, but the dog's excitement surpassed that of sensing Bambi's cousins.

Fine hairs lifted on his nape, yet he didn't reach for his Glock on the side table. The Lexi-type manifestation in his imagination had happened yesterday when Diego raised a racket, yet he'd received no callers.

Matt, his oldest sibling visiting at the time, constantly harangued him about needing security cameras outside. Perhaps he'd give it more thought and make them happy.

The soft, tentative knock on his door barely registered and would've been drowned out if his TV had currently been running his favorite sitcom. Through the peephole, he saw nothing.

The knock came again, this time answered by Diego's excited chuffing.

"If you guys are reduced to pranks, that means your time is—" He expected one of his brothers to startle him with one tactic or another—a stun gun, dart gun, or perhaps his mother's disapproving scowl as she marched in and exclaimed how he needed a woman to care for his home.

"Hi. Mind if we come in?"

He didn't expect the wind to blow in a tall, chestnut-haired young woman with emerald-green eyes hidden by dark shades. And a dog? The mixed breed canine beside her stood hip high and eagerly sniffed at Diego.

The punched-gut feeling received in the hospital upon seeing her replicated in him now. Momentarily frozen, his entire nervous system seemed to come alive in her presence, everything heightened, more sensitive.

He couldn't quite define the faint but enticing aroma that ensnared his senses, yet she appeared oblivious to her allure and pulled him in just the same. Desire sluiced through his blood, compelling him to reach for her.

She sidestepped but proceeded forward. "Nah, I got it without help." The large, brown paper bag in her arms, contents unknown, appeared heavy. "Wouldn't want you to hurt yourself." She didn't remove her sunglasses.

You've already invaded every aspect of my being, why not my home?

Seeing there would be no difficulty between the dogs who greeted each other with play bows and false starts of energy, he hobble-stepped behind her after she'd brushed past. "Where's your car? I assume you didn't walk here."

"Never assume anything." No hesitation slowed her step en route to his kitchen. Diego trotted beside his guests, accepting Lexi's hand on his head as if they'd befriended each other years ago.

Several thumps from the bag's contents on the breakfast bar had both dogs' attention. "Ya know, you really should think about feeding raw. Diego would be healthier."

Why is she sure that I don't? "How do you know his name?"

"You think I'd come here without due diligence? Really? I'm glad you picked a good veterinarian. I'd take my furbaby there, too, if I didn't already have a great vet." Her smirk gave away nothing.

She probably has my digital life on file.

"What can I do for you?" He'd given up on her coming and wondered how she'd traveled since no vehicle sat in his driveway. Furthermore, he felt deprived as he couldn't see her eyes.

"Wasn't going to come. But you'll need my help to catch Frannie's killer, and since I've kinda gotten used to working with you, I figured we might as well finish this."

Pulling a baggie of small, brown squares from her care package, she inspected her surroundings. "Nice place, by the way."

"Glad you approve. Exactly how is it that *I* need *your* help?" In fact, he was relieved with her arrival for reasons that had nothing to do with the sudden electrical hum touring his nervous system.

"And by the way, one of our IT workers and several colleagues are trying to determine your identity since you've given us good leads. They don't trust anonymous sources. Curiosity is killing Carl in forensics. I think he'd like to be the ultimate hacker and might be a bit jealous."

Larrick had spilled the beans to his brothers about a mysterious female visitor in the hospital. Few could prevail against a tide of determined McAllisters.

Despite his excuse of anesthesia numbing his senses, his brothers hadn't bought the "maybe I dreamed the conversation" scenario.

They don't know your approximate age, hair color, ethnic background, etc.

She shrugged. "No one has a clue who I am, and I intend to keep it that way." The snap of her baggie opening drew both dogs closer.

Whether from body soap or shampoo, her ambrosial scent urged him closer in the guise of looking over her shoulder.

"What's in there?" A slow breath kept his deep inhalation quiet.

Her body tensed. "You need to train Diego not to accept treats from strangers." That directive issued, she promptly gave said dog a small, brown square from her baggie.

"Imagine that. What are you hiding?" Though he still wasn't in any shape to interrogate a suspect, he couldn't pass up the opportunity to elicit information. His most important clues when deciphering a person's deception came from observing the eyes, which he still couldn't see.

"Hiding? Nothing, I just like my privacy." When her own dog nudged her leg, she relented and held out a snack.

Diego's eagerness to steal his guest's goodie resulted in driving Ethan forward and off balance.

His crutch clattered to the floor while he scrambled to

stay upright. With one hand on the counter and his other on the curve of her hip, he realized his list of errors. Removing his hand from her body cost him his equilibrium, his trajectory leading to the floor.

"Damn."

Flailing limbs and mindless cursing would've earned great marks in his brothers' mocking comments, each declaring him hopeless in one form or another. Larrick's, *You're a hopeless romantic,* speech mocked his less-than-smooth move as pain expanded outward from his wound.

Lexi's quick reflexes softened his landing, but her strength was no match for his greater size. Her body followed his trajectory, landing on top of him with an *"Ooof."*

Muscles in his thigh contracted with the agonizing burn flashing down his leg. He heard more than felt his head thudding on the kitchen floor mat. Gradually, other sensations took root in his mind and sent signals to his body he couldn't avoid.

Face to face, neither one moved. He couldn't breathe with the shock of the connection reaching a deeper part of his spirit. She felt it too, evidenced by her quiet gasp and slackened jaw.

The arcane connection forged months ago allowed him to remove her shades and delve deep within her gaze to cobble together a network of cues for which he could neither summarize nor define.

Her hair, flowing softly to embrace his head, cocooning them in their own world, her scent that inexplicably drew him in against his will, and the languid heat singing his hands where they touched her flanks, all combined to leave him paralyzed.

Her muscles went lax and became pliant for several

shocked heartbeats while her legs on either side of his own created a cradle, one his baser instincts recognized and responded to instantly.

She curled her fingers against his chest, marking him in a way only Lexi could, by blasting filaments of small charges to squeeze his lungs.

Nothing had ever felt so good as his body hummed with the sparks firing through his nervous system to leave him in a state of confused craving. The shocked expression delineated by her open mouth and softening body stood forefront in his mental catalog of memorable experiences.

Months ago, he'd saved her from a homicidal pimp, yet circumstances—namely her hasty escape—had denied him the pleasure of anything more than a quick visual. With time, her occasional texts and through the less frequent but humorous gag gifts, they'd forged an otherworldly connection he couldn't deny.

He distantly wondered what horrific experience had briefly crushed her spirit. In his heart, he recognized her invisible armor as a shell built from grief, disappointment, and pain.

Diego and Hoover broke the unnamed vortex of swirling emotions with slobbering kisses by clambering on top. The resultant pile-up compounded his discomfort on several levels, forcing their bodies to lock together. The crimson tide creeping up her neck from under the long-sleeved tee indicated her acknowledgment of his problem. She looked away and took a deep breath.

"Diego, you furry brat. Knock it off." Ethan concentrated on the dogs, anything but the soft, pliant flesh under his fingers.

"I think he's adopted me as his fairy godmother."

"Sorry. Let me help you up." With a clearer understanding of and respect for personal space, Ethan eased her up with both hands at her hips, curling his body at the same time. Due to her t-shirt riding up, his fingers rested on the smoothest skin he'd ever known. He didn't miss the full-body shiver that shook her frame.

Once set to rights, the tightening of her shoulders spoke volumes. Her gaze touching everywhere but his face gave further evidence of her inexperience with romantic entanglements. The deep flush of her skin was adorable.

"You all right? I wouldn't advise entering a crutch race anytime soon. You just don't have the coordination." Her attempt at humor didn't change the course of her obvious thoughts. Deepening crimson rode high on her cheeks as she pulled her shirt down.

The reactions were unexpected from someone so bold and self-assured of her place in life. Unable to cover her physical responses, she turned her face away, the long fall of silky waves hiding her expression as she retrieved her shades and his crutch.

"I'm fine. Growing up with four brothers ensured nothing could hurt my head. Sorry. I guess Diego really likes your treats."

Ethan rubbed his hands on his jeans in a failed attempt to halt the tingling sensation spreading up his arms. "Where were we? Oh yeah, we were talking about invading privacy." Anything to keep his mind off her body's privates.

"I happen to like my personal information to remain unseen." The rise of her chest delineated the quiet, deep breath taken as if sampling the heady mixture of something forbidden, exotic, toxic.

"But don't mind invading other folks' inner sanctums?"

He then realized that maybe she was just as he'd first thought—a young woman who appreciated solitude.

"Like you don't do the same thing on a daily basis?" A slight shake of her head illustrated her confusion.

Dissecting others' lives is what I'm trained to do.

"I hacked some reports. Frannie's dog was drugged with an ACE-like compound. The report said the son of a gun used a steak laced with tranquilizer, then waltzed right into her home to terrorize and cut her up."

This time, when Diego attempted to take the offered treat, she snapped her hand closed with a "leave it" command. "See? This is how you start. Give it a try. When you're ready for him to have it, just tell him to take it."

Shocked that someone could whirl into his life, his home, his private sanctum, take root in his mind, and issue commands left him speechless. He accepted the moist, tasty treats while a mental picture as to the nature of this young woman's ulterior motives refused to take shape.

"So, you read the dog's lab reports. What else did you find out?" *She's more efficient than some of our officers.* When Diego reached forward to take the morsel from his hand, Ethan closed his fingers and issued the directive. After several tries, the dog merely waited until given a verbal command to take it. "I understand the need for training your dog well, but I doubt the psycho will be visiting *my* home."

"This is for Diego's sake, not yours. I didn't pick up much else in my electronic inquiries. The path reports on Frannie showed a small amount of an unidentified drug in her system. However, the dirtball you shot overdosed with the same drug used on Frannie's dog."

Diego whined.

"And you'd know that how?"

"Cross-referencing their bloodwork. Your shooter was identified onsite through the biometric scanner." She huffed a breath as if waiting for him to catch up.

"Guess I underestimated your efficiency. So the guy I winged hooked up with a day trader who doesn't even have a parking ticket *and* has a permanent address in Delaware. A stock market whiz *would* be very familiar with technology. Maybe he was the one to send Frannie the text." Ethan added, "Why don't we have a seat in the living room? Would you like something to eat or drink?"

"I can stay for a bit, but I'm not hungry. I know your family probably brought you food, but I brought a bag of Diego's food just in case." Setting the twenty-pound bag in the pantry, she added, "Let's talk about raw feeding afterward."

"How'd you know... Never mind. I'm thinking there's never gonna be anything private about my life again. Am I right?"

"Hey, it's a world of ones and zeroes. Join the twenty-first century. Be careful with your step. You're not exactly Fred Astaire."

"Yeah, yeah, sit down and tell me what you know, if not your full name." Ethan sat on the sofa, watching as she perched on the opposite chair. The lithe grace with which she sat couldn't be taught, more likely ingrained naturally to those rare creatures who stood out from the crowd.

Despite her air of self-assuredness, a slightly narrowed gaze and stiff gait had indicated she lacked the projected confidence, or their collision had affected her as much as it had him. "Let me guess. You parked down the road so I couldn't get your tag."

"Well, you are a cop, even if you don't know one end of a computer from the other." As if competing for her attention, both dogs attempted to sit with her in the chair, managed only by her pushing back and elevating the footrest. "As far as your guy who coded in the hospital, I did find that he was divorced."

"Yeah, several years ago, living on the East Coast at the time."

"Yep, I took the liberty of looking into his ex-wife. Her name is Bethany Jameson, and she lives in Callouston." Lexi studied her surroundings as if further gauging his character.

"So he did have a tie to someone in this area."

"She went back to using her maiden name after the divorce."

"I guess I should thank you for this and your past help three months ago. You're bold, but you've shown a great knack for placing yourself in danger. If that pimp had caught you stealing from his safe, he would've killed you just as he did the prostitutes."

The thought of her broken and shredded tightened his gut. By bringing up her past, perhaps he'd learn more about her.

"He *did* catch me, yet I got away. Street smarts. As a result, he's on death row, and his former *employees* are now safe and have begun new lives." Pride edged her tone.

"But you were never one of his girls." Despite her toughened exterior, Ethan sensed a tender vulnerability that begged for exploration. The only glimpse he'd gotten of her without anesthesia in his system had been months ago and fifty yards away as she'd dashed into the woods. At the time he'd had his hands full with subduing the pimp who'd tried to kill her.

"No, his girls took me in when I was orphaned, gave me a place to crash and managed to keep my presence a secret. I owe them everything. It could easily have been me you'd found in the alley, carved up and left for dead."

"So they spared you their fate, and in return, you used your skills and risked your life to free them." Loyalty, courage, and determination, as well as a natural grace that accompanied the innocent, encompassed her spirit.

If he could, he'd personally thank those working girls for protecting Lexi. The intricate and convoluted web accounting for how she remained an obvious innocent despite her upbringing was a mystery he had to disentangle. Dressing conservatively, shunning makeup, a quiet confidence uncorrupted by false pretenses were all things he'd observed in his assessment.

"You're plotting something. I can see it." Raking her bottom lip between perfect white teeth failed to restrain her impulse to take an aggressive stance.

"Merely trying to get a read on you." *And wondering if the rest of your skin feels as soft as satin.*

"That's why I love animals, always straightforward and honest about what they feel. Their intentions are written in their body language with no subterfuge, no conditions." With each stroke of her hand down her dog's back, tension seemed to drain from her body.

Non sequitur, or sideways accusation? Her gaze gave away nothing.

"Huh, looks like you should sit on the sofa to accommodate your admirers." The comment had nothing to do with the fact that he wanted her closer to catch the scent of her shampoo and feel the stronger sizzle of excitement with her proximity.

"I came here to give you info you can't access."

"Really?" Somewhat skeptic of all things electronic, Ethan

gestured for her to continue, hoping to discern more about her motives. If she'd intended to disrupt his investigation, his intuition would've rung the alarm by now. Oblivious to her beauty and its effect hammering his concentration, she spoke with conviction.

"What do you know about Tor?"

"Ancient Norse God of all branches of the Germanic folks before Christianity came to town. Known for courage, sense of duty, physical strength, and *Mjolnir*, his hammer." He realized she'd referenced technology but wanted to see her smile.

It worked.

It was breathtaking.

It was out-of-bounds thinking that distracted him from his work.

"You're dying to waggle your eyebrows." She shook her head and briefly closed her eyes. "And now back to our regularly scheduled program. Let's unpack those letters. *TOR* stands for The Onion Router, which also goes by dark net, deep web, and many other names."

Rubbing behind Diego's ears appeared to smooth the lines furrowing her brow as she took a deep breath. That same look had graced his brothers' faces many times when they tried to convey a complicated idea.

"You play there?" To his knowledge, only the criminal element along with some private investigators like his brother Caden surfed the dark net. Hoodlums looked for illegal drugs, porn, and murder for hire. Others were merely curious. She didn't seem to fit any of the former categories.

"Not usually, but I like to understand its workings. Digging for clues to Frannie's murder led me in that direction. I found someone who might be connected, might not. It's too early to tell." A long blink later, she continued, "He asked if I wanted to join the game."

"What game?" Those words claimed his full attention as he leaned forward.

"It's a killing game of some sort. If I'd found it on the light net, I'd have assumed it connected with a video game. However, this is some sick dirtball's idea of entertainment."

"Can you trace it?" He had to swallow hard as he imagined her face superimposed on Frannie's body in the crime scene photos.

"Possibly, but it wouldn't matter since he's only a spectator and wouldn't provide a direct connection to the killer. Looks like someone is using the dark net as a betting ground. People place bets and offer suggestions for targets. I'm not yet sure what the winner gets."

"So, how did you answer?"

"I haven't yet. I don't want to appear too anxious or ask too many questions. I wanted to talk with you about it first, but I also don't want to get caught up with your brothers. I was thinking maybe I could nudge your IT department in the right direction if they're capable enough. But I'd have to do it in person."

"Why not electronically?"

"A, I need credibility, so they don't end up focusing on dissecting my life, a waste of precious time. And B, I want physical access to Frannie's computer and phone. I can spot any malware on it."

"I think you should bring your computer here and send your messages from this IP address in case the killer does trace you." Taking her to the station and keeping her anonymous equaled an oxymoron.

"With your brothers dropping by daily? I don't want

frequent interactions with them."

"Look, they didn't get anything from the hospital cameras, so they've no clue to your identity. Larrick will keep his mouth shut, to some extent. They'll think you're my girlfriend."

"You don't have a current girlfriend that I've found. Matter of fact..."

Is she fishing? "No, I don't have a current girlfriend. Don't go there, you're starting to sound like my sister." *But you sure don't look like her.*

"Why not?"

"I'm tired of bottled blondes and empty-headed twits." He squeezed his eyes shut as if in pain. "Sorry, I didn't mean it that way. I just want—more out of life. I do respect women of all types."

"Must be all that meaningless sex that's fried your mental circuits while giving you that GQ bod. Hope you didn't catch something bleach wouldn't scrub off."

"I'm not like Caden. He's the gigolo."

"Ha. All men are ruled by their joysticks."

You were just as affected by our fall...

"As far as talking with our IT folks, I can speak to Carl. He's a friend that works in our forensics lab." Everything she'd said made sense and was logical. It didn't mean he had to like it. Ironic how he wanted nothing more than to analyze every aspect of her life yet keep said knowledge from anyone else.

"Okay. Good. As far as sending a reply email, I can deal with this and stay anonymous."

"You're not equipped to handle these killers. Who knows how many are involved and the extent of their reach? Maybe these two are part of a larger conspiracy and will track you down."

"You can't surf Tor."

"My partner isn't sure to what extent you're involved in this mess." He continued the standoff in his determination to exert his will.

"One hundred percent. Frannie was my mentor and my friend, yet I failed to protect her. Now, she's dead because of me."

"No. She's dead because some sick screwball chose her for his sadistic sense of sport. We need to figure out how, where, and when he's gonna strike again."

Years of investigative experience discerned the great depth of her guilt as real, something that would haunt her in the coming years.

"I figure he might be accessing someone's database to dig through personal information. He hacked her cell phone account and who knows what else. I need to see her computer." Lexi grunted when Diego pushed off her abdomen to hop down from the chair.

"So the twisted psycho spies on them electronically, learning their routines, and nails down his timing?" Ethan sat back, thinking of how easily a cyber-snoop could accomplish that goal.

Unfortunately, he couldn't hack records worth a darn and didn't want to pull Lexi in any further. He couldn't ignore her not-so-subtle request to examine police evidence, which could only be done as a consultant.

"From what I understand, you got nothing from the clue he left?" She was fishing with an expectation of a solid answer.

"It seems you understand quite a bit from—" He shouldn't have been surprised that she could keep abreast of current events right down to the smallest detail. Her determination would see her underneath the killer's vicious torment if he couldn't sway her steadfast objective to *help*.

"Electronic reports." The slightest of smirks tilted one side of her mouth.

"Figures. The script was too degraded by fluids. Listen, since you've hacked every aspect of this case, what's to say the psycho hasn't already found *you*? If he's good enough to play on the dark net, why wouldn't he be hacking police files at the same time?"

"Yeah, it's possible." Sucking her bottom lip between her teeth, she cocked her head side to side before answering. "Guess I would if I were in his shoes. All right, I'll bring my laptop and communicate from here."

"I assume you can make your reply bounce off different servers." The more information he could obtain, the sooner he could close the case and prevent another murder.

"Yeah, all around the world, but with enough time, anything can be traced."

"You can have the spare room. No strings." In his mind's eye, his brother Billy lectured him about picking up strays. On the other hand, if they didn't appear totally involved, Caden would ask her out, and that wasn't going to fly.

"No thanks." Pink tinged her cheeks as she picked a strand of hair from her jeans. "I have a friend I can stay with 'till this blows over. I'll just communicate from here." She returned a grin for his frown. "I'll come back later with my laptop. You need anything else?"

"Yeah, some help programming this TV for streaming. Never thought I'd want it, but now that I have all this time off, I might as well try it. This solitary and sedentary recuperation is for the birds."

Frustration twisted his gut with the guilt that had edged her tone. Beneath her narrow-focused determination, he sensed a strong code of street-style ethics that demanded justice for her mentor. He needed her help to catch the killer, but in return, he couldn't ensure her safety if she wouldn't remain close.

It appeared that anything furry or electronic in her hands would instill a certain amount of diversion or relaxation. As she flicked through screen after screen in setting up the TV, her natural curiosity illuminated the path of her thoughts.

"So, are you a runner?"

How would she know that? "You mean you don't already know the answer?"

"I know you regularly purchase sportswear, but that could be for show even though you don't seem the type."

"You're the ultimate Christmas shopper, never have to ask questions." He smiled at the blush climbing her cheeks. "Yes, I've run a few marathons and mud races."

Relaxed conversation enlightened him to the depth and variety of her personality's layers. She refused to speak in anything but generalities concerning her private life, either deflecting or answering specific questions with ones of her own.

In the briefest of outlines, she described her life. If she'd ever thought fate had beaten her in any way, it didn't surface in hard-boiled cynicism or resentment. After extracting her promise not to send any more embarrassing *gifts* to his precinct, he could appreciate her mischievous streak without being its recipient.

"What a contradiction you are, sending cuffs and dainty unmentionables to me via the station yet texting clues about dangerous criminals." The reminder of her sexual innuendo was aimed at bringing color to her cheeks.

It did.

"I was bored, and I like pulling pranks. Don't get excited or read anything into it."

Too late. "You'd love some of my brothers. They're all about monkey business." *That came out wrong.*

"I doubt that. They're all cop types."

Intrigued didn't come close to describing his feelings, but the physical reminder that someone with his appetites should steer clear of innocents stuck in his crawl. She deserved slow, artful caresses, patience, and a tantalizing seduction.

"Your shepherd has a routine vet appointment scheduled next week. Can one of your brothers take him? He shouldn't miss it."

Her words catapulted his thoughts back to reality, one where her armor-shielded innocence remained intact. "And why am I not surprised you'd know that? Billy already volunteered."

Genuine concern for his dog etched her features, dispelling the irritation over his life presenting as an open book.

He'd learned long ago that reactions to and treatment of animals revealed a wealth of information about a person's character. What he saw now notched a new level of understanding in his mind and nurtured his burgeoning attraction.

By the time she headed toward the door, they'd at least established a rudimentary, if confusing, working relationship. He'd never been one to mix business and pleasure. Separating the two would prove as difficult as protecting her anonymity.

"It's 'bout time you got security cameras around your house, Ethan. Lucky for you I know my stuff and had the extras on hand. The cameras out front aren't long range, but I'll replace them when my next order comes in."

A stiff gust of wind muffled Caden's words as he stood on the ladder and adjusted the angle of the front porch lens. "Want me to stay with you a few days 'till you're on your feet again?"

"No. I just want to see what's around my house and what's turning in my driveway." He studied the winding asphalt carving a tunnel through the woods, its deep curve hiding the entrance.

"Why the rush? Is this what you've been thinking about for three days while sitting on your butt?" Caden's arched brow spoke volumes.

"No...I just want them in place. Okay?"

"Got it. Advanced warning devices for the technologically impaired on the lookout for Grendel and other mythical creatures. I'll put in lane sensors and attach wireless devices on trees at either side of the entrance so you'll get a bit of notice when someone comes. No one will see them unless they're looking hard. Then I'll set up the receivers in your study and connect it all to your phone."

"No! I don't want them connected to my phone." Lexi had enough insight into his life without him adding more.

"Why not? You've never been paranoid about security."

"It's just that I like things separate. I want to see what's coming when I'm home. That's all."

"All right. Separate circuits. Got it."

"Thanks, Caden. I do appreciate your time."

"Anything else?"

"No. Well, maybe but not today. I'll need some tags run—but off the grid with the family, okay?"

"Why not do it yourself?"

"I'm off duty. I don't want them run through police channels."

"Let me guess. You're not the type to touch someone else's woman, so this must be the elusive prankster or tipster we've been trying to trace...unless they're one and the same. What's she look like? We've all been dying to know. Billy wanted me to set up cameras on your house so he could get a look at her."

Everyone needed brothers who couldn't stop *poking*. "Kiss my butt."

"Ha. I thought you carried mistletoe in your back pocket year round for the girls who drool over you. Expanding our appetites, are we?"

"Sod off."

"I'm not the one protecting a witness, or whatever." Caden raised both hands in surrender as he reached the bottom rung of the ladder.

"How good are your computer skills? Any chance of putting that expensive education to work?" If Ethan could get Caden up to speed with the dark net, he could remove Lexi from danger.

"Fairly decent. What d'ya have in mind?"

"Dark web stuff."

"Oh. I've done a little exploring, but I'm not a nightwalker. I'll see if any of my friends might be able to navigate it a bit better. Give me a starting point." A wry twist of his mouth and drawn-in brows intimated Caden's kindled interest.

"I'll let you know tomorrow."

"So when do I get to meet her? I won't tell the others. At least not for a bit." Caden's show of sincerity was lost in a gaze dancing with devilment.

"Her who?"

"The woman I'm doing all this extra security for. You aren't worried about yourself."

"Sorry, dude. It's gonna be a while. Matter of fact, make sure you call before you come next time. I don't want her spooked."

"Ahh. So it is the girl from the hospital, your secret admirer checking up on you."

"Darn Larrick, anyway. Figures he wouldn't keep his mouth shut."

"Not against a united front of McAllisters. We've been trying to give you time to adjust to the idea of us knowing."

"All right. Come in for a drink, and I'll get you up to speed. Crap. That's why you rushed out here with all this stuff as soon as I called." Fading sunlight slanted through the oak and sycamore branches, unable to dispel the growing sense of foreboding that coiled in Ethan's chest.

Chapter Six

A night without sleep compounded with hours of brooding hadn't brought new insight or alleviated Ethan's stress over his dilemma. His only lead, if honest about her motives, lurked in a world where he exerted no control and couldn't monitor.

None of his brothers or Carl from IT could do much better. The idea of drawing his family further into this murky case soured his stomach. *Like I could keep them out.* After his being shot, nothing would keep them away.

To expose Lexi to the department's IT nerds would risk her anonymity, something she guarded like a Doberman pinscher. She'd understood that, yet determination to draw out Frannie's killer had driven her to extreme measures, given her actions so far. His family considered him as one who fiercely protected his privacy, yet Lexi took that trait to a new level of conviction.

Breakfast consisted of cold cereal and milk while he waited for the decaf to brew, his thoughts drifting to light brown, wavy locks with auburn highlights that curled down to a slight waist. Intelligent emerald eyes didn't detract from her appeal, merely added another hurdle for him to navigate.

If the freshly installed cameras picked up her license plate, he'd have a starting point in tracking her movements. He contemplated asking Caden to stick a tracker on her car during her visit, but its likely discovery could cost him the case and possibly Lexi's life. She wasn't the type to quit digging into the seedy underbelly of the web.

Restraint was not his strong point.

The coffee pot's beep coincided with his doorbell chimes

announcing a visitor. Intuition dictated Lexi had arrived, probably expecting to find him in pajama pants instead of showered and dressed. His eagerness to get the door cost him his balance but not a face-plant on the hardwood floor. The hobble-step crutch walk was getting old. Opening the door equaled a breath of fresh air.

"Huh, fresh as a freaking daisy. I was hoping to not catch you in a scruffy beard and BVD's."

And then there's the attitude. "Not so bad yourself. Come in and join me for coffee."

"Thanks. Hoover found me AATK this morning."

"Is that slang for—"

"Asleep at the keyboard."

"Just what I was thinking."

She snorted.

Diego and Hoover's excited reunion appeared well rehearsed as the shepherd mix bounded through the doorway. Energetic hopping about preceded good-natured doggy roughhousing.

"Hoover, knock it off."

Too late, her command didn't prevent the crash landing of an end table lamp and the crushing of its shade.

"Crap. Sorry, Ethan. Hoover gets a bit excited. Keep them in the kitchen area, and I'll clean it up. And I'll replace the lamp."

Ethan sighed. Knowing the dog was an integral part of Lexi, accepting one meant taking in both with all their idiosyncrasies.

"Don't worry about it." He disliked the lamp anyway. "So, unicorns, huh?" The fanciful design on her t-shirt made him smile. "And here I thought you'd stick with the geeky logo stuff."

"Hey, nothing wrong with either." Lexi headed straight for the kitchen with Hoover bouncing at her heels. The open floor plan afforded him a view of gently swaying hips and the swing of luscious curls caressing a nipped-in waist. She shrugged out of her backpack and deposited it on the table.

"Kind of a strange-looking lamp. Where'd you find it?"

"It was a housewarming thing from Matt, calling me a nihilist and drawing me into the art world in one fell swoop. Apparently, that represented Diogenes, a rebel against cultural norms. Matt's way of calling me a nonconformist." *Which fits your personality more than mine.*

"I assume your broom is in the closet here?" Without waiting for a reply, Lexi opened the small door. "I'm glad you're not a neurotic type-A kind of guy—but being less than a hundred percent must be driving you crazy."

"Yeah? What type do you take me for?" Contemplating her equaled a study in contrasts, form-fitting jeans and solid self-assurance compared to an underlying vulnerability that only surfaced when reminded of her sexuality.

"Not the type to live in a snow globe. Your leg must be hurting pretty bad." To make her point, she snared a small tuft of hair kicked up with the dogs' play. "Then again, Hoover is starting to blow her coat, so it's only fair that I help."

"Mhmm, sorry. I hate the idea of hiring a cleaning service. I prefer to do it myself, but..." Something about watching her perform a simple domestic task in his home, maybe her innate grace or perhaps her assumption of his acceptance, stirred a primal reaction he'd never known. Maybe her presence was a good thing.

With the last of the mess cleared, she pulled the treat bag from her jacket pocket. "No problem. I can help a bit. It just seemed a little incongruent with what little I know of you."

"Leg's getting better each day. I'll be up to snuff in no time."

After clearing the mess and with practiced moves, she again played the *leave it* game with Diego. "Have you had breakfast? I don't mind cooking."

"I was just getting ready to fix some eggs and bacon." Light thumps defined his crutch's placement in his faltering steps across the floor.

Though he'd already consumed a bowl of cereal, the simple act of sharing breakfast imparted a domestic atmosphere unlike any other. The fact he preferred to not have overnight guests made his one-evening stands short-lived.

"Sit, I'll cook while we talk." Minimal wasted movements betrayed an organized mind as she moved around the kitchen. "Love the new hardware, expecting trouble?"

Whether she referred to the cameras around the house or near the end of his lane remained undetermined but might clue him into her perceptiveness. "No. Since I've been injured, my brothers think I'm an invalid."

"Spoken about a male, a McAllister at that—huh." Cracking eggshells attracted both dogs' attention. "No, guys, these aren't for you. I assume Diego has eaten already?"

"Yeah. So, did you learn anything new on the dark net?" As he watched her retrieve bacon and a frying pan, Ethan's thoughts fast-forwarded to an image of this becoming routine.

"Not really. I'll answer the email to tell them I want to play, but I'm afraid that's just gonna encourage our psychopath to kill that much sooner. Any news on your end?"

"Not yet. We're looking into another one of the hospital administrators. It appears he was in competition for a step up and pay raise. He also has a computer science and business background." Ethan smiled as the sizzling bacon caught Diego's attention, accustomed to his own slice.

"I wish she'd told me more, something specific."

"Since the clue with Frannie was, um, degraded, we've no idea about his next target's identity. Larrick spoke to the shooter's ex-wife, who said she hadn't seen her husband since moving across the country. She didn't sound to surprised that he was dead."

"I'll start doing a little more research on her. Seems weird he'd come all the way out here and not contact her, unless he wanted to harass her anonymously, maybe set her up as another victim."

"I'd like to know where he was hanging out. The only address on record is in Delaware."

"I'll see what I can dig up. CSI turned up absolutely nothing at Frannie's house? Not even how they got in?" After pouring herself some orange juice, she nodded in question then poured him a glass.

"Apparently she had a membership to the gym down on Wyneth Street and walked on a treadmill three times a week. I'm wondering if someone broke into her locker and duplicated her house key while she was there." He made a mental note to ask Larrick to examine any security footage when checking out the health club.

"Would've been easy enough to do. I kept telling her to tighten her security, but I don't think she ever listened to anything I said." Lexi took a deep breath and let it out slowly.

Breakfast was a solemn affair, giving each time to evaluate their situation.

"Did you stay at a friend's house last night?" He wondered just who she'd put at risk. She probably counted her close friends on one hand, and he couldn't imagine her bringing trouble to any of their doors.

"No. not yet." She paused in raising the last forkful of eggs, her expression thoughtful.

"Where do you work?" The silence stretched out to the point he figured she wouldn't answer.

"For a tech company. But I work from home."

"Ah, like-minded people, united confederation of hackers?"

"Some of them are, on the side, yes. Some just want to be the one to write the next coolest program. Understand this, I don't steal, and I don't share what I've seen unless it's with the police." After seeing he was finished, she scraped and rinsed the dishes as if she'd always done so.

"Like when you sent me information on the pimp killing the prostitutes?"

"Yeah." The moment taken to close her eyes seemed to settle something in her mind. "I'm going to boot up and answer this email. What time are your brothers coming?"

"I told them to call first, which doesn't mean they will. Heck, they'll probably call from my front stoop, now more curious than ever."

"Smooth move. Thanks. I'll be quick in sending this. I've taken the liberty of increasing the security of your net connection."

The off-hand comment indicated a *thank you* was in order. He did so with a nod.

"From poking around last night, it seems there are a few murder-for-hire sites."

"Is that how you tipped me off with the Whittaker case?"

Several months ago, the anonymous lead had led to the arrest of the victim's greedy son-in-law.

"Yeah. Sorry I was too late to help him."

"At least we got him justice." The *we* had a nice ring to it until he remembered she lacked official training.

"The longer it takes us to find the leads, the colder the trail gets. Though I have to admit, you drove Carl, our IT guy, absolutely wild." Her laptop looked so ordinary, yet in her hands, he knew it was as deadly a weapon as any gun.

"Huh, if I hadn't been able to trace it back to the exit node, I wouldn't have accessed the information. That killer must've been new to the dark net and not the brightest bulb."

"I won't ask you to define an exit node."

She merely grinned.

"It looks like our psychopath is getting ramped up on the bids and suggestions he receives. I'm replying that I want in on the action." Steady clicking and extreme focus indicated she was in her element, soothed by the motions yet inspired by anticipation of justice served.

"When you get a reply, come over, and we'll evaluate where we stand." Considering her penchant for privacy and independence, he wanted her correspondence occurring where he could keep an eye on her progress.

Her presence offered a comfort he greedily sought, and he mentally searched for a viable topic that didn't imitate friendly interrogation, yet curiosity twined with a heavy dose of lust left him in a state of flux.

Snapping her laptop shut, she eyed him with a mixture of confusion and suspicion. "You're not what I expected for a cop. I'm glad we can work together. Do you need anything when I return?" She stood, indecision written in her expression.

"Yeah, some rocky road. Come, sit, and let's talk for a bit." For once, maybe his partner's envious bitching about good looks would come in handy. He offered his most sincere smile in the face of her obvious suspicion.

"Hmm, my favorite treat." Tilting her head to the side, she continued, "You want information."

"I'm a cop."

"I won't forget."

A long minute passed as she visually evaluated the situation. Her nod was all the encouragement he needed.

"How long and how well did you know Frannie? What is your history with her?" *And my mouth jumps right into the sore spot.*

"All right. Just for the record, I'm sorry about the timing of my text and you getting shot. I had no idea what was going on in Frannie's house."

The virtual weight on her shoulders dropped her to the sofa before memories poured out about a ragamuffin caught red-handed in the hospital's server room, altering records.

"I was erasing one of my friend's files. They'd been sheltering me for three years. Instead of turning me over to security, Frannie offered me a simple meal with no strings attached after determining my intentions. That led to another meal the next day, accompanied by a gift, a blanket."

"She gave you a blanket?"

"Yeah. Normally I wouldn't have accepted it, but Frannie was—persuasive, special. Over the course of several months, we cultivated a friendship that grew until I developed a sense of self-esteem and ambition."

"How old are you?" Her need for privacy negated him asking where she lived. Curiosity about many aspects of her life kept his thoughts swirling in a vortex of cosmic dust and unable to settle on a method of approach. The question stemmed from desperation, a need to know he didn't lust after jailbait.

Her eyes narrowed as if zeroing in on his intention to further define her. "Twenty," she grumbled. "You have less than ten years on me."

He didn't object to Hoover overlapping her small frame on the furniture. The two appeared inseparable with the dog infusing a sense of comfort he understood.

Further details of how the hospital administrator had domesticated a street kid and set her on a new path pulled at his heartstrings. Fierce determination and a strong code seemed to come with Lexi's self-assurance package, but each time he tried to fit her into a specific mold, she redefined the boundaries.

Enough details wove her tale into a believable history, including the triumph of returning to an offshoot of society's mainstream and excelling in an online gifted program, poignant moments of attempting to help homeless street rats, and most of all—hope.

His respect was generally hard won, but not this time, not with this girl. *She's so young.* Everything he observed indicated Frannie had found an exceptional if determined girl with nothing other than a brilliant mind then maximized her potential.

With no indications of subterfuge and no glaring holes in her story, he saw little hope in altering her course of searching out the killer, considering her perseverance and devotion to the administrator. Protecting her in whatever way possible presented his best option.

Their easy conversation stretched out until afternoon sun pouring through his bay window roused his awareness to time's passage. Lost in the moment was not a cliché generally associated with his character until stumbling upon this wary, young woman.

With the passing of time came a loosening of her tightly gripped control, a few relaxed smiles, and his need for more of the same. A gleam of interest broadcasting from her gaze kept him tuned to every nuance of her demeanor, the results forming a slideshow to replay in his dreams.

"I'll come back as soon as I have more information."

"What if I need to contact you?"

"Write an email and save it as a draft."

"To whom?"

"Yourself. Just put Hoover's name in the subject line, and I'll know to look at it."

"I really don't have any privacy. Every electronic connection is open to your perusal. Tell me, you don't have the phone wired, do you?"

"No..." Simple and direct, with no hidden agendas.

His brother Matt used to employ the same tone when frustrated with his younger siblings as if they were all idiots.

To watch her go created both anxiety over her safety and a burning need to learn more about her and their unsettling situation. What if some elite hacker wanted to teach her a lesson?

To throw an informant into a precarious situation without backup existed in no rulebook or police procedure he'd ever read. Despite her unwavering decision to fly by the seat of her pants, he'd knowingly placed her in danger.

Unacceptable.

The minute she strode out, he headed for his study only to learn that when she reached the end of his driveway, she'd parked too far away to discern anything more than her car's model. *Is Lexi even her real name?* "Wow. Tracking her down is going to be difficult."

Even after a cold shower, he spent the rest of the day fumbling around his house in abject frustration while Lexi's clean intoxicating scent clung to his thoughts.

Chapter Seven

Seclusion, if for the benefit of peace and solitude, refuted the very notion of loneliness, yet with the next sunrise, Ethan eagerly anticipated his guests.

Lexi's life experience mitigated their age difference while her intelligence and wit drew him into her unique and complex world. Several calls to family members the prior evening afforded him another day without unexpected company.

Hopefully.

Midmorning, Lexi and Hoover arrived in time to keep his world in a continual state of tilt. Form-fitting jeans seemed to be her norm. Removing her hoodie and exposing the wolf's head t-shirt with jaws that appeared ready to latch onto her curves further defined her in a way his subconscious obviously appreciated, judging by the redistribution of his blood flow.

Getting right to the point, she headed for his kitchen table to boot up her laptop and show him the email. "Okay. I got an answer last night but didn't open it."

"That must've driven you nuts."

"Yeah, you almost had a midnight visitor. How's the leg today?"

Not that he would've minded the late-night visit, but it would've been difficult to remain professional. "Better. Listen, I hate to bring this up, but Frannie's funeral...You really shouldn't go. Plainclothes will have it staked out."

"I know. Seems wrong, disrespectful."

"I want you off everyone's radar for as long as possible."

Ethan didn't want to poke a wound after heaping misery on her shoulders, but the closer he kept her, the safer she'd remain. "Also, about going out…"

"I work from home, remember? Considering how driven most of us are, the boss doesn't even track our hours, just the results."

"I have an office. If you'd like to work from here, it's no problem."

"Hmm." Tilting her head to the side, she ignored his offer while her gaze remained locked on the screen. "Hey, he's asking for a bid and a choice for the next victim. He sent out a multiple-choice questionnaire. The sick dirtbag."

Ethan shoulder-surfed to read the rest, quietly enjoying the scent of freshly shampooed hair. He smiled at her shudder after he blew out a breath that ruffled the soft waves. "Bids close in less than two weeks. Possibilities include a nun, a grade-school teacher, or a politician, plus an opportunity for write-in suggestions."

"Bitcoin index is up."

"Sounded like a porn thing when I first heard the term." Not where his mind needed to go.

"Decentralized digital currency. Money. Right now each coin is worth a little over six hundred bucks."

"So what exactly does it buy here?"

"The opportunity to vote and watch the *procedure*, as he calls it." Again, the clickety-clack of her keyboard brought up strange-looking screens. "The winner receives a video with extra scenes."

"Sick bunch of creeps. I wonder if the vote actually counts or is just for hype. Most serial killers target a specific detail or characteristic of a person. Seems odd that he'd offer choices." Ethan had investigated enough crimes to see the results of man's greatest cruelties, but watching the preliminary setup offered a viewpoint of a whole new level of psychosis.

"Yeah, but if you want to have a chance at narrowing it down, I'd vote for a nun. Easier to protect them since they'll be together." Again, her analytical mind selected the most logical choice, unfettered by society's moral etiquette.

"The captain's going to have a coronary. Can you trace this?"

"I'll work on it but probably not in time."

Placing the bid was the most morally reprehensible thing he'd ever done. He'd be dancing a fine line in talking with his captain, explaining how he came by the information while protecting Lexi's identity.

Nothing he could do would stop the bidding process, and no other acquaintance held such an advanced level of technological skills. The best he could hope for was to track and catch the killer before he tortured and mutilated another woman.

"Captain Faulkner's a shrewd interrogator with decades on the force. My conversations with him are safer, not to mention more pleasant if one remains an open book." Even through something as nominal as a telephone wire, the man knew when someone withheld information. "We'll be treading a fine line here."

"CIs are accorded anonymity, so just tell him I'm a confidential informant."

"That's discretionary in most departments. Captain isn't hard and fast on either side. Your tenuous invisibility will only last so long as we prove successful."

"I won't fail."

"I spoke with Carl. I can take you to the station, and he'll let you look at the hardware as long as he's present."

"Good. I'd expect nothing less if I were in his shoes. I've never let anyone near my electronics."

"How about some breakfast?"

Bacon sizzling on the cooktop kept both canines close while Ethan studied Lexi, who blew a stray lock of hair from her brow, oblivious to the reality surrounding her digital world.

She struck him as a solitary soul who preferred animals and bytes to human interaction, yet underneath the layers of skin, muscle, and sinew lay a spirit needing the same spiritual nourishment as any other being, regardless of how deep she buried the yearning.

"You okay with French toast?"

"Sure. I like mine drowned in a sea of molasses if you have it." When he set a plate beside her computer, she closed the lid and studied him. "You're really not what I expected."

"You mean after snooping through every aspect of my digital life?"

No telltale sign of embarrassment reddened her face as she changed the subject. "Considering how much you care about Diego, I'm surprised you don't feed raw. Most people wouldn't spend the time to do the research while others just don't realize how much healthier their dogs would be."

"And kibble hasn't been around forever." He sighed. "I know. I'll look into it."

"Yeah, sorry. Guess I'm passionate about my furbaby." Her gaze slid to the living room as if searching for a different topic.

"How good are you with that 3D chess set? You and your

brothers play?"

"Yeah, we usually get together on Sundays, alternating houses, eat, play, and catch a game."

"You going today?" Something akin to disappointment crossed her face.

"Nah, I told them I needed a break from their nagging, had plenty of food, and could catch up next week."

"I can leave..."

"No, you're fine. How about a match after we eat and while we're waiting for a digital reply?" His breath stilled as he waited for another layer of intricacy to be unveiled.

"You're assuming that not only can I play, but I understand the three-dimensional version."

"Yep."

"All right then. I'm black, but I haven't played the tiered adaptation."

Three games later, she'd given him a run for his money. Within a week she'd probably crush each one of his brothers. Imagining innocent wagers induced a smile.

By lunchtime, their online bid had joined countless others, bringing him down from the fascinating if temporary interlude.

"Okay, we're in. Let's see how this system works." As if nothing else existed, once again she dove inside the world of sick and forbidden pleasures for twisted minds.

Hours later, Ethan placed a sandwich and glass of tea by her laptop without uttering a sound. Wordlessly, she consumed both without breaking gaze with a screen full of lists, numbers, and indexes.

A compulsion too great to ignore pressed him to dab the corner of her mouth with a napkin, her sudden flinch preceding a long blink and shy smile.

The increased pulse in her neck and owlish gaze hadn't escaped his notice. Their implicit connection sizzling in the atmosphere between them could no more be defined than ignored. Something in her demeanor drew out his protective streak, wanting to secure her to his side while delving into the mysterious depths of her character.

He'd learned long ago to compartmentalize the many facets of his job, to keep them from intruding and overtaking his personal life, yet with Lexi thrown in the mix, all bets were off. Larrick, a prime example of *leaving your job at work*, had set the bar high when they'd first met and would be disappointed.

When the sun hung like a ball on the horizon, Lexi leaned back and cracked her knuckles. "Freakin' sick dirtball is clever as the devil and smart as any psycho who ever walked the Earth." Blinking several times and lubricating what must've become dry eyes, she looked around in surprise. "Oh, you did the lunch dishes. Thanks, I'd have done them."

"No problem. Also walked the dogs, cleaned the house, and solved world hunger."

"Yeah, um, sorry. I kinda get lost in my work."

"It's all right. It's fascinating to watch someone get so absorbed in something that nothing short of a dirty bomb explosion could get their attention. Speaking of work..."

"I'm caught up for now on my current project. Just waiting for one of my cohorts to finish his algorithm."

The afternoon's odd companionship had allotted Ethan time to touch base with Larrick and his brothers. Preventing them from dropping by involved many prank-type threats since their ever-growing curiosity over his mystery woman would soon outweigh the fear of retribution.

"How about I cook us dinner? I brought an eye round

roast we can share with the fur kids." Her determination to feed Diego a raw diet held fast.

"Sure. Nice evening to sit on the porch and enjoy a sunset." Rarely did his softer side venture forth, but something about her easy comradery and the way they seemed to fit made him want more.

"You? A romantic?" A fake cough didn't cover her delicate snort. She failed to meet his gaze.

Yeah, the same thing is on her *mind.*

"Nah, just bored, cabin fever." How did one successfully break through the emotional defenses of a prickly pear?

"Oh, I forgot to mention. I brought you a couple movies to watch. They're in my backpack."

"Chick flicks or action?" He couldn't help but grin at the thought of her watching a tearjerker.

"Science fiction, aliens, predators, and cowboys. What d'ya think?"

"It's a date." Perhaps he should consider Matt's advice and socialize more—outside of the bedroom. "Uh, I mean, sounds good."

A split second passed before she closed her mouth and her gaze slid away. No denials came forth.

Each morning, Lexi arrived to fix breakfast while Ethan sat working with Diego and nipped at her social armor. It seemed they'd reached a truce.

He didn't pry into her life, realizing she'd offer information as she learned to trust, and she returned each day, their mutual sharing of information a fragile bond. By the end of the week, he knew little more about her than when they'd first met, but the obvious mutual satisfaction derived from their odd companionship provided a basis from which he could work.

He'd hoped she could track the killer without physical access to Frannie's laptop and phone, thereby preserving her anonymity. As yet, she'd been unsuccessful.

"Larrick's coming by again this evening to keep me updated. I think he wants to check up on you. At least he's warming up to you."

"Yeah, I researched, *How to win a redneck's trust*." Lexi snickered, her gaze locked on her computer screen. "You've encouraged him to keep my upcoming access to your IT department quiet?"

"Yeah, he wanted to bring Carl by tonight, but I told him we'd stop by the station tomorrow. I don't want a lot of folks knowing your whereabouts. Larrick at least promised that much."

"Good. Thanks."

When his partner had stopped by on several evenings to provide and update on their progress and the captain's increasing demand for results, Lexi walked him through the basics of the dark net's intricacies. Judging by the slight glaze that had crept into his partner's eyes, Larrick understood little more after the lecture than before it had begun.

He put up a good front.

Holding off the family took a daily, monumental effort, their suspicion about his relationship growing to epic proportions. By now, Caden had looped himself into the network's installation and kept track of Lexi's appearances. *And gives Matt a daily update.*

"I appreciate your visits. The mental stimulation takes the sting out of enforced limited activity." She'd joined him during his short hikes, insisting he might fall on one of the wooded trails surrounding his home.

Her presence added a layer of serenity never enjoyed. The fact she spent a growing portion of her days with him, still avoiding specific personal details, revealed her inner conflict over privacy.

"Well, I gotta make sure you live long enough to catch this psycho, don't I?"

Each day, he'd find reasons to stand close, touch her shoulder or lay a hand on her arm, whether from reaching something from a shelf or leaning close while she explained some fine detail of the net. Each day, she tensed less, even smiled on occasion. In truth, he was gentling a filly.

* * * *

"Don't be nervous." Ethan opened the glass door to the police station.

"I just don't like being around so many cops. Are your brothers working now?" *The last thing I need is to run into them.*

"Matt's K-9, so he generally works evenings. Lucas works in the narcotics division, so he's out in the field. Billy works criminal division. He's somewhere in the building, but Larrick's keeping him busy. Caden's a private investigator and is working an insurance fraud case. We should have a straight shot to the IT department with few obstacles at this hour."

"What made you want to work homicide?"

"It was the only division here without a brother in it." Ethan rolled his eyes.

Up the steps and down the wide hall, they nodded to several officers in passing before pushing through swinging doors leading to a smaller hall with a stairwell. None of the uniformed men showed any signs of recognizing her.

Once on the lower level, Ethan again opened the door for her, waiting as she took a deep breath before stepping into the forensics lab. Her body took on a will of its own, using small, hesitant steps.

According to earlier discussions, most of the department considered the *geeksters* competent if a bit odd, always toeing the line and protective of their information, at least to public scrutiny.

Given the workload, their office should've rated a better area. Budget cuts and overhead scrutiny relegated them to a smaller space with block walls, bleary lighting, and lots of stairs in getting to work.

"Where is everybody, Carl?" Ethan asked and then murmured to Lexi, "There are two other techs in this section of forensics."

"You said you wanted to keep this meeting as small as possible. They're working on a burglary scene uptown, something high profile." Carl offered Lexi a shy smile before turning back to Ethan, "How's the leg? I didn't know you were back to work yet."

"Technically, I'm not on the clock. Leg's better, no crutches. Thanks for seeing us, I know you stay busy."

The technician's stool squeaked as he swiveled around and offered Lexi his hand. "Hi, I'm Carl."

Lexi extended her sweaty palm along with a tentative smile. "I'm Lexi."

Though the techie wasn't a cop, per se, she didn't give her last name. Everything in her screamed a warning to dash from the building. Cops had never been people she'd called friends.

So what is this thing with Ethan? He seemed to draw her into his web without conscious effort using a mere gaze, a touch, or a soft-spoken word.

"Don't worry. This is a private meeting. If anyone asks, I'll say you're an outside source I consult when I have a difficult case." Carl's white lab coat added a bit of professionalism while obscuring his shape, but a well-muscled neck below a lean face instilled the sense of a muscular frame. Thick black hair framed a pleasant, symmetrical face while something about his eyes, gray with hints of brown, hinted at a shrewd intelligence.

If they're friends, what has Ethan told him about me?

Instinctively, she looked around, noting one other exit and three small windows set high in the wall which put them below ground level. Brash lighting completed the dungeon feel, giving way to thoughts of spider-infested corners and shackles on the walls.

Duct tape patched the seat Carl patted in an invitation to sit, his smirk challenging her with his assurance of dominance in the field.

She mentally cringed, wary of usurping his imagined status. In sitting, her concentration narrowed to the devices on which she'd work.

Frannie's computer and cell sat side by side on the table, evidence of Lexi's failure to act. "I appreciate this a lot. I know how protective I am of my stuff. Well, most good technites I know are neurotic about their equipment." She couldn't determine the source of her ratcheting anxiety, hence chalked it up to the environment.

"I've already taken a crack at her cell and laptop and couldn't trace a darn thing. If you can help us catch this guy, I welcome the assistance." The statement was a challenge, one nerd to another.

Since she'd set this machine's security up and had an idea of what to search for, if anyone could find the evidence, she could. Unfortunately, none of her installed programs were present.

"Why don't people keep the apps protecting personal information current?"

"Guess nobody thinks they're vulnerable. Did you install them?" Carl's gaze narrowed, the kind of look that scrutinized while inner thoughts whirled, placing one edge of a puzzle to another in an attempt to find the right fit.

Have they never seen Ethan with girls?

She understood his love 'em and leave 'em attitude, even respected it. She'd kept her world simple, bits and bytes, cables and cache, less complicated than the fringes of romance. She'd never had a long-term relationship. She'd never had a romantic entanglement at all.

Not knowing what Ethan's earlier conversation with Carl entailed, she decided to play the generic card. Nerds always evaluated each other.

"Nah, every machine comes with a temporary program. Look at this." She pointed to the date on an antivirus program. "This is over two years old." She wasn't about to give out surplus information. To have anyone other than Ethan watch her work induced a bit of queasiness, but she blanked her expression as if this were just another routine day. "Looks like the psycho deleted his tracks if he was even here."

"Yeah, that's what I figured." A tinge of admiration, possibly envy, colored the tech's tone. One didn't have to be a psychopath to appreciate high-level digital skills.

Minutes later, a frustrated sigh blew a lock of hair from

her face. The killer was the cleverest deviant she'd faced. Not a trace of her security measures existed, and no path led to the timing of its tampering. There was a finality in closing the lid she couldn't explain.

"Did you know the vic?" Carl set the laptop in an evidence box.

Now he's just getting too personal, a side effect of hanging around cops. She shook her head, the denial bitter in her mind. *Wouldn't you do the same if you were in his shoes? He's responsible for helping solve this case. He's Ethan's colleague and friend.*

"Is there anything you all can determine from the computer?" Ethan redirected Carl's attention to himself.

"No, it's pretty much been wiped—if the information was ever there."

"You guys mind if I take a look at her cell?" Again, someone had erased the security measures she'd installed on the device.

Had Frannie been communicating with the killer for some time? Maybe they had some type of relationship that allowed him access.

Lexi had never dug into Frannie's personal life and didn't know of her romantic entanglements. Images of her friend pleading for her life washed a new stain of guilt over her soul. It was all she could do to keep a stoic expression.

Considering the whitewashed state of the computer, she hadn't expected to find anything on the phone.

"Looks like it's another dead end." Her gaze instinctively sought Ethan's, needing his strength. She didn't flinch when he settled his arm around her shoulders, his breath feathering her hair and sending an entirely different message through her chest.

Whether he'd intended to provide a cover as his girlfriend or was just lending support when she needed it didn't matter. She accepted it with gratitude.

"Figures. We're chasing one nerdy ripper." Carl pushed to his feet and placed the cell in the box labeled with Frannie's name and date of death.

Just because Carl was shy and protective of his domain didn't make him an enemy. If he was Ethan's friend, she could at least extend an affable pretense. "Thanks for letting me take a look. I think catching this guy is going to take a bit of luck and a lot of time on TOR."

"I've been exploring that area myself but haven't come up with anything yet. Since we're approaching from two different angles, we'll find something." Turning to Ethan, he added, "Hey, you want to bring your girl and go bowling with me and the guys? I've been thinking of joining another league and need the practice."

Horrified at the thought of being around so many cop types, Lexi couldn't help the shiver running between her shoulder blades.

Ethan's response of rubbing her back multiplied it exponentially. The grin hiking up one corner of his mouth provided evidence of his awareness.

"Um, not anytime too soon, my leg isn't ready for that. However, how about we get a small group together for a barbecue?"

"Sounds great. I'll bring marinated ribs."

After a promise of a friendly gathering, Ethan escorted her out. "You okay?"

It came as a bit of a shock she didn't need to gulp a huge breath of air. "Actually, that wasn't too bad."

"You sound surprised." Leaning down so his warm breath

brushed her ear, he murmured, "We cops aren't as bad as you think. Give us a chance."

The shudder racing down her spine originated from the husky whisper promising a sizzling encounter, if only in her imagination.

Chapter Eight

The following day, Ethan woke at six a.m. to a pounding on his front door, early by Lexi standards. Answering the barrage bare-chested and wearing only jeans, he was surprised to see her hunched over her satchel, dripping wet.

The bigger shock came in the form of her vehicle parked in his driveway. *Finally.* He imagined it registered to a false address, the coordinates somewhere in the middle of the Kanuai River. Still, it was a step in the right direction.

"Come in. Jeez, you're soaked. I'll get you a towel."

Strands of her ponytail stuck to the slopes of her shirt, defining the curve of her breast and the indent of her waist, a distraction he didn't need.

Think about how Caden used to put itching powder in Matt's hair while sleeping, and then play with the water supply when he took a shower.

"Thanks. I believe we have a direction. I'm thinking the killer has made a decision."

She didn't wait, just headed toward the kitchen as he snatched a towel from the linen closet and concentrated on the case. *Not on her wet t-shirt, or the best way to warm her up.*

"Rats, I thought we had another week." Crutches were a thing of the distant past, but a slight limp reminded him he wasn't yet a hundred percent.

Minutes later, Lexi sat on a towel-covered chair in the kitchen. "Our screwball has chosen to do a politician. Didn't clarify what level, if it's state, federal, or local."

Now that he'd have to involve the department, Ethan prayed the closer scrutiny wouldn't hamper their growing rapport. Natural curiosity outweighed respect for legal parameters in her digital snooping, which meant she would continue to cross lines.

His brothers and Larrick would understand and accept the indiscretion, but others—not so much. Yet another slippery slope.

"All right, let's eat while we flesh out our plan."

Stop thinking about flesh.

"First, I'm gonna go grab a shirt." He grinned after catching her studying his chest. As her fingers flew to open her computer, he realized his gym membership had more benefits than anticipated. She wasn't immune to his proximity, not by a long shot.

A quick stop off in his study yielded a small surprise, something he should've seen coming. A few clicks of his keyboard brought up the camera feed from the front of his home. His chuckle elicited Diego's whine.

"Huh, she smeared her license plate with mud and...something to make it stick, considering the rain hasn't washed it off. Then she parked under the tree. Should've seen that one coming." Diego nudged his knee. "It's all right, boy. We're making progress."

Breakfast passed in quiet conversation with the burden of another person's life weighing heavily on their shoulders. She didn't have the same knowledge of community, but her moral ethics seemed to always point toward life. Regardless of how her mind tried to solve the puzzle, a flush rode high on her cheeks every time her gaze swiveled to his chest.

He didn't try to hide his smile.

Lane sensors alerted to incoming vehicles. *No. Seriously?*

A moment of panic crossed her eyes before she carefully blanked her expression, necessitating his impromptu plan.

"Hey, it's either Larrick or one of my brothers. They're cool. You know Larrick, and you can trust my family. Heck,

Abagail's an attorney and tight-lipped as a calm. If you'd rather pretend to be my girlfriend..." Surely Larrick had filled them in concerning their arrangement, but the idea of keeping her close would warn his siblings to back off.

"I've never been anyone's girlfriend and have no idea how to pull that off." Worrying her lip between her teeth, she was adorable.

"Really? You're Twenty...right?" Ethan ran his fingers through his hair. Some women tried to appear anything but their age. Lexi wasn't that type. Her inexperience widened the gap between them.

"Close your jaw, you goof. You know I'm not jailbait. Since Caden looped himself into your security system, he's known about my visits and hasn't shown up until now. Either they know something's up, or they have information."

"Just act like you always do around me. We'll play a game of chess 'till I can clear them out." At least they'd formed a basis for a friendship that allowed him to carry a semi-believable conversation.

His heart softened with seeing the slight tremor in her fingers. Knowing how abrasive his family could be strengthened his resolve to protect her.

When he moved to stand beside her chair and give her a quick hug, she leaned into his chest. The heat sizzling between them held him prisoner, the uncharacteristic silent plea for assurance something he treasured as they both appeared on the precipice of an epic emotional breakthrough.

Later, when the video replayed in his memory, he would further define her weaknesses and supplement each with his own strength.

"I've never before pulled into your driveway or shown up

at the crack of dawn. They've been waiting for a break..."

His oldest brother opened the front door, followed by Billy, Caden, and Lucas. None appeared repentant for the unannounced invasion. *Knocking is for polite society.*

"Figures you guys would show up. Couldn't use Ma Belle? You each have a phone." Frustration leached from his voice, but Ethan knew they wouldn't leave until satisfied.

"Hey, you missed family time and have been avoiding us all. We wanted to see what the fuss was all about." Caden's gaze latched onto Lexi with appreciation. "Been mudding lately, hon? Your tags were a bit smeared—with some type of sticky mud—so I cleaned them off for you." As if proof of action, he wiped his hands on his jeans.

Lexi's glare made her point.

"Knock it off, Caden. Off limits, got it?" Ethan blocked his younger brother's approach to Lexi. "Why don't you guys have a seat while we finish clearing the table?"

"Sure. Need to use the can first." Matt made his way toward the bathroom. He'd ascertain if feminine products filled half the medicine cabinet and subtly broadcast his findings.

Lucas moved the chess game to the table between two chairs in preparation for a match, taking the farthest seat. His brothers intended to stay a while.

"No, dude. Lexi and I have the first game. It's tradition," Ethan warned his older sibling. With the dishes stacked, he guided his young bundle of nerves to sit where she could keep everybody in sight while playing chess. Taking the opposite seat put his brothers catty-corner to Lexi and let him keep an eye on all.

"Huh, a little over a week and you've established traditions? You move fast." Smiling at Lexi, Lucas added,

"Nice to meet you, but if you get the urge to trade up, I'm Lucas, the fun brother."

"Ah, the one that enjoys reruns as premiers... every time." Lexi's taking the offensive, albeit jokingly, came as no surprise.

"Naw, hon. That's just my younger sibling trying to make me look bad. I'm the brains of the family."

"Shame you're sitting on them." Matt entered the room, an almost imperceptible shake of his head toward Caden conveying a world of information.

"If you're done with your inspection, how about getting to the point?" Ethan watched Lexi closely, her nervous gaze scrutinizing each man before moving to the next. Her tension radiated through his siblings, judging by their close regard.

"Hey, we just wanted to check and keep you up to date on the investigation." Sitting on the opposite couch next to Billy, Matt frowned as if trying to figure out the motives of the technological enigma.

"At this hour? Let me guess, nothing new." Ethan moved a pawn forward on one of the lower levels. *She's not going to concentrate well.*

"Nothing of significance. How about you?" Caden asked, his question directed at Lexi.

"Nothing more than you've found, until this morning."

"And how is it you're aware of my progress?" Caden asked, the crinkle between his lowered brows the only outward indication of concentration before a dropped jaw indicated enlightenment. "Elite hacker. Son. Of. A. Bitch!"

"In case you haven't come to realize the difference, my mother wasn't a dog, and I'm nobody's *son*." Lexi paused in her next move until Caden caught the joke.

Chuckles around the room ended with Billy's whoop. "Hey, you *are* a keeper, aren't you?"

Her gaze flicked over the chessboards as she brought everyone up to date. "His next victim is going to be a politician."

"What? There're only thousands of them," Matt grumbled. "Do we have a timeframe?"

"No, but considering the location of his last two victims, we have to assume he's making Callouston his current playground, so that does limit the field somewhat." Ethan scowled at each of his brothers as Lexi squirmed under their continued regard.

"Senator Tuckerman lives within city limits, along with Congresswoman Rufer, among others in our thirty-five square miles." Lexi grimaced, her gaze roaming out the window as if trying to excise the sharp talons of bitter memories.

"Ya know, with your wit, looks, and intelligence, hanging around with Ethan here must—" Caden began.

"Finish that thought, and you'll suck liquid nourishment through a straw for six weeks." Ethan spat the words between clenched teeth.

Surprise etched each man's expression with various placating gestures. Having never taken such a stand with his brothers, Ethan knew they'd back off.

As if someone flipped a switch, conversation detoured to whitewater rafting, hiking, and other activities the brothers had enjoyed growing up. Long minutes drew out before Lexi's shoulders lost their stiffness in favor of the slight tremor from subdued chuckles.

A certain wistfulness about her eyes hinted of a deep-seated desire for comradery, or family, perhaps the precious commodity of her dreams. In turn, each brother took his chance in a battle to best her at strategy.

The close-knit relationships inherited from a large family characterized by laughter, trust, unwelcome advice, and unwavering support formed a solid base and a wealth of confidence in each sibling. Ethan wondered about her life before her parents' accident. Thus far, she'd only shared a few details on their daily hikes.

"C'mon, Billy, make your move. Your king is gone either way." Matt laughed with his younger brother's chafing.

"Looks like he went down a water slide without the water," Lucas added.

"That's why he doesn't have a girlfriend. Doesn't believe in lubrication." Caden cleared the glasses from the coffee table.

"You're toast, man. She had you from the get-go. I'm next. Don't want her to think we're a family of mental wimps," Matt confirmed.

"Actually, he's done very well." A strange wistfulness underlay the resolute determination of her voice, like a thread of envy coiling in her gut causing a subtle discomfort.

Over the next several hours, she won their respect, if not their confidence. Experience dictated their show of solidarity was tempered with myriad unasked questions, answers to which Ethan also wanted but would tease from her in slow degrees of healing a wound she thought buried under sass and sarcasm.

Patience was not a common virtue among McAllisters.

Chapter Nine

I run but not walk.
Thoughts are not far away, but I never seem to connect.

A full moon enticed enthusiastic night callers such as northern mockingbirds and whip-poor-wills from the woods while night herons from adjoining wetlands made their presence known. Squawks, cackles, whistles, and sirens filled the air as Arvel crept along the back of the decorative wooden fence.

The silvery bells of wind chimes serenaded his arrival. After the near disaster at his first victim's home, he'd decided to enact a contingency plan and carried a knotted rope draped around his shoulders like a bandolier. The minor inconvenience served as a reminder of his ability to learn and evolve.

The melody of night crooners soothed his mind, calming the voices within and allowing him to concentrate on the task at hand. His best work materialized when the sun's absence urged his unique genius to new levels of creative brutality, encouraged by phantom shadows and blessed obscurity.

Like the bush crickets or katydids grinding their sweet song in the night, he would also produce a symphony, albeit in a different medium, preferring the beauty of muffled screams amid crimson spray from his chosen honorees to decorate in a multi-sense palate.

This resident's ankle biter had eaten the specially prepared steak almost sixty minutes ago, watched via the camera set up during reconnaissance at the beginning of the week. The dog slept peacefully by the back door.

He loved secluded homes. The tranquility of nature's

white noise, remote setting, and manicured backyard, appealed to his mellow side. His transceiver's screen displayed the large yard, empty except for young flower shoots surrounding a lone maple tree that provided dappled shade for the patio.

Buttery soft light spilled from the rear slider to highlight the empty deck chairs and table with a closed umbrella. Other windows revealed no light at all. A picture of serenity begged for approach.

The whinnying of a screech owl startled him as he unclipped the camera from its tree branch overhanging the fence. His last experience had taught him the value of maintaining a tidy scene. An uncharacteristic fumbling had resulted in the camera breaking off from its supporting clip.

He'd managed to retain the ball-shaped globe and concluded the hillbilly and straight arrow would not likely find the remains. The clip didn't matter since the meticulous use of gloves prevented anyone lifting his prints.

On the other hand, the excitement of the infamous duo finding the dropped piece and anticipating some small thread on which to pull led him to leave it. Another crumb of information he'd deny the badge monkeys.

A rear gate to the property, secured with a drop-lever latch, opened without a squeak. No security lights adorned the rear or side of the house to give away his presence.

In that instant, he knew destiny favored him this night, for the deluge of images flooding his mind of both past and future playdates would enrich the lives of his audience.

The video of tonight's performance, with intricate blood spray patterns and intimate poses of a victim, beaten and vulnerable, submissive in her helplessness, would reach epic numbers, each fan expressing his adoration with higher bids toward his next artful expression.

Despite what his fans requested, he'd already decided on his next two stars. Now that he'd eliminated his sloppy partner, he didn't have to contend with another's insistence on helping to choose the victims.

Tonight's performance was a final tribute to Dooley. It would've been disrespectful to toss aside the finished prep work in setting up the show. On the upside, he no longer had to contend with an inferior mind who insisted on bringing his dog on surveillance. In addition, he'd left enough digital clues in Dooley's past to lead the pigs on a merry chase.

Back to business.

Perhaps existence as a public figure infused his new client with a distorted sense of power. The recently appointed council member was about to learn a new meaning of terror and how one utilized true strength.

He would've preferred selecting the congresswoman and still might, but integrity dictated he honor his fallen comrade with the dead man's choice.

A surge of adrenaline signaled his readiness to begin. A few deep breaths and concentrating on relaxation helped contain his excitement and normalize his pulse despite the sweat beading his face as he thought of the evening to come.

Silent steps carried him up the deck stairs while the sudden appearance of a second story television's glow provided a muted, eerie light through the lacy window curtain. The thought of creating a delicate pattern using the gauzy dressing gave him chills of inspiration.

Hmm, outside slider in an older home. Love it.

From his bag, he removed the screwdriver and inserted it between the door frame and door about six inches from the corner, diagonal from the latch. Prying upwards tilted the door and lowered the latch, releasing it from the bracket. Without a chock stick in place, the door glided smoothly in its track. Prior research ensured no alarm existed to disrupt the evening's program.

The inside offered a woodsy pine aroma mixed with spice and chocolate to soothe his excited nerves. Perhaps she'd baked cookies earlier. Meager light from the kitchen affirmed his notion of the layout, open with elegant furniture and expensive rugs adorning hardwood floors.

In honor of his protégé's memory and to take a poke at Callouston PD's finest, he'd brought and now carefully placed the banded Amaranth on the counter, its bright red flowers a memory of his dead partner's ineptitude. Chosen partly for its common name, pigweed, its innuendo would be lost on the police.

He sighed. At least his fans would love the added touch.

When the forensics team studied his offering, he hoped they'd be diligent enough to uncover the clue he'd left. After all, obtaining the shipment from the East Coast had cost one of his contributors special time and expense.

God, I love the internet.

A bottle of wine sat on the stone countertop, something to enjoy later with whatever sweets he might find. Quietly, he placed the unknown vintage in the fridge beside the Beluga caviar.

Houses in the neighborhood rivaled the most expensive real estate in the area. He detested rich people. Considering his own wealth, that made him a hypocrite.

I use mine for the betterment of the art world. He never flaunted his money.

Splashes of color couldn't define the pictures decorating the wall, probably some expensive Impressionist crap that made little sense to anyone but the amateurish hack who created it.

The stills he'd capture from the video of his artistic endeavors epitomized the height of digital composition and artistry.

Quiet murmurs from the TV upstairs camouflaged his telltale squeaky ascent on carpeted stairs curving in a way that screamed aristocracy and filthy rich. In a socket low on the landing's hallway, a nightlight shed weak beams to welcome his presence. More pictures adorned the walls with family portraits, an adolescent riding a horse in a show ring, and a smiling couple sitting with two small children in their laps.

Disgusting.

The top of the stairway divided the hall with one doorway to his left and one to the right, the latter failing to contain the commentator's drone about the uptick in the housing market. He licked his lips in anticipation.

The voices in his head grew louder, waiting for blood to flow and the inelegant screams to beg for mercy. He loved the screams, each depicting a depth of emotion that words and even visual recordings couldn't begin to express. After all, since he'd done due diligence in selecting his actress, her debut film should render the scene in a multi-faceted demonstration of his exceptional skills.

Once at the stairway's top, he extracted a small disposable camera from his cleverly designed tote. Great expense had gone into crafting the carryall that doubled as a modified body suit.

If one were to scrutinize his appearance, he'd give the impression of an obese sloth who drank to excess and shunned the very idea of exercise. Yet reality proved stranger than fiction as his detachable potbelly not only contained his tools but also was arranged to not restrict his movements. Wearing this getup continuously would surely induce bulging spinal discs due to the odd distribution of weight.

Excitement quickened his pulse and filled his mind with exquisite images of the canvas he'd create, something to keep his admirers begging for more while he digitally stalked his next star.

In the back of his mind, he envisioned a tall, young woman with chestnut hair, but it wasn't time to eliminate the hounds on his trail just yet. That didn't stop his mind from wondering how the pig had hooked up with a geek.

Not his usual type at all.

The swath of light slipping through the open door beckoned a stealthy approach while his hand shook with the frenzied passion of a child eagerly awaiting cookies. After tonight, he'd make his name known to everyone on the dark net, not to mention earn enough to elevate the complexity of his next performance, something unique and exquisite.

Bedcovers rustling denoted the occupant getting up. A lamp's soft click increased the light spilling from the room before she turned the TV off.

No remote control?

Creaking floorboards detailed her approach, necessitating a slight adjustment to his plan. Too bad he didn't have time to set up his video.

First interpretations of horror and outrage always provided the best footage, which demanded the right tool for the job. Damn, he hated being deprived. A slight ache in his fingers inspired him to release the grip on his camera before his finger pressed the power button.

Perhaps she fancied some sweet confection before bedtime or just wanted to let her dog in for the night. A damn shame Fido had to stay outside for the duration, but unless it awakened and created a racket, Arvel wouldn't chance the mutt messing up his carefully choreographed scene.

Her evenly spaced footsteps whispered encouragement as he flattened himself against the wall, waiting to honor her with his gift of immortal elegance.

A slight creak in the door and her thin body blocked the light before some unnamed quality of the night alerted her to his presence. She swiveled her head, providing a backlit expression worthy of a poster-sized frame.

Perfection was the first glimpse.

He snapped a picture, the momentarily blinding flash allowing him to savor her shock.

Dropped jaw, impossibly widened eyes—priceless.

One quick chop to the throat sent her down and gasping for breath while negating her ability to scream. Another picture. Like most sixtyish bodies, her neck couldn't endure much pressure and facilitate a decent air exchange.

I've got to be careful.

Inability to issue an alarm heightened the terror infusing the air around them. With her fingers scrabbling at her throat, white circling her pupils, and her mouth opened in a silent scream, she made a divine, frame-worthy illustration epitomizing the look he'd wanted to achieve.

The rag he stuffed between her lips on her next inhale contained enough hallucinogenic to quickly subdue but not render her completely insensate. He had tasks to perform before filming began and didn't want the nuisance of tying her to the bed.

Perfect.

Voices in his head clamored for attention, each giving a different direction, regardless of his meticulous plan. Grinding his teeth, he took a deep breath to placate them, once again reviewing the images he'd force into reality.

Her soft, gray hair seized in his fist reminded him of his late mother's and the way she'd pampered herself with endless expensive shampoos and rinses, all the while touting scriptures and axioms referencing clean living.

After months of planning, he'd taken great delight in filming the transitions of her demise, securing her on the antique dining table she'd treasured and burning patches of her hair. And the cuts—oh, those first cuts were better than any orgasm he'd ever experienced.

Now, lifting and dragging this geriatric replica back to her bed, her struggle increasingly uncoordinated and ineffective, inspired only a fraction of the thrill he'd once known.

It's past time to evolve and move on to a younger generation.

"Figures you'd spring for a fancy four-poster, seeing these ostentatious drapes and Persian rug. Still, the lace underlays are something I can definitely put to good use."

Tears squeezed from closed eyes flowed toward her ear's helix and into the auditory canal. She no longer attempted to move, defeat written in the lines of her face and the flaccidity of her arms. Even her shaking had stopped.

Was the drug too strong for her? Damn. Her statue-like demeanor during his preparations disappointed him. Considering her political status, though local, it should've engendered more spine.

Never judge a book by its cover.

"If you think submission will decrease the length or quality of our playtime, you're about to learn differently."

A thin whine was her only response, her eyes glazing from the combination of fear and the chemicals in her system. Defeat was a wonderful look.

With camera and tools set up and once again at her side, whispered intentions in her ear after removing the gag induced her low, keening cry. Keeping his body from blocking the camera's sight line would allow his viewers to see the effects of his words breeding panic in her slight frame.

"I realize you don't understand the transcendental legacy we're going to create tonight, but I will immortalize you in ways never before seen."

"S-sick scumbag. You're nothing but filth." Minutes passed as her gaze adopted the understanding of what she faced. "I know you."

"Ah, but you know what they say about one man's trash being another man's treasure. You, my dear, will be treasured by millions." He hated editing his videos and was disgusted when she'd called him a scumbag. He sighed. In the end, everyone was entitled to their point of view even if it was wrong.

He hadn't realized how much time had passed until predawn patches of gray sullied the perfect darkness outside. Disappointment over how fast time had flown slowed his final touches to the not-so-living canvas. He still had the note to leave and her electronics to collect.

After packing up, he headed downstairs while reveling in the fond memories made that night. A quick celebration was definitely in order.

In the kitchen, he found the cookies whose aroma had snared his attention earlier, some version of cinnamon chocolate chip that would complement the wine he'd put in the fridge.

How thoughtful for her to provide refreshment. The vintage spirit was a little dry for his taste and didn't sit well with the caviar, but the cookies were divine.

When finished cleaning and wiping the glass and arranging the riddle on the counter, it was time to take his leave and publish the cherished memories. He hoped Ethan solved the riddle leading to the clue to his next victim in time. He'd purposefully made it easy in light of the dull minds of his pursuers. After all, his fans expected some sport.

With a pensive yearning for more performances like this one, he knew he'd think fondly of this night for years to come. Exiting through the back door and locking it behind him, he left as quietly as he'd entered.

The dog slept peacefully.

An interminable ride home increased frustration when he wanted nothing more than to upload his newest video and collect his reward for work well done. The clue he'd stuffed up her nose would lead them to the tasty morsel he wanted for his next masterpiece if they found it before the chemicals degraded the paper.

And if they're smart enough to figure it out.

Unlike the modest house maintained for his public persona, his second home was small by comparison to the snooty councilwoman's but suited his particular need for privacy while modified to his specific standards. The current nesting place was where he created epic works of art.

Upkeep for two houses was a necessary evil but occasionally yielded other benefits. He didn't often entertain in his primary residence since pasting on smiles and talking social dribble wasn't his forte.

When forced to endure their company, he relished rubbing elbows with the snobbish elite while inwardly laughing at their pathetic, dull lives that plodded from dawn to dusk, never realizing the great adventures he enjoyed reviewing in his cozy bungalow. What the tax assessor might think of the home's exterior induced a smile.

The driveway gravel was darkened and dew-damp, the rising sun sending its first dreadful rays creeping over the treetops and crawling into his front yard. With no neighbors for miles, he'd passed unseen with no one to suspect the wonderful night he'd secretly experienced.

Despite the exhilaration of work well done, his body couldn't escape the lassitude ushered in with the sun's bright rays slanting around his closed living room drapes.

The interior was another example of his bold deceptions, a contradiction to the slovenly kept exterior where scrubby landscaping and the home's remoteness deterred ambitious salesmen. He preferred the inside stay immaculate, free of dust bunnies, signs of neglected maintenance, and clutter.

After securing his pouch and equipment in the hidden control room designed with painstaking attention to detail, he headed for bed. A few hacking coughs during his short phone call convinced his co-workers he couldn't come into work but would stay overtime on the morrow to catch up. If it weren't so much fun dealing with the peons, he'd quit and live off his inheritance and the money taken from his dead partner.

Stretching out on his bed lent great comfort after a night

of strenuous exercise, which in the past had led to a good day's sleep. His subconscious would not only provide a smorgasbord of vivid memories but also a fanciful array of new ideas to explore, tweaking until perfect for future ventures. Part of the fun of having an intellectually superior brain was that it never turned *off*.

Silence greeted him upon waking in a dark so deep it soothed his soul. The extra insulation and custom drapes were worth every penny. Sights and the feel of the city enticed him to play like a much-cherished lover, but the serenity of the countryside drew him back to nest each morning. A good day's sleep had furnished for his body what his sophisticated moral activities provided for his spirit.

The rest of the week would demand much of his time, but considering how he'd toy with his pursuers, it would provide Oscar-worthy moments when they arrived at his intended conclusions.

Inside, he laughed daily at the cops scurrying around, snooping for any scraps he deigned to throw them. Intellectual superiority allowed him to laugh at the McAllister brothers' collective efforts. They'd never give him a run for his money. If they ever did get out of hand, he'd eliminate one or two to throw them off their game.

Come to think of it, I could use one as a test subject for a new project.

The special room devoted to his extracurricular work always welcomed and beckoned him to sit comfortably while he shared his favorite pastime with like-minded souls, the digital images far exceeding what his thoughts conjured despite frequently flexing his mental muscle.

Snagging a chocolate sprinkled donut from the nearby box, he uploaded last night's video to the highest bidder then sent out suitable offerings for his next undertaking.

The next performance would be special beyond comparison, both in selection of target and methodology of execution. A unique harmony between his exceptional intelligence and acquired skillset facilitated his physical art career. It was sad to admit he wasn't perfect.

Selecting an incompetent apprentice ranked an embarrassing blunder. At least he'd corrected his mistake and left an interesting if faint trail.

One of the marvels of the dark net was that it allowed him to obtain supplies without setting foot in a store or risk losing his anonymity. No one could trace him. He had quite a list for his next project. Unfortunately, he'd have to personally retrieve them.

Considering he'd planned for the next two performances, he might as well solicit all the needed supplies at once. His fans might make suggestions, but none were intelligent enough to dream up his intricate scenarios. At least they felt they had a say in the planning.

The next theme required battery acid from an older man in Seattle, pulley systems from a promising young sociopath in California, and a cane concealing a poison-tipped needle just in case it was needed—all obtained without spending a dime. He could make his pickups over the coming weekend. He intended to pull out all the stops for his next exploit.

"I don't remember how long it takes to purify sulfuric acid to my specifications. Time for some research."

Gotta love the internet.

After the police had disrupted the first kill outside the city, he'd decided a tariff was in order. The lead detective would suffer on a dual level. In time, Arvel would immortalize Lexi, Ethan's beautiful piece of fluff, and eliminate the possibility of her tracking him.

As if she could.

A dark premonition briefly warned that allowing Ethan's girlfriend to continue sending the detective tips was dangerous, but he couldn't resist playing with the morons for a few more weeks. The detective wasn't smart enough to catch him and could barely keep his hands off the girl.

Even after a few minutes of spying on them, Arvel knew she wasn't the type to play games and wasn't feigning infatuation. Ethan and Lexi were hot for each other despite her obvious inexperience, which would make his pain all the sweeter.

For reasons he couldn't define, the bone-deep gratification from posting last night's work didn't come. Like a stone in his shoe, something niggled at his sense of accomplishment and festered until he could no longer ignore it.

Another look at the cameras used to record the comings and goings of police and medical examiner from Frannie's house might supply the needed information before he removed the hardware. So far, they'd provided details of the main players and allowed him to focus on McAllister and Robertson.

Whereas Robertson didn't utilize outdoor cameras, Ethan employed several, newly installed. Frustration soured his mood when he again failed to hack McAllister's security system. Obviously, the little twit had a hand in it.

Chapter Ten

"So you're finally getting off your butt tomorrow and going back to work. How's it feel?" Lexi dropped her queen down two levels to take Ethan's rook, knowing her attempt at distraction was ineffective.

Playing chess with Ethan had initially equaled verbal hopscotch, dodging his persistent questions to land on a safe subject and exchange necessary information.

With each passing day, she found herself opening up a fraction more and wanting him as a semi-permanent fixture in her life, something never before experienced.

Close friendship with a male had never made it on her to-do list. The fact her concentration took a dive every time they locked gazes hadn't eluded his understanding if his half grins were any indication.

Her logical brain understood the attraction and chastised her for the weakness. The rest of her turned to mush when his penetrating regard reached inside and coiled around her heart, melting the walls she'd painstakingly erected.

Combined with his not-so-subtle touches, she found herself leaning forward more attentively, thinking about him even when home with Hoover. Ever since their collision that tumbled them to the floor, he took every opportunity to graze her arm or shoulder as if trying to tame a wild horse.

He has no idea.

Diego whined then nudged Hoover's shoulder as they lay side by side watching their masters' virtual combat. It was a warm, family setting, cozy and intimate.

"Feels great, looking forward to grinding my nose in the pavement, not waiting for backup, and Larrick blasting my ears with hillbilly music." He grimaced.

He'd bested her in half their games, the sneaking suspicion that he toyed with her instigating a smile. "You know, you have a tell when you hold back."

"Sorry. I wanted to give you time to get comfortable with the game." Worrying his upper lip between his teeth and the expanding dimple in his right cheek foretold of his restraint in subduing a chuckle. Yet the humor dancing in his gaze said it all.

She'd never shared such a comfortable comradery with a male and couldn't help wondering where it would go if she allowed it free rein.

Daily visits consisting of chess matches and verbal sparring filled a portion of her life she'd not recognized as empty. Ethan's home served the same purpose as her own yet felt warmer, cozier, and different in ways unfathomable, which brought with it an unwelcome envy.

Every night, she'd spent hours trying to discern the exact nature of the heat welling up inside when his intensity held her prisoner, and his touch melted her resistance.

They had much in common, from music to vintage and scary movies, hiking, or merely enjoying a quiet afternoon on the porch. She'd taught him to navigate some difficult paths on the internet while culling anecdotes of large family living. Time spent unraveling the killer's convoluted digital path equaled fate's counterbalance to the new and strange developing relationship with a cop who turned her mind to mush.

"Hmm. You don't seem as uptight when my brothers or sister visit."

"I leave that attribute to you, especially since they've noted my positive effect on your disposition." She couldn't help but smile.

His sister's visits were something she actually anticipated. Abagail broadcast warmth and acceptance with easy smiles and a quick wit. They'd even talked about *girl stuff* in light terms. Apparently, Lexi had passed each of the, *are you good enough tests*, to be included in their inner circles. As much as she wanted to read their emails to each other, she'd refrained, holding on to her strict moral code.

"You've grown on me." The slight arch of his brow and raking of teeth over his bottom lip begged for a response.

"Kinda like a fungus?"

"Fungi are paramount in the making of certain medications..."

"So—I'm like a drug?"

"No, you are a drug. A necessary one, at that."

Sudden heat in her face and a virtual lump swelling in her throat prevented her from continuing the banter. Looking away, she let the fall of her hair cover her reaction. He'd never been so direct.

"In the past several weeks, you've demonstrated training tips for Diego and actually learned cooking techniques here while teaching me about the internet. We seem to be good for each other."

As if I hadn't noticed. Her laptop on his kitchen table had become part of the decor. When her email program chimed, her stumbling rush to check it elicited a snort from Ethan.

"Graceful fungus." A muffled laugh took the sting out of his words. "Any news from the onion field?" His words belied the respect shown for the vastness of the dark web.

She snickered at his analogy to the many addresses she'd worked on tracking. "Yeah, he's collecting supplies for his next performance—pulleys, a special type of cane, and acid." She hadn't heard him pad up behind her, but the warmth of his breath forced a shudder to ripple across her shoulders.

"So, we're looking for a cripple wanting to build some type of lift and is in need of exfoliation. How's he acquiring the supplies? Maybe we can catch him that way." Disgust laced Ethan's tone.

"I'm thinking he's only using a few known contacts. I suspect it's people he's dealt with before. If I appear pushy, I might lose the thread, but I can make an offer."

"Yeah, okay. But go easy. I spoke with Larrick yesterday. There's nothing new on Frannie's case, so this is all we've got."

"I've kept up with the record flow, and I went to her house last night. Before you freak out, I wore dark clothes and had my hair up. I know we're missing something, but I'll be damned if I know what it is."

"How'd you get in?"

Very slowly, he lifted her to stand and turned her to face him. Expressed within the expected heat, a concern that reached the pitch-dark corners of her heart warmed yet warned of something deeper yet to come.

He stepped close enough that only her hair separated their bodies, his minty breath mingling with her own. The anxiety always nipping at her mind with his close proximity overwhelmed her reasoning for maintaining distance with a cop. *He's not just a cop.*

"Picked the front door lock." Her tongue stuck to the roof of her mouth.

When he bent his head in slow degrees of torturous anticipation, Hoover's whine cleared her thoughts. She tucked her head against his chest.

"And?"

"Nothing out of place, nothing missing. I just don't understand the why of it."

"Don't try to get in a psycho's mind. You'll end up lost or damaged."

She'd always shied away from physical relationships but pressed closer when Ethan's hands circled her waist. He wasn't conceding the battle, more like giving her time to adjust.

The tentative friendship they'd formed was so new, her feelings raw. At some point in her nightly deliberations, she'd concluded some barriers were destined for demolition since she's erected most of hers when hiding from a vicious pimp. Now that the predator was in jail—could she have a normal life?

She'd never had a boyfriend and wondered what it would feel like to kiss him when just being in the same room heightened her senses from the adrenaline rush. Now, her over-sensitized body tightened and ached in a way that begged for more.

It felt natural to have Ethan's hands caressing her back. They just fit, despite the different backgrounds and perspectives. Each uniqueness complemented the other's personality in a way that designated them corresponding halves of a whole.

"We'll figure this out, Lexi."

The case or our strange relationship?

"I think..."

Words were a useless commodity as his head lowered, slowly, asking permission even as he intended to take.

The brush of his lips across her own incited a low groan. Gently, he captured her mouth, her soul, quietly demanding her surrender. The warmth of his tongue delved inside her mouth, slowly at first, flirty, dallying with his prize.

When she melted against him, his hand smoothed down the curve of her spine to gently mold her butt, kneading and shifting until they fit together perfectly.

Conscious thought wasn't required for action, but the silky-soft texture of his hair twined in her fingers made her want to explore more of his body. A slight slide of her hips against him produced a rumbling in his chest, felt against her own.

As if realizing where this was going and unable to continue, Ethan lifted his head, her regret reflected in his eyes. "Yes, definitely a drug."

"We shouldn't be doing this." Yet her body pressed tighter to him, needing his warmth, his strength, his passion.

"Not yet. There's a time and place for everything. For now, we shouldn't get sidetracked from the investigation."

"I owe Frannie more than you could ever imagine." She groaned when he leaned back, missing his warmth. "I spent three years with the prostitutes, trying to avoid pimps and other creeps.

"Then Frannie caught me and for some reason decided to take me under her wing. A couple nights later when I ended up in the ER, she swooped in and kinda took over and shielded me from endless questions." Lexi smiled at the memory of Frannie declaring her a friend of the family.

"That night, she introduced me to Father Thomas from the Episcopal Church. I helped him with his computer. When Frannie learned the extent of what I could do, she helped me get a job and off the streets. As I said, I owe her everything."

"How'd you become so digitally adept while homeless?"

"I did have a life before I hit the streets. My parents indulged my electronic obsessions. They were great."

Another bittersweet memory invaded her mind. "When they died, I went into foster care...for less than twenty-four hours." The touch of his fingers petting her hair and making swirling motions on her nape raised goosebumps.

"What sent you to the ER?" His frown declared he'd search through hospital records for any scraps of information they would offer.

She'd long ago erased any digital record of her presence. Of all the people to orbit her world, Ethan embodied a new realm, one she couldn't quite define or categorize.

According to his record, he was a top-notch investigator, shrewd and intelligent. Reality contradicted files in that he wasn't the ruthless dominant she'd expected. Apart from their work-related skills, they shared many traits.

"Violent schizophrenic decided I was an alien in need of eliminating. I thought I'd learned to respect others' personal space, but apparently, the distance is greater for abductees." The incident's far-reaching effects still gave her nightmares.

Her attempt to lighten the matter didn't fool him. He'd see more than surface expressions, his discerning gaze plumbing the depths of her soul where life's lessons twined with old habits to keep her in a state of insecurity concerning relationships.

"So nothing struck you as *off* in Frannie's house?"

The warmth of his touch circled each vertebra then spread out to stimulate her numbed nerves with languid heat and quieting the ever-present urge to bolt when near a man.

"No. I'd only been there a couple times. I couldn't tell you if the, um, items left belonged to her." Determination to exact justice fortified her reserves and denied the stinging under her eyelids to release her grief. Teasing swirls of his fingertips on her arms further distracted the direction of her intended focus.

Does he know what he's doing to me? Conflicting emotions would soon tear her apart.

"You know, mourning a friend's loss doesn't make you vulnerable or weak."

Some men's gazes could pierce the thickest and smoothest of lies without the deceiver realizing he'd been made. Ethan's quiet intensity had the added ability of quietly delving through emotions, watching, assimilating, yet not forcing his will and overriding her restraints.

The self-contained force of nature was one step away from zeroing in on her deepest pain and exposing it for all to see, her oldest wound. Loneliness. Yet it was just the two of them. What did he want from her?

There was a personal edge to his nonverbal, something she'd paid close attention to in hopes of solving the Ethan puzzle. The dichotomy of electronic reports compared to flesh-and-blood man left her confused since she had no personal experience of close-up encounters of this type.

"Yeah, yeah. I don't need sappy friends." The fact she no longer had friends within the city probably wouldn't surprise him.

He obviously wanted more than friendship yet held back while giving her time to assimilate her feelings. His heat spoke of secreting her away from the world, but underneath, there remained an innate sadness she couldn't fathom, like a desire never to be fulfilled.

Life had also taught her to dissect a person's motivations and desires. Could she throw him off balance—return the favor? She molded her body to his, watching his eyes briefly widen with the shoulder-to-knee contact.

He stroked her back, her arms, her cheek, offering a comfort she'd never known. Yet fear skittered down her back when his eyes darkened, the hunger within dominating his gaze and reminding her that this was his world, one where he obviously excelled.

"I've never kissed anyone before." The words blurted out before her thoughts filtered the blunder.

His response, taking a deep breath that softened her chest against his solid wall of muscle. "You're young. There are a lot of things you haven't done...yet."

His grazing touch branded a trail down her neck then back up to skim over her lips. The fiery tingle left in his wake blazed a molten path to her chest, stretching, aching for something undiscovered. Heat gathered in her low belly, an embarrassment never suffered.

Closing her eyes only aided the tsunami of emotions consuming every aspect of her being.

"Open."

Simple, direct, and immediately obeyed.

He was a master.

He was the fire burning in her soul.

He was—

Melting the last of her invisible armor.

In slow degrees of heart-pounding anticipation, he lowered his head until his lips lightly skimmed over her brow, placing a kiss and then moving lower. Whispering in her ear, his words barely made sense, his heat all-consuming. "Soon."

When he finally took her mouth, his gentle touch grew stronger, unleashing something wild and urgent inside she couldn't stop. She couldn't deny her response.

The sweep of his tongue demanded entrance then twined with her own, exploring, writhing in an imitation of the full-body dance for which they both hungered.

There were so many reasons to pull away, but her body betrayed conscious thought, her fingers twining again in his hair to pull him tighter. The rumbling in his chest echoed her need.

When he pulled back, she was breathless, boneless, and unable to process her swirling emotions.

What am I doing?

"We shouldn't..." Doubt braided with lust etched his expression.

Regret was a cold stone in her stomach. "Why not?" No one had ever breached her personal walls before.

"I'm not the man for you. Your innocence..."

"Everybody starts somewhere—"

"I'm not a gentle lover."

"Gentleness is vastly overrated. I was a street rat."

"You're inexpierenced."

"It doesn't make me weak."

"Your first time should be with someone who spends hours preparing your body with soft caresses and mild petting. I want you so badly I don't think I—"

"Are you saying you're into whips and chains?"

Oh, God. I sent him fur-lined cuffs as a gag.

"No, I'm not. But I'm hard on a woman's body."

"Ever had complaints?"

"No, but that's not the point."

"Yeah, it is. Enough talking."

This time, he didn't take her mouth. He stormed her senses, wild and thorough, plundering her depths and leaving her exposed as never before. Yet hadn't she learned to trust him? He could've turned on her any number of times yet continually protected her at every opportunity, even from his own family.

Everything inside her burned, encouraged by his bolder caresses. His fingers massaged her waist as he nuzzled her neck, little bites trailing to her jaw then her mouth. When he cupped one breast, she groaned before gasping as his thumb grazed over the crest. Every part of her body tightened.

With his other hand on her waist, he pressed her hips tighter, rubbing back and forth to create the most delicious friction she'd ever known.

"I want more." Mumbled words against his mouth.

Doorbell chimes broke the spell. Ethan lifted his head, his darkened gaze leaving no doubt of his desire.

"Tell them to go away."

"First, I need to see who it is." Ethan rolled his shoulders and adjusted himself, letting her know what the future would bring. "If it's not important, I'll shoot 'em and be right back."

"Wow."

"My thoughts exactly."

A determined stride carried him across the room, his smile disappearing when he opened the door. "Damn. Like you don't have a phone?"

"You took Lexi to the station? What happened to keeping her out of the limelight?" Matt glared at his younger brother. "And why am I just finding out about this?"

"She needed physical access to Frannie's electronics to see if the killer left anything traceable. I see Larrick failed in his attempt to keep his mouth shut."

"You think the killer, an expert in the dark net, won't learn of her involvement?" Matt turned to Lexi. "Sorry, hon, but at the moment you're our best shot at this psycho. Taking you there was—"

"A calculated risk. I get it. But it was *mine* to take. I would've gone with or without Ethan's help." Lexi realized they were in for a long afternoon of explaining how nothing made sense, and why she'd obtained no information from Frannie's electronics. Would Ethan's brothers question her involvement?

"Yeah, I get it. You two are a perfect match," Matt quipped. "Bull-headed."

Chapter Eleven

"What, no coffee? Where's my morning cup of joe?" Larrick's snark earned a glare. "I hate working crime scenes before I'm caffeinated." Larrick parked behind several patrol cars in the long drive.

"I've been up for hours, a little chore with my oldest brother before returning to duty. And before you ask, I don't want to discuss it. 'Sides, I'm not a rookie trying to impress his partner. While we're at it, thanks for spilling the beans to Billy and Matt. You were supposed to keep quiet about Lexi's visit to IT. We would've shared any new information."

Ethan's slamming car door startled several dozen bushtits and other songbirds in the nearby wood line. Their sudden exodus exposed a foot-long gourd-like nest made from spider webs, moss, grass, and other plant material. Extra space for the unlucky males not finding their own mates provided room for those helping to raise the young.

Ethan had always likened himself to the extra male in that his search for female companionship led to simpering, fragile women unable to keep stride with him, physically and mentally.

Larrick's continued quips about abbreviated relationships would earn him a black eye one day.

"Yeah, save that energy for a certain long-haired brunette. By the way, how is Lexi?" Larrick nodded to the uniformed officers posted by the front door, each handing out gloves and crime scene booties.

"Knock it off. We've got work to do." His feelings for Lexi were complicated, evolving, and tangled. How could he explain a connection he had yet to understand?

Two weeks of recuperation would normally have driven him crazy, but with Lexi's daily visits lasting from early morning to late in the evening, he'd settled into a routine he wanted to incorporate in his life.

Last night, he'd encouraged her to visit after work today with the claim he'd like to continue training Diego and watch a movie together. The fact that she enjoyed his cooking helped.

Since she'd investigated every other aspect of his life, surely she'd know when he returned home. He wondered at what point she'd hacked his security system.

"Yeah, please direct your attention to the job. If you get hurt again, your brothers are gonna send me on a one-way trip to someplace very unpleasant."

"If I don't do it first for snitching." Perhaps some Limburger cheese placed on the engine manifold of Larrick's truck one cold morning might reinforce the point.

Ethan mounted the elegant stone steps and smoothed his hand over the ornate ironwork handrail. "He seems to control every aspect of his endeavors, meticulous in not leaving DNA. Serial killers don't start with perfect skills. If we could find his earlier victims, we might draw a lead."

"You think he has many priors?" Larrick rubbed the back of his neck as if ethereal fingers ruffled his hair.

"He's organized. That takes time and experience." No case had ever challenged Ethan with such murky leads.

"He certainly has a knack for picking secluded spots."

"I think he's watching us remotely." Ethan's over-the-shoulder scrutiny couldn't pierce the low-level fog, yet some unnamed presence pricked his subconscious as if he stood in a killer's crosshairs.

"Let's check the surrounding wood's edge when we're done inside."

"Lexi showed me last night where he's tracking our

progress online, even posted our names on a site as 'up-and-coming' detectives. Maybe we'll get lucky and find something."

"Is he posting details only found in the papers? And is it on the site where he solicits bids?"

"Nope to both. He's blatantly giving away the fact that he either has an inside source or he's hacking us. It's driving Carl batshit crazy."

"Speaking of hackers..."

"No. Let's not just now. Did you find anything new on the hospital administrator, Daryl Johanson?"

"Not yet. His wife was out of town visiting her sick mother while he attended the function earlier in the evening. He's got no alibi."

Era-appropriate furniture monopolized the space with intricately carved chairs boasting rounded arms, sofas covered in luxurious jeweled fabrics fastened with nail head trim, and side tables perpetuating an Old World charm.

If he hadn't worn booties to protect the scene, Ethan would've taken off his shoes. Not a dog hair or dust mote blemished any surface until reaching the bedroom where the carnage indicated a killer who'd planned and taken the time to savor his psychotic fantasy.

"Yuck. This guy's wormy brain must've started rotting at birth." Larrick snatched a handkerchief from his jacket pocket to cover his nose.

Three years of detective work in a large city department hadn't yielded a fraction of the sickness displayed in the two unsolved murders. "I came back here to work in hopes of a lighter caseload."

"Naw, Ethan, you came back to roost with your family."

On the bed, blood spatters soaked into and distorted the

lacy pattern created by the torn window shears while severed body parts painted a gruesome story of a hellish descent into a death no one deserved. Even the crime scene techs forfeited their gallows humor, their grayish complexions warning of unrevealed abominable details.

Rounding the opulent footboard, the horrific sight made Ethan remember that trying to rationalize a psychotic's behavior could drive one nuts. A cause-and-effect relationship did not always exist within a damaged mind. On occasion, acceptance of the inexplicable led to dealing with bizarre circumstances on its own terms.

"Why?" Ethan knew terror had filled the woman's last hours. He wondered how long she'd stayed conscious.

"I guess like a lot of psychos we catch, this one just needs someone to hate." Larrick briefly closed his eyes before visually searching the room. "He's targeting wealthy and powerful older women. Gotta be a story behind that."

"Yeah, more information for our profiler."

"We'll have another chat after our assessment. But I bet this will confirm her theory." Larrick stood aside for a technician in coveralls carrying out a container of trace evidence bags. The green tinge surrounding the veteran CSI's mouth spoke volumes.

Two crime scene techs moved about, methodically dusting each piece of furniture for prints while another used powder and an adhesive lifter to obtain a latent shoe print from the hardwood floor.

"What size, Jordan?" Larrick asked the kneeling tech.

"Hmm, I'd say, thirteen. This is a common tread pattern. I'll know more once I recreate it from the print."

"So, we're looking for a big guy, probably six foot. 'Bout the size of the dirtball who shot me. Darn shame he wore a mask."

Moving closer to stand beside the coroner now bent over the mutilated body, Ethan took a slow breath to impede his throat's knot of disgust dissolving into acid.

"What was he trying to do?" Moisture dotting Ethan's forehead and slicking his palms warned he wasn't a hardened detective. "And why drag her to the floor when clearly he tortured her on the bed?"

The victim lay curled on her side with blood spray saturating the rug around her. When they lifted her body, an outline of blood would delineate her final position.

"Maybe she said something she shouldn't have." The coroner studied the victim from several different angles while the photographer finished taking his pictures. "Different MO, but I'd swear it's the same killer. How many whackos can there be?"

"What about her neck? What is that all about?" Larrick grimaced, approaching from the other side.

"Well, the idiot severed her spinal cord while drilling a hole at her nape. Looks like maybe he was trying to pull out the bundle of nerves. The sick moron." Dr. Kefner shook his head.

"So, the blood looks diluted in spots because..." Some darkened recess of his mind forced Ethan's feet to reposition himself at the victim's head. He immediately regretted the need to acquire all information through visual examination versus a written report.

"We'll find cerebral spinal fluid with the breach of her column. If there's semen—or other fluids mixed in with it, I'll let you know."

"Dear God. How can a human become so twisted?" Ethan turned away.

"Who knows? By the way, we've identified the drug added to the ACE." The medical examiner shifted back for the photographer to snap some close-ups. "It was an anticholinergic. Took a while to identify because it wasn't pharmaceutical grade. The killer apparently makes his own deliriant distilled from the Nightshade family, Datura. Death came from shock and respiratory paralysis."

"Jeez, who needs friends? How many people would have the knowledge to do that?" Ethan grumbled.

"Anybody with a computer and an internet connection. As far as the ACE is concerned, all you need is a script written by a vet. Unfortunately, we don't monitor veterinarians and their prescriptions. Hell, you can even order it online from out of the country."

"Where's her computer and cell phone?" Ethan's nod to Larrick instigated a quick visual search.

"Didn't see one in here. Haven't seen the other rooms," Dr. Kefner bent over the body for a closer inspection, his voice trailing off in distraction.

"What about a riddle? Did he leave a riddle anywhere?" Ethan asked.

"I heard someone mention that—on the kitchen counter by a bunch of flowers. I'm a bit occupied here."

Vibrations from his cell phone signaled Ethan's incoming message. "Who the heck is sending—" As soon as the words left his mouth, he regretted it.

"Well?" Larrick, halfway out the door, stopped. His smirk warned the question was rhetorical.

"Did you guys find a dog?" Ethan wordlessly cursed for not silencing his phone. Awareness of Lexi's tendency toward helping via electronic stalking would inevitably lead to trouble. He merely frowned at Larrick to head off questions until they spoke in private.

"Yeah, a uniform found one out back. Looks like someone drugged it. One of the officers took it to the emergency clinic." Dr. Kefner shook his head. "The killer mutilates the woman but leaves the dog with just a hangover. What a sick, twisted mind."

Further details failed to illuminate the inner workings of the sick mind behind the vicious murder.

By the time they exited the gruesome scene, lacy filigreed light sweeping the front sidewalk had given way to brilliant sunshine but failed to lighten Ethan's spirit. As long as he lived, he'd never understood man's compulsion to instill abject terror and dispense unmitigated pain. "He kept her conscious as long as he could."

"Leave that in the house, Ethan. I'll buy you a beer after work. We have priorities." Larrick paused before unlocking their SUV's doors. "Unless you have something better to do?"

"Actually, I'll take a rain check. Tired after the first day back and all that." His bogus excuse went unchallenged.

"All right. Let's decipher the riddle. *I can run but not walk*, could have various meanings." Larrick slid into the driver's seat. "A computer? After all, he's digitally inclined."

"A car or a nose." Ethan thought of how many times he'd sneezed when Larrick replaced the homemade air freshener.

"Both sound reasonable."

"The second part, *Thoughts are not far away, but I never seem to connect*, could definitely refer to her nose," Ethan added. Finding a clue to the next victim's identity might save a life.

"I'll call the coroner and tell him to check for anything up her nose before she'd transported and the clue is degraded."

Ethan sighed. "If we can unravel this riddle, maybe we can beat him at his own game."

"I'd like to be waiting at the next home he visits."

"Darn shame we couldn't find this victim's cell or laptop." Ethan checked his phone again for messages.

Rip-roaring guilt over Lexi's involvement stemmed from his need to protect. However, her stubborn streak ran wider and stronger than anyone he'd ever encountered. She'd do this with or without his help.

At least their current arrangement allowed him to keep tabs on whatever trouble she'd find. Yesterday, he'd come one step closer to convincing her to stay with him until the nightmare blew over.

Progress that might have succeeded if not for my brother's interruption.

As a detective, Ethan had worked with CIs before, but this scenario involved a different realm, full of mental minefields and tangled emotions. The tense ride back to the precinct allowed time to contemplate his thoughts and the riddle. "Two murders back to back with no evidence and no leads. Why did he start here, now?"

"Maybe he didn't. Maybe this isn't his first playground. He's had to have made a mistake sometime. We'll catch him." Larrick cornered his next curve abruptly, his speed commensurate with the tightening grip on the wheel.

"Yeah, after how many more of these scenes and riddles?" Ethan asked. "Dooley was from the East Coast, but we've found no matching crimes from his home court, nor any connection to anyone else in this area, except his ex-wife."

"Who claims she hasn't seen him since the divorce. And

we've found no connection to Daryl from the hospital. Ugh, back to basics. Maybe this victim didn't have a computer. She was pushing mid-sixties. Not everyone thinks in bits and bytes."

"Your idea of modern computers is a redneck abacus with wildfowl leg bands and neckbands sliding on guitar wires."

"Funny. Not all older people keep up with the digital age."

"Seriously? Everyone has a computer these days. Heck, pre-kindergarten kids have computers. 'Sides, she was a councilwoman. I looked up her email addresses—one for the city, two for personal use." Again, Ethan's preoccupation had disengaged his brain's filter. Nothing like easing into a conversation.

"Okay. We couldn't find her computer or cell phone, yet you already know how many accounts she has? How much is Lexi *helping*?" Larrick pulled into the station's lot, the abrupt stop proportionate with his obviously jaded thoughts. Silence ensued as he cut the engine and pocketed the keys.

Ethan merely grunted. "She texted me." Shoving his door open invited honeysuckle and other soft scents on the spring breeze to remind him that yes, nature had a bright side.

"She's thorough. Has she had any further digital contact with our psycho?"

"No, but I'll talk to her tonight." The distant blast of a semi's high-pressure horn prodded images of a less complicated life, one he'd briefly contemplated long ago in hopes of a freer lifestyle and travel. "I could've been a truck driver."

"Yeah, I can see you in a big rig now. Your brothers would ticket you every time you drove through town." Larrick preceded him inside and up the stairwell to the second floor's open squad room.

Multiple back-to-back desk units filled the center while single desks lined the walls between countertops filled with printers, copiers, and various terminals for specific record searches.

Ethan had replaced the token coffee machine residing in the corner with a state of the art espresso and latte machine capable of piloting the next spaceship, according to his colleagues. Long hours accompanied the job, necessitating occasional survival on caffeine infusions.

"I'll start the abbreviated paperwork if you wanna check the lab. Then we can hit the streets." Larrick's chair scraped against the tile floor, his attention already riveted to the computer screen on his desk.

Advertising his redneck status were other items including a cartoon hunter flip calendar, a camouflage gun mug, and a hillbilly dashboard dancer, its head wobbling when Larrick bellied up to the desk.

By the time Ethan returned, the opposite side would consist of sticky notes lined up in alphabetical order, precision-stacked papers, and an odd assortment of pens placed in the cup holder to deliberately refute the normal chaos.

Every partnership entailed idiosyncrasies that frustrated as well as confused. The court of public opinion had long denied their compatibility, but it seemed the differences separating them established a bond that braided them together to form a unique working relationship.

Some things just worked, like a straight-arrow detective and a smart-mouthed hacker.

"Hey, Carl. Anything new?" Forensic studies had long fascinated Ethan, the myriad ways microscopic evidence could condemn criminals mind-boggling. If not for the stifling effect of being stuck in an office, he could see himself sifting through and studying evidence for that one filament connecting predator and prey.

"Yeah, Toby found something for you in the litter box."

Named because of the criminologists specializing in the study of everything dirt related, Carl's obvious attitude came with a slight twist of his lips. The other section of the lab included a larger footprint with tables and counters full of various analytical equipment.

"He's out at the moment, but we've been discussing the case," Carl added. "I can give you the highlights while I'm eating."

"All right. Thanks." Ethan took a deep breath. "Hmm, smells like seafood."

Carl had always flavored friendliness with a slightly awkward shyness yet was quick with a smile and offer to assist. When Ethan had moved into his new house, Carl arrived to help, bringing crab bisque to share afterward.

"Yeah, I love this stuff. Park it and we'll put our heads together. Toby and I were discussing how to catch this clever little shit, and he was telling me what he found." Carl's excitement over the new findings was evident, his energetic smile displaying several crooked teeth while advertising a degree of success.

Ethan pulled a swivel stool closer to the tech's workspace, wondering what the whiz kids had discovered this time. "What'd he find?" At this point, any evidence would be welcome.

"Pollen."

"Pollen?"

"Whereas this guy is smart enough to not leave fingerprints, he *did* leave pollen. In this case, just as good."

"How so?"

"Because the spores they found didn't come from native trees. Unless Frannie recently visited the East Coast, our killer is someone who travels."

"Can they narrow it down?"

"Maybe, but it'll take time."

"Anything else? Anything with the new victim's email accounts or cell messages?"

"I can't trace anything back yet. It might be different if we actually had the hardware." Carl pinched the bridge of his nose before adding, "This killer might be better than me." Frustration clenched his jaw as he shook his head. "We'll track him, eventually. Nobody's perfect."

"The coroner called with the riddle he found up the victim's nose. Larrick and I were trying to decipher it. *'I detect the ill winds of fate. I travel with hurricane force despite the load I bear. Once begun, only death can stop me.'* I think my brain is on overload, though, because I can't make sense of it."

"Um, I'll have to think about that one, Ethan. I have no clue what twisted thoughts are swimming in this guy's warped mind."

Something had to break soon. The longer they took to solve the case, the greater the likelihood the killer would find Lexi.

"What about your girlfriend? She have any ideas?" A slight edge of frustration, possibly desperation, dusted Carl's voice.

"No, but she knows some other techies that according to

her are more adept at the keyboard. She's going to check with them." The lie tasted like betrayal yet added the thinnest layer of protection. An all-consuming need to shield Lexi from prying eyes consumed him.

Chapter Twelve

"You know, for a cop, you sure don't believe much in security measures."

The fact Lexi walked into his house unannounced felt comfortable and right. Though he always locked his door at night before retiring, he didn't bother after coming home from work.

Between his training and Diego's advanced warning, he'd square off against any intruder. Furthermore, there were enough walls, albeit invisible ones, between them. *They're coming down one by one.*

"What if I was entertaining a lady friend?" Teasing her was his favorite pastime.

"You don't have lady friends. You have family, a dog, and I'm guessing, one-night stands."

Was she afraid of becoming a statistic? Wariness had given way to wistful smiles during his brothers' visits and had revealed her only known vulnerability, a yearning for family. He knew when she committed to a man, it would be forever.

"I just got home." Ethan watched Diego and Hoover's tumble greeting with a small grimace. Since the canines' second meeting, they'd smashed no other furniture but not from lack of trying.

"Good, means you haven't eaten. I'm hungry." En route to the kitchen, she handed him a bag of doggy treats.

"What's this?"

"I brought food and something for you to have analyzed. Not in the same container." Setting the large paper bag on his kitchen counter, she handed him a smaller one, the kind school kids used to carry their lunches.

"What? Where'd you get something that would need investigating?"

Hesitation in her tone shifted his thoughts from her form-fitting jeans to a cryptic smile he wasn't sure he wanted to decode.

"It's a sample from Frannie's place. You should open it *after* dinner."

"Why?" Frustration saw the bag opened in short, jerky movements. Inside, a plastic baggie held two long, white cylindrical objects. Even through the plastic, the smell delineated the specimen's source.

"Its dog crap. Let's eat before discussing it."

"What the heck?" All prior interactions had led him to believe Lexi existed as a mysterious force of nature, well balanced despite her craving for privacy. "I prefer my presents wrapped, thank you very much."

"It was in Frannie's backyard, beyond the fence."

"And you don't have enough, such that you have to import it? Why would you even go looking?"

"I wasn't looking for *that*. We're missing something, so I took another look around. I'm glad I did. Frannie fed her dog kibble." Her tone suggested anyone not understanding the obvious meaning was an idiot.

"And—"

"That is white, which means it's not from her dog."

"Explain."

"Raw-fed dogs have a higher calcium intake. Hence, their feces turn white within a day or so. Frannie fed kibble. *And*, her furbaby was quite aggressive, so this wasn't left over from a doggy playdate."

"You think the murderer brought his dog to the scene and left him outside the fenced area?"

"Well, he is a psycho. Why not? He could've brought him during surveillance or whatever. Maybe he wanted to get

Frannie's dog used to the idea of him passing through... I don't know."

"Which means if you're right, we'll have his dog's DNA. But with nothing to compare it to." *How am I gonna explain this to the crime techs?* "What made you go back and look?"

"The fact that nobody's perfect. He had to leave *something* for us to find and use against him. I just couldn't accept it otherwise. This is the only discrepancy I could spot."

"*Okaaay.*"

"Did the second victim feed kibble?" Lexi removed a package of ground beef from her grocery bag and placed it in the fridge.

"Don't know yet, but I'll check out her finances and her house tomorrow. That's not something the techs would've documented." Ethan placed the plastic baggie back in the smaller paper bag and set it aside.

"If the dog marked the territory, you might find some."

"Tying the two homicides together." *She should've been a detective.*

"Actually, we've already done that. I found clips of the second victim's ordeal on the dark net." Lexi slid the strap holding her carrying case from around her neck. I can show you as soon as this boots up. I've made a copy for you to take to your lab."

"Thank you, Lexi."

"Since we joined his little club late, he sent us the previous filming of Frannie, as a bonus." Her shoulders tightened while her head dropped forward, composure a hard-won commodity.

Ethan closed the distance, sensing she needed the contact but would never ask for comfort. With an arm around her shoulders, he pulled her into a hug while her laptop's *whirring* forewarned of a somber evening ahead. Her sob against his chest signaled her acknowledgment of everything her friend had endured.

"I'm sorry, Lexi. I'm so very sorry." *Finally, she's grieving.*

Long minutes passed where Ethan grazed his hand up and down her back and held her through the racking shudders until her breathing evened out and her snivels abated. From the crime scene photos, he knew Lexi's mentor had suffered things no human should ever experience.

In slow degrees of awareness, the fresh but subtle floral scent of her hair invaded his senses, twining around aspects of his soul that should've remained unavailable to the persistent entanglement of reckless determination and vulnerable complexity. Their mutual familiarity pointed to an innocent intimacy born of understanding and affection but had grown into something defying definition.

Ethan tucked a lock of hair behind her ear before she pulled back, the loss of her warmth instigating a sense of deprivation. With her emotions under control, he released her to sit and delve into the dark highways few others could navigate.

Minutes passed in a respectful, subdued silence as he waited for her to dissect digital pathways and form some semblance of order. It didn't take long.

"I found something in common in their bank records."

"You…" Nothing about her should have surprised him. "What is it?"

"The second victim bought kibble from the same store as Frannie. Different brand but same place. Pampered Paws Pet Store on the corner of Rose and Cannon Streets."

"Who owns it?"

"Um, oh. Oh, my God. It's owned by Bethany Jameson, ex-wife of Dooley Sonnenfeld, the man you shot."

"Really? I'll call Larrick. We'll check it out first thing in the morning." It was more than coincidence, but he couldn't imagine a woman moving across the country from her ex then helping him and another sociopath commit mayhem. Larrick had already spoken with Dooley's ex-wife. If a current connection had existed, his partner would've picked up the vibes.

"The sooner we figure this out, the more lives we save."

"I found another site where the killer is posting part of his videos. It's called Playtime. He's listing items needed for his next job and offers suggestions as far as possible victims." Turning back to the kitchen table, she withdrew into her own world.

"How did you find it?"

"Through the onion sniffer. It's a dark net search program."

"But this is still bouncing around other servers to keep him anonymous?" Watching her bring up an unknown browser, Ethan felt more out of touch than ever.

"Yeah, there's still only a slim chance of finding his psychotic butt. I found a social forum that talks about him, but nobody knows where he's located. They offer to obtain things he needs for his next job. I'm guessing he contacts them privately like he did with our email."

"Why separate sites?"

"Hmm, the second is loosely chained to other destinations. I think he keeps it up for bragging rights but who knows for sure."

"We could offer to obtain supplies, might gain access to him or one of his trusted subordinates. Does he have more than two videos posted?" Discussing this went against everything ingrained in him since childhood. The slight quiver in her lower lip and stiffening shoulders boded ill.

"Yeah, partials posted on the second site, but I don't know who they are or where they're from. It also doesn't preclude him having other sites for one reason or another. I just haven't found them yet."

"How about similar murders? Can you do a search that way?"

"I've been looking, but this guy changes his MO. What if he does that every time? I have no specific parameters with which to search."

"Then we'll work with what we have. I'm still wondering if he moves around the country, transient work. He's clean and organized."

"Hmm, he's posted again. Voting has started on the next choice of victims, and his ratings have gone up. This is just more encouragement." Her flurry of digital motion increased in speed and coincided with grumbled expletives.

"He's starting again, without taking any kind of break."

"Looks like this is his antisocial forum. I think he's getting high on all the comments and encouragement," Lexi added.

"He's giving a choice between a college coed and a high school student. That just narrows it down, doesn't it?" Ethan snarled.

Lexi picked up his thread of thought. "If owning a dog is some kind of connection, we still can't narrow it down much. There are too many college kids commuting, and according to the ASPCA, between thirty-seven and forty-seven percent of U.S. households have a dog. Considering the city's size and how long that pet store has been around, there's no way to narrow the search."

"Oh, look at that. Bidding is going through the roof." Man's capacity for inhumanity never ceased to amaze him. "Is he doing something special with this one?"

"It's probably because of the change in the victim's age. Jeez, look at the current bid. There's no way to top that."

The next hour provided little further information. Lexi's obvious frustration gained momentum with each dead-end link.

"Let's call it a night, have some dinner. Yes? You need to take a break." Slowly, he closed the laptop after she shut down her browser and powered off, both literally and figuratively.

She appeared totally wiped. Helping him prepare a simple steak and salad gave her mindless tasks to divert her thoughts. Throughout the meal, he knew the direction of her focus as she kept circling to the root of their problem. As per their routine, each helped clear the dishes.

"We've got to find his one mistake, an earlier victim or weakness. What is he planning with car battery acid, glass barrels, and pulley systems?" That baffling combination would keep him awake long into the night. "I gotta make a call. I'll join you in a few."

It didn't take long to give Larrick the updates, scarce as the information had been. *At least it's a start.* They finally had small threads on which to pull.

And it turns out to be dog crap and a pet food store.

When he returned, she hadn't moved. A combination of circumstances had obviously drained her energy and laid her soul bare. The need to give comfort transcended his physical realm upon cataloging her signs of exhaustion.

Without words, he scooped her up and sat on the sofa, her body's instant tightening earning an admonishing, "Easy, tiger. Just going to sit here, nothing more."

Despite her nearness and her hair's fresh scent frying his brain cells, he simply held her, feathering his fingers across her shoulders and down her spine until she relaxed into his embrace.

Intermittent conversation detailed the incredible relationship she'd shared with Frannie and the dreams she'd formed as a young girl before orphan status derailed her life. Quiet intermissions provided equal if parallel comfort. Words weren't necessary to cement their bond.

The intimacy of the moments startled him into realizing that this connection, this communion of souls was something he'd never shared with another woman, nor would he seek with anyone other than the mysterious conundrum snuggled in his arms.

When she awoke later, it took all his strength to let her go. Watching her leave with Hoover by her side created a new and unwelcome tightness in his chest.

Early-morning meetings with the brass telegraphed trouble on the horizon. Larrick's ominous message had come before sunrise in a short burst of grumbling complaints reminiscent of Matt's demeanor.

Now, recognizing the commissioner's car in the department's parking lot magnified the possibilities exponentially. This was shaping up to be a crappy day.

Larrick's car stopped in front of their lieutenant's parking bumper as Ethan reached the glass front doors of the station. A lop-sided smirk was the only indication of the intentional offense.

"The office pool is up to fifty bucks that you get towed,"

Ethan murmured.

"We'll be gone before Lieutenant Sunshine arrives."

"Captain's call must've woken you before the first rooster's crow." Ethan smiled at the memory of their first days of working together. He'd quickly learned not to speak to Larrick before his first cup of coffee.

"On top of that, my partner interrupted a very interesting evening to discuss the intricacies of dog poop." Larrick adjusted his deer-head tie before snagging his briefcase.

"I couldn't resist."

"Waiting for your partner before doing battle at the puzzle palace? You know the captain is gonna want to meet your girl who not only thought of but also found distinct evidence at a crime scene."

"Two crime scenes. I found more at the second vic's home." Ethan waved a small paper bag holding the plastic evidence bags. "Might as well share the wealth with my partner, right? 'Sides, he won't know *who* found it. We are detectives."

"That's your call. I'll back you on it."

Ethan inwardly sighed. For all their differences, Larrick always had his back. "I can see the captain now, pushing a stack of papers for me to fill out for my CI. Darn if he doesn't love his backup hard copies."

"Hey, at least we have a lead. Soon as we're finished with the zookeepers here, let's have a chat with our pet store owner." Ethan sighed. "I have to drop these samples off at the lab. I'll join you in the chief's office."

"So our psycho's dog is marking his territory? I've searched for a lot of things in my time. Dog feces hasn't been one of them." Larrick glanced at Ethan's specimen bags and grimaced before adding, "Might not be from our second killer's dog. What if the dog belonged to Dooley?"

"Gotta start somewhere. There was only one sample at each house, so the deposit wasn't made by an animal that frequented the area. Plus, we've found a white pile outside *both* victims' yards. What are the odds we have a match?" Ethan paused before opening the glass door while several uniforms nodded in passing.

"If those samples *do* match, it would be a step in the right direction, placing the same animal at both crime scenes. Either our lone shooter has a dog, or it came from Dooley's dog, and the killer is carrying out his dead partner's wishes."

"Let's hope the DNA matches. It would be nice to start connecting the dots." At the head of the steps, Larrick turned left, slapping his keycard against the reader then pushing through the double doors into the squad room.

Ethan pivoted in the opposite direction to head for the lab.

After a short discussion with a forensics tech about analyzing dog manure, Ethan dropped off the thumb drive containing the gruesome videos to Carl.

"Pity us poor bastards watching this today." He accepted the media with a grimace, complaining about sickos and psychos.

Contemplative strides carried Ethan to the conference room, his quiet knock answered immediately. "Good morning." He'd expected his partner, the captain, and the commissioner, but the conference table yielded more stern looks. Two other detectives each shuffled files back and forth after studying them.

"Sit." Commissioner Franklin was a man of few words and fewer moods, both equally succinct and dark. "I understand you have several leads. One that may tie these two murders together. Another concerning a pet store. Explain the latter."

Right to the point. "Yes, each victim bought dog food from a pet store on the edge of town. Larrick and I will check out the owner when this meeting is over. Ms. Jameson also happens to be the ex-wife of our dead perp."

"Yes, and didn't Detective Robertson already interview and clear the woman?" Captain Faulkner slid a file on the conference table to the commissioner.

"Yes, but now we have this second connection. I don't believe in coincidences," Ethan replied.

"Do you realize that nearly half the population owns dogs? Not to mention the fact that there aren't many pet stores in town. Since I've been told the second victim's computer and financials haven't been disclosed yet, how do you know where she bought her pet food?" Captain Faulkner raised a questioning brow to one of the silent detectives and received a nod in return.

Ah, the heart of the matter. Giving Lexi's identity away now might sabotage his case if she bolted. It would also leave him with a very large hole in the vicinity of his chest. Without her sharing information, not only would they lose their best shot at catching the killer, but also Lexi's persistence would see her in the predator's crosshairs.

"I have an informant, sir." Tightness around his mouth stilted his words.

"And did she educate you about colored dog crap?" Skepticism laced with condensation flavored the commissioner's tone.

Ethan headed off the next questions with an explanation. "She was a friend of the first victim. When she showed up, I walked with her around the backyard." A slight stretch of the truth with the benefit of not implicating his partner. "I went earlier to the second victim's home and checked the yard."

"And did you find anything?" The captain adopted his *stone face* as if infusing a final argument with irrefutable logic.

"Yes. More of the same," Ethan replied.

"Or, it might be from a wild animal," the commissioner added.

"So how'd you know where the victims shopped? Financials on the second murder haven't been released yet." Few people could divert the captain's focus.

Here was where Ethan needed to tread carefully. "My informant is well versed, actually better versed on the deep web than our department's tech specialists. Because of her digging, we now have more information. The killer set up a betting platform and is posting partial videos on another site called *Playtime*. The first site links the women's murders and offers a selection of the next victims along with new MOs."

"And..." Thunderclouds were brighter than the captain's expression.

"High school kid or college coed. The killer's looking to gain supplies. Battery acid and pulleys."

Steepled fingers carried the façade of the captain's relaxed contemplation. Nothing appeared lax about his upper body. "I think the pet store is a red herring. If you know what he needs to accomplish his next kill, concentrate on that. Now, I'd like to meet your informant."

Not freaking likely.

"First, the killer's acquiring his *tools* through contacts that we haven't been able to identify yet. We're working on it. Second, my informant insists on anonymity. If you pull this person out in the light, our information gathering on the dark web will cease to exist and the investigation will stall, if not fall flat.

"Furthermore, are you telling us not to investigate a substantial lead as far as the pet store is concerned?" Policy backed Ethan in denying bringing his source forward as long as no laws were broken. He was treading a very thin line.

"There's a serial killer on the loose, and you want to play house?" After heading the department for over twenty years, not much escaped his boss. "This hacker that you're playing footsie with, she can't trace this guy? Is she involved with him, too?"

"First of all, sir, I'm not involved with her." *Yeah, I am.* "Second, the dark net is a very complicated animal. Our techs can't begin to navigate it the way she can. She's our only shot at it. And—I haven't received an answer about the pet store." *Why are you directing us away from a perfectly solid lead?*

"What are the chances the killer can trace her?" Pursed lips and a deep frown betrayed the captain's devious mind.

"We're not using her as bait. She's found his site, deciphered his intentions, and is keeping us up to date."

"Perhaps we should put her on the payroll."

Devious. "Which means records, so, no."

"If we bid high enough to receive the souvenir, could we catch him that way?" Larrick's timely intervention in offering another tact had just earned him a free coffee and venison burger.

"No. I believe he has intermediaries and keeps his distance from his clients," Ethan replied. "But we are looking at Daryl Johanson, also from the hospital."

"All right. What about Dooley, the accomplice? Did we learn anything about him?" The captain's focus narrowed on

Ethan.

"Killed by the same drug used to dose the victims' dogs, just a higher concentration. And no, we got zip." Ethan shifted in his chair.

"Well, isn't that something. If he strikes again, or when he strikes again, it'll be strike three, and we'll have the feds all up in our business. Find this idiot. Now."

Chapter Thirteen

"So what do we know about this shop's owner?" Delicate beams of sunlight crested the building across the street to warm Ethan's face while light traffic bore early shift workers into the city.

"Aside from being a prominent, well-connected divorcee, not a lot. She's loaded. Started the pet shop as a hobby. My girlfriend says they're opening another one across town. Apparently, this lady supports the Mutt Strut each spring." Larrick tugged on the locked glass door while Ethan tossed their empty coffee cups in the trash.

"Patience, man. I'm glad she agreed to meet us here before opening."

"She said she has a business meeting this morning but agreed to see us first."

"Good. Speaking of Charlotte, when are you guys going to tie the knot?"

Larrick snorted. "Charlotte's a good woman, and I've been thinking about it. But wow, I don't know." Larrick's shudder spoke volumes. "I hope we can get a peek at the shop's records without a court order."

"We won't get one unless we can prove some type of communication or current connection." Ethan wondered when his friend would succumb to the sanctity of marriage. He'd never seriously considered it before but couldn't stop envisioning Lexi as a permanent part of his life.

"Mhmm, piece of cake. You could get it, I'm sure." Larrick muttered.

"Like any judge would sign off on a subpoena? I can see it now. Yes, Your Honor, her ex-husband from the East Coast was involved in a murder. No, she's had no contact with him in the last two years that we can document. The last two victims bought their dog food at her store, and we have reason to believe that the next victim will also. We just need to pry into every customer's life and figure out which sweet young thing is gonna be the next target."

"I'm sure you'd pull it off. Just use that McAllister charm. Women love you. Unless you've considered narrowing your selections to a certain emerald-eyed brunette. With your silver tongue..."

Years of investigating had honed his analytical and intuitive talents to the point he rarely traveled false paths for long, but Lexi proved a dangerous distraction.

Light beamed through the glass window and over interior shelving of dog toys and canine clothing, racks of bowls, leashes, and harnesses. Signs denoting cat supplies, aquatic materials, and an area partitioned off for grooming depicted a serene atmosphere through the front glass doors.

From his partner's description, Ethan expected a woman who obviously took care of herself. First appearances made a big impression during investigations, but he hadn't expected heels and an expensive suit on a young and well-toned body. She was about his age.

Larrick cleared his throat. "Showtime."

Keys jingled as she inserted one in the lock and flipped a release lever before pushing the door open. Despite the easygoing politician's smile pasted on her face, tension radiated in waves from her tightened jaw down through her shoulders.

Only a fool would've failed to recognize the shrewd intelligence emanating from her gaze. Perhaps the form-fitting skirt was meant as a further distraction since any man's scrutiny would travel from two-inch heels over the shapely calves and the teasing glimpse of thighs that surely belonged to a runner.

"Hi, I'm Detective McAllister. This is my partner, Detective Robertson."

"Gentlemen, come in. I don't have much time, and I won't be late for my meeting. We'll talk in my office."

Without further introduction, she turned and headed toward the back, the precision clicking of heels on painted cement coinciding with her rigid back and severe *updo* hairstyle.

After the forthcoming conversation, Ethan realized he'd probably never purchase supplies here since Larrick was sure to straddle the line of questionable behavior. The captain's subtle bent of leading them away from this path meant Larrick would trample all over it.

Crisp steps led them down various aisles before a wide hallway revealed several open doors. The first revealed a moderate-sized break room containing a small table and two chairs in a kitchenette.

The large office they entered continued the owner's bent toward upper crust living. A mahogany executive desk remained clear except for two folders. With his luck, they contained dossiers on two detectives for whom she intended to make life difficult.

How is she connected to the captain?

"Have a seat, detectives. What can I do for you?" High cheekbones reinforced the piercing effect of deep-set eyes capable of freezing hell on a whim while perfectly painted lips bearing a hint of liner emphasized her ability to decapitate with mere words.

"Thank you for meeting with us, ma'am. I know it's early." Ethan's smile usually received like in kind. *Not this time.*

"Let's cut to the chase. Like I said, I have an important meeting to attend. What do you want and why?"

"Ms. Jameson, as I said on the phone last evening, we're trying to track down a suspect who shared a connection with your ex-husband." Ethan wondered if her superpower included launching icy exhalations that could encase her opponent's frame in a frozen tomb.

"I've come to understand he was involved in the murder of a hospital administrator. I've had no knowledge of him and no contact with him for years, nor can I offer you any information. I've no idea what he has done or why."

"But someone has contacted you about his death?" Larrick asked.

"Of course. You two aren't the only police officers in the department... certainly not the highest ranking." The twist of her lips likened to someone having sucked on a lemon. "As I said, I have nothing to contribute to your case."

"Did your ex own a dog back when you were married?" Ethan kept his tone and expression neutral.

"Yes, we both doted on Bull. He won custody."

"Did he feed a raw diet?" Larrick asked, his practiced smile giving nothing away.

"Yes. The dog ate as well as we did. Are you happy? I don't know if he still has the dog. As I've said, I haven't had any contact."

"Who set up your computer network?" Larrick apparently decided to bat the virtual bee's nest.

"I did. I'm not incompetent."

"Great. Did you study computer science or programming?" Larrick's baiting her would only tick her off more.

"No." Spoken through gritted teeth. "I'm sure you already

know my background. I didn't go to college nor a trade school, but that doesn't make me stupid." Realigning her calendar seemed to give her fingers something to do.

"Oh, I thought it took a good bit of knowledge to set up your own LAN. That stands for Local Area Network." Judging by the small twitch at the corner of his mouth, Larrick was getting too much enjoyment from antagonizing the woman.

"I know that. Dooley taught me—" Her mouth firmed into a straight line as her gaze hardened. "I was married for five years. Yes, during that time, my husband, at that time, taught me a lot about computers, networks, and how to set them up. Satisfied?" Her hands briefly fisted on the calendar before she dropped them to her lap.

"Ma'am, first, we're not investigating you." *Though maybe we should.* "We have reason to believe that our suspect may have access to your business records." Ethan kept his tone calm, normal procedure in dealing with any agitated suspect.

"As I said, I haven't seen my ex, and if I had, I wouldn't let him into my home or place of business."

"Maybe he has shared a connection with one of your employees without your knowledge."

"That's absurd. There are two male employees here. Whistler is the mousiest man I've ever met, loves dogs. I can't imagine most murderers do." She took a deep breath before continuing, "Lucca is a college student studying marine biology. You think one of my employees is a serial killer?"

"What makes you think we're looking for a serial killer?" Larrick's challenge received a short huff of derision in return.

"I make it my business to stay informed, Detective, through my *personal* connections." After pointedly shuffling her files to the side of her desk, she continued, "If you'd like to speak to my employees, you're welcome to do so. Eric Whistler is one of two males on my staff unless you'd like to start an inquisition with my female clerks."

She wore condescension the same way other women applied makeup, layers that blended seamlessly with her façade.

Larrick tapped her desk for emphasis before standing. "We'd also like to take a look at your client list. We have reason to believe one may be a target." Without legal access, any information obtained otherwise would not stand up to a judge's scrutiny.

"No. That's ridiculous. The numbers alone would prevent you from filtering the list down to a manageable point."

Though a sideways approach usually resulted in the desired outcome, Ethan realized this shark would see it coming, was ready for it, and would block them with her right to privacy. Slow degrees of tactful invasion generally bore the best results.

Straightening her jacket added emphasis to her standing, the meeting's conclusion evident in her gesture toward the door.

By the time they'd made their way to the store's front, a gangly young man was setting up his register. A slight frown contradicted the smile he'd pasted on his face. "Good morning, Ms. Jameson." His suspicious gaze darted from the officers back to his employer.

"Whistler, these *gentlemen* are detectives and would like to ask you a few questions. They do not have a warrant to access our records, but you may answer any personal questions they ask. I will be here until they leave, which will be shortly." With her directive issued, the shark retreated to deeper waters, her sanctuary.

Surprise gave way to distrust before Whistler's shoulders hunched in, and he turned away from his interrogators. At over six feet with a wiry build, he appeared able to easily overpower a smaller woman. A partially open chamois shirt hid the breadth of his torso while underneath, his t-shirt read, *Bad cop, no donut.*

Ethan hadn't missed the clenched jaw before the clerk turned back to arrange a dog tag rack next to the register.

"What do you want?"

"Nothing major. We need to find out a little about your clientele, Whistler," Ethan replied. If guilt carried pounds, the man should've crumbled under its weight.

If I can't put him at ease, it'll be difficult to pick up his nonverbal tells.

After three years of working with Larrick, Ethan always took point at this juncture.

"I don't get friendly with them. Sorry." An indifferent shrug accompanied enough belligerence to rival a dozen toddlers.

Though his gut put him on alert, Ethan relaxed his shoulders and leaned against the counter. Without knowing the specific reasoning for the clerk's tension, it was difficult to navigate the conversation. After a bit of small talk, Whistler faced them and loosened up.

"One of your customers is going to die if we don't intervene." Larrick circled the long counter to approach his objective whose gaze snapped up in frank awareness.

"Then do your job and let me do mine." The clerk's gaze searched the store as if looking for help, a reaction to an innate understanding of Larrick's dominant approach.

"Well, see, the thing is, we need information. We believe

someone might be finding his victims from your customer list. Maybe he's a real dog fanatic. Do you have a dog, Whistler?" Larrick toyed with one of the displays.

"Yeah, I have a dog. Everybody has dogs these days."

"Me, too. I was thinking of changing his diet. What do you recommend in the way of food?" Ethan drew a bewildered frown from his subject.

"It's all pretty much the same except for the label and price. Pick one." Whistler's gaze swung back and forth between Larrick and Ethan.

Clearing his throat, Ethan again became the focus of attention. "I've heard some say that raw feeding is the healthiest. What do you think?" Expecting more of a reaction led to disappointment.

Again, the employee shrugged a shoulder. "I hear it's a lot of work, but then there's all flavors of crazies out there. Take your choice."

"I noticed you have a fenced backyard here. Why is that?" Larrick gestured to the rear of the building.

"Because we're allowed to bring our dogs to work as long as they get along with people and other animals."

"Did you bring yours?" Ethan asked.

"No, he's not friendly."

"Since there aren't any customers yet, why don't you show us around? I'd like to get a feel for the place." Long shots rarely paid off in Ethan's estimation, but this was a stone worth turning over. Even if this clerk wasn't guilty of murder, he'd been intimidated by something other than Larrick's size.

"Yeah, as soon as this numb nuts moves, I'll let you out back."

"Where do you take deliveries?" Ethan looked around the

upscale doggy boutique. Along the sidewall near the back, a personnel door read, *Employees Only.*

"Storeroom's in the back right corner. Entrance to the yard is from the other side." Circumventing Larrick, Whistler darted around the counter and shuffled toward the back. "I'll wedge the door so it doesn't lock you out." His expression declared that a satisfying possibility.

Sunshine failed to penetrate the shadows of a large oak tree after they stepped through the doorway. Considering their discussions on dog training, he wondered what type of gear and obstacles Lexi utilized.

Not surprising, several pieces of agility equipment, including a teeter-totter, elevated dog walk, and tire jumps, provided an alternative to canine boredom. Larrick followed him out, inspecting the neatly trimmed yard contained by a six-foot wooden fence.

"Not a trace of white." Though he didn't expect to find any fecal matter considering the store's clean interior and the owner's fastidious attention to detail, Ethan wanted to end this case and move on. Making a connection through a dog's DNA wasn't going to be easy.

When they caught the butcher, would Lexi cease to visit? The past several weeks had changed his perspective on life and the benefits of a long-term relationship, making each minute in her presence a challenge to remain platonic.

"There's a trash can for waste. I'll check the perimeter." Metal hinges protested Larrick's exit adjacent to the building, leaving Ethan to verify the garbage container was empty. A roll of colored poop bags hung on a post beside the can.

A small ravine separated the backyard from the woods while loose gravel lined either side. The right border held enough space for large rigs to maneuver during delivery. A short distance to his left, a donut shop offered the welcoming aroma of fresh-brewed coffee.

Without the slightest breeze to dry it, morning dew sparkled on each manicured blade of grass despite the warming rays of the sun. He studied Larrick striding back through the gate. Tight posture and a small head shake confirmed what they'd both expected.

Nothing found.

"Figures. I wonder what type of dog Whistler owns." A wooden wedge holding the door ajar clattered to the concrete as Ethan tugged on the back door, a small swish of stale air caressing his face. Before swinging the door wide, he turned to his partner. "Whistler's hiding something. Let's do some digging before having another go at him."

Larrick would have picked up Whistler's multiple channels of nonverbal indicators even during their short discussion, their combination a warning sign of deception.

A longing glance toward the coffee shop confirmed Larrick's need before answering. "Yeah, but right now, I could use some caffeine."

"Fine, we'll chum the waters a little bit first. Maybe we'll get lucky."

"Careful, better let me do that. Captain seemed awfully protective of this shop or owner, and he already hates me." Larrick smirked as if proud of the status.

"Those two files on her desk had significance to her."

"Looked like she enjoys flaunting her connection." Larrick waggled his eyebrows, the desire to snoop written on his face.

"Maybe the captain and the shop owner love to tango. I see trouble on your horizon if you pursue it."

"It could just be a meeting of *physical needs*. He's married." Larrick's reminder of Daryl's callous admission of adultery revealed his partner's monogamous personal standard.

"Too many maybes..."

Ms. Jameson remained as stiffly polite during conversation as when they'd previously spoken. Further discussion enlightened them about two particular employees, unattached females before moving on to the other male.

"Lucca is an air-headed college kid. I highly doubt he'd be any value in your investigation." Perfectly painted fingernails drummed a staccato beat on her desk before her countenance turned sly. "Based on what you've told me, you certainly don't have enough information to obtain a warrant for viewing my records. I also assume you've been *asked* to not harass me?" A delicately arched brow completed her look of disdain. "Which means we have nothing further to discuss."

"So you have a friend in the department. Congratulations. Unfortunately, it won't prevent or even sidetrack us from doing our job."

Ethan silently groaned at his partner's lack of tact. Previous discussions of honey and traps had fallen on deaf ears.

Chapter Fourteen

"You know words like subtlety and diplomacy are in the dictionary for a reason, right? And I do recall you mentioning the fact that you went to school." Ethan placed his order at the cafe's counter, silently comparing the fresh-faced coed's fluid movements and easy demeanor to the cold meticulousness of the pet store owner.

"School in the bayou is different, more practical."

Ethan's groan went ignored.

"The best schooling I've gotten has been from the streets. She wasn't going to give us a thing, not that she probably knows much. It's just a power issue." Larrick never hesitated to share his point of view, especially when he knew he was right. He accepted his coffee and apple fritter then turned toward the floor-to-ceiling windows, contemplation furrowing his brow.

"Ah, but the things we learn by watching are sometimes more important." Needling his partner came with a price, eventually, but Ethan couldn't resist the temptation. "So what did grasshopper learn?"

Larrick smiled and took another bite of his fritter.

"While you were baiting her—"

"That was intentional, and you know it."

"Really?" Ethan asked. "You can control it? That's new. As I was saying, while you drove her to distraction, I studied her desk calendar. She has a meeting with CF this evening." Blatant interest from the young clerk received Ethan's bland smile.

"Upside down? Kudos, Sherlock. That doesn't necessarily mean Charles Faulkner, our captain. Maybe she's involved with a man named Cedar Fink." Larrick's tone betrayed his interest. "What time? And do note that the captain is married."

"At seven. And it didn't stop the hospital administrator, who has a weak alibi. Doesn't anyone stay monogamous these days?" Another reason Ethan avoided long-term relationships. He wanted to be absolutely certain of his partner and have the kind of connection his parents enjoyed.

A sip of his coffee brought a semblance of sanity before he turned to follow Larrick out the door where distinct golden beams pierced patchy clouds to warm his face. "So you want to pick me up about six?"

"No, I'll cover shark lady. You have a computer nerd to protect." Larrick bit into his apple fritter then sighed in ecstasy. "Besides, the captain hates me anyway. If he catches me sniffing after his fluff on the side, it'll just infuriate him that much more."

"A condition you aspire to inflame. Fine, let's go visit the other employees, see if we can turn up vats of acid or pulley systems. One's in school so that visit will wait till afternoon."

The morning had proven fruitless in their hopes of collecting usable information. After interviewing all but the high school student, they'd not made any progress. No nervous tics, reflexive breathing pattern changes, rigid stances, or other signs of deception accompanied their tense replies.

Anxiety came naturally to interviewees since everybody had done something that remained uncovered and made them uneasy. As far as involvement in the murders, none appeared to hold any knowledge of the victims, the serial killer, or even the dark net.

Back in the station, each detective followed his own hunch in searching through records. "Hey, lookie here. Our little Whistler has a colorful rap sheet. Two sexual assaults, an attempted robbery, and breaking and entering." Larrick shoved backward, his chair's wheels clicking on the tile floor. "Here, take a peek."

"Then how'd he end up working for someone who's connected?" Ethan studied the sheets handed him, not able to form a plausible scenario.

"Maybe shark lady's connection is new..."

"Possibly. Either way, let's have another run at him. He's off parole, so we don't have as much leverage."

Snagging the jacket from the chair's back, Ethan pushed to his feet. "I'll drive. It's the only way I can arrive with my senses intact."

"No. I'll drive. We can stop by my house. Charlotte fixed lasagna last night. Leftovers."

"Hmm, heartburn and car sickness from a ride from hell, or more fast food."

"Stop whining, her cooking is epic."

"Yeah, I'll make sure the next ER doc treating me for food poisoning remembers that point."

"Hey, that wasn't her fault. The company recalled truckloads of that ice cream." Hollow echoes of their footsteps followed them down the steps and into the parking garage.

Despite the warming temperatures outside, the underground space boasted cool shadows stretching from each corner and rimming every vehicle. "Good thing you park in the back. Our colleagues are too lazy to walk the distance to mess with our car."

Several sedans parked toward the front had acquired oily

stains from the rusty water drips common during and immediately following storms. "Either that or they're leery of going near your truck parked beside it...Afraid some type of snake or other natural defense system would swallow them whole."

The sedan chirped with the push of Larrick's key fob. "Funny, partner. Very funny. I figured with your lack of a love life, you needed the exercise." He smirked over the roof before climbing into the vehicle. "Though maybe with your *new flavor of the day,* we can start parking on the open lot more often."

The throaty rumble of the car's engine obscured his next words.

Ethan flipped him off. It wasn't that he didn't enjoy sex. On the contrary. He merely preferred to not become a hound dog, which would've been a reality had he accepted half the blind dates his family tried to set up.

The weight of his body against the seat's back increased as they accelerated out of the garage. Station Avenue held little traffic at the early hour, a fact that would reverse with the nearby hospital's shift change.

"So, what time is Lexi visiting tonight? You don't talk about her much." Larrick's probing had a purpose. It always did.

"Probably around five or so. Why?" Studying his partner's profile, Ethan couldn't discern ulterior motives but didn't like her being the topic of discussion.

"Just wondering. Wanted to keep up with the hubbub of the dark internet."

"You think this Whistler character might be supplying information?" Ethan's assessment of the employee didn't match his idea of an intelligent serial killer, which didn't preclude someone using him as a pawn.

"Don't know, but it sure would be nice to have another clue to unravel."

Most civilians Ethan knew held the belief that police work largely entailed shootouts or eating donuts. Much of the time, the gray area between kept them busy. During his conversations with Lexi, it appeared she had a grasp of his work life, probably due to her time on the streets and penchant for digital snooping.

When Larrick pulled into the store's parking lot once again, they were armed with Whistler's rap sheet for leverage. Large posters partially blocked sight of the employees' counter. Reaction from a surprise entrance might tell them a lot.

The small bell over the door announced their arrival, snapping a young woman's attention up to assess them. Narrowed eyes and pursed lips marked her deliberation.

"What can I do for you officers today?" Honey dripped from a hard-edged tone as she hung more dog treats on their ordered hooks. Lack of recognition supplied understanding that Whistler had detailed their earlier presence, with prejudice.

"Looking for Whistler. Is he in the back?" Larrick edged closer to her kneeling form, his common intimidation tactic wiping the disdainful expression from her face.

"No. He works this weekend, so his hours are shortened during the week." Wariness transformed into sullenness after she scooted back and stood, a bout of sneezing interrupting her obvious disapproval.

Larrick offered his handkerchief. "Catching a spring cold?"

She refused the offer. "No. Severe allergies. I won't let them keep me from what I want to do."

"Zoe, I appreciate the protectiveness of your friend, but we have a few more questions for him. Where'd he go?" With lack of patience came diminished tact. Larrick stalked forward slowly.

Her collision with the block wall halted a retreat and a low grumble, signaling her surrender. "I don't know, but he's a great guy and hasn't done anything wrong. You shouldn't harass him."

Though ignorance sometimes heralded bliss, it could also be the precursor of not just regret but a deadly encounter.

"Hey, it's not like we're arresting him, this time, or even charging him with rape, armed assault, or breaking and entering...*now*." Each offense that Ethan listed widened her gaze.

"H-he's done all that?" Fear provided a sudden wake-up call, followed by another sneeze.

Though Larrick had backed off, Zoe stepped forward, tentatively reaching out a hand but stopped short of contact. Each second marked a new shade of pale in her complexion as her mouth fell open.

"H-he said the cops hated him because his brother blew the whistle on some kind of underhanded sting. That's why he adopted the moniker."

"Criminal records are public information. Go to the courthouse and do your own research." With enlightenment came disgust at the way predators lured in their prey, one lie at a time. "Do you know where he went, Zoe?" Ethan regretted her new layer of wariness.

"H-he said he needed to straighten his house and get some air."

"Well, all right, then." Ethan removed a business card and reached around Larrick to place it in her shaking fingers. "If you have any problems with him, give me a call."

"O-okay. I will." The one-eighty in her demeanor was sad to witness, her shattered naiveté replaced with a new deliberation and respect.

"How old are you?" Larrick asked, their partnership having induced a parallel type of thinking.

"Um, seventeen. I'm a junior at Callouston High."

"Which doesn't give you immunity from dirtballs. Live smart, stay safe, and never underestimate a predator." Larrick's final warning was as much as he'd say.

"Uh, I'm not going out with him again. No, sir." Moisture brimming her eyes and a trembling bottom lip betrayed the line of her thoughts.

Ethan wondered what misguided encounters sprinkled the teenager's history, though it appeared she'd avoided the baser side of evil so far. Now wasn't the time to push. They had a person of interest to question and a murderer to catch.

Outside, the air was thick with pollen and the sounds of early spring. The soft breeze whispered of honeysuckle and quiet evenings on a porch, listening to nature's music.

Larrick gave him a thumbs up. "At first I thought you were kind of hard on the kid, numb nuts. But you may have just saved her future and a world of hurt."

Loose gravel crunched under Ethan's steps, barely heard between the screams of a red-tailed hawk soaring high above. He hesitated briefly with the warm door handle under his hand as he looked over the sedan at his partner. "Maybe we'll get lucky, and Whistler will lead us to the psycho killer."

Our cases are never that easy.

"Stranger things have happened. Somebody has to be

doling out information, somehow, whether it's intentional or not." Larrick slammed his door and keyed the ignition.

"I don't think it's Daryl, the administrator."

"Me neither," Larrick murmured.

"What's with the pouch hanging from the rearview?" The residual twinge of discomfort from Ethan's wound shot through his thigh, necessitating a repositioning. Perhaps it provided a warning the same way an amputee's phantom pain acknowledged a missing limb.

"Hey, it's Charlotte's way of bonding, letting me know she's with me. It's a special air freshener with bamboo charcoal that purifies the air."

"Yeah, I'm feeling the love. Looks like an altered nickel bag. Great accessory for a cop's car."

Increased traffic meant navigating among school buses, shoppers, and the homeward bound. The quiet drive allowed different scenarios regarding their approach to Whistler twine through Ethan's mental wiring, producing various consequences, most of them ending in bloodshed. He didn't want to become a cynic any more than a corpse.

"So how'd your session with the shrink go? She ask how you allowed a shooter to get the drop on you?" Larrick had tried to broach the subject several times, always shut down. "I know how you chafe at mandatory meetings and stuff."

"I'm fine. Cleared for duty, obviously. You worry too much." The sweat popping out on his brow had everything to do with the sun's strong rays magnified by the windshield and not the memory of a bullet burning through his thigh. Every member of his family had nitpicked his refusal to take more time off.

His oldest brother, Matt, had been the first to take him to the firing range for practice the morning of his return to duty, scrutinizing his every move. By the time his younger brother called, the possibility of selecting different and livelier targets had become an option.

"Okay. Just checking. My turn to go in first and even friendly fire wouldn't feel so good." Turning off the state highway jostled them both.

County road workers had recently and inefficiently patched several holes, the jarring results felt in Ethan's thigh.

Pieces of the darker tar and chip sparkled like wet jewels or blackened blood in Ethan's mind. "I doubt he's even home. Probably skipped, figuring we'd run his record and come back."

House and lot sizes dwindled the farther they drove as if mocking Ethan's need for open spaces. A worn sofa and rickety table with a *For Sale* sign associated its homeowner with a quiet desperation common to the neighborhood. The even rhythm of his pulse sped up to rival the hum of the tires on asphalt but was unable to catch and contain his wayward thoughts.

"Okay, rubbing one hand on your slacks might ease the ache in your thigh, but both, that's drying them off. This can wait."

His partner easing off the accelerator produced an immediate deceleration inversely proportionate to his heart rate. "No, Larrick. I have to do this. Now."

"Partner, you can't remain conscious without blood flow to your big head. Right now I think that's a problem. Tell me you're not lightheaded."

"I'm not lightheaded."

"Once more with meaning?"

"Damn it. I have to do this." Breath came faster if still

quiet.

"Hmm. His house is at the end of this next street up ahead." Larrick edged the car onto another narrow street lined with tiny houses, some with tall grass and unkempt hedges. "I'm going to pull over for a minute so we can catch our breath."

The quiet rush of blood became a booming cadence in Ethan's ears with each of his heart's contractions. "Yeah, okay. Thanks." Ethan appreciated the support and knew his partner would back him up with whatever help was needed.

Quiet gasps pulled air into his lungs while he took the handkerchief from his pocket and wiped his brow. He'd seen the effects of PTSD but had never thought he'd be ground under its heel. Him, the brother acclaimed for steadfastness.

"What are partners for? So you haven't told me...Have you gotten Lexi's ankles behind her ears yet?" Even Larrick wouldn't have been so crass unless he wanted to provide a diversion.

"None of your business." It was all he could manage under his partner's intense perusal. Gray edging the periphery of his vision appeared as an encroaching fog ready to devour his mind.

"That good, huh? You know, if I wasn't otherwise attached—"

"Don't go there. Mine." Uttering the words shocked him, for they wouldn't have surfaced if he hadn't subconsciously considered it.

"Well don't be too slow on the draw, so to speak. She seems kinda special." Larrick smiled in the face of his glare. "And I heard Caden is angling for a date with her. The other day, Matt said he'd choke the kid if he made a move on your girl."

The growl erupting from Ethan's throat was primal, guttural, and instinctual.

"Now if you'll just yawn, I'll pull out the stick lodged in your colon."

Minutes passed as his partner kept up a steady stream of crass verbal deflections while outside the world turned as it always did, oblivious to his plight. When his breath came easier and his vision cleared, he met Larrick's concerned gaze.

"I'm all right now. Let's go."

"Show me your hands."

He hadn't realized he'd fisted them on his lap. Holding them out and straightening his fingers, they barely shook. Adrenaline crash and washout prolonged the vestiges of his ordeal. "Need some sugar."

"Sorry, I'm not that type. You'll have to talk to Lexi about that." The snap of his glove box preceded Larrick retrieving an energy bar. "Here, it's the best I can do at the moment."

"I hope this isn't made from venison, possum, or the roadkill flavor of the week." Even ripping the wrapper seemed a monumental task. The mechanical function of chewing drained his energy.

Larrick continued smartass comments through the recovery phase.

When the bar was gone, Ethan inhaled his first deep breath. "That hit the spot. Thanks." To prove his point, he held out his hands, steady and strong.

Though his expression held the doubt he wouldn't voice, Larrick shifted gears, mentally and physically, then eased down on the gas. The steady acceleration gave the vehicle's jarring an odd rhythm from bouncing over ruts.

I can handle this, whatever comes my way.

Pulling onto the grass shoulder before reaching the suspect's house gave them a chance to observe the surroundings before approaching. Ethan took a final moment to steady his emotions.

"We can hold off if you want," Larrick murmured.

"No." Simple, clean, adamant. Ethan was ready—no, *needed* to take this litmus test to see if he could confront whatever demons decided to take a swipe at him, real or imagined. PTSD held as many manifestations as the mind could conjure. "I don't think this dirtball has any information. Still, I'd like to kick his butt along with every other sexual predator I find."

Larrick's assessing gaze was expected. The following sentiment, not so much. "Suits me. He shouldn't be chasing jailbait at the pet store anyway."

Unlike the previous situation, they weren't walking into the current milieu blind. They'd seen and taken Whistler's measure earlier, which gave Ethan a slight mental advantage.

The dented pickup in the driveway boasted rusted fenders and a sagging bumper. One side panel provided a study in contrasts, its gray base coat a contradiction to the lime-green door.

"Good. Looks like our boy's here after all. Let's go get 'em." Ethan shoved his door open, needing the fresh air as much as confronting his inner demons.

Flattened grass gone to seed left a trail of footprints to the front door, its paint peeling from neglect. On the frame, a bare wire hung from what appeared to have once been attached to a doorbell.

Each man stood to the side of the door as Larrick reached over to hammer the meaty side of his fist against the wooden barrier, his other hand behind his back and surely resting on his gun handle.

Along the street, all appeared quiet, no children playing in the cul-de-sac, no one sitting on a front stoop. Yet Ethan couldn't shake the feeling of someone watching him, cataloging their movements for future dissection.

Just as Larrick prepared for the second round of banging, the door creaked open, stopped abruptly by a security chain. His partner had taken the bleeding side, the one most vulnerable to a shooter if the occupant were so inclined.

"Whistler, we have a few more questions. May we come inside?" Larrick's tightened frame didn't flinch, his gaze steady on the other man.

"Not without a warrant. But I'll come out." The door shut briefly before the slide of the chain and slight clink preceded the rush of stale air out.

"Fine, if you don't care what the neighbors hear, why should we?" Larrick maintained his position on the moss-covered cement steps, allowing Whistler to brush past.

"You have a dog in there?" Ethan asked.

"He's in the backyard. And he bites." If sullenness were a blanket, the many layers wrapping Whistler would've denied penetration by words or light.

"I ain't done nothing wrong, and you know by now I'm off probation. What do you want?"

"Just wondering what you've been up to lately. You hear about the two recent, brutal murders?" Ethan's voice drew the younger man's attention.

"Yeah, so what? I ain't had nothing to do with them. I was at the bowling alley Friday night when the first one bought it. I stayed until midnight. My buddies can vouch for me. The second one, I was home." The clerk's rubbing his decidedly paunch belly refuted the idea of regular exercise.

"Aw, Whistler, I'm surprised you keep up with current events." Ethan mentally noted the younger man's lack of diplomacy and tact when on his home turf. "Anyway, we don't think you killed those women unless you're stepping up your game or acquired a buddy. However, they were both murdered in the middle of the night. You live alone, yes? No one to vouch for you at the time each one died?"

"My woman left me. It's just me and the dog. But I ain't never killed no one."

"We're just looking for the person supplying information." Larrick had picked up the conversation, giving Ethan a chance to observe the nonverbal. "After all, both women bought dog food from your store, and you're the only full-time employee. You probably know them, maybe even talked to them on occasion. Though the snobs probably wouldn't give you the time of day, would they?"

Whistler's lip curled, his upper body stiffening progressively as Larrick spoke.

"I see them come in, the stuck-up bitties. Do you know how hard it is to make nice when they think they're better than everybody else?"

"Ever have anyone ask about them? Where they live or what they do? Maybe someone just admired a cute little dog in a woman's purse and wanted to know the name of a good breeder," Larrick added, his upper body remaining tense, ready. "Let's not forget your penchant for dealing with women, even if you normally do like the younger ones." Larrick nodded to Ethan, who pulled out the rap sheet.

"I can see my partner's point. Looks to me like your boss is a classic case of what you proclaim to hate." Ethan's commiseration appeared to loosen the suspect's shoulders.

"She is, but at least it's a job, and I get a discount on dog food. Makes it a little easier to deal with them, like inside, I can laugh right back. But ain't nobody asked me for nothing. Not that I'd give them anything, anyway." Whistler held Ethan's gaze, steady and unwavering, with a minor twitch at the corner of his right eye.

Larrick cut off Whistler's retreat to the house, letting him know they weren't finished. "Do you have a computer?"

"What? Like I can afford one? No, I don't."

"Ever play around with the dark net?" Ethan asked.

"What is that? Turning out the lights and putting on women's nylons?" Whistler sneered before taking a step back.

"Mind if we walk around your place?" Larrick stepped aside to let Whistler pass.

"Why? You lookin' to buy some upscale property?"

"Curious about the neighborhood." Ethan watched as Whistler mentally weighed his response, confusion and mistrust filling his expression. They didn't need Whistler's permission to walk the surrounding area but used his answer to assess the predator's position.

"Long as you don't come inside." A slight head shake and shrug of his shoulder indicated his assessment of the detectives' mental health.

Larrick gestured toward the neighboring houses. "We'll be checking up on you."

"That's harassment." A jagged scar ran the width of Whistler's chin, barely visible under the light scruff.

"No, that's investigating. Right now, you're our best lead. See you around." Larrick rubbed his chin and nodded to their suspect. "Did you get that in prison or as a permanent souvenir from one of your victims?"

In response, Whistler glared, backing up the steps and sidling into his house. A slamming door and the metal glide of his chain finalized his retreat.

"All right, poop patrol?" A wry grin twisted Larrick's lips.

"Yeah, but if it were gonna match our DNA sample, he would've balked."

"Unless he thought his dog was better trained than to dump in someone else's yard."

The home's tiny footprint equaled most others in the rundown neighborhood where scraggly rosebushes and undefined leggy flowers struggled against weedy invaders to provide an intermittent spot of color.

Weathered wood provided a termite smorgasbord in the neighbor's yard separating the adjacent share of unkempt ground while missing boards defied the term privacy.

Gaps in the barrier remained small enough to keep the large lab's head within its boundary. Raucous barking was answered in kind with increased volume by Whistler's dog toward the rear of the property.

In his mind, Ethan pictured a large Rottweiler ready to hurdle the barrier and tear into the first warm body. Shock filled his mind with a glimpse at the backyard. A rusted, wrought iron fence stood three feet tall and enclosed a well-manicured lawn. A teeter-totter and agility tunnel kept company with other training apparatuses in what looked like a good-sized run. As predicted, the Rottweiler snarled and bounced on front feet, alternating with jumping on the fence.

"Who'd a thought this guy would own, much less care about using a weed-eater but only in the backyard?" Ethan shook his head, bewilderment and frustration warring for supremacy.

"Hmm, someone who might care enough to feed their dog raw." Larrick's inching steps toward the fence hesitated when the dog's vocalization increased exponentially.

"Don't make eye contact. He doesn't like it."

"Who are you, Dr. Jung for dogs?" Larrick took a step back.

Three inches between iron pickets allowed the dog's snout to break the fence's vertical plane as the animal's retracted lips displayed sharp canines.

Ethan approached while keeping his face averted and holding his hands down straight just outside the dog's reach. "How about I make nice with Fido while you check the outside perimeter?"

Tall grass beyond the fence covered the short distance to a wooded expanse. "Yeah, he's gotta dump the crap somewhere. But please, don't get bitten. Your brothers will chop up my body and feed it to the sharks."

The back of the house incorporated three decent-sized windows and a sliding glass door. Fabric pulled shut on each window eliminated the possibility of seeing anything inside while vertical blinds swung as if recently closed.

The Rottweiler's snarling ceased with his partner's retreat. Ethan remained, time well spent in visually searching the yard for white fecal remains. Moments later, the dog's aggression transformed to curiosity with intermittent sniffing.

"Good boy. Smell all you want...No taste-testing."

Its black fur gleamed in the sunshine, changing the dynamic of his coloring with the rippling of its muscles. Relaxation of ears and mouth along with a lowering tail signaled the beginning of acceptance. Though he didn't break out in a play bow invitation, he was approachable.

Moving his hand a bit closer, Ethan waited.

Within several minutes, a wet canine tongue roughened the back of his hand. "Nice. Very nice. You sure are a pretty boy. Lexi would go nuts over you. I think you have it good here, though. Sure wish you could talk. I'd love to hear about your adventures."

Despite Larrick's return, the dog's demeanor remained one of friendly acceptance. "Good thing we carry evidence bags. Looks like it was over his property line, which makes it fair game." Larrick held up a baggie, displaying the now-familiar white barrel-shaped specimens.

"I figured as much," Ethan replied, his heart rate picking up a bit with the hopes of having a DNA match. Instinct and a love of dogs allowed him to reach over the top rail and pet the dog, who accepted his touch with a small whine. "If it is a match, considering Whistler's record, we'll be able to get a court order to see if it matches this dog."

Several strokes later and he knew they were past aggression, for the moment. The dog's tail wagged side to side so hard his entire back end moved. A fact that could change with the owner's command.

"How'd you know he wouldn't bite your hand off?" Larrick asked.

"Simple. Dogs laugh with their tails. Look at him."

"So, he's laughing his tail off."

Chapter Fifteen

It was supposed to rain tonight, a mixed blessing. Nefarious activities were both hampered and aided by nature's life-giving natural shield. It came down to a matter of perspective.

Breaking and entering during the dead of night seldom made Lexi's to-do list, but tonight's priority included a multipronged approach. Find evidence, either some type of key logger or malware among the store's digital files, then bridge a backdoor connection between the LAN and the internet.

Disabling the pet store's alarm had been child's play. Years of street life had equipped her with the tools to gain entrance through the side service door, exchanging deep shadows for the pitch blackness of the stock room.

Something's not right.

A dark and silent foreboding traced each nerve in her body, laminating each dendrite with a veneer of quiet dread. The prostitutes had taught her to listen to her instincts, but she wouldn't let fear thwart her from reaching tonight's goal. Logic dictated this next step in her bid to collect necessary information despite intuition's warning.

A small flashlight shaded with a blue lens emitted enough light to navigate around pallets of dog food, boxes of aquariums, and bird supplies that contributed to the musty air constricting her chest muscles and necessitating shallow breathing. Otherwise, the store room was neat and orderly.

Pulling her turtleneck over her nose granted a more normal breath. It wasn't the first time she'd broken into a building. *Murdering pimp caught me the last time.* She currently invaded a pet store, not someone's private residence.

The slight dampness on her forehead was nothing compared to the cold sweat encompassing her body. Clammy fingers dropped her mini flashlight and left her rooted to the cement floor like a giant oak, inflexible and vulnerable to anything in its environment.

Despite her inability to see effectively, she constantly looked around in search of an unknown evil, sensed but not seen. Pallets stacked against the wall made it impossible to protect her back with the surety of concrete.

After fumbling and retrieving her light, she darted its swath to a small scurrying noise ahead. Small, beady red eyes held all the malevolence of Hades in spite of the mouse's diminutive size. As much as the vermin's presence made her shiver, they were probably a problem for every pet store since any food would draw them, their entrance granted through the smallest of holes.

She hadn't realized her lungs were paralyzed until the creature disappeared around a pallet of dog food. A gulping breath preceded her quiet whimper.

God, I hate those freaking things. Realizing one's fear as irrational didn't conquer it.

Each furry scrabbling on the concrete elicited a cringe while images of them swarming a bound and helpless victim swept through her mind.

No more horror movies. When she finally located the door to the store proper, its hinges announced her presence with an ominous groan that echoed within the concrete-and-glass walls. She left it open in case a quick escape became necessary.

Previous daytime visits and some light hacking had furnished knowledge of the security cameras located at the service and back doors along with one focused on the front parking lot, all currently suffering a malfunction. She'd never been inside the manager's office but figured the security feeds led there.

Considering the situation, starting her search at the main counter was less risky and more likely to yield the results she sought. Fragments of moon light slashed between the window posters to illuminate sections of the main counter near the store's front. More than a dozen aisles ran front to back, loaded with all types of animal paraphernalia.

Sour dread squeezed her chest and qualified the lump in her throat as impassible, not a problem since little saliva inhabited her mouth. Every sound, however small, brought life to the monsters in her vivid imagination, seen as shades of black and gray in her shadow world.

Each sheath of cells and connective tissue surrounding the individual hairs on her arm contracted to pull their captive shaft erect, goose bumps another indication she wasn't cut out for spy work.

Bearing in mind the time spent with Ethan and her growing infatuation, she should've resembled an evolved Moloch. Instead of soaking up moisture through a thorny hide like the monstrous devil, her skin absorbed atmospheric tension.

The light jacket she'd worn tonight failed to stop the shiver bridging her shoulder blades. As if on cue, the sensation of a pimpled flesh wave swept up her neck.

She knew better than to ignore her gut feelings, but desperation to find a connection to Frannie's killer drove her forward. Pulling her cap lower on her head snagged her braid but increased her false sense of security.

Rounding the edge of the counter, she stepped up on the raised dais and approached the register, careful to avoid the paler patches of light infiltrating through the front windows. Several racks displayed designer tags and collars among small containers of paw-shaped doggy treats.

Shaking fingers slipped twice on the keyboard after the computer's screen glowed a soft blue then filled with an underwater screen saver, reminding her of a burial at sea. A quick connection to the internet would allow her to surf the computer's files from home.

Desperation forced her hand to sweep the store with her mini flashlight once again, but its low voltage fell short of the first aisle. Her back stiffened, along with other major muscles, in preparation for fight or flight. She preferred flight.

Her conversation earlier in the evening with Ethan about the store had led her to believe they might find a solid connection, one she'd decided to pursue since he lacked enough evidence to obtain a warrant.

If Whistler were involved, she wouldn't find any malware on the computers. He'd access the information directly, but she could connect the victims' information with the dates their file had been accessed.

And install my own digital spying program.

She felt watched.

Hunted.

She felt like prey, the moth caught in the spider's web, suddenly unable to move.

A whisper of something sliding drew her attention, cloth against cloth, near the east rear wall.

She couldn't envision anyone dressing the mice in colorful silks. Her attempts at softening the horrific images in her mind failed. A slight shift in the atmosphere, perhaps just her imagination, declared a presence near.

Lack of noise didn't equal safety. At the moment, even beady red eyes were preferable to what her dark thoughts conjured.

If a stalker cut off her escape route from the right, she'd hop the counter and slip through the rear door leading to the dog yard. If he approached from the middle, she was dead meat.

Someone cleared their throat.

Screw me!

A low hum broken by a chuckle snapped her attention to the right. *He must've followed me in here.*

Soft steps whispered closer while the quiet tune ratcheted her heart rate to new heights. No form took shape from the shadows, the murky blackness obscuring the hunter.

She hadn't finished her electronic search after installing her program, the least of her worries. Instinct told her if she didn't stay focused, she'd lose her head. In backing up, ambient light spilling through the front windows backlit her presence.

"Hmm, looks like one of my quarries has come to me. Such a pretty girl. What a lucky break." An intense curiosity infused the harsh whisper as if planning to study her under a microscope.

"Pictures from a distance don't do you justice, Lexi." The low tone defied definition of a regional origin.

"Who are you? Whistler?" Each object she grasped in fumbling for a weapon proved unsuitable. Without diverting her gaze, she finally latched on to her mini flash. Her fingerprints garnished everything she'd touched, not a concern of any cadaver.

A deep chuckle was her only answer.

Crap. If only she'd told Ethan where she was going. He would never know if Whistler was involved and wouldn't have access to the computers. *I might take my lack of information to the grave.*

A tall, black-clad form took shape across the counter. The ski mask covering his face contrasted the whites of his eyes, highlighted by shafts of ambient light.

The demonic contrast intensified her panic. She'd felt terror before. This was different.

Without changing his focus, he sidestepped around the counter toward the opening. Despite the height difference created by the dais, he was tall. Unable to discern specific details about his form, she did notice a thickness about his midsection.

"I'm preparing a special show for you. My fans will love it. You're going to look great on film."

How does he know me? "I don't buy food here." Two sidesteps ended with her hip's collision against laminated wood. Her knee bumped into shelving she prayed would support her weight in her coming scrabble for freedom.

"Oh, I know everything about you, even things you don't realize for yourself. I hadn't planned on acquiring you until after my next performance, but now I've decided to enjoy some interesting playtime until your turn comes."

Scraps of light dully illuminated his form several yards from the steps. With hands on the counter, she raised her foot to the ledge to use as a push off.

"I'm so glad you provided this opportunity, Alexandra. Or do you prefer Lexi? You've given me quite a run for my effort. Time well spent, by the looks of my prize. You had me fooled at first, pretending to be the pig's whore."

"I like my privacy, moron." Antagonizing a psycho

probably wasn't her smartest move.

When he gained the first step, she bolted over the counter, anticipating his rush. The ensuing heavy footfalls from behind boosted her adrenaline reserves.

Something sharp jabbed her right hand in her awkward bid for freedom but didn't slow her down. Each heartbeat of time either aided her cause or allowed her pursuer a fraction of a second's advantage, depending on his speed and agility.

Instead of scrambling across the counter as she had, he'd leaned over in a desperate attempt to latch on to her. Though her body held enough mass to touch down quickly, her long braid was caught in his grasp. Pain exploded in her scalp as he yanked her backward. Her cap tumbled to the floor.

"You're mine, now." His slow exhalation down her neck induced a shiver.

"Never, you screwed up piece of crap. Who are you?"

"Your gateway to stardom. I like your penchant for wearing t-shirts. What do we have on tonight?" Giving thought to action, he slid his hand underneath her jacket and squeezed her chest.

In a frantic rally of strength, she pivoted and punched blindly with her flashlight, striking a bony part of his cheek. The mini flash held tight in her grasp added weight to her thrust.

Sudden freedom and explosive curses rewarded her effort. Without hesitation, she raced for the back door leading to the yard, realizing if he backtracked down the steps, her path would lead away from him.

Before she'd gained the end of the second aisle, staccato squeaks marked his advance from the dais. He hadn't attempted to follow her path, instead choosing to retrace his steps and depend on his longer stride to catch her.

In blind panic, she navigated the remaining aisles toward the emergency exit. Precious seconds marked her stalker's charge as she fumbled with the back door's lock.

When she threw the door open, fresh air bearing a light drizzle foiled her view, a reminder that her cap was back in the store and left to be discovered by employees.

Knowing the security cameras pointed to the door from her right, she kept her face averted in her race toward the rear fence. The rain would help deter identification.

Unless Ethan or Larrick view the footage.

A moot point since she'd left her fingerprints everywhere. She'd knocked over enough display items on the counter to draw suspicion from whoever opened the store in the morning.

Evidence can be lost or labeled incorrectly—with a little digital footwork.

A heavier cascade of rain silvered by distant security lights slicked her path, yet years of street life saw her navigating the few obstacles to the rear while stashing her flashlight in her waistband. In her mind's eye, she saw him racing across the lawn as she came to the fence. Six-foot wood pickets necessitated rails, which she used to gain a foothold in her climb.

Just as she swung her left leg onto the top band, the psycho snatched a handful of her jacket and yanked. The force pulled her arms back and her jacket off, along with her center of gravity.

Free falling ended with the hard ground knocking the wind from her lungs and pain shooting through her right shoulder. Gray edged her vision. If she passed out, she'd die.

"We have games to play, Lexi. But not here." Gloved

fingers held a white cloth, probably laced with some type of drug.

"Not tonight, dirtball." Before he could move to her side, she mustered her strength to kick out at his groin, landing a square thrust at his junk. He dropped to his knees amid muffled curses.

Pushing to her feet, she scrambled up and over the fence then dropped to the other side. Flashbacks of witnessing creeps on drugs and other crazy idiots with near superhuman strength and resistance to pain encouraged a faster pace to the woods. An unforgiving shape bumping her abdomen reminded her she still had her flashlight.

At this point, distance was more important than stealth. Retrieving her light, she used it to navigate the narrow path through tangles of briars and around small saplings. Here, she could lose him. Even if he knew where she'd parked her car, she'd beat him to it.

****

Grinding and crunching gravel under skidding tires quickly followed the sensor alert of a car turning into Ethan's driveway. Intuition warned that his mysterious sidekick had failed to outrun whatever demons gave chase. His brothers would give prior warning of trouble.

Shirtless and shoeless, he'd been preparing for bed, pondering over Lexi's earlier evasive demeanor. A full-body shiver after opening the door hailed as much from dark premonition as the misty air washing under the porch roof and over his bare chest.

Heavy rain drummed the hood of Lexi's car, the pounding beat augmenting his escalating pulse. After she'd claimed exhaustion earlier, he hadn't expected her return tonight.

With no rain gear, she was instantly soaked, hunched over and walking in an odd and stilted shuffle step. It appeared one arm was injured in whatever reckless task she'd undertaken. Hoover kept pace, whining and bouncing all around her companion.

"What's going on, Lexi?" LED security lights, hindered by the downpour, gilded the odd coloration of her fingers clenched over her satchel.

Pulling her inside, he noted the blood on her hands, scratches along her cheeks, and the wild look in her eyes.

"What the heck?" He couldn't resist crushing her to his chest, thanking God she was alive and in one piece after whatever foolhardy mission she'd adopted. Her edginess earlier had pointed to some form of upcoming mischief but lacked clarity in details.

Softening his touch, he searched for signs of injury, finding nothing more than scratches, scrapes, and minor cuts accounting for the crimson splotches on her tee. She winced when he touched her shoulder.

"Um, I met our serial killer. He says hello."

"Jesus Christ! What have you been doing? Wait. If it's illegal, don't tell me. Just point me in the right direction." Never in his life had he wanted to kill a predator so badly. A ferocious storm built inside his mind with the panic in Lexi's eyes. He clenched his fists in boiling rage. *Freaking coward picks on women.*

"I, um, was thinking of buying some kibble. Thought I'd do a little real-life research."

"Oh, no. You didn't." Again he pulled her in for a hug, unable or unwilling to let go this time. "Was it Whistler?"

"I don't know." She wrapped her arms around his waist.

"But he knows my name."

"Aw, no. Didn't you have Hoover with you?" As much as he wanted her to stay with him, their companionship growing into something—more—this wasn't the scenario he'd had in mind.

"I'd left her in the car."

"You're moving in with me. Now." There was no question in his tone, no hesitation. He would keep her safe. "I have a spare room. We can pick up your things tomorrow."

She didn't argue.

After depositing her satchel in the kitchen, Ethan led her into the spare bathroom and settled her on the counter.

"For now, let's get you cleaned up." Her reported trip through the woods had yielded multiple abrasions and small cuts on her face and hands. "Doesn't look like anything needs stitches." At her questioning glance, he added, "Four brothers, remember?"

Various rips and holes left her shirt unusable after the mad dash through the woods. "Let's get you down to your underwear so I can see the rest of the damage." Her jeans and tee soon joined the socks set aside.

A light touch cleaned minor wounds, yet his gaze returned to capture hers to let her know without words that every one caused him pain. Each time she drew in a quick breath, he stilled for a moment to let her absorb the hurt. "Your skin is so soft."

Now's not the time, she needs reassurance.

Never had he shown such self-restraint, his body humming with need and his mind yearning for a deeper connection. Her small gasp when he touched the right side of her back equaled a cold shower.

"Um, I kinda fell on my back. I was climbing over a fence."

"Ah, sorry." There'd be a bruise, but after compressing her rib cage slightly, he sighed. "I don't think any ribs are broken."

"Nah, I don't break easily. Trust me."

"I do."

With his mind settled as to her level of injuries, he skimmed his fingers lightly up her sides, reveling in her darkening gaze and quickening breath. Unable to keep his hands off, he'd use their mutual attraction to her benefit in distracting her from the injuries.

Loosening her braid unleashed some unnamed torment to wind its way through his system, tangling his emotions and wrapping around his soul. Wet hair resisted his efforts to sift through the silken strands while her skittish disposition failed to conceal the deeper link to her heart.

"Did he track you on the dark net?" Desperation pushed at his mind and forced him to consider the depth of his feelings for her.

"No. He knows how I like to dress and called me your girl."

"Hell. That means he's had eyes on you more than once."

No force on Earth could stop him from brushing his lips across the crown of her head and inhale her unique scent to hold close in his memory. He kept the cage of his arms loose, yet when she rested her cheek against his chest, the icy chill of her skin seeped through to his heart.

He could've lost her tonight.

Holding a near-naked woman in his arms stirred a strong base reaction, ignored in light of her trembling body snugged against him. She slid her shaking fingers around his waist to link at his low back, their chill seeping into the base of his spine.

Dear God. I need to think with my other head.

If she noticed his state of arousal, she gave no indication.

"I know you haven't been there in the past couple of weeks, but how often do you normally take Hoover through the hospital wards? Everybody remembers a therapy dog."

"At least several times a month, and I always check in first to let 'em know I'm coming."

The words he'd flippantly spoken to Larrick about near-death experiences surfed through his thoughts. Buried deep in her body was definitely on his mind as his fingers brushed the soft skin along her spine. The inappropriate timing of his desire didn't register with his southern head until she winced as his fingers smoothed over a scrape on her flank. Switching mental gears, he simply held her close.

"Ethan..."

He was prepared for her refusal and would have none of it. "Forget it, Lexi. You're staying with me. At least until we catch this creep. I'll show you a mugshot of Whistler."

"He wore a ski mask and talked in a hushed voice."

"Which means I need to take you to the hospital and pet store. Maybe hearing their voices will trigger something..."

"I prefer to avoid the store. I kinda lost my cap and jacket tonight, not to mention the small cut when climbing over the counter. And it wasn't cold enough outside that I'd remembered to wear gloves."

"Ah. The black jacket with the quote?"

She hadn't admitted specific criminal activity—directly. If he pulled her into the investigation's spotlight, she'd just make a better target, something he wouldn't allow. "Never mind. Don't answer."

"Wasn't planning on it."

"All right. Here's what's going to happen. Tomorrow afternoon, you'll stay in the car and listen over the radio while Larrick and I talk to Whistler, then Daryl. We'll see if you can identify either voice."

"All right. I pray it's one of them. After what I've been through—I have no idea where else to look."

"Why don't you grab a quick shower and I'll lay out one of my t-shirts for you to wear to bed."

Yeah, her lying half-naked in his spare bed. Just where his thoughts needed to go.

Listening to her move around and start the shower lent a small semblance of calm to his soul. After fighting the urge to give her one of his older snug shirts, he dropped a t-shirt on the bed then realized she wouldn't have clean panties. *Ahh.*

"Lexi, I'm gonna come in and grab your dirty clothes. I'll put 'em in the wash, so they'll be clean for tomorrow." The grating slide of rings on metal defined the shower curtain's movement.

"All right. You can come in."

The fact he only saw her outline through the semi-opaque lining didn't stop his mind from creating perfect pictures. Pictures formed from a career of discerning details.

Steps to the laundry room faltered with his current thoughts. Perhaps he shared at least a few characteristics with her stalker considering the way he wanted to linger in the bathroom to question the motives behind her harebrained idea.

He entered the pervert zone in taking a whiff of her clothes before dropping them in the washer. Thank God, she was in the shower.

By the time she came out, he'd gained control of his

senses and bodily responses. The robe she'd accepted and wrapped around her thin frame imparted a pixie look, dwarfing her in the thick material.

"You look like you feel a little better. How about some hot chocolate, and I'll brush out your hair while you drink it?"

She perched on a stool while he heated a cup of milk in the microwave, then added cocoa powder and sugar.

"I usually add a touch of cinnamon and vanilla creamer for flavor if you'd like to try it."

"Sure, sounds great." Her voice retained the calm thoughtfulness of one who'd resolved an inner debate.

When they settled on the sofa with her sitting cross-legged in front of him and facing away, he took a deep breath. He'd fantasized about getting his fingers in her chestnut hair, kissed by the sun and smoother than silk. Even though it hadn't occurred through the preferred sequence of events, he'd take what he could get.

"Since he knows my identity and our relationship, he'll guess I'm staying here. Maybe not such a good move for your safety."

The uncertainty filling her voice strengthened his resolve to protect her. "I'm thinking he set up surveillance cameras outside Frannie's home to watch her comings and goings before deciding the best time to attack. That's how he knew Larrick and I are leading officers on the case. We'll do another sweep tomorrow morning, and I'll check around my house, too."

"Okay."

You're not going anywhere.

"Besides, now that he has a fix on you, there won't be a safer place to stay."

It was going to be a long, long night filled with visions of

Lexi naked, underneath him, screaming his name as she flew apart in his arms. Yet for the first time in his life, he wanted more than sex. He wanted to know her on an elemental level, everything she'd endured and hoped to do, every nuance of her life.

This wasn't the lust he'd felt with beautiful women, this entailed a desire to merge, become one mind, full of dreams and cozy nights, days of discovering new delights, and providing her with a buffer from the harsh realities of life.

Chapter Sixteen

Ethan's new morning ritual entailed watching Lexi sleep while he sipped coffee and contemplated their future. In his mind, his bed was where she belonged.

After letting the dogs out to the fenced-in yard, he made a large pot of high caffeine nourishment. With little sleep last night and less on the horizon, the *northwest speedball*, minus the marijuana, would keep him alert.

Now I'm thinking like her.

She'd left her bedroom door ajar last night, allowing him the opportunity to lean against the jamb while deliberating on her latest escapade. Rendered mute by her fearless and loyal soul, he considered her the embodiment of every cop's wish in a partner.

Or every man's wish in a mate.

Obviously, she'd broken into the pet store and could've died as a result. If her stealth skills equaled her keyboard snooping, she'd not made a sound to give away her presence. The killer had either figured on Ethan's return for some late-night meddling or had caught wind of Lexi's virtual scent, figuring one or the other would show up. The question remained, were the two mutually exclusive? Instinct dictated he go back to the store and look around.

Why target patrons of the store in the first place?

Was it Dooley's way of drawing attention to his ex-wife's new endeavor, a sick sort of harassment? If so, was his partner also from the East Coast and continuing the initial quest?

Lexi had left her jacket, cap, fingerprints, and DNA. If her assailant had gone back and checked the store's computer, perhaps *his* prints were present. Anything lifted would require cross-checking with employees. Since their killer had never left prints before, there was little likelihood he'd done so now. There was no choice but to look.

Handling the situation with Larrick and his brothers would require tact and planning. He'd have to divulge some information to ensure Larrick's help, not to mention enlisting his brothers' cooperation to ensure her safety when he wasn't home. Even without their vested interest in catching a killer, they'd help. They were family.

As if sensing his stare, she opened her eyes, her rich-green gaze warm and appreciative. "Hey, what's up?" Long chestnut waves shimmered like fire in the morning sunlight while her yawn followed by a long stretch tightened the t-shirt across her chest. Her slight grimace spoke volumes.

He couldn't look away.

Ethan pushed off the doorjamb supporting him in his wayward deliberations. "Just checking to see if you wanted some coffee and how you're feeling."

"I found some new muscles in my back."

"Yeah, everything stiffens up the next day." Instead of heading toward the kitchen as his conscience dictated, his feet carried him forward until he stood beside her bed. "Roll on your stomach. I'll work the kinks out." *The t-shirt stays on.*

The new territory dictated caution but remained in the safe zone of platonic alliance. *Unlike the kisses we've shared.* He'd love to cross that line again, but he'd never been one to mix business with pleasure and couldn't compromise their investigation.

As if having her stay here isn't doing just that.

"Um, o-okay." Uncertainty mingled with trust in tone and gaze, but the result saw her rolling over, shoving her pillow away and resting her head on her folded arms.

Setting his cup on the side table, Ethan sat and brushed her silken cloud of hair aside. Leaving herself vulnerable portrayed the trust they'd developed, a good place to start. He'd chipped away at her wariness of cops and proved they were human, with the same aspirations, fears, and needs as everyone else.

It didn't take long to loosen the knots in her back while the quiet stillness grew to fill the room with a peacefulness, a nonverbal communion enjoyed between good friends.

Gradually, her silent breaths quickened.

Taking advantage of the situation, he massaged her neck and noted the increased pulse. Still, tension drained from her tissues amid low groans and appreciative sighs. A quick intake of breath alerted him to any painful areas in need of special care.

"Hold on a sec. I'm gonna grab some lotion."

His last shopping trip had yielded more than groceries in light of their developing rapport and hopes for—more. Shifting to his feet, he contemplated her complexities and the way fate seemed to bring them together. Whether they shared a quiet time on the porch reading or a short hike through the woods, they just fit.

Waiting until he returned with the scented lotion to snap its seal informed her of its virgin status.

That's a virtual cold shower. He smiled at her having tucked the sheet tight to one side and the pillow on the other side of her now-bared back. Six-hundred thread count cotton covered the gentle slope of her rump.

With her head turned to the side, she murmured, "Hmm, what's the scent?" A soft smile and lower lip pulled between her teeth combined with the tiny crinkles about her eyes invited him into her world, relaxed and pliant.

For all the time they'd spent together, she still inhabited a mysterious domain he could neither enter nor fathom. Though like an onion, trust came in layers he'd peel back until she allowed him to her center. The current exercise uncovered at least several.

"Vanilla and cinnamon." The cool cream drew a small gasp. "Sorry, I'll heat it in my palms first."

Smooth move, Ethan.

The feel of her satin skin under his touch stimulated more than his mind, yet this wasn't about him, just a need to coax a deeply relaxed state in a woman who'd just last night fought for survival.

Unfortunately, life happened while he made plans. "I'm going to wait 'till the end of the day to take you by the hospital and Whistler's house to see if you can identify your attacker. Larrick will be with us."

Just in case one is the predator and has a new accomplice. "I want you to stay here with the dogs while I'm at work." *One of my brothers will be close by.*

A grumbled growl accompanied her small nod. "I can't figure out how he found me unless you're right and he'd placed cameras outside Frannie's house."

"He's connected you to this case, probably through Frannie. So I'm thinking either phone records or cameras." Ethan gritted his teeth when her warmth invaded more than his hands.

"No. My cell is clean, not connected to my name or physical address."

"Did Frannie ever call your employer?"

"No, she always called my cell."

"Email?"

"No, another dead end."

"Then I'll check the area around Frannie's house first thing."

Another of her groans would put him in an embarrassing situation. A surreptitious adjustment eased his predicament.

"Thanks for the rubdown. I think it loosened me up."

"I'll go and start breakfast." Only an ice bath would cool his non-thinking head.

"I'll be up in a few minutes."

Already there.

* * * *

"Coffee smells wonderful. Thanks." Accepting a cup before taking her seat at the kitchen table, Lexi inhaled the fortifying steam. "I'll check and see if there's anything new." Every inch where Ethan's strong fingers had massaged felt supple and relaxed.

The detective in him wouldn't have missed the goosebumps and shivers from his ministrations, nor the smothered groans she couldn't hold back. In truth, her muscles had been tight for the first five seconds of contact before every fiber melted under his scorching heat.

The conditions of being naked, vulnerable, and semi-relaxed in a man's presence had been a new experience, one that left her nerves in a tangled mess and begging for more. Something had changed between them, a line she'd crossed when she'd flung herself into his arms upon arrival last night. Underneath his acceptance, she'd sensed his fear and anger—that she could've been killed.

He cares, not just about the case or getting laid, but about me.

"You're welcome. I'm still amazed at the layers of obscurity in the dark net. You definitely have a gift."

Fingerprint security unlocked her laptop before arrhythmic clicking gained entrance to her virtual home, a place she'd always preferred before meeting a strange cop who somehow managed to hover around her wavelength. Navigating her links took time due to security and inherent intricacies of the world of perverts, but what she found turned her blood to ice. "No." The word escaped before she could stop it.

"What?" Ethan was shoulder surfing in the next instant. "Damn it. I'm going to kill that pervert."

"He's making a game of me. Last night he said I was on his list, but not next." She should've informed Ethan last night.

Snapshots of her walking around Frannie's backyard exposed her identity right down to the small beauty mark on her right temple despite the ball cap on her head.

"He's put me up as a contestant. These photos were taken a few days ago at twilight. I couldn't bear to go inside but wanted to see how they gained entrance."

"Turn it off. Turn that effing thing off!" Ethan snatched the laptop from under her fingers and slammed the lid down.

"Ethan, this is our only way to track him. Look at the angles of the shots. We can backtrack and find his cameras."

"Enough. Don't you get it? He's tracking *you*! He's listing possible methods of *your* execution after his next *performance*. I won't have it!"

"He's confident that he'll get the next victim and we won't be able to stop him."

"We'll stop the lowlife."

"I saw the bidding. It's already more than anything prior,

but we can't let this stop us from searching. He would've found me eventually anyway."

"You're riding with me today."

"No, I have the dogs. At least mine won't eat anything I don't give her. And...he said I'm not next." For a moment, she didn't think he'd acquiesce, but on a long sigh he turned away, fists repeatedly clenching at his sides.

To find a man protective of her was new, comforting in a way never experienced. For so many years, she'd had to protect herself, rely on herself to remain safe, yet there was a relief in giving up control that she couldn't refuse or define.

"All right. But you stay here, and we'll have regular check-ins."

That concession must have cost him dearly.

"I'll need to get some clothes." The memory of fighting off the prick last night reminded her she wasn't helpless. She'd bested him once. With her dog and on familiar ground, she could do it again.

"No. We cut all ties to your loft. I'll ask my sister to drop off some stuff. We'll call her in a few minutes."

"Like your own personal WITSEC program. I'll go stir crazy. 'Sides, with so many cops in the family, she'll know it's not kosher to stash a witness." With her encounter last night, she'd established herself as a person of interest from both sides of the law. Cap, jacket, DNA.

"We'll tell her—I don't know. I'll think of something."

"If I could've finished what I started with the store's computer...I didn't have enough time."

"No! Don't say another word. He plays for keeps, and I am *not* going to lose you." Angry strides carried him to her side before he plucked her from the chair. His grip on her upper arms was just short of leaving bruises, but she couldn't pull away from the intensity of his gaze.

"You're so concerned about everybody else's welfare that you have no sense of self-preservation. Unlike the pimp who caught you stealing from him, this killer has specifically targeted you. If the bidding on this next victim is any indication, he has hundreds of other like-minded felons ratcheting the rat-infested, deviant thoughts circling his twisted mind. His—"

Switching tact in mid-thought, Ethan drew her body against his larger frame, the abrupt contact emphasizing his strength. Placing his hands on either side of her face, only inches away, he opened and closed his mouth several times.

His pupils expanded, edging out the dark green to mere rings. The silent internal debate lasted seconds before his mouth crashed down on hers. No hesitant request, just seize and capture, demanding surrender in the space of a heartbeat.

Her hunger echoed in his touch and his need for control, emotions left over following a harrowing experience.

Gentling his touch, he demonstrated his feelings with a heated graze of finger pads drifting down her neck and the back of her arms before settling on her hips. Shivers of anticipation sent a sensuous warmth coiling in her abdomen.

Warm breath bathed her neck then swept over her ear and along her jaw. By the time his lips settled over hers again, a blast of heat had spiraled then expanded throughout her body.

The slightest glide of his tongue opened her mouth, their mutual tasting, testing, and exploration an exciting investigation and preview of the adventure to come. For in her mind, every minute in his presence had become a marvel, a journey to a new and wild pursuit she'd never traveled but couldn't wait to ride.

"Jesus, the thought of losing you is driving me crazy, makes me want you even more." Whispered words against her neck distributed the moist heat of his exhalation over her sensitive flesh.

"Lexi, I'm not the man you think I am, not the type of lover you need. I like control." The quiet admission held little meaning when the clean scent, all male, all Ethan, pressed her tighter to his chest.

"I know exactly who you are. And I'll determine my own needs." Control was something she'd always exercised, but the thought of relaxing and letting him have his way was oddly exhilarating.

This was the joining she'd fantasized about, the coveted compulsion to tear his shirt off and marvel at the corded muscles awaiting her exploration.

"I'm not gentle." As if giving definition to words, he gripped her t-shirt and yanked it over her head, tossing it carelessly aside.

"I don't want gentle. I want you, unleashed and unhinged. I know what lies beneath the smooth exterior, and that's the one I want."

His growl against her throat erupted in a deep, primal expression that defied definition. Nips on her flesh stung and begged for more. Using his teeth, lips, and tongue, he brought her to a fever pitch of lust while underneath his shirt, she explored the rippling of his powerful muscles, the washboard abs framed by the well-defined V disappearing under his waistband.

"I want this first time to be slow, but I have no brakes around you."

It was too much and not enough at the same time.

Gasping breaths didn't help her gain control. "Ethan... please."

Sweat dampened her skin as moisture saturated her panties. Still, he continued his ministrations, making her moan, squirm, and shiver with need. Every facet of him turned her into a lusting, mindless wanton guided by animalistic instinct.

Everything she'd ever heard about sex was the antithesis of the sizzle and fire now swamping her system as millions of electrical prickles skated along each nerve, breathing new life into her spirit.

The women who'd taken her in had described a painful, revolting invasion that burned their throats with acid even as they tolerated the sexual onslaught.

The fire consuming her now would leave nothing but ashes in its wake. The fine silk of his hair twining around her fingers provided a grip to hold him tighter to her as he laved first one then the other dusky peak.

When his gaze lifted, the smile and heat combined to deny her mind access to words, instead, letting her body speak for her in ways she'd never imagined. Since meeting Ethan, she'd known a difference, a new path, as when meeting the girls who'd offered protection and again when Frannie had opened her eyes to a new world.

No one had ever described or instilled hope for such a union before Ethan, yet now she craved it from the depths of her spirit. He wrapped her in a cocoon of hunger that denied intrusion by external stimuli. She refused to let the world disrupt this perfect time.

"I'm going to take you, Lexi. And I'm going to keep you. Do you understand?" Whispered words trailed a path up her throat while his hand blazed a trail from breast to hip. There was no escaping the determination in his voice.

"Now. Please." Buttons plinked to the floor as she ripped his shirt open, the broad expanse flooding her mind with new possibilities. A shrug of his shoulders sent it drifting to the floor. Skin to skin contact brought a new level of heat washing over her sensitized flesh.

"Say it, Lexi." The command emerged as a growl.

"I-I'm yours. Forever." Even if she hadn't spoken the words, in her heart she knew it as fact.

"Yes. Until our last breaths."

"Bed." She couldn't verbalize anything more.

"Too far."

He'd told her he wasn't a gentle lover but prepared her body to accept him. He'd said he was rough yet plied her flesh with caresses until she screamed his name.

Moments passed before their breaths came easier, their shudders calmed, and he pulled back. In the past, every life-changing experience brought reflection, doubt, and uncertainty.

Not now, not with this man. Sated in both mind and body, she knew she was where and with whom she needed to be, regardless of what the future held. The gentleness of his touch worshiped her body in a way only lovers could share.

Smiling, he helped her to sit, her dazed mind taking in his intense satisfaction.

Without asking, he scooped her from the table and cradled her to his chest en route to the bathroom. "Let me introduce you to a new delight with showering..."

Chapter Seventeen

After striking out at Frannie's house, Ethan's mood soured. "I thought for sure we'd find a hidden camera. Something to show how he knows relevant details not released to the press."

"It was worth a try." Larrick's tone reflected rising frustration as he set his blinker and turned back to the highway.

With each successive mile driven, Ethan's stomach knotted while his mind conjured images of Lexi's body dismembered in some new grotesque scheme designed to please a psychotic's twisted imagination. He'd sealed their fates by claiming her and would damn well end the psycho.

Sometimes the deadliest weapons are those we don't see coming. The killer wielded a tool Ethan didn't fully understand and couldn't control.

Larrick's voice droned in the background, blending with the quiet hum of tires on asphalt. Every so often Ethan added a, "yeah" or, "uh-huh" to appease his partner as his thoughts kept circling their scant known information.

"So, you gonna do it?"

"Yeah, sure."

"Like—pick up your phone and do it now?"

"Yeah, okay. Wait... What?"

"You said you'd call the State Highway Administration and ask them to move the Deer Crossing sign since it's located in an inconvenient, high-traffic area. It'd be safer if the critters crossed somewhere else."

"What?"

"You haven't been listening for the last ten minutes, partner. What's up?" Larrick's tone held the determination of a pit bull. "I've given you as much slack as I can stand. Now, give."

Last night's rain left glistening drops sparkling along the hillsides like thousands of tiny blades reflecting fragments of light. His glance out the car window at the rolling countryside normally brought a sense of calm, but Ethan's belligerent subconscious conjured image after image of a disemboweled Lexi.

"She's been targeted by our psycho. She's on his list." His partner would understand whom he meant. Bile rose to the back of his throat. He shouldn't tell Larrick specifics about Lexi's late-night adventure and how the psycho had attacked her.

"How did that happen? I thought it was difficult to trace onion addresses." Larrick took a long swig of coffee.

"It is. He's seen her somewhere and made a connection to the case. I think when she found the dog crap in Frannie's yard, he still had a camera out back. I was pretty sure we'd find some cameras today." He'd never lied to Larrick before and knew the truth about Lexi's midnight escapades would come out eventually. Not to mention the fact he'd have to explain why he needed Lexi to hear Whistler and Daryl's voice. The sooner they'd dealt with it, the better.

"And—I hear something more in your voice." Larrick took another swig as if needing a distraction.

"Um, there is another reason. Lexi kinda had a run-in with him last night."

Spewed coffee embellished the steering wheel, dash, and windshield.

217

"What the hell?" After setting his travel mug in the cup holder, Larrick yanked several napkins from the glove box and wiped at his shirt. "Spill. Now!"

"She didn't tell me the exact circumstances, but I believe she went...someplace last night, searching for some type of key logger, a place that *previously* had no connection to the internet. Before she could finish, she had company. She got away, but barely. The bastard got his hands on her before she nailed him with her flashlight. It was close."

"And you were waiting to tell me? 'Till when, Christmas? What's wrong with you?" Mumbled threats and grumbles about compromising an investigation detailed Larrick's thoughts. "Anything else you want to throw in now? Like— did she get a DNA scraping, by chance? Was she anywhere that might have surveillance? No wait, if I don't know, I can't be complicit."

"Sounds like a plan." Silently, he thanked his partner for the support.

"Let me guess; now you have a hankering to take Lexi to the hospital while I talk with Daryl before going to the pet store at the end of the day." Larrick pressed the heel of his hand against his forehead as if trying to fend off a headache.

"Now that you mention it, why not?"

"All right. Anything else you want to unload?"

"I bagged the flashlight, but..."

"But it incriminates her, so we can't take it to our lab. Right?"

"Caden's gonna stop by the house and pick it up. He can send it to a private lab. It'll take a while to get results even with his push."

"If we can get a lead, we'll connect the dots another way, a legal way. Got it?"

"Yeah. On a more delicate note, she did manage to lose her jacket and baseball cap. Plus, she lost a little blood."

"The blue cap that says, *My kids have four paws and a tail?*" Larrick tossed his napkin in the spare cup holder. "That won't be hard to identify at all, now will it...Screw me. Meanwhile, *we* will go and look for this logging key, or whatever. You can explain what it looks like on the way."

"Good idea."

"Captain's gonna think we're trying to tick off Ms. Jameson. He made it crystal clear he doesn't like us near the shop," Larrick replied.

"And why do you think that is, I wonder?"

Larrick grinned. "Don't know, but I can't pass up such a golden opportunity. At least there's a bright spot in the day.

"You're always stirring the pot."

"Keeps me from getting bored."

"At least I do it in slow degrees of progression. You go whole hog." Lack of traffic meant his partner's illegal, mid-road U-turn went unnoticed. "I don't use a stick of dynamite."

"No, I save that for fishing."

Ethan smirked at the man who'd always had his back.

"Ethan, this is getting so screwed. How long until the screwball figures out Lexi's staying with you?"

"I think he already has. I've asked my brothers to take turns babysitting, but she won't have it—yet. Says she's not next on the list."

"Oh, wonderful. Now she's waiting for her *turn*." Larrick grunted in disgust.

"She has her Ruger, my backup weapon, and the dogs. Promised to stay put. And I'll be calling her frequently." Ethan blew out a sigh, trying to focus his thoughts.

"She has her own gun and knows how to shoot?"

"Yeah. We picked it up when we gathered some stuff from her place. She's practiced." Ethan sighed. "I wasn't going to let her anywhere near her loft, but since the stalker already knows pertinent information..."

"Dare I ask on what, or who she's practiced?" Larrick kept his gaze on the road.

"Bottles, so she said. Now, who did our shark lady Jameson's liaison turn out to be?" Ethan ejected the image of Lexi shooting her stalker from his mind.

"Don't know. She spotted me. And to top that, I blew off my girl for nothing."

"Did you screw up or was she watching for you?" Ethan knew the precautions Larrick took were above and beyond when it came to surveillance.

"She torpedoed down the road from her driveway then ducked behind the quick mart on the corner of Lynch and Main. She was waiting to see..."

"No kidding."

"Yeah, then she pulled out and waved to me." Larrick rolled his eyes.

"She knew you were waiting for her."

"Yeah, but she couldn't have seen me from her house. So how did she know?"

"You tell the captain you were gonna go on a stakeout?"

"Really? You need to ask?"

"All right. I'm sure that after our meeting, he probably figured you'd do it just for spite since your disrespect is mutual."

"This time when they pulled in the store's parking lot, customers were milling around inside. "I don't see Jameson's car." Yesterday morning, the BMW parked next to Whistler's truck had margined the class difference with the same condescension which had vibrated in her personality.

"Explain more about this device. If there's one here, we need to find it." Larrick's fingers tightened on the wheel before cutting the engine off.

"It could be anything from a small flash-type device hooked to the computer, software on the darn thing, or a remote device forty feet away catching electromagnetic emissions. The clever killer is inventive if nothing else."

"Well, shoot. Better hope it's not software, 'cause then we're up the creek. It's not like they'll give us access. You think her ex created a backdoor into the system and our killer has been combing her files all along?"

"I only know one person who could tell us for sure. After she came to my house last night—"

"Don't say any more."

"Yeah, I'll let you know what I find." Ethan popped the latch and shoved his door open. "We'll have to alternate tags to do this."

"At least with customers in the store, Whistler's gonna be easier to distract." Larrick's door slamming echoed in the quiet morning as he eyed two young women crossing the lot to their small compact.

"After we have a good look around, I want to examine the backyard."

"Hoping to find a black jacket and ball cap? We could hit the local mall that's having a sale..." Larrick's early-morning quips could test anyone's nerves.

Inside, Zoe offered a shy smile with their entrance. "Good morning, officers. What can I get for you?" Her shoulders hunched slightly before glancing warily in Whistler's direction.

Dusting inventory must rank her at the bottom of the totem pole. Ethan wondered if she'd confronted Whistler about his criminal background. The sullen expression on the young man's face represented his natural state in their presence. "Nothing. We just thought we'd stop by."

"Morning, Whistler. How's business? We were in the neighborhood, and I thought I'd stop in to buy a new chew toy. What do you recommend for a large dog? One that likes to gnaw and tear into meaty things." Larrick motioned the younger man down the toy aisle while two other customers discussed differences in dog food.

"Take your pick. They're all recommended."

Larrick's natural ability to guide someone with nonverbal proved as skillful as it was beneficial. Once the two were out of earshot, Zoe sidled closer to Ethan.

"Has he done something—else?" Her ponytail swung over her shoulder as she kept a suspicious eye on her coworker.

"Sorry, I can't answer that." He wasn't ignoring the question but wanted the girl to be cautious. He got to the heart of the matter. "Zoe, anything unusual today?" Knowing she'd think he referred to Whistler was only a little misdirection. "Anything out of place or odd?" By asking the questions, Ethan kept his partner a little further from the tenuous legal lines he was obliterating.

Youth and inexperience cosseted her in an innocent shield that wouldn't hold up against a clever predator. With a tilt of her head and a barely there whisper, she rounded the counter and headed toward the register. "He yelled at me. Said I left the counter display a mess. But I didn't. I swear it was right when I left yesterday evening. The heavier tags always go on the bottom of the display, but this morning, he said they were on top and out of order. I didn't mess with them. Why would I?" Fear crept into her voice as she continued. "You don't think he'll hurt me, do you?"

A healthy dose of caution was good. Paralyzing fear helped no one. "No. He knows we're watching him. Just keep things professional. Since you're not the last one out of here at night and you still live at home with your folks, you should be fine. Just be smart and use common sense."

Her shoulders relaxed as she took a deep breath. "Okay. No problem."

"You mind if I dust this keyboard real quick for prints?" It was a chance and a long shot, but Ethan had to take it. He prayed the fine powder would adhere to the skin oils of someone other than shop employees. "Have you been busy this morning?"

"No sales yet. Just people browsing."

Ethan removed a container of fine powder from his jacket pocket. Using the soft bristled brush, he dusted the keyboard while Zoe watched with widened eyes and dropped jaw.

As place keepers, the letters J and F were his best bet. None of this would be court admissible, and he had no viable cause for a warrant. If he did, instead of using dust to obtain prints from a nonporous surface, he'd employ superglue fumes, or cyanoacrylate ester, to convert any latent prints. He just wanted an immediate, solid lead. Within several minutes, he'd used his phone to photograph several prints.

"What are you doing around the register?" Whistler approached from the aisle but remained on the customer's side, leaving him at a distinct height disadvantage with the register blocking sight of the keyboard.

The raised voice impelled Ethan to hurry in wiping the hardware clean as Larrick redirected the male clerk's attention. "I hear you've been harassing this young lady. Considering your record, it would be a shame if we had to haul you in, wouldn't it?" The challenge muted outward hostility.

"I didn't touch her."

Zoe mouthed the words, 'Thank you,' when Whistler glared at Larrick.

"Harassment comes in many forms, doesn't it?" Larrick continued the thread, drawing the younger man's attention and allowing Ethan to quietly slide the small brush and container in his pocket.

"Larrick, I want to check out the backyard, again." Turning to Zoe, he continued, "Are there any dogs out there now?"

"Yes, my golden is probably sleeping under the tree. He's friendly." With a calculating glance at Whistler, she added, "Unless he's protecting me."

"Should I be glad you didn't find any clothing?" Larrick backed into his usual parking space in the department's garage. "Or did you?"

"No, nothing. I could see some scuff marks on the counter, and Zoe said someone had tampered with the display rack, but nothing was missing." Ethan pinched the bridge of his nose between thumb and forefinger as he let out a long sigh. "I doubt we'll get a hit since the bastard never leaves a trace. I'll run this through Caden's PI labs."

"I didn't see anything resembling what you described as a key logger or sniffer, or whatever." Larrick shoved the keys in his pocket before exiting. "What time do you want to take our little snoop over to the hospital and Whistler's house?"

"Pick me up at six." Ethan thought of Lexi, working at his home, probably feeling the onset of stir crazy.

The drive to the hospital defined a new side to Lexi as she withdrew into her shell. Each mile driven shaved a layer of self-assurance from her bearing.

The wide-brimmed hat and trench coat likened her to a character in one of the old movies she liked to watch while tension radiated from every pore, concentrically, until Ethan's hands fisted at his sides. Seeing her fear take form sharpened his resolve to end the nightmare, regardless of the cost. He wished he could smooth away the small worry lines from her face.

Larrick's rhythmic squeezing of the steering wheel and periodic glimpses in the rearview mirror illustrated the cost of his overflowing energy while intermittent attempts to lighten the mood met with one-word answers.

In the hospital, Larrick spoke with the administrator in the empty cafeteria while Ethan stood with a nervous Lexi in the prep area listening over the two-way radio.

"Larrick's not crossing legal lines?"

"No, as long as they're standing in a public area and just shooting the breeze, he's fine."

"I can't tell. Daryl's talking in a normal voice, and the killer spoke in a harsh whisper. Whenever I came here with Hoover, I always connected with Frannie. I don't know Daryl very well." She swiped at the tears weighing her lashes.

Ethan hit the squelch button on his radio to signal Larrick. "All right. Let's head to the car." There was nothing more they could do there and watching Lexi's silent suffering was killing him. He imagined the memories of Frannie assaulted her mind as he led her away.

Lexi huddled in the back seat as Larrick pulled to a stop ahead of the sexual predator's house. Listening to the ensuing conversation over the walkie-talkie had kept her presence hidden and allowed her to concentrate on the voice. Larrick once again had pulled the creep mentally off balance to get him babbling while Lexi attempted to identify her attacker.

Ethan realized that confronting the killer, even indirectly, might change the timeline of his intended assault since he obviously didn't approve of live witnesses. The risk of direct confrontation didn't compare to the consequences of not exposing the pervert. He couldn't prepare for an attack when he had no information with which to work. As when listening to Daryl, Lexi couldn't positively identify her assailant.

Larrick's concern was evident when they dropped him off at his car. Ethan's assurance to keep her safe met with a dubious smile.

The return home entailed long sighs and watching Lexi's torso slowly relax after they'd gotten coffee from a drive-through and she'd switched to the front seat.

"I'm sorry I can't be sure. Last night, I was so panicked..."

"It's all right. We had to try. Just like I had to lift fingerprints from the keyboard and search for a physical key logger."

"Which doesn't mean there isn't malware on their system. I just haven't found it yet."

"We've done all we can in that direction, at least for now." Nothing the killer had done made sense. "I'm surprised we didn't find another camera when we re-checked Frannie's house."

"Which doesn't mean he didn't have one up until yesterday. It just means we couldn't find one today." Lexi shook her head.

"This guy is smart, staying one step ahead of us."

"Yeah, and the thug from last night has my jacket and cap, not to mention I cut my finger when I scrambled over the sales counter and probably left a blood smear on the back fence."

"I checked the counter and display items. Both were clean. If he wiped up after you, he might have *your* DNA."

"He already knows who I am. Shoot. Why would he want my DNA?"

"Enough for tonight. Let's go home and grab a bite to eat." *As meticulous and clever as this dirtball is, he probably knows where she is every second. But how?*

He'd checked the perimeter of his house. With each new turn in the case, Ethan's fear of losing Lexi cultivated insecurity and questioned his competence to the point he wanted her by his side at all times.

"I have an idea, but you probably won't like it." Lexi bit her lower lip, her wavy locks sliding forward to cover her uncertainty.

"If it's not completely above board, don't tell me. Unless it helps me keep you safe. Then, by all means, talk." Knowing Lexi stood front and center in a killer's crosshairs necessitated he might blur all kinds of legal lines, something he'd never done before but wouldn't hesitate to do now.

"Let me work out the details first."

* * * *

Each morning, Lexi woke in the spare bedroom, sore from Ethan's vigorous lovemaking and amazed at the incredible direction her life had taken. Yet an ingrained sense of self-preservation dictated she sleep alone.

Years of being shielded by the prostitutes followed by three years of hiding from a vicious pimp made ingrained habits difficult to break.

After digitally connecting with Ethan months ago, she'd never foreseen herself engaged in screaming, sheet-clawing sex. *I never imagined it could be like that.* Too much was happening for her to gain a semblance of balance.

She'd also never imagined how such a shrewd, straight-arrow cop could be so inventive and kinky. Last night seemed to have settled something in his mind, an unspoken claim, a decision firmed but not voiced. When questioned, he simply smiled with a determination she recognized as part of his iron will.

Renewed motivation to locate the killer before another victim fell echoed in the firm set of his jaw and a new tension that only crumbled when they joined as one. The fact the twisted psychopath had her blood was as unsettling as her destroyed anonymity. No one had ever tracked her down before.

"So what's on your agenda today?" Cooking breakfast established a routine that lent a sense of normalcy to her life, one she'd never experienced but found addicting. Both Hoover and Diego looked up expectantly as she placed bacon and eggs on a plate.

"Lucas is gonna hang out with you this morning." The tired argument accompanied their morning rituals.

"No. I'll be fine. I'm not next on the list. He said I'd been added, but he's already planned for his next..."

"And psychotic killers are always honest?"

"I'll be okay." Lexi held out the plate for him to take. "I've got your backup weapon."

Ethan accepted the offering before pulling out a chair and sitting at the kitchen table. "Just how good a shot are you?"

"The end with the hole goes toward the bad guy before you squeeze the trigger."

Minutes passed as he contemplated her smart mouth.

"Have you ever pulled the trigger under stress?"

"No. It was after the pimp got a hold of me that I started keeping a small Ruger in my nightstand."

"All right. After breakfast, we're going out back. I want to see how well you handle your weapon."

"Fine. What are you doing today?"

"Larrick and I are meeting with the captain and starting over from scratch. We'll look at every piece of information we have, re-canvass the neighborhood houses, and review records. That riddle is driving us nuts."

Bidding on the next victim had closed after a week of escalating demands for more gruesome and inventive murders while the section for suggestions grew exponentially. To see her own name, the only intended victim whose identity was advertised, had spawned a new level of urgency to her digging.

"I've established another persona online and rapport with Zoe from the pet store. She doesn't work until this evening, so after I've dug through the store's files, I'll send her an email and see what's up. I'm already in Daryl's system but haven't found anything yet. Both Frannie and the councilwoman belonged to several civic organizations. I'll do some research and see what overlaps."

The slight tightening of Ethan's lips signaled his understanding that she intended to hack private systems and shed light on how the psycho obtained his information or at least find his next target. She'd start with employee records.

"Let me know if you come across any helpful information. Aren't you finishing up a project?" Ethan's intent gaze held more than curiosity as he crunched on the crisp bacon.

"It's done. I've got a couple days before the next phase starts."

He was probing, looking for signs she might be planning another adventure and placing herself in danger. Taking a sip of coffee meant breaking eye contact, but she couldn't hold his gaze considering that was a definite possibility depending on what her exploration uncovered.

"One thing I don't understand. After the psycho cornered me in the, ah, well, after I escaped, he could've gone back inside and cut my digital connection to the store's LAN. Yet he didn't. Why not? I would have."

"Maybe he didn't have the time, was distracted, or maybe he's just that cocky. Has he referenced the incident on his site?"

"I'll look and see, then probably spend a good bit of time surfing the dark net." According to the murder site, a young woman would die within the next twenty-four hours, then another one soon thereafter. Ethan bore the weight of that knowledge in the circles under his eyes and the constant tension in his shoulders.

"Be careful. Keep the dogs inside with you. My phone is always with me. But why don't—"

"No. I'm not going for a ride along, and if one of your brothers arrive, I'll go run errands. I'll be fine."

"All right. I get it. You're independent and can take care of yourself. Got it."

"Ya know, I've been thinking. We didn't get the first riddle. The second one was meant to lead us to the third victim." Lexi needed to make sense of a psycho's babbling. With her plate cleaned, it was time to put away thoughts of resting sated in Ethan's arms and get to work.

"Or maybe not the victim, maybe her location." Ethan finished his breakfast and cleared his plate.

"*I detect the ill winds of fate*. What if he didn't mean that figuratively, as in someone's mental perception? What if he meant it literally?" Normally, puzzles intrigued Lexi, but this one held deadly consequences, thereby adding a new and complex layer to the compulsion to solve. "Like something you'd smell."

"Okay, but winds that travel with hurricane force and can't be stopped? Plus the fact they're carrying something."

"He's indicated the next victim will be a college coed or high school girl. Someone fast could mean promiscuous." Plates clinked as Ethan placed them in the dishwasher.

"There are three high schools and one college in this city, which is too much to narrow down." Her mind raced as she slid her laptop into position and signed on. "Jeez. I'm on his list. How'd I get so sloppy?"

"Not gonna happen, babe."

So in tune, he knew the direction of her mental meanderings.

"I'm gonna see what else I can find." Some unnamed entity niggled at the back of her mind. All the needed information was present but remained out of order. "A female track runner who smells bad?"

"And I really don't want to know how you'll be checking."

Despite his words, Ethan rested his hand on her shoulder, his breath blowing out a long sigh to warm her neck.

"Neither woman was sexually assaulted, except with inanimate objects, right?" The chorus of clicks and clacks precipitated a flash of insight.

"Those women might have been selected by Dooley. We don't know."

"So, if this guy has some aversion to sex, maybe the speed he's referring to isn't a reference to that. Maybe he's subtly pointing to something else." Lexi opened up her social media page.

"Really? You're going to take a break and make new friends? Now?"

"No, no. I saw some pics online. One was of Zoe and her family, but the tag, the tag was weird." Pulling up the photos, she showed Ethan the one that had bothered her but couldn't figure out why. The answer hit her with the speed of a lightning bolt, its sizzle electrifying her fingers as they flew over her keyboard. "Look, this is Zoe."

"Yeah, she's one of several thousand young girls who could be a target. So?" Ethan studied the pictures.

"What's she doing?"

"Looking at the camera," Ethan replied.

"What else?"

"Sneezing. She has terrible allergies." Ethan's grip tightened.

"Look at the tag. The hacker must've altered it. See? Who would label themselves 'booger face'?" Lexi murmured. "Holy Hanna. Faster than the wind. A sneeze."

"Yes. Text me her address. I'll call Larrick on my way to her house. Lock up after me, Lexi." Snatching his shoulder rig from the chair, Ethan raced to the back door. "And don't open this door for anyone but me. You understand?" Both Hoover and Diego startled with the door slamming.

Lexi texted the address to Ethan's cell and tried to call the teenager. Her attempt to warn of possible danger went straight to voicemail.

Chapter Eighteen

Easter Friday, what a fantastic opportunity to make this family's holiday a picture-perfect memory.

Arvel glanced over his shoulder at the silhouette of the drugged retriever by the corner of the house. *Good boy.* Early morning rays of sunshine would soon turn his coat a burnished gold. The perfect anecdotal photo to end the morning's video.

Thirty minutes earlier, he'd watched Zoe's father and mother leave for work, not knowing that their only child would soon be elevated to celebrity status.

With schools closed, he'd have all day to watch his carefully laid plans come to fruition as his newest star's life ebbed away in painful degrees of melting skin and agonizing screams.

At least the family had the right approach to life. Country living was the best. The house was located on a secluded cul-de-sac, trees adding a sound barrier to the neighbors several hundred yards away. The rear being backed by a nature preserve meant no one witnessed his approach.

He'd taken extra care last night in hiding crucial supplies amid the thick brush, now carted away to leave no evidence except the wagon's common tracks.

The easily picked back door provided an invitation to enter. *How thoughtful that there's no alarm system to fiddle with.* Considering his next living toy's age and looks, today promised a physical fulfillment he hadn't enjoyed with other victims. Would she appreciate the scotch-flavored condoms?

His observations proved her a little adventurous, if not intelligent. After all, dating a sexual predator from work—

not so smart.

For once, he was glad of the meddling detectives, for their intervention had prevented the pervert from the pet store stealing the grand prize, assuming the girl was still a virgin.

Overall, he didn't find sex that exciting, but with the way his audience clamored for expanded horizons, how could he resist? It was a small sacrifice to please his fans.

She didn't usually emerge from the house to play with her dog until after nine. For expediency's sake, he hoped to catch her still in bed. He'd put his time to good use in quietly hauling today's tools and ingredients onto the back porch. Open rafters provided just the needed configuration for the pulley system. Twice, he had to stop his preparations to see if the slight noise had awakened the star of today's film.

Upon entering the back door, he appreciated and expected the pristine stainless steel and stone kitchen, complete with double ovens and a wine fridge.

Perhaps he'd sit on the back porch enjoying a glass while watching Zoe descend into the carefully prepared barrel of acid.

The downstairs carried a loft feel, open to his view but segregated by thick rugs and heavy furniture that probably cost a fortune. The method of Zoe's disposal forced him to leave his next riddle on the kitchen counter.

Stupid cops needed all the help they could get. Since his encounter with Lexi in the pet store, he'd kept a close eye on the pigs' digital records and movements, waiting to find new evidence that might bear his DNA. So far—nothing.

When the litter hacker had clocked him, he'd bled a slight bit. *Doesn't take much.* Soon, he'd get to return the favor, tenfold.

Lack of noise drifting down the stairway encouraged the

belief he'd catch Zoe still asleep. Already, his member swelled at the thought. The small creak made at the top of the stairs received no audible alarm from his target.

Shoulder straps from his backpack chafed slightly as he shrugged it down one side. Leaving his molded bodysuit behind today was a small price to pay for using the cart to carry the extra supplies needed. Extracting the cloth with his procured sample, he would leave a smear or two in the bedroom and teach his next victim a lesson before her final curtain call.

This ought to confuse the forensics team.

His small camera would catch the first reaction, the anticipation sending chills of excitement circling his chest. *This is the best part.*

Delicate snores overshadowed the door's low creak. No surprise she'd decorated the large room in soft pastel shades. Thick, cream-colored carpet muffled his steps to her side.

He watched, waited.

Would she wake from the weight of his stare?

No. *Ah, the sleep of the innocent.*

A deep breath before clearing his throat.

The first blush of horror, orgasmic. Zoe's youth added a certain appeal he couldn't deny. Maybe he'd stick to the younger ones in the future.

Before she could gather the breath to scream, he snapped the picture then dropped the camera on the bed. A muffled whimper emerged after he shoved the cloth in her mouth and descended upon her, using the bedspread to pin her arms underneath and to her sides. Since deciding to take her sexually, he wouldn't drug her just yet.

"Now, Zoe. This is going to happen just as I've planned.

How much pain you experience is up to you. If you're a really good girl, I'll even drug you for the second half of the entertainment."

As prey sensing the inevitable, she stopped thrashing. Oh, but her eyes. Defeat was a wonderful look on her. Green irises surrounded by so much white and brimming with tears that trickled over her temples was a turn on he'd not experienced. *Definitely sticking with the younger ones in future.*

To test her resolve, he withdrew to the bedroom door to pick up his backpack. She neither moved nor made a sound despite the continued flow of tears. Panic twining with defeat in a young girl proved a tantalizing and seductive lure he'd come to crave in his artistry.

"You know what they say, the devil's in the details." From his pack, he removed the knotted length of rope. "I love four-poster beds. So practical." Looping the end around a bottom post proved a little difficult, but was necessary for his peace of mind. With the length coiled underneath the open window, he could exit the home in seconds, a lesson learned at Frannie's residence.

Successive shudders rippled through her body when he snatched the cloth from her mouth. She heeded his threat and didn't make a sound.

"Hmm, I'd planned on securing your limbs to the four corners, but I'm wondering..." Several yanks and snaps saw his tripod unfolded and set up with the video camera ready to go.

"Please, mister. Don't tie my hands and feet. I'll do what I'm told."

"Ah, such a good girl. Why don't we give it a try?" *Will my fans like that?*

* * * *

Ethan eased his SUV off the road and parked behind Larrick's sedan. *Thank God he waited. I wouldn't have.* The soft snick of his door opening and closing resounded in the crisp morning air.

"Glad you decided to show up." Larrick's gun sliding from his shoulder rig belied the flippant tone. "No traffic in or out. You really think she's the next victim?"

"It's a good probability. I just hope we're not too late. He's always struck at night, but this is a family home, not a single woman."

Ethan palmed his own weapon, the weight secure in his hand. "At least the winding lane gives cover until we reach the yard. Lexi texted details of the house and family."

Fine hair at Ethan's nape snapped to attention while his pulse pounded in his ears. "There's no landline here, and the parents are at work. The kid didn't answer her cell."

"Whoa, your girl's efficient." Larrick squinted at the strong sunlight cresting the treetops. "This is a different setup. How do you wanna go in?" Quiet words filled the situation with uncertainty and doubt.

"If we knock or go around back and her dog gives us away, we lose the element of surprise. He's never left a live witness." The thought of minor damage and being wrong didn't compare to saving the kid's life.

"You bust in the door, I'll go in first," Larrick whispered.

"No. It's my turn to go first." Ethan darted forward beside the crumbling asphalt to let the grass deaden the sound of his approach. Once off the county road, thick woods concealed their advance along the twisting driveway.

"Either silent entry or busting the door will leave us open to being shot by the homeowners." Larrick's caution was understandable—and inconvenient.

"They're both at work, according to Lexi's initial research. This house sits back several hundred yards. It's a two-story with no fence in the back." Ethan paced his partner around the first bend.

Arching branches of oak trees overhead cocooned them in a picturesque world of peace and tranquility forbidding monsters to enter. Yet in his gut, Ethan knew the psychopath was here. The teenager he hoped was still alive wasn't much younger than Lexi, yet miles of intellectual and life experiences distanced them.

"Think he's chosen a new partner?" Ethan whispered.

The normal sounds of nature offered no comfort as they picked their way up the drive, each remaining vigilant in unfamiliar surroundings.

"Hard to tell. He hasn't done one predictable thing yet, except for hunting Lexi."

No noise broke the morning's silence. Perhaps they were too late. He'd rather believe the kid was still asleep, safe in bed.

According to the previous scenarios, he'd drugged them before the assault but ensured they retained the ability to fight. Each one had defensive cuts and bruises. His hunch told him Zoe would submit.

Morning sunshine punched through low-lying clouds and shifting leaves to spotlight intermittent clumps of weeds poking up along the road. The two-story colonial ahead stood proud among the older silver firs, mimosas, and red alders, a testament to its age and stature. Round columns ran the height to support an elaborate roofline not common to the region.

"Open area, let's hoof it," Larrick whispered.

Ethan's palms grew moist as they raced for the front door, all pretense of stealth gone. A silent mantra kept him focused on his goal while controlling his breathing. He could do nothing about his racing heart.

Larrick lifted his foot to kick the front door until Ethan raised his hand to stop him before smoothing his fingers over the solid surface. 'No,' he mouthed. A quick hand gesture suggested they circle around back.

"Thanks, guess I got ahead of myself," Larrick whispered.

"That's got to be solid oak, plus a deadbolt." In his race to the backyard, Ethan noted the first floor had intact closed windows.

At least there's no fence.

Screaming from inside the house briefly froze him in his tracks. A glance at the second-story window revealed it open. The curtain swayed in the light breeze. Peripheral vision revealed Zoe's golden lying flat at the corner of the house, drugged, as evidenced by its lack of movement with the girl's scream.

"Let's get inside," Larrick urged.

Ethan scanned the house. Off the kitchen, a large brick patio provided wicker seating and a fire pit. Adjacent to the patio, a moderate-sized screened porch with an odd configuration of furniture blocked any view through the sliding door.

A small gap between the kitchen's slider and its frame presented their easiest access. "We've got a way in." Larrick nudged him forward.

Another muffled scream inside detailed proof of life and terror before a crash and snarl of rage broke the morning stillness.

Zoe was alive and probably fighting, for the moment.

Larrick followed Ethan, canting his body to keep an eye on their backs as they rushed through the kitchen.

Blood roared in Ethan's ears while his gun hand shook. *Damn.* Understanding the different aspects of PTSD didn't grant him control over his shallow breathing or the sweat coating his palm. The tap on his shoulder grounded him.

'We good to go?' Larrick silently formed the words.

Ethan nodded. They couldn't save Zoe if he lost it. *Get it together.*

Shadows stretched from the kitchen entrance into a large informal dining room. Hardwood flooring squeaked under their cautious steps while Ethan formed a mental picture of the layout as a matter of habit.

An open doorway led to a large living room where thick geometric-patterned rugs anchored two seating areas, their sofas angled in front of a stone fireplace. Each step animated Ethan's sly imagination into conjuring one deadly scenario after another, all ending in death.

Another bloodcurdling scream amid curses and several thumps defined the ongoing fight upstairs. *What's going on?*

Carpeted stairs to his right blocked Ethan's view of the foyer, while invisible bands squeezed his chest. The quiet gasps impeded his desperate attempt to inhale deeply. The next scream dissolved the imaginary sludge impeding his forward momentum and galvanized him into action.

Upstairs, a heavy thud followed a man's enraged howl. Zoe's guttural scream filled the home.

Two or more involved. He nodded to Larrick, knowing through their weird bond they were on the same page. Against how many, one or two?

Something heavy banged against a wall.

A sturdy banister leading to the second story contained detailed carvings beneath and winding around each spindle, further hindering his view. It appeared the upstairs hallway led to bedrooms off to the left as well as the right.

A gunshot echoed through the house before a flash of pale skin and long, dark hair caught his attention. Zoe streaked from the left side past the top of the stairs. The sound of the bedroom door slamming off to the right reverberated in the momentarily quiet house.

A low growl declared the chase unfinished. From the left, a door slammed open against its supporting wall before booted steps thundering in the hallway focused Ethan on the masked intruder.

On the bottom step and fully exposed, Ethan froze. His mind formed the details of the masked assailant fumbling with his jeans, the hem of his black turtleneck caught in the zipper. He held a gun in the other hand.

Eyes, nose, and mouth seen at that distance gave no clue to identification. Ethan's gut said it was his shooter despite the difference in the silhouette. Even as he raised his gun, Ethan noted the discrepancy in body type, this man lacking the expected potbelly.

"Your girlfriend is next, Detective." The harsh whisper eclipsed identification.

"Freeze." Ethan squeezed the trigger twice in quick succession. The first shot killed a riser midway up the steps. The second slammed into the wall near the thug's head.

The assailant's own shot went wide, its hiss all but kissing Ethan's temple.

Larrick's return fire forced the target to retrace his steps. With two-to-one odds, the intruder backed behind the balcony wall. The slamming of a door indicated he'd retreated into the bedroom.

"Let's check the girl first. Make sure he doesn't have a partner. He's got nowhere to go." Larrick's nudge brought reality back to the surreal situation.

Ethan followed him up the stairs. At the top, Larrick kept watch over their six while Ethan moved toward the rooms on the right.

Several thumps from behind gave Ethan pause. As much as he wanted to pursue, Zoe took first priority.

The ripple of shudders welling up inside him inspired a look over his shoulder. Larrick nodded toward the next door. Three doors stood along the hallway, each closed.

"Zoe, we're the detectives who spoke with you about Whistler. I'm coming in to check on you." As much as Ethan's mind urged him to rush, he wanted to avoid another bullet more.

The middle door opened quietly under his light touch. *Probably a guest bedroom.* Spartan and clean, the neutral shades and lack of personal knickknacks indicated it rarely saw use.

Quick steps carried them toward the room where he suspected the girl had taken refuge, probably a master suite considering it spanned the width of the home. The question in his mind...*If this is the master, do the parents own a gun? Will she use it, reflexively, before realizing the identity of her target?*

"Zoe. It's Detective McAllister. I'm coming in, hon." Ethan tried the door handle. It gave quietly.

The room's interior reeked of fear, matured into a palpable entity thrumming in the air and clogging his throat. The contrast of sensory stimulation was worthy of a dark poet's best work as brilliant morning light highlighted an elegant room in shades of cream and maroon through a sweep of large floor-to-ceiling windows. Only one corner contained enough shadows to partly conceal the young girl visibly shaking, gun in hand.

"Zoe? Have you been shot?" He couldn't bring himself to say more in the face of her terror.

The slightest shake of her head gave him a glimpse of tear-stained cheeks through a tangled mass of hair. Her gun pointed at the floor, vibrating with the hand controlling it.

"Are you alone, hon?" He padded forward in slow, quiet steps.

She nodded, words failing to confirm her panic and pain.

"Is there just one man or two?"

"One." Her voice was barely audible.

When he stood within reach, he gently took hold of the gun, waiting until her brain registered his control and released her grip. "I'll be back in a minute, Zoe. Stay put. We're going to secure the house. Is any other family member here?"

A negative shake of her head.

A glance at Larrick in the doorway revealed him moving forward and snagging the bedspread to cover her.

Ethan handed the gun to his partner.

"Larrick's gonna stand in front of your door while I go and check out the rest of the house."

His partner conveyed his concern with a touch at his elbow. Ethan gave a thumbs-up signal.

"I'll be back in a second. He's got nowhere to go unless he jumps." Ethan swallowed hard, determined to see the nightmare through.

"Rope." Zoe's harsh whisper made no sense except

maybe in her mind.

Inaudible tread carried him to the last door.

Remembering his previous confrontation, he stood to the side and tried the handle. The door was locked, which made little sense unless the killer was buying time. *Why?*

Hesitating a split second before pounding on the frame failed to enlighten him as to the assailant's possible plan. Waiting for a blast to punch through the door, he took a deep breath.

Nothing.

A nod to Larrick and he centered himself before driving his heel into the wood near the lock. Immediate splintering saw the door flying inward to bang against the wall. Ethan darted to the side to avoid acquiring lead.

Directly opposite the door, an open window allowed a soft morning breeze to ripple the ruffled curtains in defiance of the atrocities that had occurred within.

A rope extending from the bedpost disappeared over the sill. The window had been open on their approach—to allow for a quick escape?

The room was empty except for residual from the brutal attack. Piled on the top sheet and duvet, Zoe's nightgown lay in shreds. Pastels and creams conveyed the girl's color preference in tasteful grace, but the light blue bed sheet spotted with blood indicated an animal in need of execution.

"Damn it! We almost had the bastard." Ethan's fury overrode caution. Rushing to the open window's side, he scrutinized the fleeing figure through the fence's back gate. Aiming his gun was reflexive.

Too effing far away. He took a shot anyway.

The average person's eye could perceive forty-five to sixty frames per second and give an accurate description of a picture. Occupations such as police officers and fighter pilots out-distanced that scale due to their training.

Burned in the back of his mind was the image of the perp who'd shot him. He'd been tall but also sported a potbelly. When this intruder angled to the right before disappearing into the bush, he was thinner and lacked the beer gut. The pack bouncing on his shoulder indicated a significant weight.

He has another partner.

It wasn't until he shouldered his Glock he realized how much his hand shook. A mental review of events assured him he'd reacted logically, if not strictly following procedure, but priorities were intact. Zoe was alive if greatly changed from her nightmare. With help, she could recover, unlike the previous victims.

Padding back past Larrick and into the room, Ethan quietly announced his presence where huddled in the corner, Zoe shredded his heart with whimpers and sobs. Larrick had draped the bedspread around her before stepping back.

"Well?" Larrick asked.

"He had a pre-planned escape route. Rope tied to the bed."

"Of course he did. I'll secure the rest of the house and call it in. The kid needs help." Larrick nudged past and away, knowing Ethan was better with victims.

"Zoe, I'm gonna stay with you. Can I pick you up and carry you?" Her shattered expression would haunt his nights for a long time. *This could've been Lexi.*

A violent headshake warned him not to make contact. She probably wouldn't tolerate intimacy for months if not years to come.

Trembling legs threatened to topple her to the floor once

she stood.

Bruises already marred the teenager's face. Shallow cuts seeped blood over her hands and thickened the hair over her blanket.

With a respectful distance, he kept pace down the stairs after Larrick's all clear from the first floor. Her tears and thin mewls betrayed her current anguish, yet she couldn't realize the misery and heartbreak yet to come.

Once at the hospital, emergency services would help her through the ordeal of recounting and reliving the event, the first of many times.

"Ethan, c'mere a sec." An odd note in Larrick's tone saw Ethan reaching for his gun while striding toward the porch.

The smell wafting on the gentle breeze stopped him cold. Due to the wind's direction and their haste to get inside earlier, he'd briefly noted it but not as a threat.

In the corner of the back porch, a contraption the likes of which unknown, brought another string of curses to rival any sailor's speech.

"No. No. No," Larrick muttered. A large barrel of liquid directly underneath a series of pulleys attached to the porch's rafter reminded Ethan of a dunking booth at the county fair.

"I don't think that's spring water." Larrick didn't have to lean forward to detect the rotten-egg odor permeating the air. "Smells like sulfuric acid. Jesus, he was going to lower her into it and film her melting body? Dear God, we've got to get this guy."

"Plural. This bastard was thinner but about the same height." Ethan couldn't take a deep breath without furthering the horrid images in his mind. He'd noticed the steel-like drum in the corner earlier, but not as part of an intricate system.

Further investigation revealed the metal tub contained a removable panel made from some type of soft stuffing between the steel and a huge glass barrel. After removing the padding and opening a door-like section of the metal, the dirtball could film Zoe as she was lowered inside, and acid disintegrated her tissues.

Bile rose in his throat, forcing him to turn away.

If they didn't solve the riddle, the next victim might not be as lucky as Zoe. "The degenerate said Lexi was next."

"Screw him." Larrick reached out to grab his shoulder. "Ethan, we'll nail the prick."

Chapter Nineteen

"I don't think I look like a consultant." Lexi's low murmur caught the attention of the uniformed officer posted by the front door.

Ethan's glare returned the younger man's gaze to the front yard. Bringing her to the scene was a calculated risk, but one they needed to take. He didn't fancy escorting her to the station again.

"Hmm, what does a consultant look like?" Larrick considered Lexi's ponytail, jeans, and long-sleeved t-shirt before nodding to the officer in passing.

"A stuffed-shirt type in a business suit." Behind them, Caden's quip received a smile from Lexi as he continued, "See, hon, we have more in common than you realize. You need to dump Ethan." The remarks, meant to antagonize Ethan, succeeded.

"Old people wear suits." Her simplistic answer spanned a culture and generation who thumbed their noses at formality and would've widened the gap between them had they not cemented their relationship. "On the other hand, nothing looks sharper than a hot guy wearing a suit." A saucy wink at Ethan promised heaven on Earth.

Ethan sighed.

"Thanks for coming. This shouldn't take but a few minutes." After the ambulance had sped down the driveway, Ethan had called Lexi, advising Caden would pick her up. She was the best chance at tracing anything on the victim's computer. Crime scene techs had started to carry the electronics away before Ethan advised he'd bring them and maintain chain of custody.

"Hey, you can call me for taxi service anytime." Caden

thumped Lexi's back before breaking off and heading to the backyard. "I'm gonna take a look around before joining you."

One tech visually combed the backyard for evidence.

Larrick followed them through the door and into the expansive foyer, the once elegant home now tainted with the invisible horrors of a psychopath's touch.

"Zoe and her parents will be at the hospital for a while yet." Larrick ushered them up the stairs. "Crime techs are done inside and winding up in the backyard."

Ethan noted the bullet hole in the riser and groaned, ignoring Lexi's questioning glance. His partner hadn't yet addressed the wild shots fired in a split second of panic, where hand muscles lacked coordination.

When his brothers learned of his faux pas, he'd enjoy multiple days at the firing range amid comments of how his targets remained safe.

Light flooded the crime scene in a challenge to dispel lingering images of scattered sheets and a young girl's fight to survive. Techs had bagged and removed the tattered nightgown and sheets. Dusting powder mottled every flat surface.

Regardless of the processed scene, remnants of the prior chaos remained—an overturned chair and a stripped bed along with enough pain and heartache suffusing the atmosphere to last for years.

Lexi's tentative steps reflected the understanding that came from surviving mind-numbing horror. After entering the room, her bearing altered to the point where Ethan stepped forward and wrapped his arm around her shoulders. She pressed snug against his chest.

"This could've been me."

The barely audible words filled his mind with an imagined

video of the killer catching Lexi at the pet store and spending the night in a sickening, deadly chain of events. Her deep green eyes sharpened on him, willing him to fully understand Zoe's terror and the nightmare of the teenager's healing process.

Careful not to add to the mental suffocation her expression indicated, Ethan refrained from pulling her into his arms. "But it's not you... and she survived."

Despite Lexi's fierce independent streak and self-control, Ethan gently rubbed her back in a soothing gesture of support, ignoring Larrick's raised brow.

"Barely, and she'll never be the same. You know that," Lexi murmured. Her small shuffle-step sideways signaled her reserves fortified.

"I know." With no way to refute her words, he handed her a pair of gloves with the hope of putting this task behind them quickly. "Let's see what's on her computer and cell, then get you out of here."

Ethan righted the chair and guided Lexi to sit. Within minutes, she was surfing through the laptop's files and email accounts. Her fierce concentration appeared to block out the horrors of the room's recent tragedy, a testament to her resolve.

A motion from the other side of the room compelled him to his partner's side. Larrick's expression merged a bit of shock with *WTF.*

"Caden said they found something in the backyard you need to see... and deal with. They've bagged it and are waiting by the van out front. I'll stay here with your girl."

After a quiet word with Lexi, Ethan strode out, puzzled over his partner's hesitant if discreet warning. To his knowledge, Lexi hadn't known Zoe personally. If Larrick had suspected some sort of conflict with Lexi examining the computer, he would've said something and denied her access.

Outside, one of the techs stood by the crime scene van's open sliding door. "Detective Robertson said you'd want to see this before we left." From the vehicle's interior, he pulled out a plastic bag containing a black jacket with a stitched quote on the back. The part visible read, *'Four Paws.'*

Ethan shoved his hands in his pockets to keep their shaking unnoticed. "Anything else?" Either the psycho was trying to implicate Lexi or left the items as a taunt. The former he could handle. There was no way the killer would get his hands on her. Most likely, his intentions would soon be posted on the dark net.

"Yeah, we found some dried blood on some branches at the edge of the woods. It'll take a bit to see if the DNA matches anyone in the database." Tilting his head to the side, the tech said, "You look pale. Everything okay?"

Lexi bled on the pet store's counter, but it wasn't there when I showed up.

"Thanks for the show and tell. Yeah, I'm all right, just a washout from the shooting."

Caden padded up beside his brother. "Your perp is having a busy morning."

Bile rose in his throat as Ethan headed around the back of the house with Caden keeping pace. It was doubtful they'd find anything, but a few minutes of fresh air would help clear his mind. His gut dictated the blood would match Lexi's DNA.

The question outstanding... *Is Lexi's DNA in the system?* Obviously, she'd removed any traces of her presence, but the killer had his own set of tech skills.

"You okay, dude?" Caden asked as they made a circuit of the yard's perimeter.

"Yeah, this guy—he wasn't the bastard who shot me. He was too thin."

"Crud." Caden rubbed the back of his neck as if trying to remove the weight of someone's stare. "Hey, Look at this. Tracks from some kind of wagon or cart. Odd since the homeowners don't seem to be big on gardening. I didn't see any cart in the garage. No barn here."

"Yeah, probably how he hauled his supplies."

"They lead to a dirt road not far from here according to the tech."

"Screwball sure does plan ahead."

"He left another riddle, Caden."

Item one is a staple for all children. Items two and three can make these curious creatures cry in desperation. Combined, they draw the last. So soft, cuddly, and warm, their chattering signals the end in sight.'

I'll be darn if I know what it means, Ethan."

"Great. We'll put our heads together and figure it out. At least Zoe is alive."

The yard search yielded nothing new except the realization that Ethan needed to face facts. He wanted Lexi's presence in his home permanent, something never considered with a woman before. She was different from anyone he'd ever known. And finally, if he was going to protect her, he needed to step up his game, despite her resistance.

By the time he and Caden had retraced their steps to the house, Lexi and Larrick were waiting by the front door.

"Find anything?" Anxiety roughened Ethan's voice. It was time to get Lexi clear of the horrific mess. The longer they took to catch the killer, the more embroiled she became.

"No, techs said they took a cast of the tracks out back. Some kind of cart. One thing... you should give your IT guys a heads-up. I assume they've already done this, but they need to put all their case notes on a standalone." Lexi took a deep breath and looked around the front yard as if feeling the weight of someone's stare.

"Standalone?" Larrick asked, keeping pace toward Caden's vehicle. "You think computers are shy?"

"A source that doesn't go on the net. If I can hack it, the killer can, too." Turning to Larrick, a bit of her former sass emerged. "And let me guess, you believe the letters *D e l* on the keyboard stand for *deliver*."

"Funny, kiddo. Very funny." Larrick's shoulder bump ended with Lexi's stumble-step into Ethan.

The smile reached her eyes, chasing away the shadows if only for a few heartbeats. Her acceptance of Ethan's hand on her waist for support felt natural and something that belonged.

All too quickly, she pulled away, the glance over her shoulder betraying the horrid images running through her mind. "Did Zoe know the killer was going to give her a fatal acid bath?"

"I don't know. I pray she never knows. She has enough to deal with as it is." Ethan wondered at the extent of Lexi's trauma in dealing with the pimp who'd stalked her months ago. It was a subject she usually glossed over except to say she was physically unscathed.

"I'll get the others up to speed." Caden's jaunty salute belied the seriousness of his intentions. "Later, guys."

Soon, each of the McAllister brothers would be all over the case. Division names never came between the brothers' assistance.

Caden hesitated before asking, "Um, Lexi, you want me to hang out with you for a bit? I'm much more entertaining than Ethan."

"Nah, I'm fine. I've got the best company anyone could ask for—two dogs."

"Ha. Put Ethan in his place. Good girl." Caden smirked as he sauntered to his car.

Ethan stayed Larrick's passage to his own vehicle with a hand at his elbow. "We need to talk. Soon."

"Station. Get Lexi settled and meet me in thirty." Judging by his expression, Larrick realized it would be a tough discussion.

A dark premonition warned of Lexi soon landing in the crosshairs of the sick mind they sought. When Ethan opened the passenger side door, Lexi was ready with the obvious. "We need to solve this riddle. Figure it out *before* he strikes."

Her tone echoed the frustration roiling in his gut. He couldn't get back on the road soon enough.

"How did he acquire that much acid in the first place?" Ethan wondered how much help their psycho had enlisted in preparing the latest scene. "Smelled like a surfeit of skunks set up camp on the porch."

"Sulfuric acid, you can distill it from battery acid obtained from any big box store. Only takes a few days, and this guy apparently enjoys his prep time."

"How's a young lady your age know that?" Scant traffic in the remote setting lent a surreal layer of woodsy elegance to the setting. His own house was equally remote.

And Lexi has a proverbial X on her back.

She just smiled and shook her head. "I studied hard to get my GED, and they started teaching high school chemistry in the twentieth century."

I'm not that old.

That reminder helped steer his thoughts away from the one activity guaranteed to clear his mind. Quiet introspection contributed to the eerie silence between them.

"I just don't get it. This riddle. Usually, I'm pretty good with puzzles." Lexi held Ethan's phone, staring at the picture of the latest riddle.

Lower lip tugged between her teeth indicated the depth of her focus if not the specific direction. "Staple for all children—does he mean a specific food like peanut butter or something broader spectrum like a roof over your head?"

"Items two and three—something that makes curious creatures desperate—does he mean cry in fear, anger, or something else?" Ethan glanced at his enigma, thoroughly immersing her thoughts in the riddle. "Cats are curious."

Lexi picked up where he'd left off. "And the last part, lots of things are soft and warm, but dangerous and cuddly? Is he talking about a rabid animal?"

"We'll figure it out." He just prayed they did it before the psycho came calling. "Listen. I need to go back to the station, if you'd like to come with me, that'd be nice." Ethan relaxed his grip on the steering wheel as each mile away from Zoe's house brought a little more color to her cheeks.

"No."

Winding through the woods leading to his home offered a new perspective on how a woman might view the setting as isolated and foreboding. When his house came into view, what he now saw was a secluded area that would set the killer's mouth to watering.

"Ethan. I'm fine. Look at the bay window. Both dogs are watching our approach. You forget how long I survived on the streets."

You still haven't felt comfortable enough to reveal all your trials and ordeals.

"All right. Tell me this. Is your DNA or fingerprints in the system? Because if they are, I need to know."

"Trust me, you won't find me in any official database, anywhere, in any form."

"You mean the last time you checked, and don't expect to get your jacket and cap back." That was as much as he'd say, though in truth, he'd already crossed so many lines it no longer mattered.

The small O of her mouth and widened gaze denoted her putting the pieces together.

"Yeah, I figured I'd never see them again. They were my favorites." The fact that her expression turned pensive should've been warning enough.

Ramming the gearshift into park didn't relieve his pent-up frustration. "It's gonna have your DNA on it." *Why am I bothering to talk in code?*

"I know, but sometimes those tests, the samples just get mixed up or tossed accidentally, ya know?" With one hand on the door handle, Lexi hesitated. Her mouth opened and closed twice before she shook her head and opened the door.

How could he explain or expect her to accept all of his protective instincts when he couldn't anticipate the killer's moves? "If not for you, Zoe would be dead by now."

Understanding someone's independent streak didn't relieve the stress or its consequences. Regardless of her skewed moral compass, her heart was pure and her objective clear, which wouldn't grant her protection from a crazed killer.

"All right. I'll check out the house before leaving. Then I'll be gone for a few hours, but I'll call to check on you. Keep the doors locked and the dogs inside."

"No, I don't need you to check under the beds or behind the curtains. I got this. I have some work to do, too. Then I want to poke around on the web for a bit." There was a hesitancy in her movements in getting out and circling the vehicle's front as if her sixth sense cautioned restraint.

He met her at the door and entered first. It was the least he could do. Both dogs bounced around in greeting as he secured his home. All the while, his conscience debated her intended actions.

She's gonna tamper with evidence. If he stopped her, other women would die.

His intuition rarely misfired, and his gut forewarned of a dark prescience in his near future. Something evil had cast its net over them both. He could feel the sick mind toying with her, but for how long? A week, maybe two? What would happen when playing cat and mouse became boring?

The ride back to the station tested his willpower when with each mile; his heart compelled him to turn around.

A firing squad would've appeared friendlier than Larrick's expression when Ethan entered the squad room. Rarely had he seen his partner's feathers so ruffled.

"Well?" Larrick looked around the room.

Two other detectives immersed in a quiet argument at their desks on the other side of the room nodded at Ethan's entrance before returning to their animated discussion.

"Tell me that wasn't her jacket and blood, *partner*."

Ethan sighed. The subsequent conversation wasn't going to be easy. "Yeah, the jacket's hers, and I'm sure the blood would match if they had anything with which to compare DNA, but they don't. And before you ask, she wasn't there before Caden brought her." The springs in his chair protested his lack of grace in sitting. The burden of protecting a witness had never become so personal.

"Fine. The *only* thing I want to know is that she's a victim and not also playing on the other side of the fence." The older detective's sotto voice alerted Ethan to the strain in their working relationship.

"Absolutely not. I'd bet my life on it. However, it *does* appear the psycho has targeted her for a specific purpose. What that is—as yet—I don't know. You heard Zoe's attacker say that Lexi is next. He wants to play with her first, prove he's better or some such crap."

"If he's that good with computers, he'd know she isn't in the system," Larrick replied.

"Unless..." Ethan's flurry of motion over the keys tapped out an increasingly chaotic beat. "No, no, no. This can't be happening. She's here. It says here she's been arrested for everything from prostitution to identity theft." Helpless rage clenched his jaw as well as his fists. "I know darn well you've run her through the system. Tell me."

"Yeah, I got her tag from your brothers. They ran it also. Which means someone added this recently. Unfortunately, it'll take time to prove that no hard copies exist and all this is made up."

"Thanks, partner."

"Yeah, but our killer has targeted your girl as both pawn

and victim. The question remains, does the manipulation have any other purpose?" Larrick's chair squeaked when he pushed back to gain his feet.

"You go talk to the captain while I explain to our digitally diseased techs that Lexi's been cyber sacked."

"On it. I'm sure he can't wait to see my pretty face."

The path to the lab was paved with doubt and frustration, symbols of Ethan's current investigation's lack of progress. Knowing that Carl, head of their IT department, was intimidated by Lexi's technological fluency didn't help her cause.

The heavy glass door swung quietly on its hinges, allowing Ethan a moment to gauge his reception and structure his thoughts. He and Carl were friends after a fashion, a situation Ethan regretted not further solidifying.

"Hey, Carl. Where are your sidekicks?" How fortunate to catch the quiet techie alone.

"Ethan. I was going to call you. Jim is running an errand, and I came to finish a case confounding Timothy, who went home sick."

An otherworldly pit opening up on the floor and swallowing him whole would've imbued less pain than Carl's solemn expression.

"What's up?"

"Lexi."

No. That about summed up his life's outlook at the moment. "What about her?"

"She's in the database."

"What? No. I ran a background check on her months ago." His brothers always pointed out his tells when lying. He prayed nothing gave him away now.

"You always run a background check on your girlfriends?"

A slight gleam added a calculating intensity to Carl's gaze.

Ethan was prepared. "Actually, it was when we first met. She kinda has the race car driver attitude. So, caution and all that. What did you find, and how could I have missed it?"

"Oh, I'm sure you wouldn't have missed this juice. If I hadn't met her and looked into her past myself when she came here, I'd be freaking out for you right now." Carl swiveled his chair back to his computer and began tapping.

"See, the thing is, when we got to talking about router rape in the antisocial network, I'd checked to see if she had some type of record before permitting her access to my computers. I ran her prints from the keyboard, and everything came back clean."

From a folder on his workspace, Carl retrieved a picture of Lexi's nerd jacket. "This jacket was found at the scene, and I remembered it was the same one she wore here. Hence, I ran her through the system again. Look what I found."

Ethan didn't need to shoulder surf to know about the damning information. "How?"

"Yeah, she's a geek chick, but I didn't take her for someone to post her lady giblets online for advertisement. Looks like someone has it in for her pretty bad. They're also talented. Since I didn't save or print out the original run, I can't prove this is fake—yet."

"Damn."

"Yeah. If you inspect this up close, you can easily see some of the pics have been doctored. This would be a lot easier if you weren't flicking her bean, man." Carl shook his head. "I figured I'd give you a heads-up before I talk to the lieutenant. I can hold off for a day or so while the blood is processing, but if someone else in our department picks it up, we won't be able to help her, especially if the DNA is a match."

"Screw me sideways. She's not aligned with the killer. The prick has her in his crosshairs because she found him on the dark net." Having already given Carl the other dark site address and explaining the warped game, Ethan prayed the techie wouldn't screw him over.

"Does she have a name or photo, anything specific? Anything we can use to trace him?"

"No. Not yet."

"I'd say that gives you a limited window to find him since he's better at this game than me."

Ethan turned to leave, buried under the avalanche of misinformation, only to have his body freeze with Carl's last words.

"Ethan, I'm pretty good at what I do. I live and breathe this stuff. It's rare I'm so far outclassed. Digging up the proof to exonerate her will take a good chunk of time considering the charges are from Baltimore and Milwaukie. If she gets picked up and run through the system, she'll end up in a cell, probably with the company of *his* choosing."

Carl shook his head in disgust. "One more thing to consider. This cyberpunk may have intimate connections to these places. Just a thought to keep in mind. The pollen we talked about is from the Baltimore area. Another connection with Lexi."

Jeez, it keeps getting better.

"Got it. Oh, Carl. I assume you're using a standalone?"

"Hey, as good as this guy is, he's not getting into my systems. So catch this creep before she gets screwed over... or worse."

Chapter Twenty

Cool, fresh air didn't clear Ethan's mind any more than stomping the accelerator. Ratcheting anxiety accompanied every sunrise, knowing he'd leave Lexi alone in his house. Her text asking when he'd be home set wrong in his gut, a red flag without specifics.

Each day's passing had seemed to give them a new assortment of problems with the investigation, more questions than answers, more frustration than hope.

His brothers had taken turns during their downtime to maintain surveillance, but the afternoon's schedule allowed for a two-hour lag with no one nearby, which meant his concentration had been crap.

Another crack at Daryl and Whistler had provided nothing new besides the small satisfaction of leaning a little harder on the pervert. The extra motivation had everything to do with Ethan's growing desperation to protect a certain green-eyed hacker.

A slight vanilla scent lingered in his car, reminding him how much he sought her presence, either in person or in the subtle reminders that kept his mind in a steady state of lust. Rounding the last bend to his home brought a new tension that would encourage tailor-made nightmares.

In defiance of the chilly nights, colorful pansies bloomed in a terra cotta pot on his front steps. "Yep, so much for staying home. She decided to go to a garden center?" Thoughts of handcuffing her to a kitchen chair, living room coffee table, or even better, his bed, rose forefront in his mind.

Both dogs stood with front paws perched on the bay window as he opened his car door.

Lexi stood behind the furballs, nibbling her lower lip before quickly turning away. *Yeah, she knows she screwed up... again.*

He expected a hard set to her jaw and determination etched in every line of her face when he entered the front door, her self-reliance dictating an aggressive defense in respect to leaving the house.

Panic set in when he found it absent. Before he could speak, her rushed speech added to the anxiety filling the atmosphere.

"I couldn't sit still. I needed to do something." Her voice was thin, plaintive.

While he finished greeting his four-footed friends and regained his composure, she'd retreated to the kitchen. "I see you've been busy shopping."

"I took Hoover with me. We were only gone for a couple hours. We just wanted some flowers and some comfort food." A pasty complexion coincided with the trembling in her voice and fingers as she removed the canvas bag from the granite countertop. "When we came home..."

"No!" Ground-eating strides closed the distance to her side. What the bag had hidden sent ice circling up his spine.

No force on Earth could've prevented him from gripping her with trembling fingers but tight enough to keep her from moving. Chest-to-knee contact was the only thing keeping him physically and emotionally together. If possible, he'd lock her to his side, permanently. Only when her body softened against him did he realize the force of his grip.

Despite fear restricting his thoughts, other parts of his body expanded, reminding him of his talk with Larrick about the fear of losing a loved one.

"It was here when I got home a little while ago. I didn't

touch it. Diego was groggy but seems better now. Must've been tranqed with a short-acting sedative."

Ethan eyed the monstrous-sized vibrator on his kitchen counter. Altered to the psycho's specifications, it contained small nails jutting outward down its length with a razor blade protruding from the top.

"Why didn't you call me! And why are you still in the house?" Other thoughts refused to form while a nightmarish reel of Lexi's degradation and murder held sway in his imagination.

"I did. I texted you. There's no use in going anywhere. He's good enough to find me. I know he's been in my home because that's the only place he could've gotten some of those pictures he's altered."

"What are you talking about?" The cold blanket of fear spread icy threads to interweave mind and body. Carl's words now came back to him, their meaning clear.

"All the stuff he put on his site. He's claimed me as a mark, upping the ante by specifically naming me *and* getting creative with his graphics program." Abject fear marked her expression. "I've always tried to be invisible. The fact there were so few digital records to be found gave him carte blanche to manufacture whatever history suited his fancy. He was quite inventive."

"I saw what he added to the database and spoke with Carl in the tech department. He ran a check on you after we first visited, then again today."

"Did he save or print anything?"

"No, which means there's no proof of the records discrepancy until we have department clerks in those cities dig into their files."

"That's going to take time. Meanwhile..."

"Yeah, you're going to sit tight. Larrick has spoken at length to the captain, explaining how you've been targeted. He also spoke to our tech guys. They're looking into murders in other cities that may or may not be connected."

Ethan ignored her raised brow. Not disclosing details would make her curious and encourage her digging. At least that would occupy her mind.

"The brass hats know we have no other place to stash you. All our safe houses connect electronically in some way. I was planning on you staying here." Ethan's jaw clenched to the point of pain. "But maybe..."

"There's no place to go that he can't find me, Ethan. I don't want you to—"

"Do *not* finish that sentence. I'll take care of this and check the house. You stay here."

"Hoover would've let me know if someone were still here. Trust me."

"I do. I *don't* trust the psychotic killer after you." How was he going to protect her from an omnipresent evil? "I'll bag that thing and ask Larrick to pick it up."

* * * *

Lexi had learned early that divulging information in bits and pieces had its advantages. Though neither she nor Ethan drank to excess, a glass of wine would serve them well before puzzling out the meaning of the latest riddle.

At least she'd become familiar with Ethan's family, whom she expected to visit shortly. Despite their crude banter and good-natured bickering, they were close-knit, something that would've made her jealous had they not welcomed her into their world.

The removal of her stalker's physical taunt allowed sanity to return in slow, even breaths. Holding in emotions was a basic survival skill on the street. Nothing in her lifetime had prepared her for the tsunami of fear, guilt, and anger now washing through her soul.

"I have no right to embroil others in this mess." She handed Ethan a glass of wine as he sat beside her on the couch. By unspoken agreement, neither reached for the chess set.

"This *mess* is my job."

"How'd he get in, anyway?" It wasn't until she'd finished the wine that her fingers stopped shaking.

From Ethan's dark and heated expression, she knew his reflexive possessiveness dictated he keep her near yet respected her need to limit their interaction to his arm around her shoulders. The comforting scent of aftershave and pure Ethan was all she needed at the moment.

Ethan glanced around, his gaze lingering in the kitchen. "None of the doors or windows appear to have been tampered with, which leaves Diego's door. It's the one access not connected to my security system, so no alarms were tripped."

"He tranq'd Diego then used his collar to come through the pet door." She would've realized that had she been able to think clearly.

"Yep. I'll convert it after dinner."

"Ethan, there's more." Lexi opened her laptop on the coffee table. "He's listed details inside your house. The sex toy wasn't just a taunt. It was a statement of intent."

"No!" The stem of his glass snapped under his rage, splashing wine on the sofa and his slacks. Both stem and bowl landed on the sofa. "He will not get to you, Lexi."

Barely controlled fury echoed in his steps to the kitchen. At least the goblet's bowl wasn't in shards on the floor.

"My brothers will rotate staying with you when I'm working. We can arrange our shifts accordingly." Ethan jabbed at the crimson stains on his shirt with a damp towel.

For a while. Then what? His expression necessitated a roundabout approach for her plan to work. Arguing with a bull wouldn't lead her where she wanted to go.

"All right." His siblings' company would come with a price. The remnants of her privacy. The truth, not the crap splashed on the net.

Cut from the same cloth, each brother would chip away at the private life she'd endeavored to maintain. *Then again, what good is anonymity if you aren't alive to enjoy it?* And why would she still want it after they'd adopted her, quirks and all?

Dinner passed amid careful planning and quiet conversation with Ethan wearing his calm façade, well recognized by now.

It shouldn't have surprised her when Caden showed up with more surveillance devices or that Matt and Lucas had come to help install them. Each had given her curious stares, questions roiling in their gazes, yet they failed to voice them under Ethan's glare.

When they were finished outside, the slam of the back door startled her as Caden and Lucas followed Matt's long strides through the kitchen.

"Ethan. We found a couple of modified scouting cameras on the south perimeter of your woods. We'll let you know what we find from them." Matt held up a baggie with two ball-type cameras.

"Damn it. I should've checked the perimeter morning and

night." Ethan's fist clenched in his lap.

"It appears you've had other things on your mind." Luc's pointed nod to Lexi earned a growl. "Hey, I get it, you're protective. But it's time we all chipped in and helped a bit more, considering the circumstances." A sharp glance at the bagged evidence conveyed his meaning.

"I'm going to take them to my lab instead of the department's techs. Maybe they'll have better luck. Plus, I can push them." Caden's contacts as a private investigator allowed for a diversity of service providers that came in handy on occasion.

Ethan slid his hand under her hair and rested his fingers between the sofa back and her neck. Tension drained from her shoulders as his touch swirled among the fine hairs even as the rest of her body tightened.

"We've placed cameras at intervals along the house, with a couple more mounted from the attic that you can't see or get to easily. They'll be on separate circuits so if he finds the first ones, he might not search for the others. We should assume he's compromised my initial setup." Caden handed him a cell phone. "This is clean. Don't use it for anything but emergencies. You can punch up any camera in line or set it to rotate." The mood lightened with the offhand comment, "Lexi can show you how to work it."

After the men defined security measures, Lexi navigated online to the killer's website. Several short videos of her in the backyard working with the dogs exposed her vulnerability to all the perverts, psychos, and immoral deviants skulking the dark net. "These naked shots in the bathroom are not of me. The hacker superimposed my face on another woman's body."

"Figures. He's trying to get more mileage from his

audience." Lucas' expression changed slightly as he bent his head, attempting to peek underneath a silky bathrobe.

Ethan elbowed him in the ribs. "It doesn't work like that, hound dog."

The brothers' presence should've furnished a certain testosterone-laden comfort as each man matched Ethan in the bullheaded and overprotective aspects. Yet their departure left her in the soothing comfort of Ethan's presence, feeling safe and secure.

"I feel like I've taken over your home and your life." Even with all the preparations done, she realized the killer could outmaneuver any electronics placed in his path. "He isn't giving us any kind of timeline now. This is on his terms."

"Well, I have to admit, you've livened up my existence a bit. Now my brothers will stop wondering about our relationship, seeing how your stuff is here."

The familiar heat in his gaze warmed parts where her stalker could never touch. "Um, Lucas and Caden—"

"Are flirts, but harmless. Are you tired? I want to hold you."

The heat in his gaze woke all the tiny nerve endings not already sparking with electrical charges. The intent communicated through his nonverbal didn't compare to his subtle urging. It was as if she'd detected and responded to the invisible pheromones wrapping her mind and body with a compulsive need she couldn't deny.

"Ethan—" How could she explain her uncontrollable obsession to be with him every night but then sleep alone in the other room? Each night they were together saw her slipping out after he'd drifted off. Some unnamed remnant of misguided self-preservation compelled her to return to the spare bedroom. Another invisible wall at which he chipped away. She trusted him with her life, but not her heart?

"I won't ask you to remain in my bed. You'll spend the entire night when you're ready. It's just your instincts not ready to listen to your heart." The sad smile gracing his lips cut deep.

As usual, he seemed to know what she was thinking, putting her at ease before she'd spoken. "We fit in every way imaginable. But…"

"Hey. Don't think about that now. Let's enjoy what we have instead of fretting over what we don't."

"I want you." In fact, she wanted it all—picket fence, home-cooked meals, and cozy nights together. It was the first time in her life she thought it possible.

From the moment she'd begun digging on the dark net, she'd known she'd somehow end up in the killer's sights. They'd done everything they could to keep her safe. Life always found balance.

Ethan was in a class unto himself, always analyzing, forever compiling information in his mind. She couldn't read him the way he read her, except when lust darkened his gaze.

"Since your bedroom and the bathrooms are lacking a visual monitor, if you take a nap tomorrow, do it on the sofa where I can see you. Regardless that one of my brothers will be here, I want to be able to see you." Without another word, he scooped her up and carried her to his bedroom, the gentleness of settling her on the bed so contradictory to the volcanic expression of his eyes.

"Maybe I'll nap in your bed, nude."

A darkening gaze joined forces with the hiss of his quick inhale to let her know she'd hit her mark. He'd suffer her longing until their bodies joined, entwining flesh and blood, mind and spirit, in a rhythm deliciously forceful and leaving them breathless and sated.

"I want to taste you. You never let me play." Each time they'd come together, he'd controlled their movements despite her pleas to let her mouth and fingers roam the thick muscles and planes of his body.

"Not tonight."

In painstaking degrees of gentle seduction, he removed her clothes, then his own, all the while holding her in place with the heat of his gaze. He embodied a mixture of dark and light, a complex weave of threads bridging a cold and dark determination with the warmth and geniality that defined his inner shell.

She recognized their similarities and wondered why no one had delved within to find the balance where peace nestled. He'd compared her to a butterfly emerging from her chrysalis with small, wet wings, not yet ready to fly.

She soared every time they came together.

His brushing glides and soft advances pressed her to the mattress in anticipation of the thrilling ride to come.

"You're beautiful."

It was impossible to look away as tiny pulses of energy flowed along each nerve pathway to tighten her muscles. She merely stared in wonder since her torrid mouth denied the possibility of speech. His steady prowl from the foot of the bed ensured her body was ready and inviting before he began his sensual assault.

As if sensing the direction of her thoughts and the heat pooling in her core, Ethan settled over her body. Face to face, he bound her with a strength of will that echoed throughout his character.

Their breaths mingled. Still, he didn't move. Instead, the craving reflected in his eyes skimmed the edge of a deeper connection, forged by mutual strengths and need through an unbreakable bond. An unspoken promise for the future. He would protect her with his dying breath.

"I won't lose you, Alexandra."

She breathed a new fire in his soul while he stormed her defenses. The backlash united them in a way neither could've foreseen, unbreakable and impermeable.

Her thin mewl filled the room.

Ambient moon glow caught the set of his jaw, shaded darker with the day's growth and hardened with determination. He owned the space with a confidence that set her teeth on edge. She'd seen well-built men before, albeit clothed, but had never felt compelled to know the feel of the smattering of hair under her fingertips.

Ethan's solid wall of muscle set the bar at a whole new level. His "V" framed the sculpted muscles that stood out from the plane of his abdomen in bold relief, begging for her exploration.

Damn.

"You okay?" He tilted his head to the side.

The husky timbre of his voice coiled around her lungs to squeeze until a quiet gasp brought a flush of heat to her face. "Of course. I was just thinking about doing some shopping." Though she'd never before worn a thong, a black lacy one just made it to the top of her list as she imagined herself posing on the bed while he was working, knowing he'd check his security system periodically.

"Shopping? Hmm, guess it's time to step up my game."

His quiet chuckle livened all the nerve endings in her lower belly. Judging by the gravel in his voice, he currently dealt with his own issues.

"Please, I need…"

"You need to stop talking and just feel."

A languid comfort settled her thoughts after their breaths slowed to normal.

When she woke during the wee hours of the morning, her first attempt to stir ended with Ethan snugging her tight.

"Stay with me." Yearning infused the request. He wouldn't force her, but the need in his voice echoed in her heart.

For the first time since she'd become an orphan living on the street, she'd found someone solid, someone permanent to hold onto with all the strength she could muster. Nestling in his embrace instilled peace and let sleep take her once more.

Chapter Twenty-One

Despite the muted rays of light warming her face, the world felt off-kilter. Without opening her eyes, Lexi listened to the quiet puffs of Hoover's breath against her wrist.

The comforting warmth of her dog against her leg dispelled years of strain from restless sleeping habits yet didn't satisfy the unfathomable need twisting her gut. An emptiness she couldn't define coiled around her heart until she realized—Ethan was gone.

The strong aroma of fresh-brewed coffee snapped her gaze open.

"Morning, sunshine. I was wondering when you'd wake up." Ethan pushed off from the doorframe to sit on the edge of the bed. A cup of coffee in each hand sent curls of steam to dissipate in the air.

"You're already awake?" How had she slept through him getting out of bed and taking a shower?

"Awake, cooked breakfast, fed the dogs, and briefed Caden." Ethan handed her a hot mug after she sat up. "By the way, he's very curious about you. Feel free to curb his questions with your usual sass. He'll back off."

"I don't need a babysitter, Ethan." Though she'd never drank it much before, morning coffee had become one of her favorite rituals. Just the presence of the inviting fragrance lent a sense of calm to her frazzled nerves.

"Did you honestly think I'd leave you here alone knowing that psycho has been here? In my *home*?"

"I have the dogs and two guns. I've proven I can hit what I target. Just like a shutterbug, point and shoot."

"Dogs can't call for backup—and shooting another human being is different from nailing a bottle."

"Fine. But I won't take it easy on Caden with chess."

"I would expect nothing less. I'll come home for lunch around noon." The furrow in his brow deepened as he looked out the window.

"I know that look, Ethan. You can't set up surveillance outside. He'll know it. He'll just wait us out."

"We've removed his cameras, but he's persistent. The only reason he hasn't gotten Zoe is because of the new identity and temporary relocation." Scrubbing a hand over his eyes existed as one of his tells.

Outside, dark clouds boiled across the sky in preparation for Mother Nature's restless outburst. Unlike Hoover, whom she'd swaddle in a snug t-shirt and make a comfortable bed in the bathtub, she loved storms. Snuggling under the covers and watching the fury of the elements lash the Earth instilled a natural calm.

"I'll be out in ten minutes. No, make it fifteen. I want to savor the coffee."

Unlike women who pampered themselves with exotic soaps and alluring lotions, Lexi had always preferred a simple scent. The drive to primp was new and layered a film of insecurity as to what Ethan would like. With no field experience, she was reduced to trial and error to see what sparked the greatest reaction.

By the time she padded into the great room, he was preparing to leave, giving his youngest brother last-minute directives as if Caden were a child. "And listen, don't give her a hard time."

Ethan's frown in the face of her extra time and applying a little makeup brought the stark realization that he'd think she'd preened for Caden. A misconception she could fix later.

"Ya know, I survived on the streets for years. I think I can manage your brother for a few hours." Lexi hoped her smile took the sting out of her sarcasm.

"Thanks, darlin'. But I don't get *managed.* However, I do think we can find amusing entertainment while big brother is away." Needling each other was what these men did—pure and simple.

"Knock it off, Caden." Ethan directed his attention to Lexi then the chess set. "Help yourself to breakfast before whipping his butt. I'll see you around lunchtime."

"And I thought you'd have nothing to do with whips, bro. Good for you, traveling to the Dark Side."

It appeared the brothers had a lot in common in their ability to hold their own. She chuckled at Ethan's contemplative expression before he popped Caden in the shoulder.

Ethan's breath-stealing kiss after wrapping her tight in his arms would leave no uncertainty in his brother's mind about their relationship. He'd already put his stamp on her heart. Now he advertised that possession to his family. The silent hallmark of ownership pronounced a new beginning for her, one where she was coveted and protected in a world of chaos and senseless murder.

An odd sense of serenity mantled her shoulders despite Ethan leaving for work. If he didn't care, he wouldn't have kissed her until his brother cleared his throat. She'd re-center his thoughts at lunchtime and make darn sure Ethan knew he owned her heart. Last night he'd laid a claim neither could deny, in breaking down the last of her invisible walls and keeping her close until morning.

Breakfast passed with pleasant conversation that leaned strongly into friendly interrogation. She'd expected it in reference to her connection with Ethan. By nightfall, the rest of the brothers would be up to date on whatever she shared.

Throughout the morning, Caden's cocky attitude distracted as well as entertained despite the stress bearing down on her like a runaway freight train. Every family needed a wisecracking smart-mouth for stress relief.

Caden fell hard in the first match but gave her a run for her money with the second game of chess. He enjoyed a fast learning curve while proving a shrewd and intelligent adversary.

"You play well. Your strategy is improving." Lexi smiled as they reset each tier and attack board.

"It's never been my thing, but I'd love to crush Ethan at least once." Caden twisted his lips in a grimace.

"Ethan employs a conservative opening but then ramps it up during the middle game. In the final stage, though, he still keeps his king back instead of using it to his full advantage."

"He's always been a bit overprotective." Caden's inquisitive frown vanished with Hoover and Diego's sudden barking at the same time the lane sensor alert sounded. "We've got company."

Lexi jumped to her feet, the previous veil of low-key banter shredded under a pall of trepidation. Ethan wasn't expected for hours, and he would've advised of any expected deliveries.

Caden nudged her away from the bay window before striding to the front door. "You expecting anyone, Lexi?"

"No, and I don't recognize the Chevy sedan in the drive, either."

"All right. Just wondering if Ethan had any competition.

Stay put 'till I see who it is." Caden's smirk detailed knowledge of her intimate connection with his brother. Only the steady fingers on the gun handle at his waistband betrayed the serious undercurrent of caution.

Acid rose to the back of her throat.

Caden peered through the peephole before his squint morphed into a smile. "It's just Carl. He must have some news and came in person for bragging rights." Caden opened the door, the gust of cool wind and fallen blossoms accompanying the wiry tech's arrival. "Since when do you make house calls?"

"Hey, folks. Sorry to barge in on you like this. Is Ethan here yet? I spoke with him on the phone, told him he'd want to see this away from the station." A sympathetic wince accompanied his words. "I came because I knew you'd want to see it too, Lexi. This waiting has to be hard on you."

Caden stepped back to allow the nerdy tech to pass. "Haven't talked with Ethan since breakfast. Join us for some coffee."

"Thanks. Sounds great, but I'll have tea. I carry a special blend in my case." Metallic clicks of his briefcase opening after placing it on the kitchen table earned Hoover and Diego's curiosity. Each continued to sniff the newcomer's khaki pants. Hoover whined before retreating to her corner bed. "Glad your kids are friendly. They must smell my Chihuahua. Wanna try some of this?" Carl tapped a small tin and waggled his brows as if he held a prize.

"Caden?" Lexi dangled a third ceramic cup from her fingers, waiting for his answer.

"Sure, why not?" Caden took a seat across from the tech.

From his colorful tin, Carl retrieved a small carton of tea bags. "Try one of these, they're wonderful. I belong to an exotic steeper's club. Why don't you guys sample this Turkish apple? It's an herbal tea that'll help whatever ails you." Carl handed Lexi two wrapped tea bags. "I'm going to have Himalayan orange this morning. I need the extra caffeine." Carl's solid frame settled into the chair before its scraping forward on the tile floor made him cringe. "Sorry." The oversized white jacket worn while working in the lab seemed to be a part of him, yet it seemed he'd gained a little weight.

Hoover and Diego both whined while Lexi nuked three mugs of water in the microwave. After placing the cups on the table and dropping a bag in each, she gave the dogs a chewy treat.

Once she placed sugar and milk on the table, she sat beside the tech in anticipation. "Okay, what did you find?"

"I was kind of hoping to wait for Ethan—this guy is clever as all get out." Carl cursed as his fingers fumbled with retrieving his laptop.

"He can catch up when he arrives. Let's see what you've got." Caden looked over the tech's shoulder until a suggestive throat clearing urged him to take a seat on his other side. "Sorry, Carl. Just anxious to get this idiot." The cup of tea failed to hide his sheepish grin.

"It's all right. I really have to concentrate and be more careful. I picked up some cyber crabs the other day."

"Time for a porn purge?"

Caden's needling went unchecked.

Small talk and a rundown of all their acquired information followed as Carl continued to relate his findings to date. "I figured if I started from the beginning, maybe I'd pick up on something I've missed, and I was right."

"This tea is really good." Studying their guest, Lexi

frowned. Something about Carl's smile struck a note of anxiety in her chest, but the remarkable blend seemed to soothe her apprehension.

"I'm with Lexi. This tea really is good. Looks like you may have a couple more members for your club. I'm gonna grab another cup. Lexi, you want some?" Caden pushed his chair back and stood, his foot snagging the wooden leg, necessitating a short hop to catch his balance.

"Not just yet."

"It has a full, robust apple fusion." Carl grinned. "I've found people dying to try it. Always singing its praises all the way to the heavens."

"Hmm. Maybe I'll serenade us with a tune," Caden murmured, his voice a little slurred.

The tech's grin dropped on one side to form a faint sneer. "What I found last night concerns you, Lexi." Carl turned his laptop for Lexi to have a better look.

Choking on the last of her tea, Lexi grabbed a napkin from its holder in the table's center. "What has that freak cooked up in his fried brain now?" The depiction on the screen wiped away any remnants of comfort, leaving Lexi feeling off balance and cold. She hated anything to do with rats.

Laughter from the forensic tech took on a more sinister flavor as he shut his laptop. Without hesitation, he began unbuttoning his shirt.

"What's happening?" Caden stumbled back to the table in disjointed steps, confusion and disorientation written in his unfocused gaze. Flailing his hands for balance meant a free fall of his drink. "I can't—" His mug shattered on the floor, sending tea and ceramic shards in all directions as he groaned and reached for his chair.

"I don't feel so good either." Lexi fumbled with her cell,

unable to focus on the buttons before it crashed to the floor.

"I figured my little concoction would work quickly on you, Lexi, being a female with a slight frame. You surprise me, Caden. I didn't take you for a lightweight."

"Bastard." Caden's attempt to sit ended with a loud thump as he landed on the floor and banged his head against the kitchen cabinet. A low groan escaped his lips. His eyelids fluttered shut.

Instead of covering a beer belly, parting his shirt revealed Carl's secret, hidden from the world. The flesh-colored storage compartments in his body suit had added what looked like twenty pounds. After lifting a hook and loop strap, he withdrew a small tranq gun.

Hoover whined, her snuffing at Lexi's knee conveying doggy confusion. Diego's nudging of Caden's chest conveyed similar worry until a dart pierced the canines' necks. Sudden yelps converted to threatening growls. Each paced several steps before dropping to the floor.

Lexi's eyelids refused her command to lift despite fear pumping adrenaline through her system at an alarming rate. Varying shadows of gray darkened her world. Still, she sensed his intentions in the cruel laughter that echoed around her.

"You prick." Slurred speech and fuzzy thoughts instilled a fear she'd never known. Realizing death approached didn't scare her as much as knowing it would be terrifying, slow, and viciously agonizing.

"Yes, little girl, that about sums it up. Simple, eloquent, and to the point." He laughed. A deep, rough grind that could sear any soul.

Distantly, Lexi realized the plastic wrist restraints Carl applied to Caden then herself signified the least of her worries.

* * * *

"I've watched and laughed at you imbeciles for months. Each day a McAllister came into my realm seeking information, I plotted the best way to reinforce my superiority in a public way but came up short." Carl snatched Lexi by the shirt collar and jerked her out of her chair.

"It wasn't until you got involved, little one, that I envisioned my greatest performance. Every minor setback you thought you delivered merely served to further my plan." Working in the forensics lab had allowed him to navigate both sides of the investigation with ease.

"Now, I can take you away from the arrogant Ethan McAllister and remove you, Caden, from your family. That'll give them years of guilt and grief." He sighed when glancing back at Caden.

"Sometimes fate just hands me a gift I can't deny. I was hoping to catch the youngest of the siblings here today. I think families grieve hardest when they lose the last born."

It took a bit of manipulation to maneuver Lexi's body over his good shoulder. "Darn cops." His left arm, grazed by a bullet, still caused him pain, but to see his plan fulfilled brought a significant high. "As much as I'd like to enjoy your body, Lexi, I'm afraid I don't have the time. I didn't even know I had a taste for young, succulent flesh until I enjoyed Zoe."

Her uncoordinated attempt to throw herself off his shoulder forced him to stumble back against the refrigerator and sent a burning sensation through his injured arm. The sudden pain from her bite necessitated drastic measures, ones he'd enjoy implementing. Yanking her braid controlled her head enough to deny her access to do further harm.

"You'll pay for that, sweets. Believe me—you'll pay. I kinda liked your spirit and appreciated your mind, one super nerd to another. I was even going to drug you, so you didn't see the end coming. Now I think I'll just let you watch. The stuff I'm gonna give you should wear off in about twenty minutes, at least the bulk of it will. Your lack of coordination and strength in trying to defend yourself will make for great footage...I can't wait for you to see what's coming."

Good preparation was the basis for success in any plan. Today was no different. Within minutes, he'd laid her on the floor of the mudroom and cut away her clothes. "It's time for you to rest. I'll come back to strip you and prepare your body."

The vial of home-crafted drug pulled from his pouch would slow her body's defenses yet allow her mind to process his actions and hear every word spoken. Jamming the needle in her arm, he smiled at her slurred epithets.

"I'll be back in a bit. I'm going to test a slow-acting, lethal poison on Caden and retrieve my supplies after taking care of security details. I'll bet you're surprised that I hacked Ethan's latest security. I can't tell you how much it drove me crazy when Caden made the first one a LAN. Once the latest cameras were connected online, I knew I had you. But to tell the truth, I've been listening to your conversations off and on since I shot Ethan."

Carl smiled at the thought of getting two birds with one stone. "I've distilled a special concoction and want to film Caden's downward spiral so I can calculate future doses based on his height and weight. Be back in a bit."

It frustrated him to not enjoy the little hacker sexually,

but Ethan had become unpredictable since meeting her. *Priorities. Always priorities.*

Erasing the feed from the time he'd arrived was easy. "And just to make sure I don't get disturbed this time, I think I'll send lover boy a message. Let's direct him to bring some crab bisque in a bread bowl from his favorite restaurant across town. He loved it the last time I was here. I've heard you two discuss it. Bet you can't figure out how. This will give me at least another hour, though it shouldn't take long to learn where Caden sent *my* cameras."

After he'd returned and stripped her naked, he smeared a specially prepared emulsion over her flesh. Her murderous gaze flashed an inner fire while he laughed at her uncoordinated attempts to move her limbs.

With the groundwork in place, Carl hustled to set his simple but elegant plan in motion. By the time he'd spread the slurry of peanut butter, moist cat food, and tuna fish all over Lexi's naked flesh, she was beginning to gain rudimentary movements.

Chapter Twenty-Two

Gray edging her vision's periphery tunneled down and threatened to unravel Lexi's waning reserves, but fear of passing out again kept her thoughts reviewing everything she knew about Carl and his dark net activities. She'd felt he was *off*. Many would say the same about her.

She'd chalked it up to being a nerd.

Terror had not co-inhabited her mind for years. Now, her heart beat so hard and erratic, she didn't think she'd stay conscious. Hours ago, she'd been in the mudroom, appreciating the separate space for keeping jackets and hats, along with having extra storage. Now, she'd die in the very room admired.

The horrific smell of the oily compound smeared over her body made her skin crawl while images of possible scenarios of her future flashed through her thoughts.

The riddle.

In the miasma of odors assaulting her senses, she recognized peanut butter—the staple of a kid's diet. Tuna fish and cat food completed the malodorous scent filling her lungs.

Cats are curious.

It was the third part of the riddle that instilled terror. Something soft, cuddly, warm, something that chatters would end her life. They wouldn't be demented kittens.

Pulling and twisting at her bindings only succeeded to further abrade her skin. Living long enough to acquire an infection wouldn't be a problem.

Tight bonds and remnants of the drug in her system made it difficult to twist her body to a sitting position. A headache was the least of her worries.

She sat naked and bound on the floor, covered in a smelly concoction with a camera set up on a tripod mere feet away. "Where's the creep and what is he doing?" Her mangled words failed to provide any illumination of her assailant's plan. "I stink."

When the pocket door slid open to reveal Carl bearing a cage, she failed to discern its contents. "Looks like a fuzzy rug. You gonna smother me?"

"Ahh, well that wore off quickly. You must enjoy a better than average metabolism, probably what keeps you in such great shape."

"Screw you."

"Unfortunately, we don't have time. I am, however, anxious to witness this scene." Carl looked at his watch. "I should have, at bare minimum, ninety minutes left. Matter of fact, I think I'll bring Caden in to watch—for as long as he's conscious."

The wire cage reminded her of a movie where similar crates housed the results of scientific experiments. When it landed on the tile floor with a thump, what she thought was a rug *squirmed*, each piece independent of the next.

She prayed it was vestiges of the drug that induced a hallucination of many rats stirring then settling.

"I'll be right back with your *protector,* dear." The sneer in Carl's tone couldn't be mistaken.

Minutes passed while the dark side of Lexi's thoughts served up bloodcurdling images of the future. Her very short future.

A desperate look around yielded no inspiration of how to ward off the red-eyed demons when they charged, and they would. She lacked the coordination to move effectively, even if her visual search had yielded something within reach to aid in her defense.

A brief glimmer of her first days as an orphan on the street flashed in her mind. A dirty alley, huddling behind a dumpster listening to a man beating his woman. Then, she saw them. Large, red eyes, the little beasts chittering as if laughing at her situation.

Several clunks and thuds brought her back to the moment as Carl dragged Caden over the threshold between hardwood and linoleum flooring and depositing him beside her.

Caden's eyelids fluttered over an unfocused gaze, his face a study of pain and confusion. His mouth hung slightly open with drool slipping from one corner.

"Here, I brought you some company. I'm anxious to see if the rats have any interest in him, seeing as how he has no aromatic enticement coating his skin." Two clicks and a green light on the video camera's front verified its readiness to record.

"I should make it a bit more interesting, though. Let's see if your new friends are attracted to blood. I wasn't quite clear with the trainer on that point." A small-bladed knife taken from his pouch gleamed in the light. "A few cuts across his forearms will do nicely."

Putting thought to action, he sliced Caden's arms in several places, allowing thin trails of crimson to ooze from each and collect on the floor. When finished, he backed up to admire his handiwork. "A good scene, well prepared. Now I can start the recording remotely and enjoy the show."

"You're a sick scumball, Carl." Lexi tried to reach Caden's neck to check his pulse. The cold tile against her bottom sent chills up her spine and reminded her she had no barrier against the small horde soon to be unleashed. Caden groaned when her bound and clumsy body fumbled, and she fell against him.

"He's still alive. Actually, he should be waking soon from the temporary sedation. The poison won't kill him 'till sometime tomorrow. Shame they won't be able to identify the toxin to make the antidote any more than trace the video camera's origins. I do love experimenting with exotic drugs."

Anticipatory glee rivaling any psychopath etched his expression as he lifted the side of the cage and locked it open. "As an added bonus for my fans, I'll add clips of Ethan mourning the decline and death of his baby brother. My ratings will go through the roof."

"Rats don't attack people. They're more afraid of us than vice versa." Lexi's bravado faltered in the face of the squirming mass stirring to life.

"Normally this is true. Kudos to your trivial education, surely learned from the gutter. However, these are all males, hormonally altered and trained to be aggressive." His cunning smile grew wider.

"I found a very unique individual who specializes with these cute but vicious little devils." From within another *pocket,* Carl pulled a small cylindrical object. "

See this? It activates the chips embedded in their necks and drives the little buggers crazy. They've been conditioned to attack and will do so as long as this is on. And for the cherry on top, I'll hide it, so that maybe they'll even attack Ethan when he arrives too late to help you."

"You're a psychotic freak."

"Hmm, maybe. But I have to admit, this is more entertaining than kidnapping and selling women."

"What are you talking about?"

"Just a loose association with *The Collector.* No one you'll live long enough to meet. And you're welcome for that."

Caden groaned and slumped toward her in an attempt to gain the fetal position. "Ahh." Dry heaves jerked his body in rhythmic spasms. Labored breathing punched the air in quiet gasps.

"Caden? Open your eyes." Lexi awkwardly rubbed his cheek, trying to bring lucidity into a world gone amok. After an uncoordinated, frantic effort, she shouldered him to a semi-sitting position to lean between her and the cabinet. It was the best she could do with her hands bound.

With a glance at the black squirming pile of fur, Carl addressed his horde. "Bon appétit, little ones." Quiet footsteps bore him backward until he slid the pocket door closed.

As if on cue, a low chattering noise grew from the mass of writhing bodies, morphing to a hissing and squeaking nightmare. Red eyes gleamed with mal intent.

If she moved away from Caden, would the rats attack him because of his bleeding or favor the coating on her skin? Instinct told her to stay close and fend off the masses as the mini demons charged with death in their gazes.

* * * *

The hair on Ethan's nape pricked again. How many times had his gut churned since leaving the house?

"Hey, partner, Lexi getting to you that bad?" Larrick smirked in that particularly maddening way that declared, *I know about your kryptonite.*

"Something's wrong. I feel it." Ethan yanked his phone from its clip. With several swipes, he again pulled up images from his exterior cameras. Everything looked as it should. Inside, Caden and Lexi were locked in battle over the chess board.

"Yeah, why don't you check your security system for the hundredth time this hour? Maybe—"

"No. That's what it is. Why didn't I pick that up before?" Lunging to his feet, Ethan grabbed his jacket then raced for the door.

"What the heck? What's wrong?" Larrick struggled to catch up as they headed down the hall and out the exit.

"The camera out back. There's a red bird on the feeder." Ethan punched in Caden's number. The call went to voicemail. Cool air brushed his face and dried the sweat on his brow as they sprinted through the parking lot.

The fob skittered across the pavement after his shaking fingers dropped it. Snatching it up took precious seconds. Time his brother and soulmate might not have. He couldn't get in his car fast enough. In the back of his mind, the killer's taunt that anything Lexi could do, he could do better, surfaced.

"So you gonna arrest a bird? Got something against the little fella?" Larrick closed the passenger side door even as the car rocketed out of the lot and slewed onto the highway.

"No. It's been in the *exact* same position on the feeder for the last—I don't know—thirty minutes or so."

"Crap. Compromised electronics. Son of a gun." Larrick used his phone to notify dispatch of their situation.

"Yeah, that wasn't a text from Lexi wanting a special lunch. It was the psycho buying more time." Never in his life had there been so much to lose. The fact anyone got the upper hand with Lexi *and* Caden both shocked and enraged him to white-knuckled status.

Mile after mile, his inner demons conjured horrific images of his loved ones dying in new and demented degrees of madness. Long before his mind reconciled the facts, his heart had claimed Lexi as essential for his future, his every breath.

When he slid into his driveway and around the last bend, he offered yet another prayer. "No other vehicles present."

"Which doesn't mean they're alone...or even in the house."

Ethan cussed while fumbling with his front door lock. Lexi's scream generated a shake that spread through his limbs and tangled his nervous system's commands.

"Move over, I got this." Larrick stood to the side and unlocked the door, reaching for his gun with his other hand.

Terror took physical form in Ethan's chest, squeezing his lungs until he couldn't draw breath. Another scream accompanied by a hoarse shout indicated both Lexi and Caden still lived.

For the moment.

In a perverse sense of fate, the last riddle came to mind. *Something small, furry, deadly.*

When he shoved the front door open, Larrick grabbed his arm. "Wait, the dirtbag might still be here."

"No." Ethan would rather take a bullet than endure one more of Lexi's screams.

"Ethan. We're no good to them dead."

Racing strides carried Ethan through the great room to the kitchen, procedure be damned. The shrillness of Lexi's voice contrasted the hoarseness of Caden's shout.

Breath means life.

Sliding open the mudroom pocket door introduced him to a new version of purgatory his mind would never delete.

"Jesus!" Two shots fired into the ceiling did nothing to dispel the mass of fur and teeth swarming over Lexi and to a lesser extent Caden.

"Electronic device—somewhere nearby," Lexi gasped, her body twisting to avoid the living evil clawing and tearing at her skin. Some twined in her hair, squealing in their frenzy to either latch onto her bleeding flesh or get free from her tangled locks.

Inefficient swipes caused from bound wrists furthered the enraged creatures' agenda. "Cylinder—makes them aggressive. Psycho's gone." She slapped blindly at the furry creatures latching onto her belly and thighs. Several rodents lay dead at her bound feet.

Caden, leaning between her and the cabinet, contorted his body, his weak attempts to thrust the rodents away or snap their necks equally unsuccessful. Though Lexi's movements were slightly better coordinated, they'd both obviously been drugged.

Two dozen vermin appeared unorganized in their frantic attempts to bite, sometimes turning on each other in mindless rage. Muffled, choking sobs accompanied Lexi's frantic movements.

"Larrick, go, find the device." Never in his life had Ethan faced such a dilemma.

He couldn't take either victim out to leave the other behind, even temporarily. In rage and panic, he crashed the tripod holding the camera against the far wall in a bid to gain space.

Smashing one rabid-acting devil after another under the sole of his shoe reduced the swarm, but even as he watched, Caden's motions deteriorated into an uncoordinated frenzy.

Each beat of his heart sent another surge of terror racing

through his system as the enemy turned to him, biting, scratching, and clawing their way up his slacks. At least that lessened the threat to Lexi and his brother.

Ignoring the ripping through his trousers, he knelt between his brother and Lexi, fighting desperately to keep the mindless killers away from the tender flesh of faces and necks.

In response, the furry mass accepted the challenge and focused on him. He'd hear the high-pitched, frenzied chittering in their dreams for years to come.

Snapping spines of the crazed rodents prevented their movement, but not their deranged prattling.

Caden's uncoordinated thrashing, wrenching, and slapping at the converted carnivores accompanied his body ejecting his stomach's acidic contents. The mindless beasts reacted with more rage even as they slipped and skidded on his chest.

"Ethan." Billy's voice. "Oh, God!"

Larrick's agitated explanation pressed his brother to help find the controlling device.

"Screw that. It could be anywhere. Both of you, grab something sharp."

Heartbeats later, Billy reappeared on the threshold with a blade in each hand. Kneeling beside Caden and handing Ethan a weapon, he joined the ongoing horror of disengaging and killing the multitude of miniature nightmares before throwing them aside.

Terror, revulsion, and trepidation spiraled time down to each second in a fight to rid the captives of the rodent horde.

"Get them on top of the washer and dryer." Behind them, Larrick continued to fend off the crazed rats. Snarls of rage from the three conscious men filled the air.

"I'll grab Caden, you take Lexi." Billy cursed as one of the horde climbed up his arm. Beside him, Larrick plucked it off and twisted its neck.

Chaos continued as Ethan and Billy lifted their ungainly handfuls up and onto the appliances. Sobs and groans punctuated Lexi and Caden's continued nightmare even after the vermin ceased to reach them.

Caden's weak attempts diminished until he slumped against Lexi, who used her bound arms to keep him from falling forward.

"How can this happen?" Billy growled in response to the small beasts' attack. "Why?"

Larrick slashed at the rats that had now turned their collective attention to the three men, his shouting a mix of panic and anger as he helped put an end to the nightmare.

In the distance, Ethan heard sirens even as they reduced the surviving mass of deadly rage. Some were so tangled amid legs and tails that it took precious seconds to free themselves, seconds the men used to drive their knives through their furious squirming bodies.

When the force of their disorganized attack ended, and the last one had been killed, Ethan shuddered. "Help me get Lexi and Caden to the kitchen."

Fumbled movements saw his partner shouldering Caden to carry him away. Ethan scooped Lexi up and followed.

No amount of therapy would ever lessen the horror of seeing her fight the swarm while trying to protect Caden. He set her on the counter by the sink and dampened a cloth to clean her face. Having none of it, she wrapped her arms around his shoulders and wretched.

Hysterical sobbing at least lent him strength in the knowledge she still breathed. She would survive.

"Ambulance is on the way. Caden's not looking so good." Larrick laid Caden on the kitchen table while Billy checked his pulse.

"It's fast and weak."

"C-Carl. Its b-been Carl all along. He's the psycho." Lexi's hiccups and unfocused gaze accompanied her thin frame's uncontrollable shaking.

"What?" Ethan wrapped his jacket around her shoulders before searching for the worst of her wounds. Blood streaked the foul-smelling paste covering her flesh. Bite marks covered her arms and legs, chest and belly. More wounds delineated the rodents' attempt to tear at her face and neck. "Our forensic tech?"

"Yeah. He gave Caden some type of slow-acting poison," Lexi gasped out between sobs.

"Larrick, send a unit to Carl's house, though I doubt he'd keep anything there." Ethan thought frantically about what he knew of the nerd. "What kind of toxin?"

"On it. Caden's not bitten as badly, but he's not waking up." Billy wiped Caden's face before wrapping dishtowels around shallow cuts.

"Ethan, I scratched Carl. I bit him through his shirt. But I scratched him at the same time."

"Baggies. I'm gonna cover your hands with baggies, Lexi." Rat DNA would be present. Something forensics would separate from human tissue. From the drawer beside him, Ethan retrieved several large plastic bags and zipped them loosely around her wrists.

As if breaching the limits of tolerance, Lexi collapsed against him, unconscious. He knew she'd enter a nightmare realm that continued her ordeal despite her body being safe.

"We've got to figure out what the slime ball gave Caden.

It's not going to be something simple. This madman thinks outside the box." A glance at his unconscious brother brought back the reason Ethan had wanted to be a cop. To protect.

Backup arrived in the form of two panicked brothers before EMS brought in two stretchers. Beginning the search for the psychopath bent on destroying his world, Ethan watched as Matt took over the scene and evidence was collected. Lucas pressed in from the side, urging him to step away so medics could tend to Lexi's wounds.

Matt snapped out orders, directing those on site and stepping aside for the medics to wheel their patients out. When the gurneys headed toward their respective ambulances, Ethan looked helplessly between Lexi and Caden. Each tore at his heart.

"Go with Caden, I'll be fine." Lexi watched as the EMTs loaded his younger brother in the back of the wagon.

"No, Ethan, ride with your girl. I'll go with Caden." Lucas gave Ethan a gentle shove in Lexi's direction.

He didn't remember climbing in, but Lexi's hand holding tight in his registered as necessary for his next breath, his life, despite the plastic separating them.

The medic had already started an IV and was asking the standard orientation questions while continuing to assess his patient.

The noxious paste smeared with her blood and heaven only knew what else covering her body registered as an offense to everything good in the world. Wounds on her arms, legs, belly, and neck brought tears to his eyes. He'd promised her protection and failed. Then came the paralyzing reminder, *Zoe was sexually assaulted...*

Larrick had always proclaimed Ethan better at dealing

with victims. As he watched Lexi's body jump at every sound, his mind tallied and reviewed the steps he'd take in her recovery. She may try to push him away, but he'd have none of it.

Once at the hospital, collected fingernail scrapings would provide the first conclusive evidence against his deranged enemy. Since the dirtball had fooled them all for so long, he doubted any electronic record existed but knew Matt wouldn't ignore any possible evidence in the lab.

How could he avoid leaving fingerprints there? DNA should be easy to find considering the tech's hours spent working—unless Carl used some type of silicone compound applied to his finger pads which prevented leaving prints.

Ethan stood beside Lexi's stretcher in the ER, holding her arm while tears of rage and frustration were held back by the remnants of terror and pain etched in every line of her body.

One nurse cleaned the noxious paste from her flesh while others collected evidence, tended to her wounds, drew blood, and set up new IVs. Throughout her ordeal, her gaze remained locked onto him, the unspoken plea willing him to remain by her side.

A multitude of bite and tear marks, single puncture wounds, multiple abrasions, along with smeared paste and blood had covered her skin. That image would never leave his mental directory of failures. Tetanus and specific infections were now a threat.

On the next stretcher and separated by a curtain, Caden remained quiet as emergency personnel scurried through similar tasks.

Lucas' panicked questions received abbreviated answers. Ethan slid the cloth barrier back to see Caden's face and the medical team working to save him.

Intermittent comments like "dilated pupils and slow reflexes" surfed through his thoughts. Caden's condition deteriorated by the minute, from semi-consciousness to a restless uncommunicative state.

Lucas would help Matt and the other detectives in the search for Carl, scouring any known haunts.

He was under my nose all this time.

"Sir, you have to wait in the reception area. We'll call you as soon as she's stable. You can talk with her then." Determination personified the slim, take-no-prisoners ER nurse who tried to nudge him away from the gurney, her voice resonating in the small confines.

"Ma'am, first of all, I'm not leaving her side. Do you know who's responsible for this? The serial killer who murdered *your* hospital administrator, among others. If we don't catch him soon, others will die—horribly." Ethan forced the words through clenched teeth. Nothing could hold them back. Brushing the nurse aside was the least of his offenses.

"Ethan? Ethan, I've got an idea." Lexi's anxious voice stirred the attention of the doctor and nurses at her bedside.

Meeting her gaze was an exercise in trepidation since her ideas frequently put her at risk. He didn't want her thinking about rats, Carl, or the reality that the deviant failed to complete his task and didn't like leaving witnesses.

Very carefully, he held her hand, unable to avoid the myriad remnants of the attack. He didn't want to cause her more pain but realized she'd need the human contact as much as he did. Shock at the determination in her gaze renewed his hope for recovery.

"Lexi, you need to rest. We've got DNA samples from when you scratched him."

"Which will take too long to get results—at least too long for Caden. Besides, he's never left DNA behind to provide a match, at least none that we know of yet. Listen, Ethan, Carl gave Caden a poison. I don't know what type. I'm sure he erased all the security footage at your house just as I'm sure he wiped all the surfaces in the kitchen he'd touched, which wasn't many, before putting on gloves."

Lexi closed her eyes and shuddered, no doubt reliving her nightmare. "But, when he arrived, he rang your doorbell, not wearing gloves. Maybe he didn't remember to wipe the buzzer, which means you might get a fingerprint."

"Ah, maybe that print will be in the system. I'll have the techs check it."

"No. You do it. Make sure it's done right. Please, Caden doesn't have much time. Stay off the radio, he'll be monitoring it."

He didn't want to leave her side. "Lexi."

"I'll be fine. I know you've posted a uniform to stay at my room once admitted. I'll stay awake until you return. Go, please?"

She'll stay awake because she's terrified of reliving her tailor-made, personal hell.

From behind, "I've already requested an officer posted on each." Larrick's tone conveyed the sympathy he'd never express in words.

"All right. I'll be back as soon as I can. Lucas is here until backup arrives." Ethan backed away, tugged to the door by Larrick. He hadn't realized his partner had stood behind him.

"Let's go, Ethan. We need to move it."

Chapter Twenty-Three

"I never realized Carl was that much of an anal-retentive prick." Ethan glared at his computer screen, frustrated with their lack of success.

"Hey. So he wiped the doorbell clean. He wasn't born with the knowledge to commit a crime without leaving evidence. No one's perfect. What haven't we looked at yet?" Larrick leaned away from his desk and linked his fingers behind his head. "We'll match the DNA from this morning to when he attacked her at the pet store..."

"Which doesn't connect us to his past and another name when he was lower on the learning curve. When he first came here—" Ethan struggled to remember their first interactions.

"Damn, this guy has altered every digital record to suit his whim."

"Yes. But what about the records that aren't digital?" Ethan's fist pump registered a solid prospect of victory.

"What?"

"When he first came here, he filled out a job application—on paper! You know how meticulous the captain is." Excitement coursed through his veins as Ethan continued along the mental thread. "Which is stored at another facility, where Carl doesn't have access."

"I'll get the file while you keep digging." Larrick grabbed his jacket off the chair's back and headed for the door. "Then we'll compare digital and hard copies."

Ethan printed out the copy of Carl's application. Everything looked to be in perfect order. *Naturally.*

Starting at the top, he began calling all known contacts, beginning with the most recent job. Each time he connected with someone, he gave a detailed physical description of the tech. With each call, digital records matched, but Carl rarely rated a memory, possibly due to the size of the departments.

I'm beginning to wonder if any of his records are real.

When Larrick returned with the paper file, Ethan prayed for a discrepancy.

"Okay, I've got the hard copy of his job application. He referenced classes at an institution in Virginia."

Ethan double-checked then smiled. "It's not on the digital file...He altered it."

"Then why write it on paper?" Larrick studied both files.

"Probably needed the reference, then deleted the digital part after he was hired. You know the captain would've called.

Ethan slapped both files on the desk, then snatched up his phone and punched in the number to the Virginia institution while praying for a lead.

After transfer to the records department, Ethan recalled everything he knew about Carl's habits, meticulous attention to detail, and appearance.

Minutes later, he had a new name of someone matching Carl's description, remembered for helping out with a network problem. He thanked the director, knowing if it panned out, he owed her more than he could ever repay. After disconnecting, he took a deep breath of optimism.

"We may have him. Back when he wasn't as accomplished at blending into the background."

Larrick glided his chair closer to better view Ethan's screen.

"They couldn't find a digital photo or anyone by the name Carl, something about a computer glitch, but she remembered someone matching his description and extremely skilled on the keyboard. Timing is right, six years ago. He goes by Carl here, but back there, the guy's name was Arvel Cranchek. I guess he couldn't resist showing off just a bit back then."

"So, he changed his digital file but couldn't erase a human memory." Larrick held his hand up for a high-five.

"No wonder our captain didn't pick up the discrepancy from the start. How many times do you ask a reference for a physical description of your potential hire?"

"Yeah, we got him now." Ethan prayed they'd find the antidote for Caden in time.

"Guess he never thought we'd put two and two together and finger him for a psycho. The arrogant prick. Let's run him and see what we get."

Ethan couldn't type fast enough while silently pleading his hunch was right. It felt right. "Ha!"

When the name Arvel Cranchek popped up on the DMV records, Ethan high-fived his partner. "I wonder how many identities he has. This isn't the address in Northwood listed on his application. Maybe it's a hidey-hole." Ethan printed out the DMV's information.

"I'd wondered why a man with his tech skills would want a job like this when he could make much more elsewhere." Larrick pushed his chair back and stood.

"Yeah, he fooled us all."

"Let's go get him. See what stores of poison he carries."

Every second counted in their bid to catch the psychopath before he could slip away into the undeclared mass population. Their race to the sedan seemed interminable while Caden's still form flashed in Ethan's mind.

All this time, the killer had been right under their noses., *I invited him into my home.* Death was too easy an escape, but survival meant the possibility of parole and another crack at loved ones.

Not an option. A glance at Larrick made him wonder if they were on the same page.

Silent speed and blaring, flashing lights kept Ethan's heart racing.

"Call for backup—use your cell phone. Dial carefully, *take your time,* partner." Ethan's carefully enunciated speech betrayed his intent to kill, the verbal shorthand understood, judging by Larrick's quick nod.

"Don't want him getting away from us or enjoying the freedom to continue his reign. Next time, it'd be my family on the line." Larrick relayed their destination and pertinent information to dispatch before checking his weapon.

Within minutes, Ethan's cell rang, the distinctive ringtone belonging to his eldest brother. He put it on speaker. "Okay, Matt, I know. Follow procedure. Got it."

"Yeah, kiddo. And wait for reinforcements. Billy, Lucas, and I are en route. The captain's trying to keep a lid on the fact Caden and Lexi are still alive, but we don't know who Carl may be working with yet."

One look at Larrick solidified his intent. "Sure, Matt. Larrick and I will be the boys sitting on the car's hood waiting for your arrival." Ethan disconnected amid Matt's diatribe.

The race against time led them slewing down winding country roads and alongside a national park. Each minute felt like hours while Ethan envisioned Caden fighting for his life, rasping breath, and unable to rid himself of the chains of unconsciousness.

He jerked the car to a stop on the road's narrow shoulder close to their target's drive. Thick woods denied them a view of the house.

"Let's go," Larrick murmured, the quiet snick of his door absorbed by the woods surrounding them. "We stick together, right side."

Multiple deer trails parted the thin underbrush as they made their way forward and parallel to the psychopath's rutted dirt road.

It seemed fate granted assistance when the trail followed their intended path. Ethan shuddered each time the briars caught at his torn slacks, reminding him of his earlier fight with the horde of vermin.

When they caught visual of the small bungalow, Ethan murmured, "Figures the creep would find a like habitat as his twisted base of operations. Carl won't know we've located his burrow." Ethan prayed to find the information to help his brother. The large twig snapping under his shoe drew Larrick's frown.

"Hey, man, you were raised among four brothers playing cops and robbers. Want a cymbal or perhaps an air horn to announce our presence?" The current section of woodland wasn't as thick and allowed for a slightly easier passage, if not quieter.

Never had he experienced a case so personal, so desperate.

Has Carl ever had anyone come this close to nailing him? Ethan mentally reviewed their known facts, fitting pieces together to form a comprehensive picture.

"You ready?" Larrick's brow furrowed with his assessing gaze.

"Absolutely." Ethan's gut tightened. "No vehicle present, no garage. He might not be here."

"Wouldn't count on it." Larrick stopped at the edge of the woods behind a wide oak tree. Twenty yards of open space filled with overgrown weeds and grass gone to seed surrounded the bungalow. Faded shutters and peeling paint depicted the lack of upkeep along with several missing shingles.

"At least there's no out buildings," Larrick whispered. "You feel like waiting? I sure as the devil don't. Windows are covered, so he can't see out—if he's in there."

"I don't think he is—but he probably believes this is a safe house and might return. Either way, he'll start over with a new look and new identity. By now, he knows his plan failed." Without another word, Ethan edged forward, gun drawn.

"Unless one of his contacts knows something specific about him or holds damning evidence. Then he might lay low until he can eliminate witnesses if only to soothe his pride."

No sound betrayed their passage. It wasn't procedure, but Caden didn't have time for them to follow policy. By now, Matt would have surmised the plan. Beside the front door, each man paused as their gazes met.

"We don't have a warrant," Larrick whispered. "But I'm game."

"We don't have time to wait. Caden doesn't have the time," Ethan retorted.

"Might be booby-trapped. That's what I'd do."

"I'll go first." Kneeling on the side, Ethan picked the lock, surprised at the lack of security with just one barrier. Larrick's warning echoed in the back of his mind as he stood and slowly pushed the front door open. Instead of the expected small explosion or blast of a shotgun, silence reigned.

"Either hiding or not here," Ethan whispered.

In the distance, the roar of engines signaled the approach

of backup, probably Matt and Billy. Ethan signaled his partner then stepped inside and to the left. Larrick followed and went right.

No furniture meant exposure to anyone already present.

The bite of a bullet never came.

"All clear."

Larrick's words echoed Ethan's frustration. He held his breath while flipping a light switch, again waiting for some type of nasty surprise.

Instead, small pools of a soft glow tinted the immaculate hardwoods in a lighter shade of disorientation. Confusion muddled his thoughts at the pristine interior, uninhabited with utilities running while the exterior coincided with a third world country.

Like his partner, Ethan had donned his gloves.

They'd cleared the small space before familiar, soft curses drifted in from the outside. Matt, Lucas, and Billy were pissed off.

"Damn it, Ethan. I told you to wait." Matt's frustration formed clipped speech through gritted teeth. "You don't even know if this is Carl's place." Matt handed Billy and Lucas latex gloves before sheathing his own hands.

"His name is Arvel Cranchek, and yeah, I am sure this belongs to our psycho," Ethan replied.

"If this belongs to Carl and it's where he dreams up his sick agendas, then we're missing something, a hidden space, whatever." Larrick moved along the living room wall, gently tapping.

"If anything knocks back, I'm out of here. This place is freaking spooky." Lucas moved along the opposite side, mimicking the tapping gesture. Regardless of his words, nothing would pull him away.

"From the guy who thinks Bambi is a role model," Ethan smirked as he and Matt went to check the other rooms. Like the other spaces, the kitchen was spotless.

Glass-fronted shelving further delineated the dichotomy of interior and exterior. "At least it's small. Though from the outside, when we approached, the kitchen should be bigger…" Again, Ethan tapped on the wallboard, listening for the slight difference that might indicate a hidden space.

Matt opened a closet door cautiously then flipped on an interior light. "Look at the floor—muddy footprints. Guess he's not as thorough about cleaning as I thought. Either that or he left in a hurry after learning Lexi survived."

Ethan and Lucas nudged past. "Gotta be a doorway or access here." Three long shelves held canned goods, plastic containers of rice, noodles, beans, and a case of bottled water. "Looks like he planned this as a safe house."

Excitement built, the atmosphere pregnant with the need to end the nightmare. Ethan tapped at the back wall, shuffling the shelves' contents until detecting a hollow sound along the paneled side.

"Here, Lucas. I found—something. A seam. But I'm not certain how to get inside."

"So that's been your problem all along, huh?" Lucas failed to brush his brother aside.

"There's a switch here, but considering its location, I'm not sure what it does." Lack of dust refuted the expectation of finding cobwebs and mouse droppings. Ethan cringed at the reminder of Lexi's wounds and near-death experience.

An audible click preceded—nothing. The silence continued as each waited for some type of repercussion.

"And of course finding a switch meant you should flip it

and hope it doesn't set off a booby trap." Matt snorted with disgust.

"Well, you knew one of us was going to do it." Lucas smoothed his fingers over the paneled wall, searching for some type of grip. A quick inhale preceded his low whistle. "I got it. The switch releases some type of lever that I can use to…"

Matt shouldered him aside while prodding at the slight opening until swinging the makeshift door inward. Stale air wafted out to engulf them and deter entrance into the hidden lair. Each stepped through, awestruck at the interior.

"Yes! I knew it. We found Carl's nest." Ethan gaped at the contents on the metal desk. Extensive shelving held more electronics to the right of the eight-foot-square windowless room.

"Hell." Several sheets of paper and a grocery list revealed the organized mind behind their ordeal. Matt handed Ethan the list. "Look, supplies and a local address."

"Peanut butter, tuna fish, canned cat food, and what is this last item? The whacko smeared the first three on Lexi's skin. I don't recognize the name of the chemical. Think it's what he gave Caden? Or some altered version?"

"Probably. This is likely the address where he picked up his supplies." Ethan stretched to boot up the computer in hopes of learning more.

"Don't. Even though we didn't find any bugs in this place, doesn't mean he's not extra paranoid about his tech stuff. He might be at that address now or planning on visiting in hopes of eliminating a witness. Let's go." Matt started for the door.

"Fine, I'll call and check on Lexi and Caden en route," Ethan snatched his phone from its clip.

"I'll call the doctor and tell him about the drug. I already got the DA working on our warrants. Soon as it's ready, our techs can *find* this room and the TAC team can head toward the address." To hear Matt bend the rules, even slightly, revealed a new side to the eldest McAllister.

Behind them, Billy voiced Ethan's greatest desire. "Suits me. Let's go end this prick."

"I'll pretend I didn't hear that. We'll do the rest of this by the book." Matt said.

"Yep, keep thinking that when the dirtball is shooting at *you*." Ethan high-fived Lucas before following Matt.

"We have to make sure they find an antidote for Caden. Think with your heads, guys." Matt's logic wasn't always convenient.

"Remember when we used to play cops and robbers, surrounding Abagail and Caden?" Matt took the curve fast enough to make Ethan swallow hard. A glance in the side mirror revealed Larrick and Billy in the SUV behind them.

"Yeah, we also picked on Ethan because he was younger." Lucas grinned from the back seat.

"Matt, I'm fine, steady as a drum. I don't need reassuring or a trip down memory lane." In reality, Ethan's damp brow belied his words. As much as he wanted to kill the one who'd threatened his family and Lexi, he understood the value of caution.

"Just checking, can't blame me. Mom will kill me if anything else happens to you, favorite child and all that," Matt murmured.

"Huh, right. This coming from the guy who's going after a suspect without calling for backup." Ethan chided his sibling.

"He worked alone today. We have all the backup we

need." Bared teeth and flaring nostrils depicted Matt's anger and intent.

The rest of the ride passed in a surreal silence that suffused the air with nervous anticipation. Country roads gave way to comfortable-appearing suburbs, the middle-class residents enjoying the fruits of nearby city life and larger lot sizes.

"You gotta wonder—some poor sap probably doesn't realize his neighbor is supplying a monster with tools for this sick charade." Ethan gazed at the competition of blossoms among the flowering cherry, magnolia, and camellias. With his past experience, it wasn't hard to imagine evil's black seed hidden among the beauty.

"Would that be the neighbor who cheats on his wife or the one who's embezzling thousands from his employer?" Lucas' cynicism echoed in Ethan's thoughts as their vehicle slowed. Two gentle taps on the breaks signaled Larrick behind them to pull over to the shoulder.

"Okay, so now we're both getting as cynical as Matt," Ethan replied as he and Lucas checked their coms and weapons.

Matt pulled over twenty feet ahead of their partners. "All right. According to the map, our psycho's supplier should live in the house directly behind this monstrosity."

"These houses sit back to back in neat little blocks." Ethan appreciated country living but sometimes envied the proximity to the city until this reminder from Hades rejuvenated his requirement for open ground.

The two-story colonial in front of them boasted a semi-circular portico and a walk-out balcony. It bore all the features of new money but lacked the sophistication to match the elegance of neighboring homes. Intricately shaped designs using various colored flowers and shrubs would soon provide a riot of color along the yard's borders.

"It's show time. We'll skirt past this home and approach the back of the target's house. Larrick and Billy are gonna circle wide to the front." Matt signaled Billy to move.

No midafternoon light poured through the home's front windows. No curtains stirred with their passing the flamboyant residence shielding their approach to the target home. Recently trimmed lawns remained slick from fresh-cut, juicy grass along the shady side as each man sidled down the lot's edge.

"You know we're trespassing, right? We don't have a warrant and aren't in active pursuit," Lucas murmured.

"Only matters if they catch us," Ethan retorted. "I don't see anything moving at the windows. Hopefully, these homeowners are at work. C'mon, let's move it."

Ethan's heart rate increased with each step forward. The image of Lexi, naked and terrorized by mindless rats in a fit of rage, filled his vision. If the situation didn't end in a permanent way, she'd never have peace of mind.

How will Carl react when surrounded by McAllisters? If he laid down his weapon, what then?

A line of cypress trees separated the backyards into neat squares. Squeezing underneath the mammoth branchlets of flattened, feathery sprays, Ethan's thoughts shot straight back to when he'd hidden underneath similar trees from a very angry older brother.

Matt's snort from the other side of the base came as no surprise. "I know where your head's going. Stay with me, Romeo."

"I'm right here."

"We want the resident alive. He's our only collaborator," Matt murmured.

"There's not much cover between us and the house." Lucas brushed a branch out of his way.

At the other back corner, Larrick and Billy were just crawling back, shaking their heads.

Matt's brief orders over the coms coordinated their intent. "We'll be vulnerable for about forty yards. There's an above-ground pool. Its decking connects to the house, probably the kitchen. One story, two sliders, and a glass-paned personnel door in the rear, three high windows, partially covered, no movement, no lights visible. Cypress trees surround the property. You see anything else?"

"No, that's it." Billy's affirmation confirmed their predicament.

"Move out." Ethan hoisted himself up and forward. Brilliant sunshine highlighted their dash and slide behind the pool. He'd expected a piercing slug to drop him as Matt and Lucas paced him to the temporary shelter.

As if holding her breath, Mother Nature had gone silent. No birds sang in nearby trees, and no flies buzzed around the soda can carelessly dropped by the pool's decking. Latticework shielding its underbelly played host to a small wasp's nest. The single stalk from which it hung boasted a large queen in the process of construction.

"So far, so good," Lucas studied the houses to their sides.

With Larrick and Billy's go-ahead to proceed, each team's running crouch ended with them flattening themselves against the home's southern wall. Watching Billy and his partner disappear around the corner began the process of waiting.

Ethan's weapon rested heavily in his tight grip while

Matt's quick nod signaled his readiness. Each padded closer to the slider. Unbidden, thoughts of Lexi came to mind.

"*I want the cash receipts for the supplies.*" Inside, a controlled fury preceded shattering glass.

"Probable cause," Lucas nudged Ethan forward a step.

"Left." Matt checked the glass door. It slid a fraction, soundlessly. After a silent three-digit countdown, he shoved the door open and rushed inside.

Stepping to the left, Lucas followed Matt.

Ethan advanced to the opposite side.

Carl hauled his hostage upright as a shield. The shocked expression on both their faces filled Ethan with a temporary satisfaction until the killer's gun swung first toward him then his brothers. Evidence of a struggle, glass shards from a lamp littered the tile floor.

Carl clamped his mouth shut and hardened his jaw. The twisted sneer and schizoid gaze rivaled any lunatic's. "How did you find me?"

"The devil's in the details, Carl, or Arvel." Matt's taunt redirected the gunman's attention to himself. "You didn't trash the paper copy of your personnel file."

"But I altered the digital records on the other end."

"Yeah, moron, but you can't erase someone's memories," Ethan confirmed with a grin. "You've finally been bested."

"So you found my name. Another one is waiting at the end of my keyboard." Waving his gun between his three opponents, Carl broadcasted his uncertainty as to whom he wanted to shoot first.

"Yes. Arvel Cranchek. We found you. And there will be no more hiding, no more names, except—fresh meat, in a prison cell." Lucas sidestepped farther left, broadening the space between brothers and negating the hostage's use as a shield from both sides.

"As for your cell mate, we'll make sure you have a special *friend* on the inside." Ethan took his cue and widened the distance.

"But you'll both be dead." Hatred radiated in waves. "You. You and your whore have been a pain in my butt. All I wanted was play a little longer before moving on to another city. Do you know how long it took me to set up this situation? Then you show up at that administrator's house and ruin my well-laid plans. It takes time to gain credibility, and now I have to start over."

"Things don't always turn out the way you plan," Matt explained with narrowed eyes.

"Kill me and you lose. I'm you're only link to the kidnapped women."

"What women?" Lucas and Matt exchanged glances.

"The ones collected and sold, right under your ignorant noses. Now, step aside and I'll be on my way."

"Yeah, about that. Looks like you'll be moving on, all right." Lucas took another sidestep.

Simultaneous events occurred.

Glass shattering from the front of the house, the front door being kicked in, and Matt shooting Carl in the neck prevented the bedlamite from executing an accurate shot. His body jerked backward. The wall beside Ethan's head received the psycho's lead at the same time Ethan and Lucas fired. Carl's body jerked twice more, allowing his hostage to crouch low.

The second shot from Ethan's gun bucked Arvel's body back another step before he slumped to the floor, his gun skittering across the tile to the kitchen doorway.

"Billy, Larrick, we're clear." Ethan grimaced. As much as

he'd wanted the psycho dead, he couldn't have killed in cold blood. He thanked God fate hadn't given him the ultimatum.

Billy and Larrick edged around the corner, each with gun in hand.

Carl's hand at his neck went slack, unable to stop the flow of his life's essence while blood expanded the pool of crimson on his chest and leached to the tile floor. Several gasping breaths detailed his vain attempt to survive. Within seconds, a short exhale received no countering intake. Sightless eyes stared at the ceiling.

The nightmare was dead.

"And so it ends." Matt circumvented the table and kneeled to check for a pulse.

"Thank you for barging in when you did. He was going to kill me. I have no idea who—" The hostage stood, his bloody lip and swollen eyelid a testament to his plea.

"Save it for the judge. We know you supplied him with tools for murder. Fortunately, this one will receive his judgment elsewhere. You, however, will be judged by a jury." Matt's statement received a stream of denials as he stood and cuffed the blubbering conspirator.

"What about that claim of kidnapped women? You think it was a ploy, a distraction?" Ethan tried to wrap his mind around the twisted events. If Carl was part of a greater conspiracy, a bigger nightmare waited for them all.

"Don't know." Matt shook his head in disgust. "One problem at a time."

"The battle is just beginning for Lexi and Caden." Ethan agreed. "I'll call the hospital again and check on them." It took two attempts to holster his weapon as Ethan turned toward the door. A little fresh air would go a long way.

Chapter Twenty-Four

"I hate soup," Caden complained.

"It's not soup, it's broth, has no solids in it." Matt pushed the overbed table closer to his younger brother.

"Then here, try this." Ethan moved the plastic cup of gelatin within Caden's reach. "The red is better than the blue stuff."

"It. Is. Still. Freaking liquid. I want a steak or at least a hamburger." Golden liquid sloshed over the bowl's side as Caden shoved it to the back of the table.

"Eat it. Drink it. Or wear it. Those are your choices." Matt pushed the hot bowl back. "If it's not consumed within the next five minutes, we'll call your nurse and tell her your gut is in extreme distress. How about a nice proctology exam? Believe me, they won't stop digging for gold regardless of what tools they have to use."

"Nuh-uh, my nurse is an angel and wouldn't believe you." Caden flipped Matt the bird.

"Yeah, you probably get her to fluff your pillows just so you can smell her up close and personal." Lucas tapped the electrodes on Caden's chest to form a sawtooth pattern on the heart monitor.

"Hey, I'm a connoisseur of women's lotions and shampoos."

"Yeah, I can imagine what women say when you find the best scent, like *'Get out of my bathroom, you pervert,'* or something close." Matt shoved Lucas' hand away from the wires connected to white patches on Caden's chest, returning the monitor's picture to a normal QRS pattern.

Snickers from behind the curtain alerted Ethan to Lexi's eavesdropping.

"Ah, so you're finally awake. 'Bout time." Pushing the dividing curtain back, Ethan noted Lexi's improvement in color.

"Who could sleep through all your racket?" A slight metal grinding accompanied the head of Lexi's bed rising.

"And that's the thanks I get for saving the chit's life. Jeez." Caden grinned past the spoon of broth halfway to his mouth.

"When we walked in, you were passed out against her shoulder like a little girl. Lexi was protecting your precious hide before her own." Ethan sat at Lexi's bedside and offered his hand. Fine-boned fingers sported bandages over the more severe bites, but her squeeze provided comfort.

"Thank you for finishing that psycho, Ethan. At least now I have a better chance of sleeping at night." It didn't take a detective to discern the doubt in her eyes.

"I know it's going to take a while to sleep peacefully, but we'll get there." Ethan couldn't hold her gaze. The cuts on her face and arms existed because he hadn't kept his word, hadn't kept her safe.

"I'll be sitting in the chair beside the bed for a while." There was no way he'd let her feel pressured into resuming their relationship before she was ready. Though she'd denied sexual assault, she'd been through horrendous trauma. Who knew what her subconscious may have blocked out?

Spewing liquid accompanied his brothers' choking coughs and muffled laughter. A murmured comment about adult education instigated another round of chuckles.

"Troglodytes. I come from a family of troglodytes." Ethan whipped the curtain in its slide to provide privacy if only visually before pushing the call light to make good on an earlier threat.

"I'd rather you slept in my bed, Ethan," Lexi murmured.

The words, softly spoken, reverberated in his mind.

"Finally!" Caden's voice. "Darn if I didn't think I'd have to break out Abagail's dolls and give my older brother some lessons."

When the nurse came to answer the call, Ethan stepped forward and put on his best-concerned expression. To see the same caregiver who'd hovered over him just weeks before lent his endeavor a little credibility.

"I'm really worried. Caden said he passed a little blood with his stool this morning. Do you think the poison is doing something wonky to his gut?" Shaking his head "no" and a wink conveyed his message clearly after all the ribbing he'd taken from his family.

Apparently, the nurse was game. As soon as she rounded the corner, Caden began sputtering denials. Matt, Billy, and Lucas backed up to give her room to examine her patient.

He left them to it and returned to Lexi.

"So it's finally over. Carl fooled us all, clever psycho." Lexi's grip tightened, as if afraid he'd withdraw.

Though the threat to her body had ended, her subconscious would replay the horrors she'd failed to escape on a regular basis. Flesh would heal quickly. The rest would follow with patience and time.

"That's not all. Turns out, his partner, Dooley, had owned a six-wheel truck under another name. We think that's what they used to pick up supplies," Ethan murmured. "Dooley's house was clean, just like Carl's *public* home. Apparently, they did their planning in Carl's remote shack. They also found my old phone among Carl's electronics.

"It had malware that allowed him to turn the device into a recorder. After I was shot, he'd brought it to me and said it wasn't working properly. I'd tossed it in my junk drawer in the kitchen. He must've taken it with him when he left."

"It allowed him to listen in on your conversations?" Billy asked. *"Among other things..."*

"Oh my God." Crimson rode high on Lexi's cheeks. Covering her face with bandaged fingers lent a greater contrast. "That's how he knew to send you a message to get a carry-out lunch."

Ethan glared at his brother. "As long as our voices were in range." He wondered how long the battery had lasted and if Carl had been in his home before leaving the taunt for Lexi, perhaps to recharge the battery.

"What about the forensics lab and his fingerprints?" Lexi's understanding of each puzzle piece and how it fit would help give closure.

"Techs found his workaround. A supply of a silicone-based concoction he'd applied to his fingertips when working," Lucas replied.

"But he didn't use it when committing crimes?" Caden asked. "Why?"

"He wore gloves, added protection from leaving trace DNA," Matt replied. "Ethan identified him by pulling his personnel jacket and calling his prior contacts with a description."

"That's one up for Captain Faulkner and his mistrust of electronics. Guess I'll have to thank him." After a disgusted snort, Larrick shook his head.

"Yep, in triplicate. That's going to be painful." Ethan grinned, knowing he'd have to have at least one picture of his partner typing the personal note.

"Carl had to know he'd leave at least some trace DNA in the lab." Lexi frowned as if trying to ferret out a lunatic's mind.

"He probably figured that A, no one would connect his new identity to a crime, and B, if we did, he could construct another identity, keeping the Arvel name clean. He just couldn't erase people's memories," Ethan supplied.

"What about the pollen he reported finding?" Lexi asked.

"I think that was his way of implicating Dooley if the need arose, having a backup plan," Ethan replied.

"We suspect he's pulled the same gambit in other cities before perfecting his psychotic technique. Now that we have his computers and his DNA, forensic techs will match his files to other crimes. Digital records have been hacked and changed, but gruesome murders stand out in everybody's mind," Matt noted.

"It'll take a while, but we'll hunt down his suppliers, too," Ethan added.

"I can track the cyber pervs down with access to Carl's computer. Unless he used a secure deletion that overwrites its data chunks, I can retrieve the files. Also, if he moved periodically, which we should also be able to track with his computer, we'll be able to connect more cases and close them." Lexi slid her hand from Ethan's grasp, withdrawing back into her own world.

"With no witnesses having seen his face, he probably thought he was home free. However, you're not going near any of this again. For now, you need to rest and heal." Ethan extended his fingers, turning his palm up, the silent request to reconnect clear.

She accepted.

In the back of his mind, Ethan considered Carl's warning and threat. If true, there were other young women out there in need of help.

Epilogue

Lexi needed time before resuming their intimate pursuits. What Ethan didn't know was how much longer he could hide his hunger behind a mask of platonic concern. He'd strived for patience and counted each day a success when she smiled.

Day after day, he waited, observing for signs of infection and supporting her in every way he could. Her ever-present four-footed companion lay by her feet.

"We've been home now for two weeks." Lexi snuggled next to him on the sofa. "And you've watched me like a hawk. I'm not going to get sick. I have no fever, rash, or anything else you've been waiting to see. I. Am. Fine. And I'd like to know how you've gotten so much time off from work."

The small circles she absentmindedly drew over his thigh fired all the wrong signals to his libido. Both her abrasions and small puncture wounds had healed without incident while her blood tested negative for resultant infection. She'd not complained about the prophylactic IV antibiotics, only his reluctance to rekindle their romance.

"After being shot, my time off was sick leave. I still had two weeks of vacation. The captain was grateful to have this nightmare over, so I have another week of leave. In addition, I know you're fine. I just…"

"You keep treating me like a victim. Or is it that you don't want me anymore." She curled her body away, retreating mentally as well as physically.

With an unrealized desperation, Ethan locked her body against his side. "Don't ever think that. Only you and your doctor know the full extent of what happened that day. I know you've not wanted to talk about the details, and it's like I said. When you do, I'm here for you."

A deep breath and he gentled his touch, stroking her hair and outer arm. "I'm concerned about further traumatizing you. I'm not a gentle person. You know this."

"The creep did *not* rape me. I've explained that. Yeah, I have a few healing wounds that might leave a scar or two, but I don't know how else to convince you."

"You've had years of people wanting only to hurt you. Our foundation of trust is new." Unable to stop his hunger from taking the lead, his gentle touch over her t-shirt settled between her breasts. His fingers itched to slide beneath the cotton and claim her once again. On some level, he knew she wanted it too. His hesitation stemmed from fear of moving too fast and causing more trauma.

"New, yes. But it's solid. When you accept it, you have to claim it all. I've never made this type of commitment. To anyone. So, you need to understand this." As if unable to find the words, she willed him to accept her, flaws and all.

"I've already staked my claim. I've put my stamp on you here." His fingers gently curved over her heart. "That will never change, never waver, and never diminish."

* * * *

"Aside from Hoover, I've always been alone to one degree or another, whether on the streets or in my own place. With you, granted it's the first time I've done this, but the crap that I've survived has not changed how I feel or what I want."

Several months ago, she'd had her life planned, solitary, independent, and void of the incredible love found in Ethan's arms. He'd proven himself a man who wouldn't abandon her, that in fact had the patience and care to help her through any trial she'd face.

"I understand, and I accept it, accept you in all your complexities. But you still need time..." Ethan stared at her, his expression warring between desire and concern.

Screw it.

"Fine." *Let's see how he deals with this.* "I need to get up."

Instantly, his hands slid to her waist and helped her to stand.

Without another thought, Lexi pulled her t-shirt over her head and tossed it on the sofa beside him. Her bra followed.

"Lexi, I don't think you're ready for this, for me." He swiped his tongue along his bottom lip. His gaze remained fastened on the bared skin like a starved man.

Her jeans and panties soon sat atop her bra and shirt.

"Lexi?" The fire in his gaze rivaled the hottest blaze in Hades.

When she reached for and unbuckled his belt, he stopped her. "You'd better be sure, sweetheart. Because I don't know if I could stop. As I've told you, this is for keeps."

"About freaking time."

"And didn't I tell you how I'd cure that naughty mouth?" Ethan stood, sweeping one hand under her knees while his other circled her shoulders. The smile curving his lips declared he could no more lay a hand on her than walk away.

Cradled against his chest, she grinned as he strode toward the bedroom. Any hesitation she'd ever felt was gone with one soul-searing gaze. This man was her destiny. Whatever trials the future brought, they'd face them together, united and strong. In her heart, in his arms, she was home.

Thank you for reading DIGITAL VELOCITY.

Lexi Donovan has found her equal, an iron-willed detective determined to rein in her compulsive need to help others. When a young woman stumbles into the police department after escaping her kidnapper, Lexi and her dog, Hoover, search for those targeting young women.

Follow their journey through Portland's Underground tunnels as she and Ethan untangle lies and deceit to find kidnapped women before they disappear forever.

Confusion and pain intertwined to delay Kaylee's escape from the depths of a nightmare. Her subconscious' attempt to alert her to some horror or another had been common the past two years, but this time the warning came with physical characteristics she couldn't ignore.

Pain was an unwelcome element for which she could not account.

Cozy flannel sheets had never felt so rough under her cheek, nor had her head ached from a glass of wine. Despite the tomboy tag since adolescence, she appreciated certain creature comforts. The rough material scratching her face didn't number among them.

A quiet foreboding swelled within that fuzzy twilight between the dream state and the hazy stages of surfing to consciousness. Sleep would be welcome if not for the musty odor and an undefined menace crowding her mind. Her brow furrowed as her pulse increased, awareness mounting with each painful throb.

Why is there dirt in my bed and what is wrong with this mattress?

With each erratic contraction of her heart, the tension in her head increased, ratcheting like the shell around a drumhead until pain reverberated along every nerve. In grim anticipation, she reached to touch her temple. A crusty line of fibrous, threadlike strands crumbled in her brow line and snaked down to her ear.

Blood? What happened?

Moving back to Portland had entailed a certain degree of compromise, yet shouldn't include a cotton-mouth morning. This was too much. A light finger-comb revealed a large tangled knot and a painful lump over her ear.

Did I fall off the mattress and hit my head?

"Hey, kid. Wake up, damn it. Hurry."

The harsh whisper embodied urgency and desperation that replicated and swelled within her chest.

What the heck? The voice in her head wasn't her own. Enlightenment would come after punching through the suffocating fog and fully emerging in the suddenly hostile world. Stabbing pain accompanied the dingy light spearing her eyes after cautiously lifting one lid.

A blur of flashbacks included sitting in an outdoor riverfront café enjoying the sunset with her favorite camera nestled in her lap. Snapping the riot of colors slipping into the ocean had equaled the day's highpoint, nature's way of assuring her she'd made the right decision in moving to Portland.

Now, for reasons evading memory, her gaze soft-focused on a scene defying logic.

"Kid, open your eyes before it's too late. Grab the small rock by your head. Hide it behind you."

Okaaay, evil mini me is crazy, and I will never drink wine again.

Five minutes of silence would help her collect her thoughts and allow time to search her virtual portfolio for whatever was causing the nausea-producing pests in her brain and stomach. Each vied for the position of top party host. Intuition whispered taking that time would be her undoing.

Instead of the distant hustle and bustle of city life swarming her senses, Kaylee found the intense quiet more disturbing than the harsh whisper. "Wait... what rock?"

Fragments of her surroundings wavered in and out of focus. Brick walls smeared with dirt were partially visible through the horizontal bars.

Horizontal bars?

She reached with shaking fingers to touch the rusted metal cylinders then tried to rattle them. They didn't budge. A cramp in her thigh from resting in a semi-fetal position grew in intensity while her feet crowded against hard, cylindrical surfaces and prevented her from stretching out.

More bars.

She didn't have the strength to yell.

The quick, indrawn breath was also not her own. "Stupid kid. Knock that off, or we're both dead."

A shower of dirt sprinkling her face and hair made her cough, the resultant sandy inhalation perpetuating the cycle.

The collaborative dream, having taken a southern turn into hell, brought another wave of anxiety along with nausea. Each of her senses plunged deeper into a dark abyss, taking logic and rational thought through a twisted, interactive roller-coaster ride.

Disorientation, chaos, and the first stirrings of panic took root like a well-fertilized seed that sent its growing tendrils sliding deep within the earth.

Loose dirt and small rocks covered the hard base and abraded her shoulder as she moved to a cramped position on her back. The changed perspective brought enlightenment.

That's why the bars were horizontal.

"Crap." Details assimilated sluggishly. Dirt-covered metal comprised a bed, but it wasn't in her apartment. Walls of brick as seen through her cage, lack of windows, and stale, dank air, pointed to an underground zip code.

Micro currents ferried a thick, putrid scent and muffled the faint, eerie groans of venting tunnels.

"What's your name?" Again, a whisper twisted with

annoyance and despair saturated the air.

Halting breaths and extreme concentration staved off the blind terror threatening her sanity.

"Kaylee. My name is Kaylee." Slowly, she searched for the irritating heckler.

"Listen up, Kaylee. The bastard who took you is gonna be back soon, probably looking for a bit of afternoon delight. And he won't be asking. He kidnapped you, too. I don't know why."

Kaylee's befuddled mind took in more of her surroundings, low ceiling, dirt floor, cramped, cave-like room, and the caged, bedraggled woman three feet away. Purple and black surrounded her right eye and busted lip. Her shirt front hung in tatters, the ripped flannel exposing a large bruise above her breast.

"How long have we been here?" A torch along the wall cast flickering shadows over the adjoining cage, just short of her own.

Flickering—indicates an air current.

"The last thing I remember is shopping." Tears trailed down the petite blonde's mud-streaked alabaster cheeks which sharply contrasted the bruises marring her face.

"There's a slight breeze coming from—that way." Kaylee strained to see where the tunnel led. Pitch black. Some apparitional entity scuttled in the darkness beyond the seedy illumination and left the impression of ghostly stalkers. Stalkers that chittered in the dark. *I'd rather see the boogeyman than rats.* "We seem to be in an underground room?"

"Yeah. I think so. I woke up just like you, but the bastard tied my hands before my head cleared." A sob choked further words as the victim's wide gaze flickered around the space.

A cursory exploration of the small perimeter marked the filthy, tight confines, then the small, sharp-edged rock which fit in her palm. Instinct saw her sliding it behind her as she shifted position. Mud covered her jeans and colored her T-shirt and jacket. Bathing was the least of her worries.

"Someone slipped us a roofie." Bruises, tattered flannel, and bound wrists conveyed the woman's recent past.

Kaylee's continued scrutiny yielded no clues of how to escape her dilemma. Even if she could squeeze her hand and arm through the bars' two-inch gaps, she didn't have the strength or leverage to break the heavy-duty padlock securing her prison.

"Yes. Yes. But at least you're not tied up, yet." The girl lifted her hands to reveal a double loop, plastic cuff. "See if you can break out."

Kaylee studied the thick padlock and the small rock. Stomach acid threatened to revolt if she moved too fast. "I don't think—"

Low, rumbling conversation in the distance indicated a quarrel. A man complained of "damaged merchandise" while another argued something about perks of the business.

The few words discerned, argued the merits and risks of something important, judging by the intermittent expletives and plaintive appeals. A third person had entered the dispute.

A female?

Thick foreign accents hindered clarification.

"Shhh, someone's coming. Lie down and pretend you're still unconscious."

Thank you for reading *DIGITAL VELOCITY* Independent authors rely on support to spread the word of their work. If you enjoyed the story and have the time, I'd really appreciate a brief review.

Sign up for my newsletter at reilygarrett.com for the first peek at new books, exclusive giveaways, and sales.

Reily's Books

Romantic Thrillers
McAllister Justice Series
Tender Echoes
Digital Velocity
Bound By Shadows
Inconclusive Evidence
Carbon Replacements
Shattered Reflections
Remnants of Evil

Moonlight and Murder Series
Shifting Targets
A Critical Tangent
Pivotal Decisions
Seeds of Murder
An Unlikely Grave
Deadly Interception
Love You To Death

Psychic Thrillers
Mind Stalkers Series
Bending Fate
Silent Depths
Shadow Guard
Whispers After Death
Mind Hunters

Guardian Series
Shadowed Horizons

Shadowed Origins
Shadowed Passages
Shadowed Spirits
Shadowed Intent

Paranormal Romance

Immortal Lovers Series
Unholy Alliance
Blood Union

Standalone paranormal romance
Tiago

Copyright © 2017 Reily Garrett
Digital Velocity

About Reily

Reily Garrett is a writer, mother, and companion to three long coat German shepherds. When not working with her dogs, she's sitting at her desk with her fur kids by her side.

Author of chilling suspense and snarky romance, her stories span the distance of romantic thrillers, paranormal romance, and erotic romance. Regardless of genre, each book delves into a dark and twisted imagination yet is tempered with romance and a touch of humor.

Reviews by Kirkus Reviews, San Francisco Bay Review, and BestThrillers.com best describe her work:

"This could be James Patterson, Lee Child, and Tess Gerritsen rolled into one, but the dark, twisted methods used by the serial killer could surprise even those readers..." - San Francisco Bay Review

"...steamy, seductive police procedural..." - BestThrillers.com

"...well-researched thriller that remains romantically genuine throughout." - Kirkus Review

Prior experience in the Military Police, private investigations, and as an ICU nurse gives her fiction a real-world flavor. Find Reily below.

Made in the USA
Monee, IL
25 May 2024

58910935R00194